HELLBOY

ODDER JOBS

From the Library of

HELLBOY
ODDER JOBS

Edited by
Christopher Golden

Illustrated by
Mike Mignola

DARK HORSE BOOKS™

Mike Richardson ✠ *publisher*

Scott Allie ✠ *consulting editor*

Lani Schreibstein ✠ *designer*

Lia Ribacchi ✠ *art director*

Special thanks to Matt Dryer, Dave Marshall, Davey Estrada,
Michael Carriglitto, and Rachel Miller.

HELLBOY™: ODDER JOBS

Text and Illustrations ©2004 Mike Mignola. All other material, unless otherwise specified, © 2004 Dark Horse Comics, Inc. Hellboy™, Lobster Johnson™, B.P.R.D.™, Abe Sapien™, Liz Sherman™, and all related characters are trademarks of Mike Mignola. Newford and all (non-Hellboy) associated Newford characters and settings are © and ™ Charles De Lint. No portion of this publication may be reproduced or transmitted, in any form or by any means, without the express written permission of Dark Horse Comics, Inc. Names, characters, places, and incidents featured in this publication either are the product of the author's imagination or are used fictitiously. Any resemblance to actual persons (living, dead, or undead), events, institutions, or locales, without satiric intent, is entirely coincidental. Dark Horse Books™ is a trademark of Dark Horse Comics, Inc. Dark Horse Comics® is a trademark of Dark Horse Comics, Inc., registered in various categories and countries. All rights reserved.

Published by Dark Horse Books
A division of Dark Horse Comics, Inc.
10956 SE Main St.
Milwaukie, OR 97222
www.darkhorse.com

October 2004
First edition
ISBN: 1-59307-226-0

1 3 5 7 9 10 8 6 4 2

PRINTED IN CANADA

TABLE OF CONTENTS

INTRODUCTION

By Frank Darabont

Every destination has a journey, every terminus a starting point. *Odder Jobs*—which I hope you enjoy, and which I'm thrilled to be a part of—is the end result of a seemingly innocuous conversation that took place several years ago at a legendary L.A. establishment that is sadly no longer with us. The place was called Dave's Laser Video in the San Fernando Valley (about ten minutes over the hill from Hollywood), and it was there that the seeds of this *Hellboy* anthology were planted. If you enjoy this book, know that you have a fellow named Paul Prischman to thank.

Paul *who*, you ask? I'll get to that, but first:

What can one say about Dave's? It's like praising and mourning a beloved friend that has passed away. Dave's was it, brothers and sisters (say amen!), *the* mecca for film lovers all over the L.A. basin. Back in the Bad Old Days when VHS videotape ruled the world, Dave's was one of the few places in this city that specialized in *laserdiscs*—remember those giant, gleaming LP-sized precursors to DVDs? Maybe you don't—many folks never saw them or even knew they existed, but film nuts like me lived for them. The sound and picture quality was nearly equivalent to DVDs today, so even though the laserdisc industry never really broke through to the mainstream consumer market (your granny buying them by the handful as stocking-stuffers at Walmart), it had enough of a devoted following that laserdiscs thrived as a niche industry for a decade or more. Ironically, it was the advent of the *new* laser format, DVD, that brought about the demise of Dave's Laser Video—when the world switched over, laserdiscs went the way of the Edsel overnight. Dave's gamely made the switch to selling DVDs and hung on for a few more years, but smaller profit margins and much wider availability (hell, you could suddenly buy DVDs at the supermarket) eventually did them in.

I was one of the earliest fans of laserdiscs, and thus one of Dave's earliest customers. I followed them through three address changes and the switch to DVD, and not a week went by that I didn't go in (except for those rare times I was out of town directing a movie). In fact, going to Dave's was always a fantastic excuse to get out of the house and away from whatever screenwriting deadline was consuming me at the moment; a way to see some daylight and clear my head. And listen, because here's the part that matters: it's not so much going and buying movies that I miss (I can do that anywhere), it's the *social* part of it. Dave's was the quintessential mom-and-pop place—not the faceless, monolithic mega-chain thang like Tower or Virgin, but more like that bar in *Cheers*. You went in, and everybody knew your name. The employees weren't the pierced-and-tattooed zombies you get at the big stores, they were like family.

Simply put, every visit to Dave's was a visit with friends—you'd chat, swap stories, talk movies or books, laugh, hang out. The folks who worked those counters were a particularly erudite and welcoming bunch, and I was always glad to see them. And almost inevitably, other regular Dave's customers would come strolling in like the wacky neighbors on some sitcom—ironically, given our hectic schedules, I got to see more of my filmmaker pal Mick Garris at Dave's than I do in regular life (his house is just up the street from where Dave's used to be, and he came in almost every day after his jog). It was there that I first got to meet Guillermo del Toro, with whom I've since become good friends (you can't *not* become friends with Guillermo, that's how affable and sweet he is). One of my fondest memories of Dave's was the evening I did an in-store signing on the occasion of *The Green Mile*'s DVD release—I was supposed to be there for two hours, but so many people showed up I was there for *seven* hours, and the shop didn't close till one a.m. (Are you wondering what any of this has to do with *Hellboy*? Patience—it's a journey, remember?)

Yeah, damn it, I miss Dave's. Los Angeles, impersonal enough to begin with, got that much more so when it went under. And I miss the people who worked there—Keven, Hobe, Graham (a fabulously dishy gay man we lost to AIDS), Jenni, Drew (a.k.a. Moriarty on Ain't It Cool News, who has since gone on to a burgeoning screenwriting career), Carl (the über-cool and funny black dude who always dressed in a '60s Black Panthers-style leather jacket and reminded me of Shaft) ... well, I won't name everybody (apologies to those left out), but the last name I'll sling at you is Paul Prischman, the guy I mentioned at the top of this intro as having caused this book to happen. (Ah, there now, see? The journey's beginning to make sense.)

Paul is an artist, and a damn good one. One day I walked into Dave's only to have Paul share with me the thrilling news that he'd just gotten a gig doing preproduction storyboard art for Guillermo on the upcoming *Hellboy* movie. Since this was before I'd even met Guillermo, Paul asked me if I'd ever read any of the *Hellboy* comics. The conversation went something like this:

ME: *No, I haven't. Is that the one about the giant red guy in the trench coat with the goggles on his forehead?*
PAUL (politely): *Uh, actually, those are sawed-off horns. He's from Hell.*
ME: *Oh. I thought they were goggles.*
PAUL (painfully polite): *Nope. Horns.*
ME: *Ah. I see.*
PAUL: *You really should read it. It's just awesome; the best storytelling being done in comics today. Hey, I'll bring in one of my trade paperbacks—next time you're in, you can borrow it.*

Paul was as good as his word—on my next visit, he handed me his copy of *Seed of Destruction*. I took it home, read it that night, and promptly fell in love with everything there is to love about Hellboy and his world. I mean, what's *not* to love? Supernatural conspiracies involving Nazis? A Bureau for Paranormal Research and Defense? A big red demon with a dry sense of humor and the deadpan delivery of Philip Marlowe? Well, these are just the parts, but obviously the sum is much greater. What Mike Mignola has done is create something very unique that not only honors the comics art form but often transcends it. And though Mike himself keeps claiming that he's "not a real writer" (and actually seems to believe it), I keep telling him he *is*—not just a writer, but an awesome one. Awesome in the sense of being a great storyteller. Awesome in that he's a guy who can crack me up with the simplest line of dialogue and then quite unexpectedly creep me out or move the hell out of me. And he does all this with mere pen and ink, and the not-so-mere power of his words and ideas. As far as I'm concerned, anyone who can deliver a story with the humor, emotion, and classic feel of "The Corpse" (which reminds me of vintage Ray Bradbury) is a great writer. Anyone who can floor you with the charm and whimsy of "Pancakes"—and do it in a *mere two pages!*—is a storyteller of rare power.

Okay, so I guess you don't need me to tell you how great Mignola is—if you bought this book, I'm preaching to the choir. The point is, Paul turned me on to

Hellboy, and I became a rabid fan. My office where I do my writing has no less than six Hellboy figures keeping me company, everything from Randy Bowen's great sculpts to that goofy bobble-head (with more to come ... man, I can't *wait* for the Sideshow stuff to come out!). I've acquired several pieces of original Mignola art, which hang proudly in my home. I bought every *Hellboy* book there was to buy, read every line there was to read (more than once). And one of the really pleasant surprises of my journey into Mignola's world was coming across the excellent short-story collection *Odd Jobs*, edited by Chris Golden.

Man, I loved the first anthology. There was some seriously good writing in there. It made me long for a follow-up book, which brings us to the final leg of the journey:

Shortly after becoming the World's Biggest Hellboy Fan (I know *you* think you are, but you're wrong), I managed to wrangle Dark Horse editor Scott Allie's e-mail address out of Paul Prischman. From there, I managed to wheedle and finagle Mike Mignola's e-mail address out of Scott. From there, I dropped a gushing fan letter to Mike himself, who responded very kindly—turned out he digs my work too, which made me feel great. An e-mail friendship ensued that culminated in the great pleasure of meeting Mike in person at last year's San Diego Comic-Con ... and just so you know, the more I get to know the guy, the more I like him. He's a terrific and funny man, and he has no filter—whatever he thinks tends to drop out of his mouth without the benefit of censoring, which pretty much leaves everybody rolling on the floor with laughter, much to Mike's bemusement.

Though a sequel anthology to *Odd Jobs* was not my motive in getting in touch with Mike, I *had* at that time been toying with the idea of writing a short story based on an old teleplay of mine. And the more I thought about telling that tale, the more excited I got about having Hellboy in it. So I dropped Mike an e-mail one day and asked him if there were any plans to ever do a follow-up book. He told me they'd given it some idle thought, but that it was a remote possibility at best—no real plans were afoot, or were likely to be any time soon. I told him if it should ever come to pass, he should let me know, because maybe I could contribute a story. He said okay, and probably figured that was the end of it.

Then I did something really sneaky—I went ahead and wrote the story anyway, and mailed it to Mike for his birthday.

I told him to consider it his first official submission for the book, and suggested that *Odder Jobs* might be a cool title. Mike really dug my story, and sent it along to Chris Golden. Chris, Mike, and Scott Allie knocked their heads together and decided this might be a great excuse to get a follow-up anthology going after all. And the word went out far and wide, and, lo, all these terrific writers came stampeding to answer the call. (Chris is the honcho to thank for most of these folks being here, but I'll take credit for David J. Schow's estimable presence—Dave is one of my best friends, like a brother, so I called him up and pretty much told him he had no choice. He rose to the occasion and came through in fine style, bless his dark and squishy little heart.)

So that's how *Odder Jobs* came into being, from starting point to terminus—and, like I said, it all began at Dave's Laser Video one day because Paul Prischman shared with me his fan's enthusiasm for a very special creation called Hellboy, by a very special creator named Mike Mignola. I thank Paul for turning me on to something that's become a real pleasure in my life—and I give him even greater thanks for the friendships with Mike and Guillermo that have resulted. These were awesome gifts, Paul.

As for my story, "The Brotherhood of the Gun," it allowed me to rediscover the joy of writing something that doesn't have the pressure, stress, and mega-dollars of a studio production attached to it, but just to write something for the pure, simple pleasure of writing. I hope you enjoy reading it half as much as I enjoyed putting it down on paper, because I couldn't have *had* more fun wallowing happily in Hellboy's world. And, hey, fellow fans—because so many wonderful writers were willing to jump in and give this anthology a go, we *all* get to wallow happily in Hellboy's world for a while. It's always a welcome place to visit, isn't it?

Enjoy the stories.

Frank Darabont
Los Angeles, California

THE BROTHERHOOD OF THE GUN

FRANK DARABONT

They appeared like a mirage in the blast-furnace heat, shimmering and weaving into view like a feverish dream. The two riders plodded across the high desert wastes, hammered at every step by a sun set in a cloudless sky seemingly leeched of color, a jury of watchful buzzards skating the thermals high above.

In the lead rode Billy Quintaine, eyes pinned to the horizon ahead. He wasn't a man who'd ever laughed at much, and it showed in his face. Twin Frontier Colts, well-worn but maintained by their owner with a devotion approaching that of a master watchmaker, rode on his hips in a matching pair of oiled holsters.

Bringing up the rear was Harley Tyrell, his horse trailing some fifteen feet behind Billy's at the end of a rope. Harley swayed in the saddle, clutching a suppurated, days-old gunshot wound in his belly. Dried blood, brown as old barn paint, had made his shirtfront stiff. He seemed to be staring down at it, his chin bobbing on his chest. A handful of flies were buzzing and crawling there, but Harley didn't notice. In truth, Harley hadn't noticed much in the last few days.

His head came up with a lurch. He stared up at the sun, mind swimming in and out of focus, his voice the sound of dry nettles in a hot wind:

"Billy? Billy, you there?"

Billy didn't look back. "Yeah, Harley. Still here."

"Can't let 'em catch us, Billy!"

"We lost that posse three days ago. Probably still chasing dust devils up in the territories."

Harley let out a wail and jerked his head about, seeing phantoms. "Have a care, Billy! They're close! I hear hoof beats! I see dust on the horizon! Looky there!"

Billy didn't. He knew if he did, he'd see nothing but desert and more goddamn desert. Harley's mind swam out again, his chin settling back to his chest. It was a mercy for both of them.

They hadn't gone another hundred yards when Billy heard Harley slip from his saddle and his body hit the hardpan. Billy glanced back, brought his horse to a stop. He dismounted and walked back to where Harley lay on the ground, arms and legs thrown akimbo. He was staring feverishly at the sky, his sight mostly gone.

Dying. No point in gilding that lily, thought Billy. A man as badly gutshot as Harley Tyrell had never really had a chance anyway. Billy'd brought the dying man along less out of hope of finding a doctor than out of simple loyalty, like for old time's sake. You didn't leave a wounded man behind as long as he could still ride, leastways not if you could help it, that's how Billy saw things. But it was time to face the fact that Harley's riding days were over. A brief flicker of regret crossed Billy's face.

"Oh sweet God and sonny Jesus," whispered Harley, the words draining from his cracked lips. "I hurt. I hurt sooo baaad. Like I'm in *fiiiire* ..."

Billy eased a Colt from its holster with a creak of leather. He aimed the gun down between Harley's eyes and thumbed the hammer back with a soft, oily click. Somewhere above, he heard a buzzard shrieking.

Harley's mind seemed to clear just then, fleetingly lucid. His gaze found Billy's, and he gave him a childlike, trusting smile.

"Billy?"

Billy felt the Colt buck in his hand, heard the thunderclap in his ears, and for a brief moment the world was all white flame.

They found the grave a few hours later, just as the sun was kissing the horizon and turning the desert the color of blood. It wasn't much to look at, just an oblong heap of rocks upon which a cluster of buzzards squabbled and fretted, prying at the stones. The marker itself was no more than a stick thrust into the ground from which a weathered gunbelt hung. The bullets had been removed from their loops, but the sidearm—a scuffed Navy Colt with a chipped wooden grip—still occupied the holster.

McMurdo fired from his saddle and blew a buzzard's head to paste. It flopped over in a geyser of feathers and tumbled off the grave, sending its colleagues screaming into the air in petulant rage. McMurdo got off his horse and strode forth, the lever-action Winchester nestled in the crook of his arm, his duster billowing up behind him like black wings. Already the air was going cold, though he could still feel the heat of the waning day radiating up from the cracked and blasted ground. He was rangy leaning toward gaunt, his face as thin and weathered as jerky, his hair tied back in a ponytail. He wore silver-toed boots with Mexican spurs, a necklace of knucklebones, and the badge of a Texas Ranger pinned near his heart.

He swept off his hat and crouched at the grave, taking it in, his sharp eyes missing nothing. Crouching there, he reminded the other men of a spider. Thin and angular as he was, it was an impossible association not to make.

Scorby dismounted and came up behind him, standing at a respectful distance. With McMurdo, one *always* stood at a respectful distance, not because it was ever demanded, but simply out of instinct.

"Here lies Harley Tyrell," murmured McMurdo. "Dropped out of this life and straight into hell." He tossed a look at Scorby and chuckled. "Well, damn me, too, if I ain't a poet."

Scorby didn't crack a smile. McMurdo was always making little jokes and rhymes like that, but for some reason they never seemed very funny coming from him.

"How you know it's him?"

McMurdo's eyes slid back to the grave. "Initials on the gun. There on the grip. Dig him up if you don't believe me."

McMurdo sensed something unspoken. He glanced up again at Scorby's face and saw a look there he didn't much care for. "You got something to say? Say it."

"Well, Mr. McMurdo ... thing is ... we been at it over a week now. Boys are tired as hell. Talkin' about turning back."

McMurdo weighed this, glanced toward the others. Some two dozen good men sat astride their exhausted horses, watching him, waiting for a reaction. He spat, more to get the dust out of his throat than in contempt, but he knew contempt was how it would be taken, and that was fine.

"This grave's only hours old. The rest of you give up if you want. Me, I'm going after Quintaine."

McMurdo rose and brushed past Scorby. He mounted up and spurred his horse on, knowing the eyes of the men were on him.

The next day, Billy saw a small graveyard on the crest of a low hill. It was nothing fancy, just a boothill, but it was surrounded by a small picket fence and was the only sign of civilization he'd seen since he and Harley had ridden hard out of Danielsville ten days ago with bullets whining past their ears like wasps. He cantered his horse up the hill with a tiny knot of hope burning in his throat for the first time in days, Harley's riderless horse trailing behind him.

His heart gave a little kick as he crested the rise. There was a town on the other side, almost within shouting distance. It wasn't much to look at, a hopeless-looking place choked with dust and heat. In fact, if God took a shit in the desert, it would bear a striking resemblance. But, by *damn*, if it wasn't salvation!

Billy glanced at the tiny graveyard and allowed himself a tired smile. "Never you mind, you boys, you just keep molderin' away. Ain't my time yet." He heeled his horse in the ribs and headed into town.

A languorous, metallic *clank-clank-clank* greeted him as he came up the town's only thoroughfare. Somebody pounding a horseshoe. From the buildings on both sides of the street came the stares of scattered townsfolk watching Billy ride in. An old man rocking in the shade of a barbershop gave him a nod. Some kids playing listlessly in the dirt paused to gape. A bony old hound squatted in the middle of the street and greeted him with a splash of piss, just for form's sake.

He followed the weary clanking to the blacksmith's shop and dismounted. The sound stopped and the blacksmith peered out, blinking at the daylight.

"Feed and water for the night," said Billy.

The other man nodded, wiping his hands. Billy dug a coin from his pocket and flipped it to him. The blacksmith examined it with a grunt, apparently satisfied, then tossed an idle glance at the two horses. "What happened to the other rider?"

Billy gave a look that chilled the other man's marrow. The blacksmith shrank back, realizing too late not to pry into a stranger's affairs. "No never mind to me," he muttered. "I'll take good care of 'em for you, I surely will."

Billy dismissed him without comment and headed across the street to the saloon. He mounted the boardwalk and was within a few paces of entering when a voice called out and froze him in mid-stride:

"Billy! Billy Quintaine!"

Billy turned. A man as thin as a whip stood across the street, leaning against the wall in the meager shade of a building. He wore silver-toed boots and a string of knucklebones around his neck. They stood for long seconds watching each other with heavy-lidded eyes. They were both of a kind, and knew it at a glance without having to speak. There would be no parlay between them, no question of arrest or surrender, none of that polite bushwah. The thin man detached from the wall and moved into the street, duster swept back and flapping in the breeze, hand hovering near his holster.

"I'm calling you out, Quintaine!"

Billy stepped off the boards and circled slowly into the street, angling for position. The sun was directly overhead and in neither man's eyes, so he knew the advantage was mostly even. He kept his eyes on his adversary, but his peripheral vision told him townsfolk were scurrying for cover.

"You the one been trackin' me?"

"Clear across the state."

"The lengths a man'll go to just to get hisself killed." Billy came to a stop, facing the other man at a distance of some forty paces. "You got a name?"

"McMurdo."

"McMurdo." Billy knew the name and respected it. "That'd be Tom, wouldn't it? Texas Ranger. Hear tell you're the best there is."

McMurdo drew a slow breath. "Gotta take you in, Billy. Your choice as how."

Billy nodded, spread his feet a bit, found his stance. His fingers flexed, hovering near his holstered Colt.

"Well then, Ranger man ... make your move."

The gunfighters stood, frozen like statues, eons passing in the space of mere heartbeats. A hot wind off the high desert blew dust around their boots. A tumbleweed rolled by.

They went for their guns, both men drawing like oiled lightning.

Billy felt the Colt buck in his hand, heard the thunderclap in his ears, and for a brief moment the world was all white flame.

Billy entered the saloon, the ghosts of the gunshots still ringing in his ears. He felt lightheaded and passing strange, no doubt a residual of his many days in the heat. He worked his jaw to clear his hearing and waited for his eyes to adjust. The place was dark but for the murky daylight filtering through the grime-streaked windows. Dozens of shadowy men were drinking and playing cards, clustered at small, round, wooden tables stretching back into the dim recesses of the room. Billy was taken aback to see so many patrons, and came to wonder if these mightn't be the men who'd ridden with McMurdo. Well, he thought, if they were, they were surely cowed to know their leader lay dead as hell outside in the noonday sun with a dumbstruck look on his face.

Billy stood his ground. If these *were* McMurdo's men, he figured there was no percentage in turning tail. Cowed men can turn brave on a dime. Like as not, they'd be after him like wolves and take him down. Better to play the odds and gut it out right here in the saloon. He moved to the bar with a show of unconcern, prepared to put a hole through the first man to make a move, and the eleven after that.

He bellied up to the rail and put his back to the room. The hairs were crawling on the back of his neck, but no sudden movement came to his ears. The bartender was nowhere to be seen, so he helped himself to a bottle of rye, pouring a shot and knocking it back. There was still no sound in the place, save for the soft rustle of poker being played and the desultory buzzing of flies.

As Billy poured a second shot, the emphatic slap of a card drew his attention. He glanced over and saw a man alone at a table, playing solitaire and slowly murdering a bottle of rum. He couldn't see the face, shrouded in darkness as the man was, but it was clear the stranger was watching him.

"You look like a card-playing man," came the voice, citified and pleasant, breaking the silence.

Billy gathered the bottle of rye and the shotglass, and drifted to the man's table. He kept alert for any hostile moves from the men in the room, but none seemed forthcoming. He found himself relaxing some, the rye warming his belly in a pleasant way. He sat carefully, eyes on the man before him. "Can't say as I mind so much, long as they're dealt straight."

The stranger leaned into the light, tipping his bowler. He was a little man with bloodshot eyes, a detachable collar in danger of detaching at any moment, and wire-rim spectacles perched on a ruddy nose. The suit he wore was threadbare and frayed—as threadbare and frayed, in fact, as the man himself.

His hands, however ... now *those* were another matter. They were more than clever and beyond fast, moving with the precision of a skilled surgeon. He spread the cards across the table with a sweep of one hand, revealing them all face up. A normal deck. A reverse sweep and the cards jumped into his hands to be shuffled through lightning-fast fingers. He dealt them facedown, five for Billy and five for himself.

"You got fast hands," said Billy.

"So do you, friend, so do you," replied the man, glancing at Billy's guns.

Billy picked up his cards, fanned them open ... and froze. They were all *identical.* Five black aces of spades. Billy glowered over his cards, slapped them back facedown on the table. "What are you trying to pull, friend?"

"Nothing, my good sir, nothing at all. Just trying to prove an important point."

"Which is?"

"That the hand ..."

His pale hand darted out and flipped Billy's cards over. They were *normal* again. "... is quicker than the eye."

Billy mulled this display of legerdemain, wrestling with a smile. If there was one thing he admired it was skill, whatever form that skill took. And he had to admit, the skill of the little gent in the bowler hat was a sight to see. Seeing the grudging approval on Billy's face, the man smiled and reached down, hefting a battered suitcase off the floor and onto the table. He threw the clasps and Billy reacted fast, a Frontier Colt suddenly leveled at the other man's forehead. It was a magic trick of his own, done before the other man even knew the gun had left Billy's holster. The little fellow went stiff and lifted his hands slowly into view with a queasy smile, his clever fingers tickling the air.

"My, you *are* fast. Forgive me. I forget a man in your line of work can't be too careful." He glanced down, indicating the case. "May I?" Billy gave him a measured nod that said *do it slowly*. The little man put his hands on the case, spun it halfway around so Billy could get a clear view, and lifted the lid. Revealed inside were row upon row of small brown bottles held neatly in place by fabric straps. Each bottle had a paper label which read: DOCTOR ARGUS'S WONDER TONIC. The man snatched up a bottle, held it next to his face, and launched into a mile-a-minute pitch:

"Allow me to introduce myself, Cornelius Bosch, originally out of Duluth, ever been to Duluth, friend?" He held a beat, waiting for Billy to answer. Billy didn't. "I thought not. Well, I'm here to tell you about a miracle of modern medicine ... the one, the only, the thoroughly amazing ... Doctor Argus's Wonder Tonic! Guaranteed to quicken the senses, sharpen the reflexes, and improve the vision! Yes, you heard me right, I said *improve the vision*. And even the fastest among us can use that extra little edge, am I right? Each bottle is being offered today at the unbelievably low introductory price of *one single dollar*. Yes, you heard that right, just one thin buck! How many will you be taking friend?"

The man's palaver was greeted with deep silence. Billy hadn't moved or blinked throughout. In fact, his Colt hadn't budged an inch and was still leveled at Bosch's forehead. Bosch swallowed, his adam's apple bobbing.

"Did I mention our special discount? A one-day-only offer of ten percent off if you buy—" He was interrupted by a soft *click* as Billy thumbed the hammer back. Bosch cleared his throat gently. "Twenty percent off?"

"Go peddle your potion elsewheres, little man. I'm as fast as there is, nor do I care much for fast-talkers and con men."

"Mr. Quintaine. Your hand *is* quicker than the eye, true enough. But even a man of your considerable skill could use a little of what Doctor Argus has to give." He placed the bottle on the table and slid it ever-so-carefully across to Billy. "Guaranteed to sharpen the senses and improve the vision. Give heed, sir. My final offer, never before made, one time only. An entire bottle of Doctor Argus's Wonder Tonic ... absolutely *free*. If you don't see a marked difference ... if things aren't clearer to you than they ever were before or you ever thought possible ... I'll pay *you* the dollar."

Billy gave Bosch a faint, steely smile. The gun dipped and returned to its holster. "I'll go along, little man. If only to teach you a lesson about playin' a fella for a fool. Mind, you'll pay more than just a dollar. I don't look kindly on bein' took for simple."

"You drive a hard bargain, Mr. Quintaine. But fair enough."

Billy uncorked the bottle, put it to his lips, and took a long pull. His face went taut with the bitterness of it. Wrestling with the aftertaste, he gazed around the saloon.

Nothing remarkable made itself known. Those same hard men sat quietly in those same murky shadows, drinking and playing cards. Billy re-stoppered the potion and slid the bottle back across the table. "Looks like your magic juice ain't but snake oil, friend."

Bosch leaned forward, eyes riveted to Billy. "Are you *sure*, Mr. Quintaine? Look again, I implore you. Look *hard*."

Billy did, feeling foolish, his gaze sliding from one shadowy patron to the next. There *was* something decidedly odd about these men ... they drank and played cards but hardly ever spoke, and then only in whispers. It also came to him to consider that the vague glimpses he caught of their faces in the dimmish light showed them to be pale ... *too* pale for men who lived under the harsh sun of a desert.

He saw a bald man lean through a spill of light. Their eyes met briefly, but then the man was gone from view, hidden behind another card player. Billy's face betrayed a glimmer of recognition. He tore his gaze away, trying to shake his disquiet.

"What?" whispered Bosch.

"Nothin'. Just that fella back there."

"What about him?"

Billy hesitated. "For a moment he looked like someone I once ..."

Bosch licked his lips nervously. "Once what?"

"... once *knew*. Couldn't be him, though. He's dead."

"Oh. I see." Bosch settled back.

Billy grew ever more uneasy, casting furtive glances about the room. He caught a glimpse of a face here, a face there, but hardly ever enough to get a good look. More unnerving still, some of the men seemed to be glancing away the moment Billy's eyes found them, as if they'd been staring at him only the instant before.

Finally, one man threw in his hand and leaned back in his chair to await the next deal, face falling squarely into a spill of light. He had a sweeping handlebar mustache and wore a black frock coat. Billy took his eyes off the man, squeezed them shut in disbelief, opened them again. Bosch leaned in, oozing concern.

"Mr. Quintaine?"

Billy's voice fell to a whisper. "That fella there. Damned if he ain't the spittin' image of Doc Jessup."

"Doc Jessup? The law man?"

"Law man, my ass. He was a lowlife bounty hunter ... till he caught up with me in Nogales, and I put a hole through that little tin star of his."

Bosch's eyes grew wide. "He's deceased? Are you *sure*?"

"'Course I'm sure. I'm the one who 'deceased' him." He stole another glance. "Damn, that fella could be his twin brother."

At that moment, the man with the mustache reached for his vest, sweeping his coat aside. A tin star was revealed there, pinned over his heart. In the center of the badge was a bullet hole, perfectly round and crusted with flecks of brown. A cascade of blood had once spilled down his front and soaked into his trouser leg, where it had dried and caked the fabric stiff as board. A few flies had lofted up from inside the man's coat as he'd opened it and were now buzzing lazily in the air. He waved them idly aside as he plucked a cheroot from his vest pocket and planted it between his teeth. He lit a match with his thumbnail and put flame to his cigar, puffing it to life. Smoke swirled up and caught the light.

His eyes met Billy's, and he smiled.

Billy looked slackly away, the color gone from his face. He glanced to Bosch, but found no help there—the little man wore a fixed smile, his expression inscrutable. Feeling like the victim of a bad dream, Billy looked again at the man with the mustache.

Doc Jessup was still watching him. He blew a smoke ring that billowed toward the ceiling, and muttered something to his two companions. This prompted the man across from Jessup to turn in his seat and look straight at Billy. It was Harley Tyrell, Billy's recently deceased partner, his forehead cracked open by a .45 caliber bullet that had just yesterday blown a hole between his eyes and splashed a torrent of blood down his face. A few flies were crawling aimlessly in the wound as if looking for treasure there. Then the third man at the table leaned back a bit, peering around Harley to also get a look at Billy. It was Tom McMurdo, the Texas Ranger whom Billy had just left dead in the street, sporting two gaping bullet holes—one in his chest, the other in the hollow of his throat. An empty string, once a necklace of knucklebones, hung loose about his neck. Billy's second shot had torn through it, blasting those bones off their string and into the air. They'd scattered into the dust at McMurdo's feet before he'd gone down. Billy had seen it happen.

Billy sat, limp, all strength drained from his arms and legs, mind reeling.

"I'm seeing things," he whispered.

That's when *I* finally spoke up. "Well, yes and no," I told him.

Billy turned and saw me. I suppose it goes without saying that his jaw dropped.

I was behind the bar. I'd been there all along, watching this whole thing unfold. Billy hadn't seen me when he'd walked in, of course, even though I'd been there plain as day, and I'm kind of hard to miss. He'd stared right through me when he'd bellied up to the bar and poured himself that first shot of rye. I have to say I'd really admired his nerve at that moment, the way he'd kept his back to the room and dared somebody to make a move. He hadn't seen me then because his mind simply hadn't been open to it, but now that it was I'm sure I struck him as quite a sight—seven feet tall, three hundred and fifty pounds, and red. Plus there was the matter of the sawed-off horns. From a distance, people have occasionally mistaken them for goggles parked on my forehead. I was almost tempted to let my tail twitch up into view from behind the bar just to see the look on his face, but I didn't give in. This was delicate business, and no time to be fooling around. Billy just sat pinned in his chair, gaping. For a taciturn man, he looked ready to jump out of his skin. He actually closed his eyes and rubbed them with his fists, like a kid expecting the boogeyman to disappear when he opened them again. I'm not the boogeyman, so I didn't oblige him.

"You're not seeing things that aren't there," I continued gently. "Or *haven't* been there all along."

Billy tore his gaze off me and put it on Bosch. He was having trouble catching his breath, but managed a harsh whisper: "What was in that tonic?"

"As advertised, sir, the Doctor's tonic is guaranteed to sharpen the senses and improve the—"

Billy lunged across the table, grabbed him by the throat, and hauled him choking out of his chair. "You slipped me some'a that Injun peyote, din'cha? I'll snap your scrawny neck, you son of a—"

The sound of chair legs scraping the floor made Billy freeze. He turned, heart hammering. A half-breed Washita Cherokee had risen to his feet at a table across the room. He had three bullet holes stitched across his chest. From the look on Billy's face, he remembered putting them there.

"Frank? Frank Little Bear?"

Little Bear gave a nod. "Been a long time, Billy."

Another chair scraped, drawing Billy's attention as another man stood. Billy seemed to know *him*, too. Chairs began scraping all over the saloon as the dead rose to their feet. They were shredded with gunfire, spattered with dried blood. They gave off an acrid reek of expended gunpowder mingled with that cloying cinnamon smell I always seem to encounter when dealing with the dead. Billy's gaze darted wildly around at their sallow faces and empty eyes. Of course he recognized them all, and why wouldn't he? He'd killed each and every one of them.

"Look around, Billy," I said. "Many familiar faces here. Many old friends."

"They've all come to pay their respects, Mr. Quintaine," added Bosch. "All those you've ever killed. You're the guest of honor here today."

Billy let go of Bosch and shot me a terrified look. "Who are you? The Devil himself, come to snatch my soul?"

I did my best not to laugh. I didn't want to offend the guy. "Naw. They call me Hellboy, but that's just on account of appearances. I'm a concerned friend, is all."

The dead men chose that moment to start closing in on Billy from all corners of the room. He took that for a bad sign and backed away, yelling to Bosch: "Then *you'd* be Satan? And that galoot behind the bar, that'd be your demon?"

"Satan? Oh, my. You do me far too much credit. I told you, name's Cornelius Bosch, originally from Duluth. A traveling salesman and sometimes gambler. Born with a gift of gab, which is why the others invited me here today. I'm not with these gentlemen, strictly speaking, though we do share a kinship. I was caught in the crossfire when you robbed that Wells Fargo office in Haddonton, Missouri." He pronounced it *Missoura*. He reached up and opened his suit coat, revealing a bloody hole in his vest. "A stray bullet. *Your* stray bullet, I'm afraid."

The dead kept advancing, hemming Billy from all sides. He finally ran out of backing-up room and bumped into the bar, watching the revenants loom closer.

He slapped leather and drew both guns, picking targets at random and blazing away. I clapped my hands over my ears and tried not to go deaf from the massive booming gunshots—holy crap, those old Frontier Colts were *loud!* I was yelling for Billy to quit it, tried to tell him he was overreacting, but he was firing shot after shot and doing some yelling of his own: "YOU'RE DEMONS FROM THE PIT, COME TO DRAG ME OFF TO HELL!" The dead men were staggered back as the bullets hit home, chewing through them in clouds of dust—but dust is all they were, brittle as parchment, and they remained on their feet. Billy's guns ran dry, snapping a few times on empty chambers. I took my hands off my ears, relieved, working my jaw. The ringing in my head was fierce, but I could still hear McMurdo well enough:

"Heaven or hell, Billy. Whatever you care to call it. It's a warm place. A quiet place. Maybe after a lifetime of tussle, somebody figured we had a little quiet comin' to us." The kindness in his voice surprised me. Even the hard men can be kind, as it turns out.

"We're all there, Billy," added Harley, flies orbiting his head. "All of us who lived by the gun. And died by it."

"We're a brotherhood," said Doc Jessup. "A brotherhood of the gun."

"You don't belong here, Billy," insisted Little Bear. "You belong with us."

"NO!" roared Billy, the ice returning to his veins. "Now you *listen!*" They stopped in their tracks and waited to hear what he had to say. The dead are polite at times, if not downright placid. Depends what mood you catch 'em in. Billy jabbed a finger at Bosch. "I'm sorry for your misfortune, friend, but I never meant for that bullet to find you! If you were standin' where you shouldn't, you only got yourself to blame! And you, Harley! You were dyin' anyhow! All I did was put you out of your sufferin'! It was a kindness!" He lifted his chin and seemed to grow a few inches, looking them all straight in the eye. Again, I admired his nerve. "As for the rest of you, I kilt each and every man in a fair fight! I never backshot a single feller among you, so you got no cause now to come a slitherin' out of your graves to complain!"

"Can't argue a bit of it," whispered McMurdo. "It's all like you say. But our time is past. You don't belong here. None of us do." He drew close, and for a moment I thought he was going to kiss him. "Like I said, Billy. I gotta take you in."

"Listen to him, Billy," I said, resting my elbows heavily on the bar. "He's making good sense. Why don't you ask me what year it is?"

But Billy ignored me, roaring in McMurdo's face: "I shot you down, Tom McMurdo! Shot you dead as hell! Least you should do is stay that way! Fair is fair!"

"You shot me dead, true enough. But you don't recollect what happened after that, do you?"

Billy hesitated. I saw confusion on his face as he tried to remember. "I ... I came in here." He tossed a glance my way as if maybe I'd back him up. I just shrugged.

"You recall walking away from his body? Crossing the street? Coming up those saloon steps? Can you honestly say you remember any of it?"

"I must've! I'm here, ain't I?"

"It's all a blank, isn't it?" I tapped my noggin with the forefinger of my giant stone hand. "C'mon, *think.* Tell me you remember anything after Mr. McMurdo bit the proverbial dust. You can't, can you?"

"'Course not," said McMurdo, shaking his head at Billy. "Stubborn as a mule and twice as dumb. You're just like us, only you ain't got sense enough to admit it."

"Accept it, Mr. Quintaine," said Bosch. "That's all you have to do. Just accept it."

The dead men started muttering, urging Billy on, ghostly voices echoing and overlapping, swelling to an eerie drone that set my teeth on edge. Billy was shrinking in on himself, and I can't say I blamed him—it was spooky as hell and whittling away *my* nerves, too. He whirled away from them and clapped his hands over his ears, slamming his elbows to the bar, his entire body hunched, and began screaming as if to preserve his last shred of sanity: *"YOU'RE DEAD! YOU'RE DEAD AND I'M ALIVE! NOW GO AWAY! GO AWAY! GO AWAAAAAY!"*

The silence was abrupt. The ghostly mutterings had stopped. So had the visitation. The saloon was empty, except for Billy and me. He opened his eyes and saw that I was still there. He jerked around and found the others gone. I'd watched them evaporate behind his back like vapor, vamoosing into thin air.

"Well, now you've gone and done it," I muttered.

"Oh, I know what *you* are," he growled, fixing me with a baleful look.

"Yeah? I can't wait to hear this."

"You're a watchacallit, a figment. Pretty soon you'll disappear, just like them others. Hell, they was never here, only that little fella, that Bosch. Only *he* were real, and he slipped me some'a that peyote like I said. I just had me what the Injuns call a vision walk. Nothin' but bad dreams and bullshit." He snapped his fingers dismissively at me a few times, demanding that I fade out like a mirage. "Go on now, figment, off you go. You disappear, too, like a good fella."

"Oh, brother," I sighed. He stared at me with contempt, *daring* me not to vanish. I scratched my head and felt stupid, trying to figure out how best to explain things and at a loss for what to do next.

Suddenly, there came the sound of boot heels thudding the boardwalk outside. Somebody was approaching the saloon. Billy fixed his gaze on the entrance, terror mounting all over again, not knowing what new horror to expect.

The footsteps paused. And then:

Big Bart burst in through the swinging doors, looking like something out of a Gene Autry musical—ridiculous white cowboy outfit encrusted with imitation rhinestones, red plastic holsters on his hips, boots glittering and twinkling with tiny inset mirrors, fringe swinging from his elbows Grand Ole Opry-style. For the second time in one day, possibly in his entire life, Billy Quintaine's jaw dropped.

I stifled a grin and silently blessed Big Bart's timing. This could actually work in my favor, and I sure couldn't have planned it.

"Come on, folks, step right in!" bellowed Big Bart. "There's still lots to see!"

He strode in, spurs jangling like cheap Christmas bells. He was an old stunt man who'd spent most of his life falling off horses and had retired to Arizona with a few bones still unbroken. Now he spent his days happily giving the tourists the big spiel. They poured in at his heels, spreading into the saloon with their ice cream cones and slushees, the cheap sunglasses coming off their faces as they looked around and started snapping pictures. Their clothing was a riot of styles and colors—loud tropical print shirts, sneakers as subtle as neon billboards, sandals and flip-flops, goofy straw hats. The kids mostly wore jams, always a stupid excuse for a garment in my eyes because it couldn't decide whether to be shorts or pants. A few of the ladies had so much sunscreen on them, they looked paler than the dead cowboys had.

I glanced over to Billy. Well, you can imagine his reaction. The poor fellow was flabbergasted, with the tourists milling around him like he wasn't even there. He waved his hand in front of a few faces, but didn't get so much as a blink. He realized they couldn't *see* him. Folks started noticing *me*, though, tossing uncomfortable looks my way. Big Bart raised his hands to get their attention and reassure them. I'd talked to him earlier and told him why I wanted to hang around, and had gotten his blessing. He seemed like good people. Reminded me of Lee Ermey. Four grandkids and another on the way.

"Nothin' to worry about, folks, that there's Hellboy, good ol' pal o' mine. Dropped in on us today just to have a little fun and check out the ghosts."

I gave a little wave. "Don't mind me, folks. Just part of the show."

That seemed to relax everybody, so Big Bart launched into his routine, and a polished one it was: "Now this here's the saloon! Here's where all the cowpokes and hombres would come to unwind and wet their whistles after a hard day ridin' the range. Don't you grown-up folk try orderin' nothin', y'hear? Happy Hour's been over for quite a while." This got a chuckle from the group. Billy turned to me with a look that said *what in God's name is going on here?* I motioned for him to listen and be patient—besides, I really dug Big Bart's act and didn't want to miss any of it. "Now, it might just interest you folks to know this saloon has its very own ghost."

A little boy looked up at him with wide eyes. "You mean it's haunted, Big Bart?"

"Why, little pardner, that's *exactly* what I mean! What's a ghost town without a real honest-to-goodness ghost?" He tossed a wink at the boy's parents and made them smile. I noticed an older kid with his baseball cap turned backwards elbowing a pal and rolling his eyes at the corniness of it. The kid had no idea, but Billy Quintaine was standing right beside him. *Yuk it up, Pizza Face*, I thought. *If you only knew.*

Big Bart leaned down and gave the little boy a mock-scared look, really playing it up. "And not just *any* ghost, mind you, but the ghost of the most notorious, despicable varmint ever to terrorize the Old West! I'm talkin' about none other than Billy Quintaine himself!" The tourists murmured, impressed. Bart straightened up and moved among them, weaving his spell. "He was the fastest gun alive ... but his luck ran out the day Tom McMurdo caught up with him. Tracker Tom, the Texas Ranger! And what a showdown it was! The two hombres faced each other on the street outside this very saloon. I tell you folks, the very earth must'a shook with each step they took."

He slapped leather—or in his case, red plastic—and quick-drew one of his prop guns. The crowd gasped. "Both men *drew!* Both men *fired!* But it was Tom McMurdo that hit the ground, cut down by the outlaw's bullet!" He paused, looking at their faces, dropping his voice for dramatic effect. "But we all know Tracker Tom wasn't alone that fateful day. Unbeknownst to Billy, McMurdo's posse was hid out in every nook and cranny of this town. And, yes sir, yes ma'am, the moment Tom bit the dust, that posse made itself known to Billy Quintaine! From every doorway, every window, every rooftop they came, all a flingin' lead!"

He quick-drew his second gun. The crowd gasped again.

"Quick as a flash, Billy Quintaine drew his other shootin' iron! Howlin' like a banshee, six-guns a blazin', he tried to fight his way across the street and get back to his horse ... but he never made it to the stable. They cut him down in the street like the mad dog he was. Billy Quintaine died a kickin' and a twitchin' in the dust, a big look of surprise on his ornery face."

Billy didn't look ornery at the moment. He was watching me with a slack expression, searching my eyes for the truth. I gave him a gentle nod.

Bart looked up at the ceiling, speaking in a low, spooky voice: "Some folks say late at night—round about midnight, in fact—if you listen real hard, you can hear the lost soul of Billy Quintaine a whistlin' and a cryin' through the eaves of this very saloon."

By now you could hear a pin drop. The tourists were looking up, scanning the cracked boards with dread as if expecting to see some pale spectral face peering down at them. Even *Billy* was looking up, eyes wide.

Bart suddenly bellowed, "THERE HE IS!" and started blasting his cap-guns at the ceiling—*bam-bam-bam-bam!* I enjoyed seeing the tourists shriek and jump, knowing *I'd* gotten suckered in myself the first time. Big Bart howled and yipped with glee, spun his six-guns on his fingers, and rammed them back into their holsters with a grin. "Got the varmint!" The tourists exploded with laughter, and some of them even applauded. "Well, folks, let's mosey on down the trail, there's still lots left to see."

He led the tour group out of the saloon. Silence returned. Billy stood for a time, not looking at me, then went to the swinging doors and peered out. I knew what he was seeing out there. A concession stand. A gift shop. A fake horse you could sit on and have your picture taken with. He craned his neck, and I figured he could see the sun glinting off the SUVs and RVs parked down at the far end of the street.

I felt for him. It couldn't be easy knowing his whole life, all his struggles and hardships, all his pain and tears, had ended here—as a cheap gimmick for the amusement of tourists. He drew away from the door and finally looked at me.

"So that's how it is?"

"That's how it is."

He moved slowly across the room to the little round table where he'd sat earlier with Bosch. I could see him trying to wrap his mind around everything as he sank back into his seat. He picked up the bottle of rye and stared at it. He saw that it was old and dusty and dry as a bone. There hadn't been any hooch in it for a *long* time.

"What year *is* it?" he asked softly.

"We're into the next century now," I said, coming out from behind the bar. "The twenty-*first*, I mean." That got him to look up. "Hey, you're not missing much. We're only a few years in, and things are already a bigger mess than ever. I thought we'd outdone ourselves in the last one, what with two world wars and all, but it looks like we're just getting started. I kinda miss the old days myself. Give me cowpokes riding the range. No bin Laden, no 9-11, no quagmire in Iraq, no assholes cooking up anthrax or trying to build nukes in their basements." He gave me a puzzled look, but I waved it aside. "Aw, crap, you don't even *wanna* know."

I came to the table, eyeing the flimsy chair Bosch had occupied. No way it'd hold my weight—I'd broken enough chairs in my day to know. I swapped it out for a smallish barrel I spotted near the wall. It looked stout and might make a handy stool. I sat gingerly on it across from him, thankfully *sans* pratfall—the barrel held. He was watching me.

"And you? How do you fit into this, if not to drag me to hell?"

"Me? I just happened by. Had some vacation time piled up, and things were quiet at the office, so I was heading down to Sedona to hang with a pal of mine. Go hiking and stuff. Supposed to be some kind of nexus of psychic vibes down there, which sounds a little Age of Aquarius to me, but I thought it might be fun." I could see I was losing him by the way his brow was furrowing. "Sorry, I'll try to make better sense. Anyway, so I was driving by and saw this place from the road. Big damn billboard, you can't miss it. Looked like my kind of tourist trap, so I stopped for lunch. I took the tour, used the rest room, spent maybe an hour—nothing out of the ordinary. But then, *bam*, soon as I tried to leave, this place knocked me right on my ass. I felt like Shemp getting hit with a frying pan. Before I knew it, I had ghosts all over me like flies on frosting."

"Ghosts?" he said, trying out the word for the first time. "Are such things drawn to you?"

"Yeah," I admitted. "Always been that way. I see dead people, like the kid in the movie. Come across it a lot in my line of work, among other things. Anyway, the ghosts in *this* place were filled with need. Since I have this sort of knack to attract the dead, they seized upon me for help. I couldn't really say no. I mean, jeez ... those guys have been trying to get your attention for, what, a hundred and twenty years?"

Though I could tell my lingo left him a little fuzzy here and there, the man was sharp and got the gist. "They ... they came out of kindness?"

"Well, kindness, yeah. But also pain. They're pretty much at rest, only it bothers them having one of their own rattling around *not* at rest. That would be you. So I tried what's known in paranormal terms as an 'intervention.' That means cluing somebody in to the fact that they're, you know, no longer with us. It's not like there's a manual or anything, so you mostly wing it. I came up with that cornball stuff about Doctor Argus's tonic. It's kind of a smoke-and-mirrors gimmick known as a 'trigger.' It's really all about the power of suggestion—give someone an excuse to really see things as they are, they usually run with it. It almost worked, too, but like McMurdo said, you're awfully stubborn."

He met my eyes. "What do you mean ... *almost* worked?"

I sighed, hating to break bad news. "Well, here's the thing, when you told them to go away, they went away. They tried their best, but you were pretty firm about it, and ghosts can be sensitive. What happens now, I don't know." I looked up at the rafters, hoping to get some residual feel, but there was nothing—no ghosty vibe at all, except for the man across from me. "This place feels pretty empty."

I looked back at Billy and saw tears shimmering in his eyes. My heart broke for him a little. He'd finally *gotten* there, finally *admitted* it, and maybe all for nothing.

"But ... I can't stay here in this strange place. They was right, I don't belong. Haven't in a very long time."

"Yeah, I know," I said softly.

He looked up toward the ceiling, no longer speaking to me. "Hey, you fellas. I was *wrong*. You hear me, you boys? I was wrong!" No reply. He rose to his feet, turning slowly, checking out the rafters. "Tom? Doc? Harley? Can you hear me? Wherever you are? Wherever you've gone?"

"Hey, Billy, listen ..."

He started shouting, shutting me out, desperate now: "I DON'T BELONG HERE! DON'T LEAVE ME BEHIND! YOU *CAN'T!* IT AIN'T HALF FAIR!" He held his breath, listening. So did I. All I heard was the breeze in the eaves. Above our heads, a spider web billowed and settled. "Please?" he added in a small voice.

I couldn't believe it, but it looked like he was about to cry. Then he stunned me by crumpling his face up. A ragged sob hitched in his chest. Billy Quintaine, a man who'd never cracked in life, finally did. I guess finding out he was dead didn't strike him nearly as hard as knowing his time was past and he'd been left behind. His tears began to flow freely and without shame. The man was alone. *Truly* alone. He buried his face in his hands and fell to his knees on the dusty floor, shoulders heaving. All I heard were his sobs and his thin, muffled pleading:

"Take me in, Ranger Man ... please ... take me in ..."

And then the damnedest thing happened. A voice called from outside.

"Billy! Billy Quintaine!"

It was McMurdo's voice. My heart did a flip. The sudden smell of scorched gunpowder mixed with the aroma of cinnamon whapped me in the face so hard my stomach lurched, and I actually had to grab the table with both hands to keep from falling over. I'm really glad it didn't make me puke, as it would have spoiled the poetry of the moment. Billy was lifting his head from his hands, hope creeping into his tear-filled face. The voice called again:

"I'm callin' you out, Quintaine!"

I looked to Billy for his reaction, but he'd pretty much tuned me out. He blew a long breath and got to his feet, trying to pull himself together. He wiped a runner of snot from his nose with his sleeve, then pulled his guns and started to load them. His movements were methodical, measured. As I watched, a startling transformation took place—the broken man was slowly replaced by the fierce gunslinger, determination and resolve deepening with each shell he slid into the chambers. By the time he slapped those chambers closed, he was Billy Quintaine again. Gunfighter. Standing tall and proud. Ready to face anybody and anything. At peace with what lay ahead.

He turned to a murky mirror, meeting his own reflection. He spun the Colts on his fingers, performing a fierce flourish and ramming them into their holsters where they belonged. He turned and walked to the swinging doors of the saloon, his boots *klock-klock-klocking* slowly across the dusty boards. I thought he'd forgotten all about me, but then he paused and looked back.

"I thankee, stranger," was all he said, then stepped outside to face his destiny.

"Oh, shit," I muttered, and came up off my barrel. I was across the room and at the window before you could blink. What I saw out there made my insides flutter. Gone were the concession stand, the gift shop, the parked cars, and the dumb fake horse you could get your picture taken with. In their place stood a man in the street wearing silver-toed boots and a necklace of knucklebones. His duster was swept back, his hand hovering near his holster. Billy was circling into the street to face him. I caught glimpses of townsfolk scurrying for cover.

"You the one been trackin' me?" demanded Billy Quintaine.

"Clear across the state," answered McMurdo.

They were playing it out. It occurred to me how inevitable that was. They *had* to, in order for Billy to move on. It was his ticket to mount up and ride.

"The lengths a man'll go to just to get hisself killed." Billy found his spot, set his feet. "You got a name?"

"McMurdo."

"McMurdo." Pause. "That'd be Tom, wouldn't it? Texas Ranger. Hear tell you're the best there is."

McMurdo took a breath. "Gotta take you in, Billy. Your choice as how."

Billy nodded, spread his feet a bit more, and flexed his fingers near his holstered Colt. "Well then, Ranger man ... make your move."

The gunfighters stood, frozen like statues, eons passing in the space of mere heartbeats. A hot wind off the high desert blew dust around their boots. A tumbleweed rolled by.

They went for their guns, both men drawing like oiled lightning.

They fired at the same instant. McMurdo—for the first and last time ever in his life—missed. Billy didn't. McMurdo caught the round in the chest and threw his head up toward the sun, features contorted in an ecstasy of pain, and managed to stay on his feet somehow. He looked down, gun still clutched in his outstretched hand, blinking in dull surprise at the gaping wound and the steady *drip drip drip* of blood pattering onto the silver toe of his boot.

He lifted his head in amazement and tried to get a shot off, but Billy beat him to it. The second bullet took McMurdo in the hollow of his throat just above the breastbone. His necklace flew apart, throwing knucklebones into the air. They scattered in the dust at his feet as he staggered back, his arm flinging stiffly to one side and discharging his gun into the ground. He choked up a startling spray of arterial blood and fell, hitting the ground in a cloud of dust. One last violent spasm, and that was it. Dead as hell.

A hush descended. Billy stood in the street, the smoking Colt in his hand. He lifted his chin and scanned the empty buildings surrounding him. Waiting. The whole damn world seemed to be holding its breath.

He whipped his other gun from its holster, one in each hand now, and bellowed at the top of his lungs: "C'MON, YOU SORRY SONS A BITCHES! WHAT'CHA ALL WAITIN' FOR, JUDGMENT DAY?"

And then the street *exploded*. It was like Big Bart said—from every doorway, every window, every rooftop they came, all a flingin' lead. You know how they say time sometimes seems to slow down and get weird when you're having an accident? It's like the seconds stretch out and the world goes kind of slo-mo? That's how I felt as I stood there watching the last few moments of Billy's life tick down, as if molasses had been poured into the very gears and cogs of time itself.

The first bullet sheared through Billy's collarbone, kicking up a spray of blood. He howled like an enraged banshee and spun, running for the stable, trying to get to his horse. The Frontier Colts were blazing in his hands, and his boots were slamming through the dust like thunder. Pistols and rifles boomed from every nook and cranny of the town, pinning him in a horrendous crossfire. He started taking hit after hit, the bullets whining in like angry hornets and tearing big, bloody holes in him.

Several men went down as Billy's bullets found their marks. One guy even cartwheeled off a rooftop and fell through a porch overhang in an explosion of splintered wood, just like I'd seen done a thousand times in countless movies. The poor fellow died never knowing what a cliché that would someday be.

Billy ran on, screaming through the brutal storm of gunfire, jerked around in a Saint Vitus dance, bullets chewing him to pieces and throwing a red mist of blood trailing through the air in his wake. He spun in one direction, pirouetted in another, and finally fell to his knees. He was still firing his guns, even though he was out of ammo and the hammers were falling on empty chambers. A few more bullets struck him, and he jerked and recoiled with each impact.

The shooting finally stopped. The only sound now was the wind whistling off the high desert.

Billy knelt in the street, swaying, staring up at the sky. His hands dropped slowly to his sides, dragged down by the now impossible weight of his guns. His head bobbed forward as his life ebbed away, and for a brief moment he looked like a man hanging his head in shame.

The last thing he did? He turned his head slowly, caught me watching from the window of the saloon, and I'll be damned if he didn't give me a wink. I swear it's true. Then he toppled and crashed face-first into the dust.

I pulled away from the window. "Wow," was all I said. It was all I could say.

I went to the small revolving postcard display atop the bar. It was like all the others around town, mounted on a slotted metal box so people could pay on the honor system. Only in Arizona will you see this sort of trust. I spun the display slowly on its spindle. It was filled with the typical array of pretty pictures captioned with slogans like *Greetings From Arizona!* and *Howdy Pard!* There were, however, a few bearing actual historical photos. I knew because I'd idly browsed one of these racks when I'd first gotten into town, before the ghosts had shown up and started haranguing me. I found the postcard I was looking for and drew it out.

It told the rest of the story. It was the famous sepia-toned photo of Billy Quintaine lying in a rough wooden coffin propped up in front of the saloon with his hands lashed across his chest and pennies on his eyes, surrounded by the surviving members of the posse. They'd dragged him off the street by his ankles, stripped his clothes, wrapped him in a shroud, and posed for pictures.

A cheap amusement even then, and the body hadn't even been cold.

I dug two quarters from my pocket, clanked them into the little box, and left the saloon with my postcard. Across the street, I saw tourists posing on the dumb fake horse.

I sighed and headed for the parking lot. A red '59 ragtop Cadillac with the biggest damn tailfins Detroit ever slapped on the ass of a car was calling my name. It was a guzzler and handled like a sofa, but it was one of the few things I could fit in, and I loved it.

It was time for me to mount up and ride off into the sunset. "Hi-yo, Silver," I muttered, forgetting to add the *"away."*

Even if I didn't stop for gas, I'd never make Sedona by dark.

FROM AN ENCHANTER FLEEING
PETER CROWTHER

O wild West Wind, thou breath of Autumn's being,
Thou, from whose unseen presence the leaves dead
Are driven like ghosts from an enchanter fleeing.
Percy Bysshe Shelley (1792-1822)
Ode to the West Wind

It is the fog that comes first.

It drifts into the small town of Dawson Corner while everyone is asleep, the entire town tucked up in their beds ... dreaming dreams of hope and safety. And normality.

It sneaks down Main Street and around the old oak in front of the town hall; it crouches in the hollows and ditches of the cemetery; and it hides amongst the trees out by the lake.

It snakes along sidewalks, shuffles past storefronts and swirls across picket-fenced lawns cut so fine they look painted. Then it banks against water butt and shingle, fall pipe and boarding, slate and wainscoting, building upon itself like aerosol cream or shaving foam, working its way past downstairs windows and up to bedroom windows, and then guttering and roof tiles until it reaches chimneypots and even the occasional weather vane.

In the beginning, the fog is wispy, like cigarette smoke, but then it thickens ... thickens until it becomes almost impenetrable.

That's when the dead come.

Some of them drift with the fog, ethereal translucent shapes, like kites or bedsheets blown in on the west wind this autumn morning, ten minutes before three a.m. ... the graveyard hour, the time when doctors and nursing staff will tell you they have the most deaths, gentle leave-takings, when folks done down by illness or the sheer accumulation of years or even, on occasion, by the medication that's been prescribed to them, check out for new adventures someplace else.

Others retrieve their corporeal states, lifting once familiar bodies from casket and grave, from mausoleum and undertaker's parlor. And then they shamble through the thick fog without so much as a single unsure step, slow but determined.

Pieces of these visitors drop soundlessly to pavement and sidewalk, plop onto lawn and porch, slide off of doorknobs and handles ... sometimes leaving mottled residues on previously smooth and polished surfaces.

Here comes one of them now ...

Matthew Fisher, a permanent eleven years, three months, and fifteen days old, fresh from the lake where he has hidden these past eight months, tangled up in weeds while the sheriff and a team of distressed relatives and stalwart volunteers combed the countryside where he was last seen, the search party finally deciding that the boy must have fallen into the fast-moving river swollen with the spring thaws and was like as not on his way to the ocean (if he wasn't there already). But here he was all the time, right here in Dawson Corner, lying at the bottom of the lake. And now he's come back to town, his face bloated and white, his eye sockets empty and sightless, one ruined sneaker still securely fastened around a foot and ankle that have nevertheless had tiny visitors, hungry visitors. And so it is that, halfway along Green Street, just a couple of houses from his old home, Matthew Fisher's lower shin bone cracks and splinters, momentarily lurching him to one side. He bends down, snaps the foot completely off and, carrying it like a grisly memento, continues his journey, swaying side to side when the shin-stump connects with the ground—*slop, clunk, slop, clunk*—until he reaches a familiar picket fence and an even more familiar walkway.

He moves up the walkway toward the house, easing himself up the three steps to the porch and the swing chair, pulling open the screen door with a hand that he absently notices is now reduced to just two fingers—at which point he checks behind him on the path, scanning with those deep black eye sockets, but seeing nothing—and then he thumps his wizened and gray hand on the door frame, once and then again and at last a third time, leaning forward until his face is almost touching the glass door that leads to the kitchen, opening a mouth that is stick-dry and wormy to say to the gowned figure that has just turned on the light and is even now standing barely ten feet away from him, her hands up to her face, and a yellow pool spreading on the floor around her feet, *Hi mom ... I'm back!* but no sounds come.

Not from Matthew Fisher, at least.

"That heavy?" the man asks, nodding at Hellboy's right arm, the elbow-to-wrist section of which appears to be encased in a red-colored dynamo or jet-engine fuselage.

"Uh-uh," comes the response. A sidelong glance takes in the identity tag hanging on a tight-linked chain around his neck: Lucius Jorgensen, the tag's lettering proclaims.

"And those—" Jorgensen nods at Hellboy's head. "Look like goggles—up on your forehead. What are they?"

"They're goggles." Who *was* this guy? Didn't he read *Life* magazine? Watch TV?

"Yeah? They *are* goggles?"

"Yeah. I'm a pilot."

"No kidding. They look like they're part of your head."

"Right again. Surgically attached goggles. Stops me losing them."

The man shakes his head and continues to stare as Hellboy shuffles his overcoat sleeve down a little before folding his arms across his stomach. He only wishes he had a sombrero as well. But things could be worse: the guy hasn't seen his tail or asked why his face is so red.

Leaning his head to one side, Jorgensen says, "They're not *really* goggles are—"

The door opens and Tom Manning enters the office. His manner is brusque, his face expressionless. He nods to the two men seated in front of his desk before taking his seat. Clasping his hands on the inlaid green leather of the desktop, Manning says, "Hellboy" and "Jorgensen," each time with a nod that is returned. And then he says, "You two know each other?"

Jorgensen turns to Hellboy, smiles and then looks front again, nodding.

Hellboy says, "We're old friends."

The Director of the Bureau for Paranormal Research and Defense grunts and shakes a Marlboro from a pack that looks like he's been sitting on it. Lighting the twisted cigarette, he says, "You okay, Lou?"

Jorgensen nods, eyes blinking.

"You don't need to do—"

"I'm okay. Really."

"Still on the medication?"

"Yes, sir."

"Helping?"

"The medication helps, yes, sir."

Another grunt and then, "Okay. Gentlemen, we have a problem."

Hellboy throws back his coat, watching Manning pull smoke out of the Marlboro and blow rings. *It never leaves you*, he thinks, *that desire to go back to it.* "Where this time, boss?" he asks, shaking off the craving.

"Dawson Corner."

Hellboy looks questioningly at Jorgensen, Jorgensen looks questioningly at Hellboy. They turn back.

"It's in Maine. Little town about thirty miles in from the coast. Farming community. Think of a *Post* cover by Norman Rockwell—barbershop, bandstand, corner drugstore where you can buy three-scoop lime floats for a nickel. That kind of thing."

"What's the problem?" Jorgensen asks.

"Fog."

Hellboy frowns the question without speaking.

"This fog is different. Some kind of gas, maybe—" Manning shrugs and blows out a thick plume of smoke. "We don't know. FBI had some people up there first thing this morning."

"What happened?" Hellboy asks.

Manning says, "Take a look," and, pressing a button on his desk, turns to face the large screen on the side wall. As the screen flickers to life, the blinds on the window close up and, just for a moment, the room is plunged into darkness. Hellboy hears Jorgensen breathe in, and then the room bursts into life.

On the screen it's foggy—thick impenetrable fog. Both traditionally suited men and women and military types—uniforms, thick boots, weapons, shaved heads, chewing gum—stumble around in front of an increasingly unsteady camera wailing and sobbing. Some are wearing masks, with respirator blocks, while others are not. Still more are in the process of ripping their masks from their faces or carrying them.

The camera is clearly hand-held. One of the men, rubbing his hand across his eyes, comes up against the camera, pauses for a few seconds, and then tears off his mask. He pulls the pistol from the holster on his belt and points it at the camera. There are no protestations, just interminable sobbing and crying. He pulls the trigger and blood-specks and pieces of what Hellboy knows is human flesh spatter the man's face. The camera falls to the ground but keeps running. Now towering above the camera, the man gives a brief howl to the sky before placing the gun barrel in his mouth—his mask hanging from his wrist—and firing. He falls forward onto the camera and the screen goes dark.

Almost immediately, the blinds open and Manning presses a button that turns off the screen.

"Thoughts?"

Hellboy shrugs. "Could use some editing."

"Lou?"

Jorgensen draws in a deep breath and says, "You been back in for the bodies? I mean, I do take it they're all dead."

"I think that's the case. But no, we haven't been back in." He nods at the now blank screen. "They were all wearing masks when they went in there."

"All of them? Seems to me most of them weren't."

Manning shakes his head. "Everyone had a mask to begin with."

"Why'd they remove them?" Hellboy asks.

Manning shrugs. "They just seemed to go—" He searches for the right word. "—seemed to go wild. It was okay right at the beginning, but as soon as they were in the thick of that stuff—every man and woman of them; hard-assed combat-ready troops and bright-as-a-button graduates alike—they just tore them right off."

"And that's all we have?"

"That's all, Lou," Manning says. "It's your ball—yours and Hellboy's—if you want to run with it."

"Hey, excuse me if I'm missing something here," Hellboy says. "If we go in there to Dawson's Creek—"

"Corner. It's Dawson—singular—*Corner.*"

"Whatever. If we go in there, isn't the same thing going to happen to us?"

Manning looks across at Jorgensen. Jorgensen turns to face Hellboy and says, "Not if we're not breathing."

"Ah, yes," Hellboy says after a few seconds. "There is that."

Outside of Manning's office, Hellboy asks Jorgensen, "So what's the problem?"

"We won't know until we get—"

"No, not with Dawson's Bend—"

"Corner. Dawson—singular—*Corner.*"

"Right. Not there. What's the problem with *you?*"

"My wife. My children." They're walking out of the B.P.R.D.'s small Manhattan office across from Central Park—otherwise known as "the Staging Post" amongst operatives ("good place to get a fresh horse and take a pee," as the word has it)—the sunshine glinting from the windows of the buildings up Central Park West and Columbus Circle. Kids are chasing each other around the park entrance, cab drivers are slapping car doors with their hanging left arms, car horns are *blarrrt!*-ing, skateboarders and roller-bladers are singing along to metal and rap piped into their cerebral cortexes.

Hellboy knows the gist of what's coming even before it comes; he only needs the fine details to complete the mental picture.

"Boating accident," Jorgensen says, checking the traffic for a break and making it sound like he's responding to someone who just asked him for the time. *Hey, sure ... it's four-fifteen; and, by the way, my wife and kids are dead.*

"I'm sorry."

"Not your fault," Jorgensen says with a shrug.

"How many kids?"

"Three. Joey, Candice, and Monty. Eight, five, and almost two. And their mom. Ruth." He turns to Hellboy. "You getting a cab or walking?"

"Walking." He waves his arm once. "Cabbies think I'm carrying a bazooka."

Jorgensen chuckles. "Yeah, sorry about that."

Hellboy shrugs, says, "About what?"

"The shtick with your arm. And the horns. Plus the heavy tan and—" He points casually to the back of Hellboy's voluminous coat. "—And that," he adds.

"You already knew all about it, right?"

Jorgensen chuckles and pats Hellboy on the shoulder. "Like I don't read *Life* magazine or watch TV, right?" He shakes his head. "I was kidding you."

Hellboy gives silent thanks for his coloring. "Yeah, I think maybe I get a little too self-conscious," he says, and then he takes a hold of his tail and stuffs the end into his coat pocket. "Come on, we got a 'walk.' We'll go through the park."

They stroll across Central Park West—Hellboy ignoring the excited mutterings and wide-eyed stares of recognition he gets as he goes by—and through the gates. Almost immediately, the sounds of the city start to fade away. After a few minutes, Manhattan is a recent memory of someplace they were but aren't anymore.

The story comes out steadily but with a degree of determination.

The Jorgensen family was holidaying. Washington State. Out on a boat. Stranded. Something wrong with the engine. Seas got choppy. Storm broke. Boat capsized. No moon. Just the five of them in the water. His hearing their cries over the sound of the wind and the sea. Frantically flailing one way and then another, swimming—no, not swimming: nothing so civilized in that sea— blind as he followed first one screaming voice and then another. The voices stopped. One by one. And all that was left was the sound of the storm. And of Lucius Jorgensen screaming their names out in the darkness, one after another, time after time after time.

"Jeez, I'm so sorry," Hellboy says.

"Like I said, not your fault."

They're sitting on a bench watching the squirrels.

"They found two of them," Jorgensen says, in a kind of oh-and-by-the-way manner. "Joey and Candice," he adds.

Hellboy waits before asking about Jorgensen's wife and the little boy. Jorgensen shakes his head.

"The medication do any good?"

Jorgensen gives a little chuckle but doesn't say anything.

"Not taking anything, huh?"

"They just want to give you anti-depressants. You get hooked on those babies, and it's night-night for good."

A big squirrel stops right in front of them, picks something up between its paws, and proceeds to eat. It watches them carefully.

"I asked Manning if I could come back. He said no. But then this came up, and he asked me. Just as well."

"Yeah? How's that?"

"If I'd stayed home—" He pauses and looks around, taking in a deep breath. "Well, there's nothing to stay home *for*. Nothing to carry on *living* for." He turns to Hellboy. "But I kept putting it off. Figured it was unfair to deprive the Company of my talents."

Hellboy nods. "And those are?"

"I've developed a solution that slows down the respiratory system without affecting consciousness. And when I say 'slows it down,' I mean it virtually stops the need to take in air at all. Through the nose, through the mouth ... even through the skin. We're going to be using it in cryogenics but it has certain benefits in everyday use. Such as in combat."

"The good ol' weapons of mass destruction."

Jorgensen nods. "With this stuff, they can throw anything they want to throw at us and it won't matter ... because we won't be breathing."

"How long does it last?"

"Couple hours. Three at the outside. We can't risk any longer."

"How come?"

"It slows the heart down—and I mean it pretty much stops it without your losing consciousness. But the downside of that—of the fact that the heart isn't pumping blood—is that you leave it too long, it starts to clot in the veins."

Hellboy follows another squirrel with his eyes.

"So, that what you think this is? Terrorist attack?"

"In Dawson Corner, Maine?" He shakes his head. "Uh-uh."

"So what?"

"I have absolutely no idea."

The town is up ahead of them, but they can't see it. Not an electricity or phone-line pylon, not a roadsign, not a distant rooftop. Nothing.

"Zilch," says Jorgensen, lowering his infrared binoculars. "Like trying to look inside a bran muffin."

Right in front of them, stretched across the road, is a wall of fog. Its sides pulsate and roil but it stays in one place—doesn't come any nearer to where they're standing.

The five of them drove over in a stretch limo that you could land planes on: Hellboy, Jorgensen, two marines who didn't speak anything except militarese, and a driver called Maurice. After a couple of brief exchanges—

You not too hot in that outfit?

Sir, no sir!

Nice weather today, huh?

Sir, yes sir!

—Hellboy thinks it's a blessing the marines don't speak much. Now they're here, the marines just stare, and Maurice spends his time chewing, shaking his head, and repeating the Savior's name as though it may help somehow. It doesn't.

Jorgensen hands a bottle of water and little plastic cup of tablets to Hellboy and then takes a similar dose himself.

"That it?"

Jorgensen nods. "That's it."

"What do we do now?"

"We wait."

"How long?"

"Half hour."

Hellboy looks up into the spring sky. The clouds are strung out like gossamer across a deep red and violet around the sun. "Sun's going down," he says.

"Yep."

Hellboy frowns. "That not a problem?"

"Why? Past your bedtime?" He chuckles. "We go in any earlier we could end up sucking on our guns." He nods at Hellboy's right arm. "Or, in your case, your hand."

"You ever considered stand-up?"

Jorgensen smiles but doesn't answer. He lifts a machine out of the back of their jeep and fastens a leather strap around his neck. He looks like a cigarette girl in one of the swanky Manhattan clubs, but Hellboy doesn't say anything. He just watches the wall of fog shimmering in front of them.

Jorgensen, now wearing some kind of earphones set attached to the tray at his stomach, goes right up to the fog and sticks what looks like a wand into it. He remains like that for several minutes, one hand holding the wand and the other adjusting dials and switches on the tray.

When he comes back, he's frowning.

"What was that all about?"

Setting the tray in the trunk of the limo, Jorgensen says, "Analyzing the fog."

Hellboy waits, watches Jorgensen check his watch.

"So?"

"So, it's not fog." He looks over at him and breathes in. He puts his hand over his mouth and nose and waits, watching Hellboy. After several minutes, he removes his hand. "I think we're okay," he says. "You ready?"

Hellboy shrugs. "I guess so. What was all that about?"

"All what?"

"You holding your breath."

"I wasn't holding my breath. There isn't any to hold."

"Huh?"

"Don't you feel anything?"

Hellboy pulls a face. "Like what?"

"Like your mouth being different?"

Hellboy looks at Jorgensen, smacks his lips, and frowns. "Hey," he says, his face lighting up like a child's. "It's working." He puts his hand over the lower half of his face and mumbles, "I'm not breathing."

"That's not strictly true," Jorgensen says as Hellboy removes his hand from his face and attempts to gulp in air, without success. "If you weren't breathing at *all*, you'd die."

"Bummer." Hellboy scowls and points at his mouth. "Sad face."

"Hard to tell the difference." Jorgensen hands a set of goggles to Hellboy, watches as Hellboy puts them on over his glare.

"*Real* goggles," Hellboy says. "You *do* care."

Jorgensen ignores him and says, "Your respiratory system has slowed to the slightest fraction of its usual rate—think of hibernation and then multiply it a hundred-fold. You'll get air but very little spread over long periods." He pulls a set of goggles over his own head. "Infrared," he says. Then he lifts a metal-handled reel of fluorescent yellow cord out of the jeep. He takes the end of the cord and starts attaching it to the jeep's door handle.

"These to help us see?" Hellboy swings around with the goggles in place.

"They're to help us see," Jorgensen says.

"That to stop us getting lost?" Hellboy asks, nodding at the cord.

"That's to stop us getting lost."

Hellboy grimaces. "Richest country in the world and we end up walking into oblivion wearing 3D glasses and carrying a length of string stretched out behind us and tied to the doorknob."

"Sometimes the least technological methods are the most effective."

"I know some politicians wouldn't agree."

Hefting the reel in his right hand, Jorgensen says, "Politics and common sense never were natural bedfellows."

"Amen to that."

"Okay," Jorgensen says, "time-to-go time." He reaches out a hand. "Hold my hand."

"Hey," Hellboy says, taking a single backward step, "don't I get flowers? Candies?"

"You got the goggles. You're turning into an expensive date. Just take my hand. We go in there, no telling what's going to happen. Could end up wandering around there until the pills wear off."

"Could be messy."

Jorgensen doesn't respond. He looks around and takes a step forward, Maurice and the two marines watching.

The yellow cord unravelling alongside them, Jorgensen and Hellboy step cautiously into the fog. Almost immediately, all reference to the outside—the sunshine, the blue sky, the clouds—disappear from sight. All that there is, is the fog—thick as cotton candy.

Hellboy shuffles his grip on Jorgensen's hand and makes to take a deep breath. Only no air comes in and none goes out. He looks down at his chest and repeats the attempt: no expansion. "I don't think I'm going to get used to this not breathing," he says. "I keep wanting to do it but—"

There's no response from Jorgensen.

"You sure it's okay?"

"It's like I said," Jorgensen says with a sigh. "And don't forget, you lived that way before you were born." Hellboy is suddenly aware that Jorgensen's voice has changed—he has turned to face Hellboy now, saying, "Assuming you were born, of course."

"A stork brought me."

"A roc more like."

They have walked about seventy or eighty feet now, and the fog doesn't seem quite so thick, although—even with the glasses—they can barely see their own hands in front of their faces.

Suddenly, Hellboy sees a dark shape pass in front of him, hears the sound of shoes on wooden boards for a few moments. Then silence again.

"Hear that?"

Jorgensen grunts.

They move on.

"Hey," Hellboy says, suddenly remembering. "You never did say ... about the fog, I mean."

"What about it?"

"You said it wasn't fog. How'd you figure that?"

"I analyzed it. Fog is pretty much just plain water—kind of vaporized into a mist-form, but basically plain water. This stuff is *primarily* water but it has two other components as well."

Squinting into the murk, Hellboy says, "What are those?"

"Well, the first one is mucin—that's a hydrophilic: in other words, it likes water."

"And the second one?"

"The second one is—or are—phospholipids."

Hellboy waits for a few seconds and then, when it's clear that Jorgensen isn't going to add anything more, says, "You're losing me here, doc. What's the significance of these extra two elements?"

"They're not typically found in fog, in mist, or even in rain."

"Where *are* they typically found?"

"In the eye. The mucin is created by the goblet cells of the conjunctiva while the phospholipids are produced by the meibomian glands. And, of course, water is produced by the lacimal glands."

"I thought you said that was just water?"

"It is. But it's also present in the eye and in a hundred other places as well. But not the mucin or the phospholipids."

Hellboy turns to face into the gloom and nods, turning the information over in his head. "You're telling me that this fog was created by an eye?"

Jorgensen yelps in pain.

"You okay?"

"Yes. I just walked into some kind of—" He lets go of Hellboy's hand and waves his hand in front of him until it connects with a clunk. "It's a road sign ... street sign, something like that." There's the sound of a frenzied rubbing of material. "Shit, that hurts."

"It'll be fine," Hellboy says. "So much for the damn glasses."

"I just wasn't watching where I was going," comes the response.

"Gimme your hand."

Re-connected and now walking on wooden boards alongside storefront windows they can just make out, Hellboy and Jorgensen choose each step very carefully.

"So, it's all been produced by an eye?"

"Several eyes, but yes ... it's produced by the eye. But only under certain circumstances."

"Yeah? How come?"

Jorgensen waits for a few seconds before he says, "It's tears."

After a while the fog seems to weaken. It doesn't fade away completely, and the intrepid duo still maintain their link, but they can soon make out the shapes of buildings and parked vehicles, fences and trashcans. And then, something else.

Hellboy watches, straining his eyes to see while Jorgensen crouches down by an object at the side of the road.

"There's two of them," Jorgensen says. "Both male."

"Dead?"

"Yep. *Well* dead." Jorgensen bends closer until the first shape's head assumes more detail. That's when he sees that the entire face has been blown off. He gives thanks at this moment that he cannot smell. Now if only he couldn't even *remember* smell, he would be fine. But, alas, he can. He can do only too well.

Is this your son?

Yes ...

And this your—

My daughter.

I'm sor—

She was five years old. Her name was—

The man pulls the sheet back but as he does, Lucius Jorgensen, suddenly feeling very old and frail, notices that one of his daughter's eyelids looks sunken ... as though there's nothing underneath it.

—Candice, he tells the man. Her name is Candice. He wonders whether he should have used the past tense.

With the sheet back over his daughter, the smell fades away a little. But only a little.

Have you found my wife? Jorgensen asks. My baby? He considers explaining that he's talking about two *bodies there, not just the one ... but he decides against it.*

The man shakes his head. Didn't find nobody el—

"You okay?" Hellboy asks.

Jorgensen stands up. "I'm fine." He shifts the reel of yellow cord to his left hand and flexes his right. "Nothing we can do for them."

Hellboy takes a hold of the man's jacket. "Looks like it's thinning out a little," he says. And it's true. As they start off again along the road—or wherever it is they're walking—they can make out building shapes, the familiar form of an automobile, and even their own slow-moving reflections walking parallel to them. Hellboy looks up.

"The moon's up. I'm getting light here."

They stop to look at the window, neither of them speaking, both of them flexing hands or lifting arms slightly, and finding something in such brief movements that gives cause for optimism ... even though they caused them themselves.

And then, from diagonally across the street, a high-pitched squeak cuts through the mist. Hellboy and Jorgensen turn around and squint into the murk where they can just make out a figure standing against a screen door. It's a woman, they both realize as the mist clears momentarily.

Stepping off from her porch and onto the path that leads to the roadside, the woman smiles dreamily, looking first at Hellboy and then at Jorgensen, her steps a little awkward, stilted, like she's maybe had a little too much to drink or just woken up. Then she looks back over her shoulder, back at the house, where the mist still swirls around the porch in blustery ribbons of gray and white.

"Ma'am?" Jorgensen says, keeping his voice calm, non-accusatory, non-threatening.

Mindful of his appearance, Hellboy pulls his gabardine coat about himself and attempts to cover his right arm—his Right Hand of Doom—with his left, and keep his tail under wraps. He's only partially successful but the woman, while continuing to look from one of their faces to the other, beaming all the time, seems not to notice.

"He came back to me," she says at last.

And it's a big Amen to that, Brothers and Sisters, Hellboy adds mentally.

"Ma'am?" Jorgensen says again, this time holding out a hand to the woman, taking a tentative step toward her, reducing the space between them. He pulls the goggles from his face and thrusts them into his pocket, returning the hand to its outstretched position.

Behind the woman, the porch door creaks open, its brittle whine cutting through the mist.

"My Davey," the woman says. "He came back to me." And she turns around, wringing her hands together, muttering.

Hellboy peers.

Jorgensen peers.

And then, slowly, falteringly, a young man makes his way down the two steps from the porch to the path before, one foot placed carefully in front of the other.

"Oh, Davey," the woman says, breathing the words rather than simply speaking them.

The man is little more than a boy, they now see as his face emerges from the swirling cotton candy that surrounds them. He's decked out in his Sunday best—a black or dark gray suit, white shirt fastened at the neck and crowned with a subtly colored tie (*red?* Hellboy thinks, looking down at his own hand which appears similar in shade and hue, though he wonders if it's the glasses). On his feet the boy is sporting sneakers, which seems incongruous with the rest of the outfit. But, around the water and coffee machines of the B.P.R.D., Hellboy has heard all about the constant battle of parenthood.

"Hellboy ... "

Jorgensen doesn't need to say any more. Hellboy has seen it for himself.

Now that the boy—surely no more than fifteen, sixteen years old—is almost upon the woman (presumably his mother), he raises his arms, hands flexed and stretched, fingers yearning for touch. He's walking very awkwardly now, Hellboy sees, his legs apparently being moved with great difficulty ... or pain? Hellboy glances up at the boy's face and sees no sign of discomfort. But those arms ...

Hellboy steps forward, throwing his coattails out around him and lifting his right arm.

"Hellboy—"

At the tone of Jorgensen's voice the woman turns, her smile fading as she sees Hellboy's arm raised. She turns fully and raises her own hands, palms erect against Hellboy, her eyes glaring wide.

"No," she shouts, "he means no harm."

Hellboy glances quickly at the shambling boy now only a few feet away from the woman's back, arms still outstretched. "Doesn't look that way to me, lady," he snarls ... but, as he watches the boy, he notices the right side of his head. And then the left. Hellboy frowns.

Responding to the frown, the woman turns and sees what Hellboy sees. The right side of the boy's head is blackened and indented; there seems to have been some attempt at covering over the discoloration but it hasn't been entirely successful. But the left side—a hair-covered flap of skin hanging over what appears to be a large hole, behind which Hellboy glimpses pieces of bone—is far worse.

"The bullet went right through," the woman says dreamily as she turns back to Hellboy. "But he came back to us from the undertaker's parlor. My Davey," she adds finally. "I think he wants to talk to you."

Hellboy holds his position as the boy finally reaches the woman and takes hold of either side of her head. He stays like that, as unmoving as a statue, and the woman drops her own arms by her side.

Hellboy takes three steps forward to take him within reaching distance of the woman. He watches her eyes roll backwards. And she opens her mouth.

Can mere sound have color?

Can it have a smell? Or a texture?

The sound that issues from Wilhemina Pritznuk has all of these things: it carries with it a blackness that is so impenetrable that mere light must attempt to go around it, casting brief reflections that shimmer and die in the mist alongside; it brings an olfactory odor so strong that Jorgensen's nose begins to bleed, and his eyes run with a yellow matter thick as mustard; and it moves toward and engulfs them with a sheer physicality so strong that it pushes them back, bending ribcage, sternum, and pelvis.

Staggering backwards, Jorgensen covers his ears ... then his nose and eyes ... and finally, he bends foward, wrong-footing himself so that he falls sideways, curling up, knees to forehead, crotch to mouth, turning his head sideways so that at least one ear is protected. Hellboy sees that the other one—the one that is unprotected—is bleeding.

We mean you no harm, the sounds say when their swirling is done.

And now the sound is acceptable; the blackness has drained from it and only the fog remains; the pressure is gone from Hellboy's and Jorgensen's frames, though the bruising remains; and the smell—either rancid meat or stagnant water—has faded, leaving only the faintest hint of staleness. The vaguest hint of cheap perfume on dirty skin.

Hellboy steadies himself and steps close to the woman.

Groaning, Jorgensen gets to his feet, mopping blood and matter from eye and ear, nose and mouth.

"Who are you?" he asks.

Me or the woman?

Jorgensen says, "Both."

Her name is Billie Pritznuk. She's my mother.

"And you are—"

"Davey?" Hellboy finishes.

Yes. I am—or was—David Pritznuk.

"Was? Who are you now."

Now I'm a shade. On the other side. But I am others, too. All *the others.*

"Why—Why are you here?" Jorgensen ventures.

To fix the break.

"Break?" Hellboy asks.

And so, through the woman's drab monotone of possession, the story unfolds.

W*hat you must understand is that the other side is a land inside a land.*

"Right," Hellboy intones.

Refusing to acknowledge the sarcastic tone, or simply ignorant of it, the woman/boy continues. *The newly dead assemble in the outer area where they wait to be acclimatized to their situation.* The voice pauses and then adds, *It's a difficult time.*

"I'll bet," says Hellboy. *He's pulling my leg*, he thinks.

Jorgensen glances at him fiercely.

"Sorry."

The grief is palpable. Millions upon millions, every day, countless thousands upon countless thousands each hour, hundreds upon hundreds every tiny fraction of a single second ... whether old or young, torn from their lives, separated from their families and their friends, coming to terms with death memory—

"Death memory?"

The woman turns to face Jorgensen. *Their bodies recall the very moment that everything closes down: the very nano-second when veins stop pushing through blood and hearts cease to beat. There is a time—the time of leaving—that they are aware, a knife-edge of understanding before they tumble over. That is death memory.*

Hellboy hears Jorgensen mutter something, but it's lost on him as the voice continues.

As I said, the grief is huge—in each case—and there are many, many cases. Try to imagine, the voice says, *the world as a whole: try to imagine—step back within your heads and picture the world, all the myriad continents and countries, the hospice bedrooms and hospital emergency rooms, the bombs, the killings, the traffic accidents, the household mistakes, faulty wiring, drownings, suffocations, fires ... the cancers, coronaries, and heart attacks ... the millions who die and the millions who are born ... the endless cycle of death and birth, birth and death. The comings and the goings. And before the newly dead can pass over completely, they must be cleansed.*

"Cleansed? Like some kind of detoxification process?"

Yes, the woman/boy says with what Hellboy thinks might just be a smile.

There is no sadness on the other side and none may take any in with them. For most newcomers, the process might last a day or two; for others, just a few hours; and for an unfortunate few, weeks or even months.

That accumulation of grief—the true, boundless grief of the death memory, built up over millions of years—

"The fog," Jorgensen mutters.

—yes, as you say, the fog, the voice adds. *It is unlike anything that exists on this side. While the death memory is being extinguished from them, these new arrivals will do anything to stop the pain and anguish. But, of course, there is nothing they can do. They must wait it out.*

"Cold turkey," Hellboy says.

Both the boy and woman nod in unison. *And so it flows and eddies and swirls about them, cutting them off from all others, making impossible any relief.*

"So the fog—this accumulation of grief—is all around this ... this waiting area?" Jorgensen asks.

Yes. The waiting area is a gray zone of exorcised grief impacted upon itself trillion-fold on trillion-fold. It's deadly to people who are still alive ... the embodiment of profound hopelessness and despair ... more than anyone could possibly bear. Well, you've seen what happened.

"With the soldiers?"

The woman nods. *They did whatever was necessary to stop it.* She shrugs. *And now they themselves are adding to it. More expunged grief.*

"And it's leaking out."

It was *leaking out,* the voice says directly to Hellboy.

"So what is this?" Hellboy asks. "Are you like the little Dutch kid plugging a hole in the dike with your finger?"

For a few seconds, both Hellboy and Jorgensen think that the woman-host is not going to respond but, at last, she says, *Something like that.* Then she lifts an arm and waves it out majestically. *And as you can probably see, the leak has been fixed and the fog is dissipating. In a few more hours it will be gone and safe for people to be in here.*

Jorgensen says, "But why did you come here?"

It's not only me. Many of the people who used to live in Dawson Corner are here ... at least all those who have relatives and friends still here in the town. Some, who no longer have access to their bodies, came in incorporeal form—ghosts, if you will—while others retrieved bodies from mausoleum crypts, cemetery plots, and, as in my own case, undertaker's parlor-slabs. The voice pauses for a few seconds and then adds, *Needless to say, the bodies they found were not always in the condition they'd left them.*

But we had to come. If we hadn't, then all of our friends and relatives here in town would have succumbed to the fog. We couldn't allow that.

"So how could you stop them?"

We couldn't stop them breathing it. What we could do was build up such a colossal weight of good feeling and optimism that it might counteract the effects.

"Sounds a little too 'new age' to me," Hellboy mutters.

The woman sighs and, behind her, just for a second or two, the boy drops his head slightly. *No, it's decidedly old age,* the voice says, the boy having raised his head again. *Optimism and faith have long been strong adversaries of resignation, acceptance, and despair. Of course, we haven't been successful in every case,* the voice continues, softer now. *But we did what we could.* After a pause, it adds, *And now I see it's time to go.*

Hellboy looks around him and sees the street is clearing. He can see store windows, an open sidewalk, parked automobiles, telegraph poles, a mailbox. And he can see a group of people ... a demonstration of sorts, all standing stock-still in the center of the street, the final wisps of gray twisting around them and dissipating into nothingness.

The people are men and women, boys and girls, young and old ...

Living and dead.

"Jesus Christ," Jorgensen says as he follows Hellboy's stare.

The boy removes his hands from the woman's head and steps around her, walking stiltedly across the street to where a gaggle of emaciated pensioners surround two badly disfigured accident victims from a five-vehicle smash-up on the Interstate five miles out of Messane, their hair burned away to stubble and their faces frazzled, one side exposing yellowed teeth and blackened gums; a young man wearing a kaftan, his face milky white, rubs shoulders with a boy of what could be around twelve or fourteen summers—it's hard for Hellboy to be more precise as the boy's skin is bloated and pallid, partly eaten away, the eye sockets empty holes ... and in his left hand he holds what appears to be a severed foot (this is confirmed when Hellboy sees that the boy is leaning to one side, his left leg ending in a ragged stump); two old women who can't weigh more than one hundred pounds between them, their hair wispy and fumbled, like steel wool, lean against the window of the hardware store, one of the women holding a small, gray-faced baby who, distinctly un-baby-like, watches the proceedings with a calm far beyond its apparent years. These are the solid ones, the corporeal ones;

there are others who look perfectly normal, undamaged and whole, holographic images hanging in the air like clean laundry, shimmering and shifting though there is no wind blowing.

"The dead of Dawson Corner," the woman says, her voice back to normal.

Hellboy sees, forming behind them on the sidewalk, the town's living inhabitants, their faces carrying tired smiles, moist eyes.

"Were you aware of what you were saying," Jorgensen asks, "when—you know—when Davey was holding you?"

The woman nods. "It was as though his voice—that wonderfully moving and familiar voice—were speaking right out of me ... right from here—" She hits her chest once, with a small closed fist. "—and I understood everything." She looks around and then squints upward. Shafts of moonlight are filtering through. She looks back at the two men and says, "Your people will be here soon."

"Is it safe?"

Jorgensen walks across to the group of corpses and cadavers, wraiths and wisps, shades and specters. "It's safe," he says, more a mumble than actual speech. When he reaches the boy—Davey—he holds out a hand.

"Jorgensen!" Hellboy steps forward onto the street, his tail and coat swirling out around him like a whiplash.

"Please ...," Jorgensen says.

Behind them, the woman says, "He can't speak. He's fresh from old Mister Swinney's funeral parlor, filled with sawdust and formaldehyde. That's why he had to speak through me."

With what appears to be a frown—his face creasing and folding like modeling clay, and his mouth opening slowly to form an almost-perfect O—the boy takes a hold of Jorgensen's hand.

Hellboy brings up his right arm and makes to spring forward, but the woman's hand on his shoulder stays him.

"Leave him be," she says. "Just leave him be. They won't hurt him."

Hellboy is not convinced but, seeing no immediate danger, he rests his arm by his side, suddenly feeling its full weight.

Jorgensen shudders, pulls back with a start though he doesn't break contact with the boy. The boy takes another step forward and places his other hand on the side of Jorgensen's face. And then he drops both hands, steps back, and, without a word being spoken, he drops to the ground.

Others—the damaged ones or the ones wearing pressed suits and best dresses—follow his example.

Then the shades fade, the storefronts and sidewalk behind them now showing through their midriffs and their legs, increasing in its intensity, until, as one, they disappear like soap bubbles, popping out of existence as though they had never truly been there.

Hellboy wonders if perhaps they never were.

Jorgensen drops his head, and for a few seconds he seems to be about to fall himself. But then he straightens, lifts himself tall, and turns. As he does so, he looks across the street.

Hellboy turns and stares.

Outside the general store there's the faintest glimmer on the sidewalk, a disturbance of the air particles, of something bending the fabric of the atmosphere out of shape. Out of nothingness, a shape begins to form, a roiling mass of color and density, shadow and substance.

"Hellboy ..."

"I'm watching it," Hellboy says, "I'm watching it," and he steps to the side, standing astride the outstretched figure of David Pritznuk, his tail unfurled and swaying side to side.

"Get the people off the street," Jorgensen says, and he takes a step toward the disturbance.

The "disturbance" is some kind of fracture in the ether, like a holographic transmission that's not quite connecting. But parts of it are now showing through as Jorgensen walks slowly toward it, showing through and then fading out again, then coming back—different parts of it—and fading again.

Hellboy moves to his left, covering Jorgensen's side and back, stepping carefully over the prone shapes, some of them on the road itself and others half on and half off the sidewalk.

As Hellboy starts to call out to the townsfolk, two things happen: the first thing is that the "disturbance," such as it is, finishes coming through and all of the electrical static charge around it subsides, leaving only a woman of about thirty-five, forty. Just before the second thing happens, Hellboy notices that she's carrying something in her outstretched arms.

The second thing that happens is someone grabs his tail. And that's when the lights go out in Hellboy's mind, leaving in their wake a dim but somehow comforting and reassuring glow. He feels himself jerk spasmodically, waving his big right arm weakly across in front of himself—it's ineffectual because there's nobody there. As he lurches drunkenly he catches sight of the boy—David whatsisname—propped up on an elbow with the other hand firmly holding onto his tail. He thinks maybe he should do something about that but that's when the voices come into him.

And then through him.

He opens his mouth to speak, wondering what it is he's going to say.

Lucius? Oh, baby ...

The words taste strange in Hellboy's mouth ... strange and wet, with an underlying saltiness of sea water. He can feel the memory of it on his face, in his mouth, up his nostrils ...

Without turning to Hellboy, Jorgensen moves forward, dropping the spool of yellow cord right where he stands. "Ruth?"

I'm here, baby. You've been worrying and you shouldn't. We're fine.

"'We're'?" He looks down at the bundle she's carrying and sees a small arm shoot upwards, wafting the air before withdrawing.

Come see him, the voice coming out of Hellboy's mouth says softly. *Come say hello to your son.*

The tiny head pushes itself forward from the bundle and turns jerkily toward Jorgensen. The face smiles.

"Monty ...," Jorgensen whispers.

Tilting his head to one side—where he sees the outstretched cadaver still holding onto his tail—Hellboy, or whatever powers now operate from within him, whispers. Exactly *what* he whispers, he doesn't know ... words and phrases, rounded syllables and stuttered consonants, vignettes and extracts, softnesses and affections, breaths and oaths. Absently, his head, arms, and legs twitching as though he's plugged into a main electricity supply, Hellboy glances up ahead as the sounds pour from inside of him. There, on the sidewalk of a midnight small-town in Maine, Jorgensen, Ruth, and Monty are re-united. They don't touch—they *can't* touch—but Hellboy sees them look into each other's eyes. Sees Jorgensen's hand move out to the bundle in his dead wife's arms ... and softly push right though it, the image swirling like colored smoke where the hand passes.

Then, all at once, the pressure on his tail suddenly subsides and Hellboy falls forward onto the pavement with a dull thud. He lies there for seconds which extend into minutes. When he lifts his head, the street is empty of shades and ghosts and Jorgensen is on his knees—Hellboy can hear the man sobbing. Alongside Jorgensen, the living townsfolk of Dawson Corner have gathered, their hands on his shuddering shoulders.

They have all lost friends and loved ones this night, Hellboy realizes as he scans the street so strewn with bodies. Either lost them or re-lost them.

"You know," Hellboy hears one woman say to another, "there's no sadder sound in the whole world than that of a man crying."

The other woman nods and then, very carefully, turns to look in Hellboy's direction.

"What about the other one?" she says.

"He'll be okay," comes the response. And then, "Well, as okay as he was when he got here I guess."

On the way back to Manhattan, Jorgensen says, "You okay?"

Hellboy nods. "Okay. Empty. Took it out of me." He looks at Jorgensen and says, "You?"

Jorgensen nods. "Better now."

"What did she say—I mean, what did *I* say? No, forget that. I have no right to ask."

Jorgensen waves never mind and says, "She just told me to take care of myself."

"Sound advice."

Hellboy sees an exit sign coming up on the right, but no sooner has he seen it than it's behind them. He turns and looks out of the rear window.

"What is it?" Jorgensen asks.

Turning around in his seat, Hellboy addresses the marines up front. "Either of you guys see that last exit sign?" he says.

"Sir, yes sir!" the driver snaps. For a second, Hellboy is afraid the man will stand sharply to attention and salute right where he's sitting, causing the stretch limo to jacknife against the traffic.

"What did it say?"

"It said 'To Arkham,' sir," the man says. "Twenty-eight miles, sir."

Hellboy turns to face Jorgensen and smiles, shaking his head. "I thought it was a myth," he says softly.

Jorgensen leans toward him and says, "That's what I thought about you."

As the limo speeds toward the waiting metropolis of New York City, the sun edges over the horizon and spreads its light westwards.

> And yonder shines Aurora's harbinger;
> At whose approach, ghosts wandering here and there,
> Troop home to churchyards.
> William Shakespeare (1564-1616)
> *A Midsummer Night's Dream*

For all the gang at the Travelling Man comic-book emporium in Leeds.

DOWN IN THE FLOOD
SCOTT ALLIE

A little more than ten years back, Hill's Clothing Store had caught fire. The flames started in the basement, although it was never determined how. The fire shot up the narrow staircase first into Men's Clothing, then filled the single-story shopping area and the small warehouse above. Below, wooden doorways connected the cellars of the commercial block, and when those basement doors burst, one after another, the fire worked through downtown. Townies had gathered around, as closely as they dared. The older ones, having seen the hotel at the other end of Market Street go down in flames twenty years before, considered the spectacle familiar. Before the site was cold, they'd picked through the wreck of the clothing store, scavenging T-shirts and shoes that weren't too badly damaged. More than one scavenger was surprised by hidden wells of flame exploding through the ash, but no one was hurt. The town's history was punctuated by fire—some more tragic than others. It was even more frequently marked by flood.

In the spring of 1994, the river rose over Market Street, swamping basements still blackened in places. The same people who had watched the last fire now surveyed the scene from rowboats and small outboards, from the roofs of buildings rebuilt between disasters. On the fifth day of the flood, two high-school boys rented a boat from Foote's Canoe, located up Ipswich River toward the edge of town. Foote's customers normally had to turn back upstream above the dam near Market Street. In the new landscape carved out by floodwaters, not one eyebrow was raised as the boys went over the dam, which was almost invisible under the heavy flow pulling them into town.

As they paddled across Estes Street, the boys saw Bill Damon and Joe Sargent wave from the relocated edge of the river. The men tossed their spent cigarette butts into the still water and turned back to Bill's car. They had used up their lunch break watching the river rock a van whose owner had remembered too late where he'd parked it, after the water had made it irretrievable.

Derek Lemieux pushed his paddle against the fender of the van, but only managed to shove his canoe off course, rather than spinning the van as he'd hoped. The river pooled and the flow eased in the wide open intersection where Market Street met Pole Alley, in the old truck-loading dock at the decommissioned Sylvania factory—not a casualty of the flood, of course, but of big businesses with little use for small towns. As the river's pull slowed in that flat expanse, the boys had to put some muscle to work to keep the canoe going. Derek barely remembered the last flood, back in that time when kindergarten first pushed him beyond his own neighborhood, out into the town that would have more to say about his future than he would ever have to say about the town.

He crouched in the half-inch of water they'd taken into the canoe and looked into the windows of the flooded restaurant, the posh riverside Chipper's. The fully stocked kitchen was completely submerged; it would still be out of business four months after the waters receded. The boys paddled back into the stronger pull as the river narrowed under Choate Bridge. Derek ducked low into the boat. The ancient keystone bridge usually allowed a six-foot clearance, but now its moss-coated underside pressed in over the highwater with the unexpected stink of low tide.

In the front of the canoe, Derek knew he was supposed to keep paddling on his right; steering was in Eddie's hands, behind him. But when Derek had insisted on the front, he hadn't meant to relinquish control. He heard a groan as he moved his paddle to his left again, followed by a light splash on the right when Eddie switched to keep them moving forward. Derek switched sides again just to screw with his friend, and Eddie's grumble bordered on verbal.

Stricken by how high the waters had stretched across Market Street, Derek hadn't considered how wide the river would be east of town, between the bridge and the wharf. The stench of the water worsened; Derek supposed it had something to do with their approach to the saltwater marshes that separated the town from the sea. The canoe rounded a sharp bend in the river by the middle school. He squinted at the wharf in the distance, thought he could recognize his father's cousin, Michael Michon. Michael backed his brand-new lobster boat into the water with the pride of the Yankee fisherman, that rare vocation in which real independence still had a place.

Something caught Derek's eye where a cluster of rocks, usually a whitewashed convention center for gulls, now barely poked above the surface of the water. The smell was worse here. Derek squinted, drew a breath through his mouth to avoid the lowtide stink, and moved his paddle back to the left of the boat. Eddie grunted, throwing a small spray from his paddle as he pulled it from the water and slapped it down on the right side.

"No," Derek said, wiping at the water Eddie had flicked at the back of his head. "I wanna get over to them rocks."

"Why?"

They neared the river's edge.

"You see that kid over there?" Derek asked.

Had the floater been face up, the two boys in the canoe no doubt could have identified him as twenty-nine-year-old Todd Russell—not that Todd was particularly well known, but in a swamp-bound old New England village of eleven thousand, it doesn't take a lot to register in someone's head. Like the people he'd grown up with, Todd Russell had swum in the river as a child, even though by his teenage years the bright brown water had presented plenty of danger if taken in through the mouth or a fresh cut; boys swam beneath the Choate Bridge wearing sneakers for stepping on unseen garbage. Todd had swum in the ocean, against the tide, had even played lifeguard one summer at the daycamp at the Don Bosco seminary, an excellent opportunity for checking out—and even once scoring with—the Catholic girls. So the fact that he washed up drowned with no sign of trauma would have shocked many in the small town, were he not the third man to be found in such a state since the flood began. The third *man*, because none of the four women who'd gone missing that week had turned up at all. Sheriff Douglas Marsh scratched his head over this latest round of deaths and disappearances for another couple days before calling the Bureau for Paranormal Research and Defense.

Abe Sapien waited for nightfall within a van unadorned by agency insignia, parked by the Christian Science Center at the base of Town Hill. His latest hand had only turned up a single face card, and he was in need of a king. For Abe to waste the afternoon hiding behind a game of solitaire while Liz and Hellboy interviewed people was as stupid as it was unfair, considering the case involved a river. If the townspeople—if America at large—could accept a seven-foot-tall, cloven-hoofed demon on the government payroll, surely they could handle a fish man. But Abe remained a secret. Hellboy's appearance on the cover of *Life* magazine had instantly transformed him from monster to celebrity, but Professor Bruttenholm had yet to arrange such an opportunity for Abe.

The sun eased into the hilltops on the other side of downtown. The drive up from Connecticut in the overheated van had left Abe spacey. Of course Hellboy and Liz wouldn't mind the heat. Sitting up front, the two of them had a rolling view to keep them interested. But now, waiting while they surveiled the town, Abe was positively restless. At least he had a swim to look forward to.

Knuckles rapped the back of the van five times in a familiar rhythm, and Abe pushed his cards together into an uneven pile, answering, "Two bits."

Liz Sherman pulled open the door and grinned, a short cigarette burning between her lips. "Mayberry's A-okay, Agent Sapien." He eyed her cigarette, and she muttered, "Oh, sorry." She took the smoke between two fingers, and her eyes flared yellow so briefly that if Abe didn't know better, he'd think he'd imagined it. The cigarette sparked like a magician's flash paper, was gone, leaving a sharp, sweet smell of tobacco—and of course not a mark on her fingers.

She slipped into the van, opening it only as far as she needed, guaranteeing that no passerby would catch a glimpse of her partner. Abe craned his neck as he moved backward in the van, sneaking what little view he could. Traffic was light at the foot of the hill, and the bar across the street was well lit, but nearly empty.

"Get anything?" he asked.

"Hellboy's talking to the sheriff. He wanted to give local law enforcement, such as it is, a heads up about you—so if you see badges and flashlights tonight, don't be nervous. I spent the afternoon with those kids who found the latest body, then I hit the library."

"How far back does it go?"

"Libraries still use *microfiche*, believe it or not. The newspapers had something from 1943. But they have volunteers at the library who know everything that's happened in the last hundred and fifty years. A guy named Doc says there were people disappearing as early as the turn of the century, and he's pretty sure it goes at least ten years further back than that. His second cousin, female, disappeared in 1921, body never recovered. When she died, there was already local lore around the phenomenon."

"Sea monster?"

"Ghosts. There was a shipwreck on a reef at the far end of the bay back in 1883. By the twenties, people said the ghosts of the sailors were gathering brides. That's why the men are found, but not the women. I looked into the crash, just for the hell of it, and it was a steam ship with paying passengers—"

"So there were likely as many men as women," Abe realized.

"Also, no one *died*. Still, there've probably been plenty of deaths in the bay, going further back."

"You think that's it?" Abe said, craning his neck and scratching at the side of his head. Liz didn't say anything for a minute. Abe recognized the look.

"Do I think it's ghosts?" she said, running a hand through her red hair as if to distract them both. "Maybe, but ..." A dull knock came at the van door.

Liz held Abe's eyes for a moment. Without looking away from her he said simply, "What?"

"Pizza's getting cold."

"Not a problem." Liz smiled, and the air stirred. She opened the door and reached for the two square cardboard boxes Hellboy held balanced atop his giant right hand.

An all-ages curfew was in effect, enforced mainly by the locals' fear of the river, so Abe didn't bother with his overcoat and fake-beard ensemble, when, fifteen minutes later, the sun and the pizza had both disappeared. "Perhaps the disguise does call some attention," Bruttenholm had admitted, "but it's so very absurd, no one would suspect it was designed to conceal anything as significant as you." Wearing nothing but shorts and sneakers—the recommended attire of the teens who still braved the Ipswich River—Abe walked with his partners to the old Choate Bridge.

A car drove by. If the driver noticed the trio standing just outside the reach of the streetlight, she was probably too distracted by Hellboy's tail bobbing above the curb to notice his partner, green skin dimmed in the blue light of the moon and stars.

Abe threw a leg over the side of the bridge, straddling the rotted wood edge of the wall. No river was clean where it ran through the middle of a town, even a town as small as this, but he found it inviting nonetheless.

Hellboy said, "Shouldn't you wait half an hour after eating?"

Liz ignored him. "Me and H.B.'ll be walking along the river to make sure no locals fall in. I found a place where we could sneak you into the water in daylight without anyone seeing. If you can't see anything tonight, I mean."

"Do you smell that, Liz?" Abe asked, gesturing over the bridge. "It's always dark under water like this."

"Right. If you find any of the women ...," Liz began, but if she had anything to add, she forgot it.

Abe Sapien made hardly a splash as he went under.

The current was strong near the surface, but a reluctant hitch in the flow told him that the flood would soon end. A couple of otters, perfectly silhouetted by the bridge's streetlight, slipped over his head, and he copied their sideways spiraling motion. Normally the water would only be a few feet deep here, but the flood provided Abe plenty of space to move around. Skimming the bottom he found the usual refuse—cans and bottles, a shoe, a crate the color of which was now indistinct. The trash thinned away from the bridge, and he found only the occasional scrap of metal, obscured and eaten through by rust, the last bits of abandoned boats whose wooden hulls had long since dissolved.

Despite the trash, the pollution, despite the stench that had nearly made Derek Lemieux turn back upstream a few days earlier, the river welcomed Abe. Just as the night takes the sharp edge off the world, the open water relaxed him, concealed him from the eyes of strangers. The burden of his secret existence—even the weight of his own lean build—finally rolled out of his shoulders, his upper back. The rhythm of the river beat in his veins. He reversed direction, flipping backward, his head slipping between his feet, and pounded against the river up toward the dam.

Liz Sherman laughed out loud when Hellboy said, "This town reminds me of Ireland—old and dark."

They walked through the outfield of a baseball diamond which was normally not so close to the water's edge. Ahead the river bent sharply around the field, so that a small section of open grass was surrounded by water on three sides. This was a place where young lovers would pause and consider one another while listening to the rushing tide. Liz knew just enough about teen romance to know that it was too early in the year for any of that, with too much of a chill on the breeze for most girls, even were it not for the threat of the drowned and missing.

"That's funny," Liz said. "When Bruttenholm got the report, he said, 'Ipswich. That's a dark town.' Did he say that to you?"

"Nope."

"This sort of place freaks me out. The second I walked into that library, they all knew I was an out-of-towner."

"Yeah," Hellboy chuckled in a rolling baritone, "I got a little of that when I popped into the pizza joint." Liz rolled her eyes, more at herself than her partner. "No place reminds me of where I come from," he said.

"I don't think I'm ready to go where you're from," she said, not realizing until the words were gone that Hellboy had meant the military base in New Mexico, nothing more alien than that. His mind went to the devil much less often than hers, especially when those thoughts were focused inward.

"Have you noticed a change in Abe?" she said; she didn't think of it as changing the subject.

"How do you mean?"

"I slipped the other day when we were watching you interview that séance medium with the wooden leg. I said she seemed kind of uncomfortable. Abe just made this real casual gesture—he still had the disguise on, and he tilted his head down and looked over his glasses and said, 'Well, Hellboy is rather tall.' His gesture just kind of struck me. I said, 'Abe, you're acting more human all the time.'"

"Ouch."

"Yeah. But he has to know it wasn't an insult, right? I mean, half the time I don't think of myself as all that human."

"The other half you wish you weren't."

"Right. That said, I've known the guy all my adult life, and he does seem like more of a ... well, more of a guy lately."

Hellboy had stopped a few paces back. Liz turned toward him now. "Hey," she said, "what are you looking at?"

The water pushed harder as Abe neared the dam, until finally he was under its direct pressure. He surfaced, held the granite wall that lined the north side of the river. It had receded a bit, so that the dam was doing its job again. Foam rose in the white rushing spill. On the far side, a gray colonial mansion stood just feet from the water's edge. They'd be having a hell of a time in their basement this week. Someone stood in a second-floor window looking out, but the darkness protected Abe from their sight, even under the winking light of the quarter moon. Downstream, the river calmed, a black ribbon uninterrupted in its retreat while foam collected along the edges. Abe let go of the granite border, waved unseen to the man in the window, and let himself be swept seaward. He slipped under the Choate Bridge, coasting on his back. That was when he noticed the gathering clouds.

The night grew darker as the narrow curve of moon was hidden. Stars lit up the silvered edge of approaching clouds, then vanished behind them. The chill running through Abe's spine had little to do with the temperature, but much to do with the water. He righted himself, kicked his feet to put his head above water. As always, the first hint of trouble made him assume a bearing better suited for land than sea, more man than fish. It wasn't always a bad instinct. He didn't have much time to consider this, however; he swam as hard as he could in the direction of the blue lights over the baseball field.

He left the river at the sharp bend. He'd lost sight of the lights at the water's edge, climbing the few feet of steep incline above the rising water. The two blue pinpricks hovering ten feet above the ground made him think of corpse candles, those clusters of light along the English coast that appear where sailors drown. He'd seen corpse candles up close, though, and these lights were different. They moved over the ground, toward the water which flowed fast around the corner of the field. Hellboy and Liz were following them.

Abe stumbled a moment as he found his land legs. He called, but they didn't respond, didn't slow, and the warning chill made his gills flare. He ran between Hellboy and Liz, turned to face them, raising his hands to stop them, but the phosphorescent blue glow of their eyes, so close to that of the lights overhead, surprised him enough that he let them step around him.

Across the field another light caught his eye, and the distant blue glow cast a halo in the rising mist. With a head full of unanswered questions, Abe knew this much: the lights were leading people into the water, taking the women elsewhere and discarding the men. He didn't wait to identify the gender of the person on the other side of the field, as his two friends reached the river.

Liz fell on her knees at the water's edge, looking up at the enthralling light, her eyes more than reflecting that unnatural blue. Hellboy hunched over, wading out into the river. Abe dove between the two into the fast-moving though shallow water. The river's pull toward the ocean was not so comforting now, with his entranced friends drawn into it, out of his reach. He turned and leapt at Hellboy, hooking both arms around the giant red hand. Hellboy's short legs and enormous torso made him easy to knock over in the water, and Abe spun him around, though the effort brought the fish man splashing down on his side. Hellboy had lost sight of the two blue lights, and scanned the clouds absently for them, his wide mouth open, upper teeth exposed in an expression fit for a cartoon mule. From the corner of his eye, Abe caught three blue lights lining up overhead, an azure belt for Orion. Something fell into the water near Liz.

It was two locals who'd been crossing the field, their eyes glazed over in ethereal blue: an unremarkable man thick around the middle and the neck, and a girl who looked either much younger, or just forever underfed. They must have ignored both the all-ages curfew and their dead and missing fellow townies. Now the man sat in the water by Liz, gazing vacantly at the lights overhead. The girl, hair that some would describe as dishwater blond dripping in stringy plaits across her glowing eyes, crawled on all fours off to the right, well out of Abe's reach. Liz got to her feet, and took a decisive step toward Abe before stumbling again in the tide. She was close enough to the man that Abe thought he could get an arm around each of them, but it would mean letting go of Hellboy, possibly losing the girl. He barely hesitated.

One arm caught Liz around the middle, knocking her down. The other looped around the man's neck and shoulder in a rough approximation of a lifeguard's hold. As Abe struggled to get his footing, Liz slid out of his grasp, water splashing over her head as she tumbled a few feet closer to the sea. Just beyond her, Hellboy slipped in past his waist.

Out in the middle of the river, five silhouettes, man-shaped but certainly not men, stared back at Abe with glassy blue eyes. Eyes like fish, like frogs. The water stopped its flow for a moment, then pressed on.

"Liz!" he cried, as she slipped toward the things in the water. He lashed out with his free arm, found her long red hair, and jerked her head back. Her eyes popped open in blue circles, flashing quickly to brilliant yellow. The riverside lit up with flame unlike any even this town had seen before, bursting from this thin girl. Abe felt water evaporate on his face—he lost his grip, but she was saved already. The things behind Hellboy were illuminated by a yellow diamond of flame shooting up around Liz, backlighting her in stark silhouette. The things from the river slipped back underneath. Liz fell toward Abe, and he saw her pale brown eyes, the eyes of a woman in her right mind, though perhaps a little bewildered by her own power. "Hold him," Abe said, pushing her at the enthralled townie, and diving after Hellboy. Water splashed over red forehead stumps. The young local woman or girl fell headfirst, arms at her side, into the undertow.

Beneath the surface the scene was both calmer and darker. Hellboy's black shape glided across the rocky bottom, seaward, the right hand kicking up puffs of riverbed. The girl's hair swam around her head in a colorless cloud. They were too far from one another for Abe to grab at once, so he planted his feet on the rocks and launched himself at the girl, slipping an arm gently across her breasts. He turned toward Hellboy, whose blue eyes still glowed underwater. Another figure slipped up between them, swift as an eel, a sudden, unmoving reef in the rushing water. Those blue eyes. Insane syllables, weird sounds that couldn't have come from a human mouth, vibrated in the water, pierced Abe's mind and made the girl in his arms cry out in a silent burst of air. No sooner did Abe realize the thing in the river was speaking to him than it disappeared.

Hellboy was also gone.

Just after dawn Sheriff Douglas Marsh, his brother Barney in tow, knocked three times sharply on the back of the van parked by the Christian Science Center. The door flew open, the red-headed girl popping out with the word, "Hellboy?!"

and spilling her steaming cup of coffee. Another person huddled in the shadowed seatbacks at the far end of the van, holding a nylon coat up to conceal himself. The folds of fabric rendered the yellow initials on the back of the jacket unreadable. Barney Marsh took a quick step back at the sight of the long bare legs—not the girl's—that stretched across the floor of the van. Translucent flaps of skin, the pale green of moss, ran up the backs of the calves, seams in shimmering silk stockings. The arms holding up the jacket were covered in a black sweatshirt, but something shifted underneath the covering, first to one side, then back, and Barney somehow knew what it was. Fins.

"Ma'am ...," Sheriff Marsh said, " ... and, um ..."

"His name's Abraham," she said. The coat came down from the large round eyes. The girl grinned at the fish man when she said, "He's a doctor." In fact, both smirked, as though they might be sharing an old joke.

"Sir, then," the Sheriff said, and frowned. "You're missing the red one, that right?"

They left the van at the foot of Town Hill and took the squad car to Labor-in-Vain Road, parking in the middle of the street in front of Orville Giddings's house. The soft shoulders on either side were already bumper to bumper with old cars and pristine SUVs. Gid waited for them by his mailbox. He ran a hand through his long hair, still black though the man was well past the age of retirement. Doris Hopping, bible clutched to her chest, came around the side of Gid's house from the backyard, weeping, and piled into her Volvo, apparently unconcerned that the sheriff had left her no way out of the dead-end road.

Gid rolled his eyes in greeting, said to the sheriff, "Crowd's gathering," and pointed around the side of the house.

Liz and Abe followed the sheriff; Barney stayed back, sharing no more than a deep sigh with the old townie until after his brother, the girl, and the freak rounded the side of the rundown colonial. It was Gid who broke the relative silence of the morning.

"You should see the one in my backyard."

"Who'd have thought, in our little town?" Barney said.

"Your town? You're not from here."

"I was born here same as you, Gid."

"Eh, your parents are from Peabody. Just 'cause a cat has kittens in an oven it don't make them biscuits."

Barney Marsh ran the toe of his boot through a mud puddle. "The girl doesn't look so bad," he said to the ground, and walked back to the cruiser, sparing a pitying glance toward Mrs. Hopping.

Gid had gone into his backyard and down to the highwater to spend a few hours fishing before his wife, a late riser, cooked breakfast. Ruth was well entrenched in the local gossip loop, had in fact been in the library when the red-haired girl started asking questions. But Gid didn't have much to say to Ruth after dark anymore. He hadn't heard about the red man who'd come to town to take care of the flood, so he'd been more than surprised to find him face down in the rocks not too far from where Todd Russell had washed up two days prior. Gid had heard of Hellboy years ago, but as their paths had not yet crossed, his first thoughts were not of a rescuer when he spotted the tail and hooves poking up from the rocks, with the tell-tale horn stubs and right-hand anchor down in the water. Instead of a morning spent fishing, Gid had turned his back on the river and run to the telephone, debating a moment over whether to call the nearby Reverend John Hooker, or the more remote police station. It was the good Reverend Hooker himself who convinced Gid to call the cops.

Liz Sherman pushed through the crowd of about twenty locals gathered at the river's edge, and kneeled in the water where Hellboy lay, unconscious and for all appearances drowned. Abe followed reluctantly, pushed along by the sheriff. The wharf across the way was also full of onlookers, fishermen delaying their work for the chance to see something even more interesting than a sleeping demon. A dinghy slipped across the river, one man rowing and another standing, barely maintaining his balance. The man on his feet had a Super-8 camera trained on Hellboy. When Abe saw the camera he spoke Liz's name, and the man in the boat shifted his attention from Hellboy to the less famous and perhaps more film-worthy agent. Abe bent down to touch Liz's shoulder, said, "Maybe I should go back to the officer's car."

"Bruttenholm wouldn't send you out if he didn't plan on you being seen eventually," she whispered. "What better place to start? You probably saved this town."

She rapped on the back of Hellboy's skull with the knuckles of her left hand. Abe steadied her when she jumped, nearly as much as the sheriff jumped, as Hellboy jerked awake. She stroked the back of his head gently, turning to grin at the cameraman who'd leapt even higher than the others. The camera had hit the edge of the boat and fell inside, but the lens cracked off and disappeared into the lessening flood.

"Jesus, what time is it ...?" Hellboy said.

"Six twenty-nine," Liz said as Gid and his wife, whose hair was as wild as Professor Bruttenholm's just out of bed, parted the crowd. Ruth Giddings smiled down at her visitors. "This fine gentleman," Liz gestured to Gid, "complained that you were scaring away his fish."

"Nah, that was Abe, last night. Hey, wait a minute—you guys waited till now before looking for me?"

"You're as likely to drown as I am," Abe said, his attention split between the gawking teenage boy on his right and the boat coming near them, the man searching his styrofoam cooler for another lens. "Anyway, we did look for you."

"For a while." Liz lit her first smoke of the morning, an extra flourish in her burning fingertips to keep the locals interested—although it probably wasn't enough to play to the cheap seats across the river.

"Nice," Hellboy said, scanning the audience. He pushed himself up into a sitting position on the rocks, letting his feet trail in the water.

"Where'd you get that?" said Abe, indicating the pale blue stone hanging around Hellboy's neck, wound in fishing line and smooth and translucent as glass. The stone lay cold against Hellboy's broad chest. There was long grass caught in the line as well, and a rusted fishing hook had found purchase in Hellboy's skin—if the tiny wound had bled at all, it did not now. He touched it with his right hand, and the stone or glass shattered silently on contact, blew off his chest in the morning breeze.

Abe Sapien laughed.

"I barely touched it," Hellboy grunted.

"I think it had a letter on it, some kind of symbol," Liz said, flicking ash in the water, then catching herself. "Oh, sorry," she said to Abe.

"Eh, what's the difference?" he said.

Hellboy rose to his hooves and hopped from the rocks onto Gid's back lawn, nearly sending the old married couple running to their door, the rest of the locals straight to Reverend Hooker. Most managed to collect themselves, if only out of embarrassment for the burst of laughter they'd inspired on the wharf side of the river. The men in the rowboat had just touched the grass themselves, and the one in front overcame his lack of coordination and dragged the boat ashore.

"Did you get a good look at those things?" Liz asked Hellboy.

"Nah. Water was pretty dark, I was kind of foggy the whole time. Last thing I remember before conking out was what that one guy said to Abe."

A few of the townies turned their eyes on Abe; others muttered his name to one another beneath their breath. He rolled his shoulders, shrugging the comment off. "What makes you think it was talking to me?"

Hellboy pulled the last of the fishing line from around his throat, and realized that the thing in the river had spoken in a language no human—not even Abe, apparently—could understand. He shrugged. It had been clear enough to his ears. These things usually were.

"Well, he had his back to me, and he said he was sorry. Something like, 'We've taken our mates from this town for ages. We didn't realize they belonged to you now.'"

Hellboy shrugged. "That was the basic gist of it, at least."

No one said a word. The locals simply turned to Abe Sapien with expressions ranging from quizzical to accusatory, and not without a little fear. The burden that had finally rolled out of his shoulders, his upper back, returned with full force under their eyes.

NEWFORD SPOOK SQUAD

CHARLES DE LINT

Now ...
   We haven't had any rain for the past few weeks, so the water level in the storm drains isn't high—a trickle in most places, though occasionally it comes up to our ankles. But not having to slosh through heavy storm water doesn't make it any more pleasant to be down here. Our flashlights cut a series of criss-crossing beams into the darkness ahead of us. The air has a musky scent, and I keep hearing things scuttling away from us in the darkness.

Rats, I guess. Nothing big. Not what we're looking for, but then who knows what the hell we're really looking for? All I know for sure is three workers from the Water & Sewer Department have gone missing down here, and no one knows what happened to them.

"What's that up ahead?" Hellboy asks.

The beam from his flashlight plays on a side tunnel. Walker checks the screen of his PDA. He downloaded the specs for this tunnel system before we left headquarters.

"It's a dead end," he says.

When we reach the branching tunnel, Hellboy plays his flashlight down its length.

"A dead end?" he asks.

"That's what's showing up on my schematic," Walker tells him.

"Then how come I can feel a breeze?"

He's right. There's a draft coming down the tunnel toward us.

I step around him and move further in, the beam of my flashlight showing nothing but damp stone walls as far as it will reach. The passage slopes away from us at a slight angle. After ten feet, it makes a turn to the left. There's no telling how far it goes.

I start to take another step, but Hellboy catches my arm.

"Wait," he says. "Hear that?"

I shake my head.

"There's something ...," he begins.

But then we all hear it. Hell, we *feel* it. A sudden pressure in the tunnel, a sound like something's shifting deep underground. Something *big*. The stone underfoot sends tremors up our legs and right through our bones.

I look at Hellboy and he grins.

"Now it's getting interesting," he says.

He sets off down the tunnel, his partner, Agent Sherman, on his heels. Walker and I exchange glances. He looks as uneasy about all of this as I'm feeling.

"Crap," I say.

I don't want to go, and neither does Walker. The hair on the back of my neck is standing up.

But we follow them into the tunnel all the same.

Then ...

My name's Sam Cray.

One week ago I was a detective for the Newford Police Department's Special Investigations Squad.

Six days ago I was put in charge of the NPD's new Paranormal Investigations Task Force.

No matter what I've been told, I figure I must have really pissed someone off to get the transfer.

"Tell me you're kidding," I say to Bill Sweet when he gives me the news in one of the downtown conference rooms.

Bill's the chief of police now, but we go way back. We came up together from the Academy, and even our rabbis were partners. We both made detective around the same time, but Bill was always more ambitious than me. Right from the start, he had a leaning toward the politics of the job, while I just wanted to be on the street, putting away the bad guys. I'm not saying one's better than the other, just that we're different. And it's worked out well, because at least we have a Chief who actually knows the job from the bottom up.

Yeah, he knows my job, but at times like this, I can't believe what's involved with his.

"You can't do this to me," I tell him.

Bill shakes his head. "The mayor insists on it."

"And there's room in your budget for something like this?"

"No. The task force is being funded by an anonymous group of concerned citizens."

"Who expect to get what out of it?"

"Nothing, Sam. In case you haven't been paying attention, a lot of seriously weird things go down in our city—not just once or twice, but *all* the time. These people are worried about its effect on real-estate values, on the tourist trade, on their ability to lure new businesses to town. So it's not like they're being particularly charitable here. But that's fine, because no matter how self-serving their motivations might be, it still gives us the budget to actually help the people who are being affected by this."

It's a good speech, but I don't buy it.

"This is bullshit," I tell him. "What exactly am I supposed to do? Track down monsters and spooks and things that go bump in the night?"

"If necessary. If that's what comes up."

He says this with such a straight face it makes me glad I never played poker with him.

"Seriously," I say. "What'd I ever do to piss you off like this?"

"This is a compliment to your abilities, Sam. Simply put, you're the best man for the job. I went to every precinct with this, and only your captain was against you being offered the position."

"Really? Well, at least Monroe's not trying to screw me."

"Don't be an idiot," Bill says. "He just doesn't want to lose you to the task force."

"I can't believe you're even calling it a task force. I'm going to be a laughing stock when this gets out. Jesus."

Bill shakes his head. "This task force won't officially exist, so no one's going to know."

Like that ever stopped information from getting around before. I swear, cops are worse than little old ladies when it comes to gossip.

"And you don't answer to anyone but me," Bill finishes.

"A task force," I say. "On the paranormal. Do you have any idea how that sounds?"

"Last week we had a rain of frogs inside the Williamson Street Mall," he tells me. "Monday a complaint was filed about something that looked like a cross between an eagle and a lion flying off with some guy's Doberman. Just this morning two female joggers reported a fishman rooting through a garbage bin who dove into the lake at their approach and never surfaced. Do you need any more? Because I've got stacks of them."

"Look," I say. "I'll admit this city seems to have more than its fair share of nutcases, but that doesn't mean we should start believing what they tell us."

"The guy who lost his dog," Bill says, "is the president of the Newford First National Bank. One of the joggers sits on the city council; her friend is VP of Human Resources at McCutcheon & Grambs."

Doesn't mean they're not loopy, I think, but I say, "Okay, so I'm supposed to do what? How is anybody supposed to figure out who's responsible for this crap? Come on, Bill. You can't arrest smoke and shadows and hearsay."

But he's shaking his head. "It's not a lot different from what you're already doing, except instead of collecting data on gangs and subversives and extremists, you're going to be investigating the weird things that go on in this city. Hopefully, you'll get to the point where you'll be able to identify and prevent the incidents from occurring in the first place."

"I don't know the first thing about the paranormal."

"That's why we brought together those advisors for you."

He's talking about the collection of misfits he's got waiting for us in the room on the other side of the one-way mirror where we're having our meeting. Like the idea of working with them would even remotely boost my confidence.

"You get to pick your own team," Bill says. "No strings, no PC processes. Choose whomever you want, and if they agree to the transfer, they're yours."

"Plus that bunch of bozos," I say, pointing to the group waiting on the other side of the mirror.

"These people can be useful, Sam. They know things we can't guess at."

Because we still have the full use of our senses, I think. Or at least I know I do. I'm not so sure about Bill anymore, because these people …

I recognize some of them—mostly from pulling them in on various charges when I was still walking a beat. There's the alcoholic priest who thinks he talks to angels and demons. The owner of The Good Serpent Club in Upper Foxville who claims to be a voodoo priestess. At least two of the people Bill's brought in do the phony oracle shtick in Fitzhenry Park, or down on the Pier.

I also recognize the writer, but not from a rap sheet. I've just seen his mug in the paper when they're reviewing his books.

"Who's the old guy beside Christy Riddell?" I ask.

"Dr. Bramley Dapple. He's got a couple of PhDs, but the one that interests us is in mythology and folklore. He's supposed to be a world-renowned expert in his field."

"And he's got time for this?"

"He thinks it's important and long overdue," Bill says. "As do I."

"You're not asking me to head up a task force," I say. "You're asking me to babysit a pack of charlatans and lunatics." I turn to look at Bill. "I have to work in an office with these people?"

He shakes his head. "This is just a meet and greet to let you all put faces to each other's names. I want you to go in, introduce yourself to them, thank them for being a part of this. That's all."

"I don't do this well," I warn Bill.

"I know. Just be nice and get it over with. After this, you'll only speak to them when you need their expertise on a particular case. And you don't even need to do that yourself. You can delegate one of your people to be the liaison."

I shake my head. Now I've got people.

"Let's get this over with," I tell Bill.

Now ...

"Is he always like this?" I ask Hellboy's partner when Walker and I catch up with her.

I can see the light from Hellboy's flashlight a good twenty yards further down the tunnel from us.

Agent Sherman smiles. "We spend a lot of down time, back at headquarters, twiddling our thumbs. Which is a good thing, of course, because it means there isn't some big crisis that needs looking after. But Hellboy likes it best when he's in the thick of the action."

"What's his real name?"

"That's it. Just Hellboy."

Okay, I think. Be like that.

"I've read the stories. Saw that *Life* magazine cover back when. But I always figured it was mostly image stuff, P.R., all that," I say. "What, was he caught in a fire or something when he was a kid?"

She gives me a look that's beyond cold. There's anger in it and ice, and just the hint of old ghosts. It stops me in my tracks and Walker bumps into me, but she just keeps walking, back stiff, long red hair bouncing against her back.

I turn to Walker. "What'd I say?"

He shrugs. "Who knows? But I wouldn't bring it up again. Maybe it's like asking if my skin's so brown because I fell down a crapper."

"Who's going to say something that stupid?"

"I don't know. Maybe some kid back when I was in high school—just before I broke his nose."

"Christ, so now I'm a racist?"

Walker smiles. "Not that I can see. Seriously, though. You think the guy's a fake? Somebody's going to pretend they're a demon? Big media hoax? Who'd do that?"

"Stranger things happen. Maybe you should ask Agent Sherman?"

Walker shakes his head. "Nah, I think I'd rather give myself an enema with a fire hose. Man, if I didn't know better, I'd think she'd done time because she's sure got that thousand-yard stare down pat."

I grin in agreement and we quicken our pace, rubber boots splashing in the few inches of water we've got underfoot. But just because I'm in better humor doesn't mean I'm not checking out the walls and tunnel roof for cracks or fissures. That sound we heard earlier, I figure it came from a piece of the roof falling in somewhere down a ways, and I don't plan on getting stuck here.

Then ...

Chad Walker is my first choice for this task force I'm putting together. He's got experience, he's tough, and at six-foot, two-twenty, he can hold his own. I've seen him in action. He can look like a street thug, and he's played the part in the past, though he can't go undercover again—not since he put away most of the Taggart Street Runners, along with their main man, Frankie Chestnut. Walker's also smart as hell, but more importantly, he's a guy I can get along with. If I'm stuck with this job—if I'm going to have "people"—at least they're going to be people I like.

Walker grins at me when I walk up to his desk at the 12th Precinct.

"If you're here to ask me if I want to join up with your Spook Squad—" he starts.

"Jesus, who's calling it that?" I say, before he can finish.

"Everybody. Come on, what did you expect?"

"Well, I knew no matter what the chief said, it was going to get out. I just didn't think it'd be this fast."

"Or that somebody'd come up with such a cute name," Walker says.

"That, too."

"Anyway," he goes on, "I'm in. Unless you're here to ask me to go for a beer, and then I'm going to be seriously embarrassed."

"Why would you want in?" I have to ask.

"Are you kidding me? This is the gig of a lifetime. I mean, think about it for a minute: they're willing to actually pay us to investigate all this weird stuff that goes down in the city. Which reminds me, do I get a raise?"

"Put it on your list of demands."

"I get to make a list of demands? Sweet. I'm putting in for a Ferrari. Maybe that'll finally get me some respect in the old 'hood."

I laugh. "But seriously," I say. "When did you get into the weird stuff?"

"Living here, how can you not? It drives me crazy trying to figure out what's really what."

"You're beginning to sound like Ricker."

"Oh, crap. You're not bringing him on board, are you?"

Alfred Ricker's been collecting data on unexplained phenomena for about as long as anyone can remember, and everybody avoids him because he's got a hundred theories—and he's not afraid of sharing them with you. At great and tedious length. The only way you can get him to stop is to just walk away.

He'd probably add a lot to the team—if he didn't drive us all insane first. I'm surprised Bill didn't put him on my board of advisors, considering some of the other winners that are there.

"No," I assure Walker. "I'm asking Ramirez next."

"Judita's good," he says. "I heard she once stood down a swarm of fifteen or twenty kids going after a couple of Arab boys outside the Williamson Street Mall. Just her on her own, no backup. Knowing her, she stopped them dead with the sheer force of her will."

I nod, wait a beat, then ask, "So is she a believer, too?"

Walker gives me a puzzled look. "I don't know. Why do you ask?"

"It's just ... everybody's treating this so damn seriously."

"And you don't," Walker says.

It's not a question, but I can see he's just figuring it out now. The Looney Tunes crap the task force is being put together to investigate isn't something the two of us have ever really discussed before. You want to know the truth, I don't like to talk about it with anybody.

"Which really makes me wonder why they've got me heading up the task force," I say.

"You're a good cop."

"I try. But this stuff ..."

"Maybe they want someone in charge who's going to stop and ask questions instead of just running with the weirdness of the moment."

"I guess ..."

Walker doesn't say anything for a long moment. He just sits there, studying my face—hesitating, I realize, when he finally does speak.

"This have anything to do with Lela?" he asks.

It's been three years, but I still feel the ground disappear under my feet at the mention of her name. Lela Searle. We were supposed to be married. She was going to leave the Job, become a civilian, raise our family. Instead, she got torn apart by a pack of dogs set on her by a crack dealer in Butler University Common. Except the whisper in the NPD is that it wasn't dogs. The whisper says it was the dealer himself, Bobby Cairns. That he goes all Wolfman three nights of the month. That she wasn't paying attention to the lunar cycle when she went to make her bust because otherwise she'd still be alive.

All of which seriously pisses me off. Lela was a good cop. Maybe she shouldn't have been out on the common at night without backup, but those kinds of situations happen on the job. In the heat of the chase, you make the judgment call. It was bad luck Cairns had those dogs. It wasn't supernatural. And if we ever pull in the murdering son of a bitch, I'll go a few rounds with him and prove he's just a lowlife with a freak for fighting dogs.

I hate the fact the whisper says she was killed by bad mojo. I want the world to know it was a man that got the drop on her, not some monster. If we buy into monsters, then what do we have left? What good are we against monsters? I mean think about it. If there really are these wolfmen and vampires and crap out there in the dark, how are we supposed to protect the public against them? We're as helpless against that kind of thing as the average joe.

Sure, there's weird shit on the street. But the point is, you get the facts, you take the incidents apart, and you don't find monsters—at least not like in some freak show. We've got plenty of human monsters as it is. We don't need to make up storybook ones.

Lela's death has to mean something. She was a good cop. She died doing her job. She didn't die because some random boogeyman stepped out of the shadows and tore her apart. She died trying to bring down Bobby Cairns, a crack dealer, end of story. Accepting anything else diminishes her death.

"No," I tell him. "I don't buy this crap for a lot more reasons than that."

"And if it turns out to be true?"

I shrug. "Then I'll buy myself some silver bullets for when I finally track down Cairns."

Now ...

When I was a kid, my friends and I were fascinated with the idea that the bedrock underneath the city was supposed to be honeycombed with caverns, some so big you couldn't see from one side to the other. Discussing the possibility of their existence was a big deal for us. We'd sit around for hours planning all these Tom-Sawyer-in-the-caves/*Journey to the Center of the Earth* expeditions that never got further than the neighborhood storm sewer, though it wasn't for want of trying. We could just never find the secret entrances.

You put that kind of thing behind you once you grow up and find other interests—like, hello, girls—but it stays there in your subconscious. Every once in a while, I'd remember. Maybe I'd be on a stakeout, and the steam coming up from a manhole cover would remind me. Or I'd read in the paper about the fire department rescuing some kid from a storm sewer.

The city's got an underground history, too. Everybody knows about Old City— that section of Newford that got dropped underground during the big quake at the beginning of the last century—but nobody goes there except for the homeless. They say there are still buildings standing down there in some subterranean cavern—that's what happened during the quake: the roof of one of those caverns collapsed, and Old City got swallowed up, buildings, streets, and all.

I'm thinking about that now as Walker and I follow Hellboy and his partner down the storm sewer, pretty sure that what we heard and felt was a cavern roof falling in. But then we get to where the other two are standing, their flashlights playing over what appears to be a large body of water. I can't see the far end. There's no longer concrete or brickwork underfoot or on the walls. There's just bedrock, with a bunch of loose boulders and stones along the edge of this underground lake.

If my childhood pals could see me now ...

"How deep are we?" I ask Walker.

He shrugs. "Hard to tell, with all the ups and downs and turns we took."

"Probably the equivalent of a ten-story building," Sherman says.

Her voice is completely normal, like she didn't give me the big ice-stare two minutes ago.

I shine my light across the water, and wonder what its range is.

"There's something moving in there," Hellboy says.

He's shining his light into the water but it's so murky I can't make out a damn thing. "Something big," he adds.

It's like he calls it to us, whatever the hell it is. I'm just aware of some large shape that comes out of the water like a whale, before the waters close over it again. The motion sends waves toward us, lapping at the tops of our boots.

"Jesus," Walker says. "What the hell was that thing?"

Hellboy grins. "It looked like a kraken."

"Yeah," I say. "You'd have to be on crack to make sense out of something like this."

Hellboy shakes his head. "I said 'kraken.' It's a kind of sea monster."

"In the city sewers?"

"It's a small one," Agent Sherman says. "But you're right, it is puzzling. I didn't think they could survive in fresh water."

"Hey, the water down here's anything but fresh," I put in.

Hellboy smiles at me, then turns back to his partner. "Remember Nazas, in '88? We had a pair of them."

Sherman shakes her head. "You were with Abe that time." She pauses a moment, then adds, "I thought they were Nessies."

"What the hell are you people talking about?" I ask.

"Do you remember those Ray Harryhausen movies with the giant octopi?"

"Sure. But what's that got—"

"They were actually kraken, which is like a giant cuttlefish or squid."

Walker grins. "Man, I knew this was going to be an interesting gig."

They're all nuts, so far as I can see. And then Hellboy, as though to drive the point home, strips off his trenchcoat. He unbuckles his belt and lays that oversized handgun of his down on top of it, but he keeps the big glove on. I'm starting to think maybe the hand inside is deformed—you know, like he's got elephantitis, which would maybe explain his size and coloring, too, but I'm no doctor. And the thing is, his hand works fine. It's just big.

"What're you doing?" I ask.

"Going to have some fun," he says.

He turns to the lake, and that's when I see it. A red tail. He's got a freaking tail. I'm still trying to register the fact when he dives in.

I take a step into the water, but his partner calls me back.

"I wouldn't try to follow," she says. "Not unless you can hold your breath for five minutes or so."

"And Hellboy can?"

"He's kind of bigger than life in a lot of ways," she says.

Walker laughs. "No kidding."

"He's got a tail," I say. I turn to Walker. "Jesus, did you see it?"

Walker only shrugs, and I make myself calm down. Okay, so he's got a tail. I guess it should have sunk in by now that he's not exactly like you or me. All along I've been telling myself he isn't what everyone says he is. But he has a tail. That one's hard to get by.

Agent Sherman sits down on one of the nearby boulders and rummages around in her pocket. She comes up with a pack of smokes.

I step out of the water and sit on a rock near her, pretending a nonchalance I don't really feel. But I figure if she's not concerned about her partner, I'm not going to be either. At least I won't let on that I am.

"Look," I say. "About what happened earlier. I didn't mean—"

She waves me off before I can finish.

"That was my fault," she says. "It's a touchy subject for me. I lost some people close to me in a fire."

She snaps her fingers and damned if a little flame doesn't appear, hovering there between her fingers long enough for her to get her cigarette lit. She offers it to me, but I shake my head. Walker accepts it, though, and I watch in fascination as she lights herself another.

"Nice trick," I say.

She nods, but doesn't explain. I guess she holds to that magician's code where you never reveal how you did the trick, though she did do it twice. Didn't help me much. I couldn't figure it out either time.

I turn to look back at the water, then check my watch. It's been almost three minutes, and there's still no sign of Sherman's partner.

Then ...
     So Bill has one more surprise for me. I'm six days on the job, and the task force is just settling into our new offices at police headquarters, when he drops by with agents from something called the Bureau for Paranormal Research and Defense. Turns out the Feds have their own full-time investigative task force.

"These are agents Hal Jones and Liz Sherman," Bill says as he ushers them in.

The man is just a nondescript suit, but the woman is a real looker. Great figure, pretty face. Long, red hair falling past her shoulders. Cool, blue-gray eyes. But attractive as she is, she can't hold my attention once the third member of their team comes through the door.

"And this is Hellboy," Bill finishes.

The third team member has to duck his head coming through the door because he's got to be seven feet tall. I've read the news stories about him, seen an interview or two. But I always figured it was just some gimmick. And maybe it is, but if so, it's a good one. I put his weight at close to four hundred pounds, but even with the trenchcoat, you can tell there's not an ounce of fat on him. So his size grabs you right off the bat, but then there's his skin: bright red like a cooked lobster. Weirder still, he's got a couple of disks stuck to his forehead—wood, bone, I'm not sure what. Except they look like they're growing there. Like maybe he had some kind of growths and they were cut off, which makes no sense at all. What the hell would anybody have growing out of their head like that? But then I don't know anybody who has his size or skin coloring either.

I can't tell the caliber of the gun he's got holstered at his hip. I just know it's the biggest damn handgun I've ever seen. And then there's this glove he's wearing on his right, doubling the size of his hand. The cloth has a texture that makes it look like stone.

And he's supposed to be one of us, one of the good guys, for Christ's sake.

I guess I've been staring, but he doesn't seem to take offense. He smiles, like he's used to it. Like I'm an idiot for staring. So I turn it around and focus on the strangeness of him.

"That's a seriously bad sunburn you've got there, buddy," I tell him.

The monster laughs and turns to Agent Sherman.

"Already I like him," he says to her.

"Now that we've established that we all like each other," Bill says, "maybe we can get down to the business at hand."

"I'm all business," Hellboy assures him, but he winks at me.

It's a friendly gesture—brothers-in-arms bonding and all that—but something goes pit-patting up my spine all the same.

Bill lays it out for us once we're in his office. A worker from the Water & Sewer Department went missing on a regular maintenance recon down in the storm sewers earlier this morning, so they sent in two more to look for him. They haven't come back either, but one of the men did make a cell call just before Water & Sewer lost contact with them. There was screaming on his end of the line, screaming so bad that the receptionist who took the call was being treated for shock at the hospital as we spoke.

"What makes it our case?" I ask.

"Stafford at Water & Sewer says his men have been talking about weird sounds coming from down in the lower sewer levels," Bill says. "Says it's been going on for some time now."

I nod, wondering if this is how it's going to be. If every time someone gets some little whiff of the weird they're going to call in the Spook Squad.

"I know you and your people only came down to introduce yourselves to my men," Bill is saying to Agent Jones, "but seeing how this will be their first active case in the field ..."

"No problem," Jones says before Bill can finish. "Hellboy and Agent Sherman will be happy to assist."

Great, I think. So now I'll have the Feds breathing down my neck while dealing with my first case.

There's a little more talk between Bill and Jones, but I tune them out. It's all bureaucratic doublespeak, making nice, we'll work together, share resources, yadda yadda. Instead, I concentrate on what I need to do once I get out of Bill's office. I'll take Walker and Ramirez. Walker to come down into the sewers with me—and won't he love that—Ramirez to set up a command post at the entrance. We'll have to grab a couple of uniforms. I'm trying to decide what the closest precinct is when I realize the meeting's come to an end.

"So what do you think we're looking at?" Hellboy says as we're walking back to the Spook Squad offices. "Giant albino crocs? Mutant rats?"

I look at him, then at his partner.

"Is he for real?" I ask.

"If this is your first time out on something like this," she says, "I guess it can seem a little over the top. But ..."

She shrugs.

"Wait a sec'," I say. "You guys have seen crap like that?"

"I just hope it's not zombies," Hellboy says. "I hate zombies. It takes forever to wash the stink away."

Now ...
       I just about have a heart attack when my radio squawks, but it's only Ramirez at the command post, checking in.

"No, we're good," I tell her. "We just found this lake, and Hellboy's gone for a swim looking for some giant octopus or something."

There's a moment's silence before Ramirez says, "You're kidding me, right?"

"I wish I was."

"But—"

"I'll get back to you, Judita."

I cut the connection, still staring at the water.

"How long's it been?" I ask.

"Four minutes," Walker says.

I turn to Agent Sherman, but before I can ask if we shouldn't be starting to worry, something explodes out of the water. No, not something. It's Hellboy. The beam from Walker's flashlight follows his trajectory as he sails maybe fifteen feet above the water before smashing against the wall to our right. When he lands, he lies still, but we don't have time to see to him, because there's something else coming out of the lake.

Now, I heard what the B.P.R.D. agents were telling me earlier about giant squids and crap, but it didn't really register. By which, I guess, what I really mean is, it was just too stupid to take seriously. But this ... this thing ...

Stupid, impossible, what*ever*—I can't deny what I'm seeing.

The water churns, and this monster the size of a small car rises up out of the lake. We play our flashlights on it, but there's no way their beams can take the whole of it in at once. I freeze when my light illuminates one huge eye along the side of its head because there's ... not exactly intelligence, but certainly a cunning that's more than animal in the look it gives me.

Tentacles ... arms ... these appendages thick as tree trunks come whipping out of the water, and then things get even weirder.

Turns out Agent Sherman's trick with lighting a cigarette is just the tip of the iceberg when it comes to her talents. She puts her hands together, and when she moves them apart, a ball of fire forms in between.

I don't know what she plans to do with it, because she doesn't get the time. One of those tentacles comes ripping out of the water and knocks her flying. The flame ball lands in the water and splutters out. She lies still.

I manage to duck as the tentacle comes for me—I don't know how, I'm just a gibbering idiot at this point. It's like everything's closing up inside me, and I can't even remember how to breathe. I've been a cop for over fifteen years, and I've been in situations before. Serious situations. I've seen shit nobody should have to take home from work. But this *thing* does what nothing else in my experience ever has. It just shuts me down.

So I don't know how I manage to duck. I just do.

Walker isn't as lucky.

He's standing there like me, frozen, just staring at the thing. He starts to move when the tentacle comes for him, but he's not quick enough. It wraps around him and tugs him up into the air.

I know I couldn't have done this for myself. I just didn't have what it would take in what was left of me. But on the job, your partner's a sacred trust. That's the first thing my rabbi taught me when he took me under his wing. No matter *what*, you watch your partner's back. You stand by him and take the bullet for him if that's how it plays out.

So seeing that the monster's got Walker is what makes me move. I know my .38's not going to do a damn thing against this creature, but we've got something else down here that might.

I take the few quick steps over to where Hellboy dropped his gear and tug that oversized handgun of his out of its holster. Turns out it's not so much a handgun as small mortar cannon with a handle, and the damn thing weighs a ton. I need both hands to hold it, to aim. I squeeze the trigger, and the blast pretty much deafens me. The gun bucks in my hand, and I feel a snap as my shoulder dislocates. The gun falls from my hand, back onto Hellboy's coat.

But I hit the monster.

Didn't kill it, I don't think, but I did enough damage that it shrieks with pain and drops Walker into the lake. Those arms of its are churning the water into a froth. My gaze goes from the gun to Walker. I don't think I can lift the gun again, even if I had another shot for it, but I don't know that I can get out there to Walker either.

Then a big shape looms up beside me, and I don't have to decide.

Hellboy stoops and picks up his gun. He cracks it open, knocks out the spent shell and inserts another that he gets from the pocket of his coat.

"I'm impressed," he says. "I haven't met many guys who can fire this and actually hit anything."

He holds the gun with one hand and fires off a round, reloads and fires again. The first goes deep into the oily skin on the monster's side. The second hits it in the eye. Bam, bam. Just like that, and the creature's falling back into the water, dead. The impact of its body sets up a wave that brings Walker in close enough that I can wade in and pull him back to shore with my good arm.

He coughs up some water, but otherwise he's okay.

I find my flashlight. I play its beam over the body, and we just stand there staring at the damn thing floating in the water. Then I think of Agent Sherman. I turn to find that Hellboy's already seen to her. She seems to be shook up, but okay.

I remember the fireball she made in her hands.

I turn again to look at the impossible monster floating in this underground lake.

"Everybody okay over here?" Hellboy asks as he walks up to us.

Walker nods.

"I think your damn gun dislocated my shoulder," I tell him.

"Yeah, it's got a kick. Here, let me fix it."

"No, it's okay. I can wait to see a—"

I don't get the chance to say "medic" before he's already grabbed my arm and popped my shoulder back into place. The pain goes through me like a white heat.

"Th-thanks," I manage.

"What happened to you down there?" Walker asks.

Hellboy shrugs. "I couldn't get a grip on its skin—it was too slick."

Agent Sherman joins us. She lights a cigarette, and I don't even blink at her not using a lighter.

"We were lucky," I say.

Hellboy shakes his head. "The hell we were. We're better than the monsters. We're smarter, and we never give up. That's why we're always going to come out on top at the end."

"I guess ..."

"I'm serious," Hellboy says. "You want to survive in this business, you need to remember that. The monsters are strong, and they're mean, and they can scare the crap out of you. But we can stand up to them. We can put them down. It's what we do."

Agent Sherman smiles. "Make the world a safer place, yadda yadda."

"But it's true," Hellboy says.

"I know it is," she tells him.

Hellboy works a kink out of his neck, then bends down to get his coat and holster.

"You know what I need?" he says, looking at us.

Walker and I shake our heads.

Hellboy grins. "I need Peking ravioli."

There's paperwork and debriefings to go through, but here's the good thing about having the Feds at your back: you can put it off until tomorrow on their say-so. We take Hellboy and Agent Sherman to Cassidy's, a cop bar on Palm Street, but not until he's had his Peking ravioli. Hell, he earned them.

"So you still think the boogeyman's all a load of crap?" Walker asks later when we're walking back to our car.

I shake my head. "I just don't get how we don't hear more about it. You'd think the papers and TV crews would be all over this stuff. You'd think there'd be federal task forces with their scientists dissecting these things right down to the cellular level. But there's nada."

"Well, we don't know about the scientists," Walker starts.

"What do you mean?"

He shrugs. "Someone's going to go down there and take that monster away."

"I guess you're right. They're just going to keep a lid on it."

"Everything's need-to-know," Walker says.

"But what about the ordinary joes who get caught up in this kind of thing?"

"I figure it's a kind of consensual denial, you know? It's easier to let it just be something that never happened. Human beings, we're good at that."

I nod. "I suppose we are."

It's another half-block to where we found a parking spot earlier, and we cover the distance in silence.

"Do you think the armory carries silver bullets?" I ask when we reach our car.

"I don't know. Why?"

"It's a full moon next week. I thought I might go hunt me a werewolf."

"Bobby Cairns," Walker says.

"Since I can't find him as a human—maybe I'll have better luck tracking him down as a creature of the night."

I can't believe I just said "creature of the night" in all seriousness. I guess I'll have to get used to it on this job.

"You doing this for Lela," Walker asks, "or for the safety of the public?"

I have to think about that for a moment. I know what my immediate answer is, but now that I've learned what I have about how the world really works, everything's more complicated.

"Bit of both," I finally tell him.

He nods. "Either way, let me know when you're going out. I'll watch your back."

Special thanks to my pals Dave Russell and Mark Finn for vetting this.

WATER MUSIC
DAVID J. SCHOW

The pull of history is tidal. The pull of *human* history can be countermanded; it occupies too scant a footing on the timeline to offer resistance. Mere mammals to date have claimed precious little additional length on that timeline. Imagine a yardstick. Human history barely fills the final 1/16th inch of the span. Mammals have yet to stake an inch, let alone a foot ... long after evolving opposable thumbs.

Nonhuman, non-mammalian creatures fill much more of the Earth's imaginary timeline. There, the weight of the past can exert an irresistible pull—a dangerous undertow, a riptide that can enfold, sometimes with toxic results. Death, even.

Abe Sapien is aware of this when he fugues. The fugue is a form of self-meditation, an almost out-of-body state vital to maintenance of mind and spirit, but as with medication, there is the hazard of overdose. One can get lost in his own genetic past, as the price for consultation with one's former selves.

Most humans lack the option, let alone the control that Abe Sapien has cultivated through deft experience. Humans, he has found, remain stranded in the backwaters of ghostly visitation, of demonic possession, of poltergeists and so-called past-life regression—superstitions they use to rationalize the preternatural.

The preternatural is already an accepted part of Abe Sapien's universe. To augment the experience of the fugue, and permit more control, he has climbed into his special isolation tank. Chemically enhanced pure water at optimum temperature; utter silence; total darkness. This helps Abe Sapien to concentrate on leveling his brainwaves to exclude the here-and-now world. To an unschooled observer, Abe Sapien appears to segue into a coma state, respirating less than one breath per minute through the delicate lamellae of his gillwork. The "floating" sensation of the buoyant solution in the tank gives way to the airborne, "hovering" sensation that is the first stage of fugue.

Abe Sapien floats—transcending the concerns of the petty or material, temporarily obviating the earthly need to indulge emotions. Like hate. Like resentment. Abe Sapien has been suffering these feelings more, lately, than he judges to be normal, even for a unique specimen such as himself. Hate, mirroring the hatred of human beings for anything different from their limited form and shape. Species hate, too often against *ichthyo Sapien*. Resentment at the arrogance of the Bureau for Paranormal Research and Defense. Lately Abe Sapien has been feeling that the B.P.R.D. has been taking him for granted, as if he had no other options in the world of humans. *Yeah, throw the freak a bone, gang him with the other mutants and misfits, and see if we can somehow profit from their investigations into spooky stuff.*

Never does Abe Sapien express these sentiments, but he cannot lie to himself— he *feels* them, from time to time, always keeping the feeling to himself. Human feelings, to his fancy, in conflict with his non-human nature; it is not a choice between human-or-otherwise. He occupies not a netherworld, but a *neither*-world. But he acknowledges that to bottle up misgivings is never healthy. They fester in the dark; they grow malignant and burst forth into black consequences. That is one of the reasons he has come to the tank tonight, to meditate, to fugue. To circumvent these confusing emotions and re-attack them obliquely, from a refreshed perspective.

Abe Sapien does not appear to age, but he is aware he is somehow outside his own skin, looking at himself, over a century earlier. He is younger, smaller. He is standing knee-deep in some anguineous backwater of New Orleans swampland, feeling the mystic transport of his fellow creatures, the water witches and the Peremelfait, shrouded festively in the ghost-shapes of drowned pirates, decorated with Spanish moss and kudzu. He feels at one with the earth, the quickmud, the backwater tidepools, all of it teeming with biology, with the reassurance of the ocean always nearby ...

... and he jolts, subtly, in his tank, from synapse shock. The warm feeling of homecoming is an illusion, a confection of his mind. The way he would like his past to have been. He has heard humans do this, too—idealize a childhood that never existed, editing out the objectionable bits.

But the fantasy refuses to dissipate. Abe Sapien knows what history claims. The theory goes that he was created in a laboratory as the first human-fish hybrid, a *homme amphibie*, nearly a century before the word "bioengineering" was coined.

For him to backtrack, via fugue, along that path is a dead end, and he knows it. That path ends in 1895.

Several decades of isolation in a water cylinder, labeled as a marine curiosity, had taught him a lot about leaving his body. About fugueing, and finding ways to "think himself elsewhere." To Abe Sapien, "Elsewhere" is a destination. When he achieves the proper mental state to fugue, he has arrived at Elsewhere ... and Elsewhere has nothing to do with being fabricated, mutated, or invented. Elsewhere pulls him gently backward along a different path, an alternate life.

And ancestry.

He glimpses his younger self—still in the fanciful swamp—but momentarily, as though from a fast-moving hot-air balloon bobbing overhead. Then he continues his journey, passing his own birth ...

Wait a minute. *His birth?!*

His sensitive dermis dances with galvanic new input. What he sees is contraindicated, yet it moves him as profoundly as any single vision could. Abe Sapien has never embraced any notion of having a real mother or father. Yet there they are, and they love him. They are regal and gracile, sophisticated masters of both land and sea.

Elsewhere blossoms for Abe Sapien, offering more, and he opts to continue his journey back along this genetic timeline.

Now he sees his progenitors as a spare and noble race—overlords of Atlantis; demigods of Amazonas; favored consorts of Triton and Poseidon (as humans had later named them, erroneously). They had developed their own culture and written language, no artifact of which survives today. The paintings of the great human masters crumbled to dust in fewer than a thousand years; the ancestral dynasty of Abe Sapien is millennia older than that.

He visualizes an earlier configuration for himself. Primordial, tougher, more brutal. Armor-plated scales, talons, an almost microscopic alertness of the air around him and the signals it imparts. With ancient, chromium eyes he can now see into the infrared. Hyperdeveloped sensors in his taste buds now convey crucial hunting data, like the smell of fear.

And it is in this form that Abe Sapien touches down on the virtual ground of Elsewhere. The hot ozone of antediluvian lightning-strikes charges the atmosphere. He stands on gray rock outcrops jutting from a turbulent, iron-colored sea, and knows humid wind is buffeting him, but cannot feel its temperature. His civilized self, back in the tank, floating, fugueing, would be handicapped here. He looks down to see he still wears his formfit tunic, because that is what his memory has provisioned for this fugue. This might be the world as it was before the aquatics crawled, gasping, onto land. The enormity of this place dwarfs both his irritation and preoccupation—the foibles and frailties he still biases as "human" in his mind.

If Abe Sapien owns a cellular history, he is the only extant repository of that line. A possible past. It is easy to extrapolate others like himself. Even his own ancestors. In this fugue, he might even be able to console his misgivings by consultation with others of his kind. *Others of his kind*—the revelation is deliriously gravid with possibility. The dormant lobes of his thinking mind, back in the fugue tank, know this is not real. But the illusion is deeply convincing.

Here—theoretically—he can be alone instead of lonely. At least, that is what he thought until he saw the visitor. Intruder, perhaps. Standing atop a rock in distant shadow, a humanoid silhouette, perched on one leg like a warrior sentry. It seemed to have just noticed Abe Sapien; both stood in regard of the other for several tense moments. Abe Sapien felt himself being sized up.

Then the other being dove into the choppy water and swam to a closer rock. It hauled itself up, sea foam sluicing from its smooth naked body, which was a dark, mossy green, mottled with brown spots. Its legs were backward-jointed, avian. Three fingers, three toes on each spindly limb—long, super-attenuated digits designed for grasping. A little pot belly like a pygmy, which did not conceal the protuberant stump of penis.

Abe Sapien knew evolution. If this were some sort of protohuman reptile, *anthroposaurus Sapien*, then the brain development required to advance a species to the status of a thinking being would induce the upright, bipedal stance of a human, and thus necessitate the ventro-ventral mode of copulation, which was a more reliable method of mating than the way birds or lizards did it.

It stood there with a definite attitude of challenge, then took to the water and swam closer. Now it regarded Abe Sapien from a reef less than thirty yards away.

This was not the "dinosauroid" posited by paleontologists, the "primosaur" theorized as a possible conqueror during a time when vastly outnumbered mammals kept to the trees to avoid predation by the dinosaurs. This was different. This was a version that had crawled from the water and learned to *climb* the trees.

It glared at Abe Sapien, waited exactly as long as it had before, then swam nearer. It was now ten feet away. It rose erect and commenced its stare-down. Its skin was scaly, probably armor-hard and elephant-tough.

It had large, oval eyes with vertically slit pupils, protected by bony, slanting plates. Definitely a nocturnal hunter, and evidence that its visual associations had shifted to its enlarged cerebrum. Lizards processed most of their visual information in the retina, not the brain.

It was not until the 1990s that scientists were able to use CT scans to map the musculature of a dinosaur heart, which proved to have a single systemic aorta, unlike the double-aorta found in cold-blooded crocodilians. Extrapolated, this meant that *anthroposaurus Sapien* would have warm blood, and a higher metabolic rate.

What would have happened? Intelligent dinosaurs might have dominated what are called the Cretaceous terminal extinctions—the so-called "Kimmeridgian turnover" of 145 million years ago, the "Aptian turnover" 28 million years later, and the "Cenomanian turnover" 22 million years after that—possibly even steam-rolling over the apes that were in power by the end of the Tertiary geological era.

In short, they might have resembled *this* guy.

Abe Sapien thought that the being's expression classified as smug. It gave a dismissive snort and jerked its head sidewise ... then *leaped* from his rock to the one Abe Sapien was standing upon. Abe Sapien willed himself not to recoil as the creature landed in perfect balance. The pads on its spatulate fingers and toes gripped the porous stone. It appeared to weigh about a hundred pounds, and its stubby tail (more a tailbone, with vertebrae) was probably vestigial.

Its snout was akin to a blunted beak, but still had nasty teeth, or perhaps ridged gums. Either way, they looked pointy and pain-capable. Abe Sapien wondered who and what this vision was supposed to represent.

I am the thing you have always feared most, the being said. But it stood there, transfixing Abe Sapien with the combat stare. It had not moved its mouth, nor spoken. Abe Sapien heard the thoughts of this being in his mind. Perhaps his brain was fabricating that detail, while putting a face to some enemy who laid traps deep in his subconscious, those unmapped eddies accessed by the fugue state.

But Abe Sapien retained his share of instinct, too, and that primordial fight-or-flight coding engaged on an autonomic level. His left hand flew up to protect his face, while his right struck with ballistic, deadly force. Crush the throat and one usually brings down the antagonist.

Abe Sapien's martial-arts jab passed through the being; it was like punching cigarette smoke. It was not corporeal.

In response came an organ-dislocating hammerblow of pain that sank Abe Sapien to his knees, as palpably as being mashed by a falling safe. Purple coronas of concussion nimbused Abe Sapien's view.

And again. Abe Sapien grimaced and tried to shove himself up from the abrasive surface of the rock, which was similar to pumice; volcanic. Pressure vised his neck and impeded his wind.

Choking, Abe Sapien felt the density of the battering waves of hatred that assailed him. The *Anthroposaur* was knocking him down with sheer hate—megatons of it, eons of it, all backed up on the yardstick of time until it became a lethal physical threat.

You persist thinking according to real-world terms.

All Abe Sapien could summon by way of response was, "Bite me, Doggie Legs."

You forget that we are beyond the realm of the corporeal.

"Not so far beyond that I can't feel this! And if you're a phantom—"

Not even that. We are not memory. Because we never existed.

In his mind, Abe Sapien began to block and parry. He could feel the killing energy invading him and fought to deflect and defuse it. He managed to rise to one knee, then stand, flinching as if pummeled from within.

"Why?" was all he said.

Abe Sapien felt the salvo ebb, just slightly. The *Anthroposaur* had tilted its head, as it had before, peering at him.

Your race eliminated the possibility of our existence. And now you are the last of your race.

The massed energy of an entire race, denied by history, was focused toward making Abe Sapien history, too.

As a civilized being, Abe Sapien was supposed to have an advantage over this ... this *joke*, this dawn-of-time mockery of evolution. At least the damned thing couldn't club him with a bone axe. In a human fight, Abe Sapien would have favored the Neanderthal by default, for savagery and efficiency in extermination. He needed to become his own version of a primal man, someone unencumbered by modern tactics or remorse.

All he had by way of return fire was his own capacity to hate.

But defending himself was also a risk. He had to expend thought toward this battle, here, now, thereby increasing the risk that he would never be able to meditate upward from the fugue state. His travels, before, had never divided his attention this way, and it wasn't as simple as clicking his heels and saying *there's no place like home.* He needed a reserve to avoid being sucked down by the undertow of this past, yet he had to summon all his will, now, to engage this unexpected foe. The fallout could be worse than death, as the atoms of his very consciousness were spread thin over the return centuries, in a dustcloud of miniscule microns. Even his own considerable mind, body, and spirit would be scattered so widely that he would run out of particles before he could make it back, whole.

Your kind exterminated my race before we could flower.

The energy of hatred pulsed from the *Anthroposaur* in wave after wave, relentless as the ocean, like magnetism that could rend Abe Sapien asunder; the hot, devastating microwave power of cosmic rays. Abe reeled as he absorbed each attack, struggling to envision himself inside a shielding cocoon of healing water. He imagined the motes of aquatic life, the quintillions of living forms in every ounce of fluid, bonding together to work with a purpose and protect him in unison. He thought the image clearly and felt another barrage soar into his guts—but this strike felt *deflected*, as if magically sapped of aim.

To prevail, Abe Sapien would have to enact a genocide unprecedented in the annals of civilized history. But at this moment, he was not occupying civilized history, and turned his thoughts to hatred.

Abe Sapien thought of being stranded in time, alone, the only one of his kind, seeking community in the company of ghosts. Of humanity's dismissal of him as a sideshow freak. Of the prejudices of little people, against him, and against what he represented. He hated humanity—and every other phylum that could despise him so much with no cause. He confronted black, primeval emotions that his modern self had learned to tamp down, restrain, and muzzle. He gave his loathing full rein against the scientists who had bottled him up for years, uncaring. His ire for the condescension of the B.P.R.D. was allowed to bloom into a scalding fireball of hatred that was both irrational and unwarranted—but he could not permit the luxury of mercy or compassion or understanding, not now. The whirling fireball took on the chartreuse cast of poison, decanted, as Abe Sapien expanded his hatred to include all air breathers, all mutants and mockeries, anything that was *not* Abe Sapien.

And he found he could stand, at last, to face his opponent.

Deep down, past the veneer of manners and feel-good drivel spoken, but not meant, Abe Sapien acknowledged that he was unilaterally hated and feared, on some level, by every living thing he had ever encountered ... and he was able to focus that hatred, that fireball, and swing it like a scythe. He brutally reduced his thinking mind to the elements: Water, from which he sprang. Earth, on which he stood. Air, which could serve as a hot conduit for Fire, which was the summation of his capacity for rage.

Coming to hate every living thing still did not include the *Anthroposaur*, who was not a living thing.

So Abe Sapien stretched the parameters of his hatred to include the dead and the never-born, all of whom had committed the sin of forcing Abe Sapien to consider his own demise someday, and his place in a world that did not want him. Even his ancestors—the ones he had never had—had stranded him. If they had existed, he wanted them to suffer. If they were figments of a dream, he wanted them to live so he could murder them, and kill anything else that had denied him a different world from the one he knew.

Now Abe Sapien could see the force being deployed against him, as an icy blue aura enveloping the *Anthroposaur*, and flowing from it to him. They both held steady, like arm wrestlers locked in tension, as the blue collided with the chartreuse. Much of the energy was canceled out by its mirror, its opposite.

And when matter and anti-matter meet ...

Abe Sapien's eyes could not see fast enough to record all that happened. But he got fragmented images: A molten sunspot in the center of the *Anthroposaur*. The ocean behind it, visible through the hole only for an instant as the hole flared, supernova bright, and consumed the world in white-out. It was like opening a porthole and seeing a star, close-up. It was too much for any mind to bear, in its vastness. It was the blinding opposite of a black hole, shredding time, ripping a gouge in the fabric of the universe.

Abe Sapien felt himself displaced.

He drifted in a gray limbo with no reference points, no up or down, gravity-less. He could see through parts of himself, not wounds, but portions of his wholeness that had ceased to be. Lacking all except the most basic urges, Abe Sapien swam—swam as his ancestors might have, without thought to time, which existed only as an ordering conceit of more rational beings. He swam as *they* would have, before evolution, before social groupings or sequential cognizance. Before right or wrong. And when he could no longer swim, he floated, unmoored ...

... until a mighty hand of stone grasped his arm, and hefted him bodily out of the isolation tank.

"We thought we'd lost you," said a voice. "Your readouts had all gone flat."

Abe Sapien could not see anything until he remembered to retract the protective membranes that had automatically snapped upward to guard his delicate eyes. He was very thirsty.

"Just what do you think you were *doing* in there?"

"Relaxing," said Abe Sapien.

He took in the concerned expression on the devilish visage of his friend. Horns, hooves, crimson skin. Yes, most humans would have collapsed into gibbering insanity upon waking up to see such a sight.

"Yeah, well, you almost *relaxed* yourself to death."

With help, Abe Sapien was able to debark the tank and stand upright—a biped, as intended. Nausea washed over him. He had returned to the world of humans, and demons, and pain without measure. But not without the assistance of a friend.

It felt good to be home.

THE VAMPIRE BRIEF

JAMES L. CAMBIAS

There was a house in the Garden District of New Orleans. A vampire was inside. I was outside. And standing at the top of the front steps was a little guy wearing thick glasses, holding up a sheet of paper the way I've seen other people hold up a crucifix.

"This is a restraining order," he said. "It specifically forbids Mr. Hellboy or any other employees of the Bureau for Paranormal Research and Defense from approaching within five hundred feet of Mr. Antoine Castelaine or his residence."

"Castelaine's a *vampire*," I said. "I'm gonna put him down."

"Officers?" said the little guy, and behind him I could see four New Orleans cops come out of the front door. They looked kind of embarrassed, but each one had a hand resting casually on the flap of his pistol holster.

People tell me I have problems with authority figures. I put one foot on the bottom step. The little lawyer went pale. The cops unsnapped their holsters. I started to figure how I could get past them without doing any permanent damage.

"Hellboy!" A hand clapped me on the back. "Nice to see you back in town! Why didn't you call me first?"

I looked down. "Hi, Eddie." Eddie Canizaro's been on the New Orleans police force since he got back from a tour in Vietnam. These days he looks more like Santa Claus than an ex-Marine.

He waved at the cops on the porch. "I'll take it from here, guys."

"So are you going to tell me I can't put this stake where it'll do some good?"

"Let's go get a drink, Hellboy. There's some things you need to know."

Ten minutes later we were sitting in a bar called the Riverfront Tavern, just under the span of the Mississippi River Bridge. The last time I'd been in there it had been a real dive—the kind of place where a couple of customers come down with "hollow-point lead poisoning" every Saturday night in the parking lot. Now it was cleaner, better lit, and filled with nice-looking young couples drinking microbrews.

Canizaro looked like he missed the old days, too, especially after he got a look at the beer prices.

"Okay, Eddie. Tell me why you and those other cops are protecting a vampire."

He looked miserable. "Things have changed, Hellboy. People think vampires are cool. Sexy. This guy Castelaine even puts ads in the newspaper." He reached over to the next booth and grabbed a discarded *Times-Picayune*. "See for yourself."

The ad was a quarter-page, white gothic letters on a black background.

Are YOU a VAMPIRE LOVER?
Meet a REAL VAMPIRE!
Antoine Castelaine
will share the secrets of BLOOD AND IMMORTALITY!
By Appointment Only
Major Credit Cards Accepted
No Personal Checks

"You're kidding," I said.

"Nope. He even does birthday parties, as long as they're at night. Welcome to the nineties."

"How can he get away with this?"

"No law against being a vampire. Not even against drinking blood, as long as the donor is willing. This guy Castelaine has half a dozen groupies who think it's the coolest thing in the world to let him drain off a couple of pints."

"He doesn't kill anyone?"

"Every now and then a body turns up in the river drained of blood. But we can't tie any of them to Castelaine. How do you tail someone who can turn into a bat?"

"So you're telling me you know this guy's a vampire, but I'll go to jail if I try to go in and stake him?"

"That's about it."

"This sucks, Eddie."

"That it does, my friend. That it does."

Julianna Butler's shop is in one of the parts of New Orleans the tourists never see, but I pay her a visit every time I'm in town. The shop is a little shotgun-style house with a faded sign on the door that reads "Mother Julianna—Fortune Telling & Voodoo Charms."

The front room is for the rubes. She's got shrunken heads (made in Taiwan), voodoo dolls (*hecho en Mexico*), and dried herbs which I know she just buys at the supermarket and puts in little cloth bags at ten dollars an ounce.

The back room is where I like to hang out. She's got old occult books there from collections in Latin America and the Caribbean, genuine Mayan artifacts, and handmade gris-gris charms which aren't in any book I've ever read but which keep evil spirits at bay.

Mother Julianna wasn't young the first time I met her, but I was still surprised to see how tiny and white-haired she was getting. Her eyes were still sharp, though.

"It is good to see you again, Hellboy. Are you married yet?"

"I'd love to be but you keep telling me no."

She smiled a little at that, showing a mouthful of gold teeth. "I heard you have come to do something about that Castelaine man. He's a vampire, you know."

"Is he a real one?"

"Oh, yes," she said, nodding. "From the dark places in Europe. The French name is surely false."

"Can you help me? He's got a restraining order against me and the city cops are guarding his house."

"What can I do? I can give you a charm to find a vampire. I can tell you how to keep one out of your bedroom as you sleep. I can tell you how to kill one, but you know that already. I cannot reach into his home and strike him down. This is a cunning one."

"There's got to be some way to get him."

"I cannot help you, Hellboy. But there is someone who can. Someone with knowledge I do not possess."

"Who?"

"You must go to Little Augie."

"Who the hell is Little Augie?"

"My grandson. He's a lawyer."

I'd seen the billboards and the ads on late-night TV. "When the big guys try to push you around, call Little Augie. I'm Little Augie Butler, and I'm on your side!"

His office was on Tulane Avenue, conveniently near the courthouse and the parish prison. Augie was evidently doing well—the carpet was deep enough to lose a shoe in and the furniture was all massive mahogany and polished brass.

Augie matched the office, in a silk suit and gold cufflinks. His tie alone probably cost a couple of thousand. "How are you doing, Mr. Hellboy? Let me tell you, it's an honor to have you as a client, and I mean that. Come on in here and sit down. Have a drink. Miss Bordelon, if the District Attorney calls, tell him I'll get back to him."

He ushered me into a private office and half-pushed me into a big leather chair, then handed me a glass of what smelled like really good bourbon.

"So what can I do for you today? Criminal defense work? Litigation? You been in an accident?"

"I'm here to take down a vampire. Your grandmother sent me."

Little Augie sighed. "I wish she wouldn't do that. I mean, I love her and all, but it's kind of embarrassing. I'm a lawyer, not a ghost chaser."

"Actually, I do need some legal advice. This vampire has a restraining order out against me so I can't get near him."

"Let me say first of all that as your attorney I must urge you to avoid any kind of violent confrontation. But *hypothetically*—what do you need to do to kill this guy?"

"Stake through the heart. Nail through the temples. Cut off his head."

"We've got laws against that kind of stuff around here, you know. Anything that won't get you a Murder One rap?"

"Sunlight. Most vampires can't stand direct sunlight."

Little Augie gave a big grin, just like on his commercials. "Then I think I can help you. We file a lawsuit and send him a summons to appear in court. Civil court only sits during the day."

"That's perfect—but can you do it?"

"Sure I can. What do you want to sue him for? Gotta be something you have legitimate standing to bring against him. He do anything to you?"

"I've never met the guy."

Little Augie sipped his own drink, then grinned again. "You read the papers?"

"Yeah, sometimes."

"Good. Then we'll do a class-action for deceptive advertising."

"How are those ads deceptive?"

He shrugged. "Who cares if they are? We don't have to win the suit, right? Just get him out in daytime."

The next couple of weeks were taken up with legal skirmishing between Little Augie and Castelaine's attorneys. I took off a few days to investigate a report of zombie pirates near Jamaica and then looked into a sighting of La Llorona near Vera Cruz. Little Augie got in touch with me while I was having some nasty cuts stitched up in a Mexican hospital.

"We've got our court date. This Friday. Do you want to be there?"

"Absolutely."

Two days later I was standing with Little Augie on the steps of the New Orleans courthouse in a pouring rain. The clouds overhead were thick and black. Even though it was eleven o'clock in the morning the day was so dark the streetlights were still on. Augie was keeping his suit and his hairdo dry under a golf umbrella, but I was getting soaked.

A limo pulled up in the no-parking zone and half a dozen people got out. I recognized the little lawyer and some security guards. One of the guards was trying to hold an umbrella over a tall, aristocratic-looking guy in a black overcoat, but the boss waved him away.

"The rain feels good, doesn't it, Hellboy?" he called out as he climbed the steps with his lawyers trailing after him. "Almost as warm as blood."

I looked up at the sky, hoping for a break in the clouds. Just one sunbeam would be enough. Castelaine looked up and smiled, letting the rain pour on to his pale face. "I had to flee Scotland a couple of centuries back because they accused me of invoking the Devil to summon tempests. That wasn't quite how I did it, but it's close enough. A useful art for a vampire to know, don't you think?" He laughed and looked me in the eye. "Now, do you actually intend to go through with this farce today? I've got a delectable young girl waiting at home to be initiated into the mysteries of the blood."

There was a wooden stake in my overcoat pocket. It would be simple: two steps forward, grab him by the shoulder and jab. Maybe I made an unconscious movement forward, because Castelaine took a quick step backwards and a couple of his bodyguards fell into place between us.

I watched them go into the courthouse and plodded after. My old coat was heavy with water.

Augie leaned close as we passed through the metal detectors. "Now what do we do?"

"What do you mean?"

"I figured the guy would shrivel up or something, so I didn't bother to prepare an argument."

"Can't you make something up? Stall him? Maybe the weather will get better."

"I'll try."

There was no jury at this trial. Castelaine's lawyers had insisted and Little Augie hadn't bothered to fight it. But now I could see he was regretting that. A jury would have let him run out the clock with a long speech. The judge was a big cynical-looking woman who didn't look like she would put up with anything like that.

"Your Honor," Augie began, looking uncomfortable. "My client is seeking damages from Mr. Castelaine on the basis of false advertising, on behalf of everyone who has been exposed to Mr. Castelaine's print and radio ads."

"Counselor, I'm afraid you're going to have to explain just how Mr. Castelaine's advertisements are false or misleading," said the judge.

Augie looked down at me. I was having the beginnings of an idea. "Tell them he's really not a vampire," I whispered.

"Your Honor, Mr. Castelaine claims to be a vampire, but we maintain that statement is untrue and misleading."

Castelaine looked amused at that. The judge raised an eyebrow. Castelaine's lawyers went into a huddle. After a few minutes the little guy with the glasses raised his head from the group. "Your Honor, the plaintiff hasn't presented any evidence to disprove my client's claim. The burden of proof is on them to show that Mr. Castelaine is not a vampire."

Augie just grinned at that. "Your Honor, I happen to have here Mr. Hellboy, a world-famous occult investigator from the Bureau for Paranormal Research and Defense. He's an authority on vampires."

So Augie got me on the stand and asked me if Castelaine really was a vampire. Since I was under oath, I didn't want to lie about it directly. "He doesn't show any of the traditional powers and weaknesses of the vampire," I said.

"What would those be?"

"They're repelled by holy symbols, but that's pretty easy to fake. They're destroyed by sunlight—"

"Objection," said the little guy with glasses. "My client has the right to refuse any test which might cause him physical harm."

"You have a point there, Counselor," said the judge.

Augie looked at me. "Anything else?"

"Well, many legends say vampires have the power to turn into animals—you know, rats, bats, that kind of thing. If Castelaine turns into a rat it would reveal his true nature."

His lawyers started to huddle, but Castelaine silenced them and stood up. "Very well," he said. "Observe my power."

It wasn't any kind of gradual change. One moment he was there in his black overcoat, the next moment there was a black bat fluttering in his place.

I leaped out of the witness stand, reaching for the bat. It circled higher, and I jumped onto the judge's desk. The room was full of shouting voices. I could hear the judge yelling at me, and the little lawyer with glasses crying, "Master!"

Castelaine tried to taunt me, dive-bombing my face and then flitting away, but I gave a jump that carried me halfway across the room and caught him in my big stone hand. I made a tight fist and heard little bat bones snapping.

I crash-landed among the empty seats behind Augie. The bailiff and Castelaine's guards were rushing toward me. Before any of them could get through the splintered wood and scattered cushions I pulled a pencil out of my pocket and jammed it into the heart of the crumpled little black creature in my hand. The body burst into flames.

"*Mister Hellboy!*" the judge was yelling. "What *on earth* are you doing?"

"Just killing a bat, Your Honor," I said. "No law against killing bats, is there?"

The room got quiet. Castelaine's lawyers were all looking at each other, except for the guy with glasses. He was trying to scrape up the bits of ash and fur scattered on the floor.

"Case dismissed!" said the judge, and banged her gavel.

Mother Julianna and I buried what was left of Castelaine where the Interstate-10 overpass crosses Canal Street; that was the biggest crossroads we could find. Canizaro told me no more bloodless bodies were found after Castelaine disappeared. For my courtroom brawl I got sentenced to a week of community service, instructing the NOPD in how to deal with supernatural threats.

And if you're ever watching late-night TV in New Orleans, watch for me during the commercials. I'm the big red guy who says, "Thanks, Little Augie!"

UNFINISHED BUSINESS
ED GORMAN & RICHARD DEAN STARR

Rick O'Malley was the private's name, which is a pretty good name for a PFC when you think about it. He was from nearby Wisconsin, just nineteen and fresh off the farm, and he was headed to Korea to get his ass shot off in what was still officially being called a "police action" by the Pentagon. God forbid you should call it a war, even though 35,000 Americans, including a whole lot of PFCs, had gotten themselves killed in that snowy wasteland.

Tonight was O'Malley's last night at Camp Pennington. By o-nine hundred tomorrow he'd be on a train to Texas. Then, after a week of special training, he'd be flown with his company to Korea.

He glanced at his Timex. It was barely nine-thirty; not quite twelve hours to go. More than enough time to finish getting drunk out of his mind and maybe even get laid.

In the rain-misted darkness of the Army town known as Grand Mound, there wasn't much else to do on a Thursday night. Some gambling was about all, but you had to be careful. Otherwise, you might end up in front of the Provost Marshall with your ass in a sling. Getting drunk was a lot more fun and, generally speaking, a hell of a lot cheaper.

O'Malley grinned and held up the half-empty bottle of Dunphy's whiskey clenched in his hand. The stuff was rough and cheap, but it sure made him happy. He couldn't give the whiskey all the credit, though—the rest went to the well packaged brunette wrapped inside his other arm.

"Jess like a mir'cle," he mumbled.

She glanced up and smiled. "What was that?"

He blinked, and then took a swig from the whiskey bottle. "All's I said was, you being here's a miracle, it surely is."

"My, what a sweet thing to say. In fact, you're so sweet, I may just have to give you a kiss!"

O'Malley could hardly believe his good fortune. Nancy Fielding, the girl who'd broken his heart during his Junior year in high school, had come to Grand Mound to show him a proper sendoff.

The last he'd heard, she'd been a nursing-school student in Chicago and was engaged to some doctor. He'd been damn surprised to find her standing along the bar at Charley's, the most popular bar in Grand Mound.

If he hadn't already been drunk, he might have been dubious about her timing or asked a few questions. How had she known where to find him? And what had prompted her sudden appearance? He also might have noticed that she was more buxom than he remembered, or that the tailored red suit she wore accentuated her every curve in ways he'd never seen before.

All he could see was the Nancy he remembered, her beautiful, smoldering eyes promising to resurrect memories he'd once tried to forget.

What had he been thinking? Forget about Nancy? That was just crazy.

The jukebox in Charley's had been playing Frank Sinatra and Doris Day, songs about loneliness and heartbreak. *Fuck lonely*, he'd thought as he took her in his arms. There was no way PFC Rick O'Malley was going to be lonely tonight.

Now, standing on the sidewalk across the street from Charley's, he knew this couldn't be the girl who'd broken his heart. This was Nancy.

She'd never hurt him. Not again. Never.

He pulled her close. "Guess I'd like that kiss now," he said, his voice hoarse with desire.

So she did, and the overwhelming scent of her perfume threatened to drive him crazy with love and lust and loss.

For just a moment he thought of the Nancy Fielding he remembered—or thought he did, anyway. The girl who was in nursing school. Who was engaged. In Chicago.

How could that be?

Then the scent of her perfume enveloped him completely and he felt his doubts slip away. What a fool he was. This really *was* Nancy. The one and only.

She took him by the hand and led him away from the lights and the bars and the safety of the other GIs. From inside Charley's, he heard Patti Page playing the "Tennessee Waltz."

He could have cared less; he was with his one and only.

The funny thing was, for a young guy who'd once wanted to make the military his life, O'Malley didn't give a damn about being AWOL. At this point, he couldn't even remember how many days it had been since he'd returned to base. Six? Seven?

He really didn't care because they were living on a different world, one untouched by the crude concerns of terra firma. Her apartment encompassed the entire universe. She had stocked up with steaks and red snapper and lobster. There was wine and whiskey and, my God, champagne. She had a 19" console TV and she loved all the same shows he did—Jackie Gleason and Milton Berle and *M-Squad* with Lee Marvin and the Hopalong Cassidy movies he'd never outgrown.

But most of all there was the dark and perfume-scented bedroom where he was reborn each time they made love. Only once did he mention how hurt—hell, devastated—he'd been when she deserted him that time.

But when she pressed herself to him and stroked his cheek with a tenderness he'd never known ... it was not difficult to forgive or forget ...

Nine days after he was last seen on base, two boys playing in a shallow timbered area behind the high-school stadium found the body of Private Rick O'Malley. By now his flesh had been pecked and ripped apart by various animals, and turned into mottled patterns of decay by the elements. What was even more disturbing than death to the boys, was the vestige of a smile on the corpse's face. Dead guys never looked happy on *Dragnet*. What did this guy have to smile about?

The man wore a uniform, one soiled with pigeon droppings, dirt, and grass stains. He was from the nearby base.

The boys ran down to a Shell station and breathlessly told the gas jockey there what they'd found. He said: "You kids bullshittin' me, I'm gonna kick your ass, you got that?" These two eleven year olds had a deserved reputation in the neighborhood for, shall we say, enhancing things a mite. But they raised their hands in the Boy Scout way and pledged they were telling the truth.

The gas jockey dragged out the phone book, looked up the number he wanted, and then dialed the base.

A Jeep-load of four MPs were dispatched within eight minutes of the call being logged in at the base switchboard.

Four days after the discovery of Private O'Malley's body, a special convoy came through the front gates of Camp Pennington without stopping at the guard shack, and Colonel Robert Blaine knew immediately that their guests had arrived.

"That's them, isn't it?" said Lieutenant Steve Wentworth.

Blaine nodded. "Yes."

He watched the largest vehicle in the convoy, a massive Army transport. No one could have guessed who was inside. Blaine wouldn't have believed it himself if he hadn't met him. Sometimes he still found it hard to believe that he had. Was it really nine years now? Too often, it seemed like a dream—although there were some who would have called it a nightmare.

"No disrespect, sir," Wentworth said, "but this is a joke, right?"

Blaine stared at the younger man. "You've been my Chief of Staff for two years, Lieutenant," he said. "Do I strike you as the type to make jokes? Especially classified ones?"

Wentworth shook his head, chastened. "No, sir."

The two men were standing on the second-floor balcony of the camp's wood-frame administration office, less than a quarter mile from the front gate. As the convoy drew closer, Blaine could make out indistinct faces inside the staff cars. He wondered if one of them was Professor Bruttenholm. He'd always liked the guy, even if he was a bit odd, and the feeling had been mutual. It would be good to see him again.

Wentworth said, "Sir, about this individual ..."

"Yes? Spit it out, Lieutenant."

"Well ..." Wentworth looked uncomfortable. "Is he dangerous? Is there anything I should know, security-wise? I haven't had the time to—"

"Relax, Lieutenant," Blaine said. "You've been briefed. Just pay attention and do yourself a favor; don't speak to him unless he speaks to you first."

"Yes, sir."

The convoy parked in a semicircle in front of the building. The Army transport shifted into reverse and lurched back toward the front porch with a shriek of tortured gears. For a moment, Blaine thought the truck might crash into the balcony. Then it stopped with just a few inches to spare. From inside the truck, Blaine heard something heavy fall and a voice say, "Crap!"

Blaine suppressed a smile. Apparently, some things hadn't changed. "Let's welcome our guests, Lieutenant," he said. "And just try to relax."

"Easier said than done, sir," Wentworth said. "You've met him before. I haven't."

At first, red was the only thing Wentworth could see. There were other colors and textures and shadows, of course, but none of them could compete with the massive crimson presence that filled the back of the Army transport. Then it moved into the light and Wentworth's mouth dropped open.

"Holy shit!" he blurted. "He's real!" Immediately, he wished that he hadn't spoken. Blaine glared at him with an expression that said, *Shut your trap right now, or there'll be hell to pay.*

Apparently, hell wasn't too far off the mark.

"Yeah, 'he' *is* real," Hellboy said. His baritone voice was tinged with irritation. He stepped out of the truck, his cloven hooves clanking loudly on the wood porch. "And 'he' can hear, too. Imagine that."

Wentworth swallowed thickly. "I-I'm sorry," he said lamely. "I mean, it's just—"

"Forget it," Hellboy said, waving his massive right arm. "I get that kind of thing a lot." He squinted down at Wentworth. "What are you staring at?"

"Nothing," Wentworth said, averting his eyes from Hellboy's right hand. At least, he *thought* it was a hand. It looked more like a chunk of rock with four jointed pieces that only vaguely resembled fingers.

"It's good to see you again, Hellboy," said Colonel Blaine warmly.

Hellboy reached out with his left hand and fingered the silver eagles on Blaine's shoulders. "You're moving up in the world."

Blaine grinned. "Working with you was considered hazard duty, so they promoted me. You've grown up quite a bit, Hellboy. Last I remember, you were three feet tall and had a face only a mother could love."

Hellboy grimaced. "I always liked you, Blaine. You were funny. You're not funny anymore, but at least you've still got your eye for the weird. I told the Bureau that if anyone knew a live one when they saw it, you'd be it. So here I am."

Blaine glanced around. "Is the professor with you?"

"Nah," Hellboy said. "I'm handling this one alone. If you've got what I think you've got, it'll be a simple cleanup job."

"Let's get to it, then," said Blaine. "Shall we?"

He stepped aside and gestured for Hellboy to precede him. Hellboy sized up the available space around the door, his red tail swishing through the slit in the back of his trench coat. Then he sighed and ducked inside. The sanded down stumps of his horns narrowly missed the top of the frame.

They moved into the outer office and Hellboy glanced at the stairs leading up to Blaine's office. "You sure you want me on those?"

Blaine shrugged. "Down here's fine."

He reached behind the empty receptionist's desk and rolled a metal typing stool into the center of the room.

"There you are," he said. "That should do the trick."

"Thanks," Hellboy said, sitting down. "So what do you have for me?"

Blaine looked at Wentworth. "I'll let Wentworth brief you. He's been the investigator on this case."

Wentworth nodded, tried to control his nerves. He stood up, the way he had in Catholic school, to give his report.

"Over the past four months, three of our soldiers have gone AWOL. One was gone nine days, one six days, one four days. When we found them, they had each been dead for approximately twenty-four hours. I was on the scene with the police and the ambulance and the medical examiner. I was liaison between the camp and the police. I mention this because I was glad I had witnesses to what I saw.

"Each man—corpse—died smiling. I asked the doc who did the autopsies if maybe they weren't smiling, that maybe there was a reaction at the point of death that simulated a smile. He said no, that there wasn't such a reaction. The men were smiling.

"The autopsies listed massive heart attacks as the cause of death. Each of them were young men. The oldest was twenty-three. They were all in excellent condition. Hearts, lungs, brains showed no pre-existing conditions."

"That's unusual," Hellboy said, "but not unheard of."

"It was the autopsies that got our attention," Blaine said. "We knew we were looking at *something* paranormal. We just haven't been able to determine exactly what that *something* is."

"Such as?"

"Well, their faces, for one thing." Wentworth said. "The smiles."

"And their eyes," Wentworth said. "That was something nobody really noticed until we all saw the bodies laid out in the morgue."

Hellboy said, "The eyes were full of fire? Not literally, of course. But there was an image of fire on the retinal surface? And the docs said they'd never seen anything like it?"

"Yes," Wentworth said, looking young and astonished. Hellboy was proving to be everything Blaine had told him. "How did you know?"

Hellboy sighed. "We're dealing with a lady of sorts here. A very special lady. I've had a few run-ins with her before. She's unfinished business from Bulgaria. But I didn't expect her to end up in Iowa."

"You said 'she,'" Wentworth said. "What do you mean?"

"Succubus," Hellboy said.

"Excuse me?" said Wentworth, unsure he'd heard correctly.

"She's a succ-u-bus," Hellboy repeated slowly. "A demon of seduction. Supposedly, she and her male counterpart, the incubus, are fallen angels and can change gender at will. Personally, I could care less if she's a demon, a fallen angel, or a lawyer. As far as I'm concerned, there's not much difference. They're all just as easy to hit."

"So how do we stop her?" Blaine said.

Hellboy looked at Wentworth and said, "I've got two bags in the truck. Would you go get them for me, Lieutenant? I just don't want anything damaged."

Wentworth knew he was being sent on an unnecessary errand. Clearly, Hellboy wanted to talk to Blaine alone. But he also knew that he couldn't say no.

He said, "Of course."

And after saluting Blaine, he was gone.

When he was sure that Wentworth was down the hall, Hellboy leaned forward and said, "Let's talk about the type of men we need."

"Type?"

Hellboy sat back and said, "Men who've experienced a bad relationship with a woman. A divorce or a very painful breakup. This particular demon can work a number of ways, but her strength is preying on men who are psychologically at a very vulnerable point in their lives. From five minutes on the phone with you, I had a pretty good idea of what we were dealing with here. And Wentworth's report confirmed it."

"How do we trap her?"

"Bait. We need three soldiers to spend a few nights in the bars along the strip, where the soldiers go. Everybody's got an old love somewhere in their past. She instinctively takes the form of that old love. We need men who have iron will and can stand up to her."

Hellboy shook his massive head. "That's why we need the toughest men we can find. The second she starts to change form, our soldier signals the MP and moves in. The MP holds her till I can get there. I'll be cruising the block where all the bars are. I'll be a few minutes away at most. Then I take it from there."

Blaine had one more concern. "I'm not sure I know which soldiers to recommend."

"We talk to the chaplain and the sergeants who run the barracks. They'll know who we should use."

"You want me to round up the chaplain and the sergeants right away?"

"May as well," Hellboy said. "No offense, Colonel, but it doesn't look like there's much else to do in this little burg of yours."

Hellboy and Colonel Blaine spent the next twelve hours talking to the staff members who could help them choose three soldiers for a special assignment. They didn't share any information about the assignment, except to describe in detail the kind of men they needed for this particular job.

Twice during the long, butt-numbing afternoon sitting behind his desk, the Colonel watched through the partially open door as Wentworth appeared in the outer office and spoke with the corporal who was answering phones and typing.

Nearing five o'clock, they concluded their interview with a private named "Touch" McKenzie. "Touch" had been a damned good high-school running back, a three-summer lifeguard, and an auxiliary policeman before dropping out of college his sophomore year because his father had died and no more money was available. Tough, sensible, reliable. The same kind of profile as the first selection, a hard, handsome Italian kid named Tommy Puzo.

"One more to go," Hellboy said as McKenzie closed the door behind him on his way out.

"I think we've already got our third man. And he's been right in front of us. Steve Wentworth is trustworthy and competent and as an investigator he's always kept a cool head."

"I was wondering about him myself," Hellboy said. "All right, that's three, then. One of them will trap her and I'll move in to destroy her."

Blaine laughed. "You're handy to have around."

"That's why they pay me the big bucks."

The Colonel placed a call and twenty minutes later, Wentworth knocked on the door.

"Come in, Lieutenant," Blaine said. "We were just talking about you."

"Favorably, I hope," Wentworth said.

Blaine said, "Of course favorably. Now sit down here and let's the three of us have a talk. We think you can help us with this succubus thing."

Promptly at nine a.m. the following morning, Wentworth, Puzo, and McKenzie met in a private consultation room with Hellboy and Colonel Blaine.

Hellboy spent an hour telling them in detail what they were to do and to watch for tonight as they began to work their way through the bars that servicemen frequented.

Hellboy and Blaine alike noticed that Wentworth looked tired, maybe even a bit sick. Blaine suspected that Wentworth had maybe picked up the stomach bug that had been felling soldiers—and keeping them close to toilets—for the past couple of weeks. But, Blaine assumed, like the good soldier he was, Wentworth didn't complain. He showed up on time and participated by asking Hellboy several questions.

In truth, Wentworth hadn't slept well last night. Following the meeting with Hellboy and Blaine yesterday afternoon, he went to his apartment, opened a fifth of Dewar's scotch, and proceeded to get, in the current parlance, plastered.

He hadn't been honest with Hellboy or Blaine in his interview. They'd asked if had ever had a love affair that he hadn't gotten over, that he still brooded about. He'd said no.

But that was hardly the truth. He'd wanted this assignment. He was intrigued, fascinated by it. And so he hadn't told them anything about Dierdre, the campus beauty he'd gone out with for five months until his jealousy and possessiveness had caused her to break it off. He spent the following three months following her, calling her, sending her flowers on the one hand, and bitter hate notes on the other. He had no doubt that he was insane during this time.

Finally, she agreed to go out with him one night if he promised he would keep things light. Everything had gone well on that night of an ice storm, until they were approaching her dorm. He sped up so she couldn't get out of the car. He drove straight to the highway. The radio had warned that all roadways were ice-packed and dangerous. He told her that he'd never let her go. He started screaming at her, so absorbed in his madness that he didn't see the long sheet of ice just ahead, nor the semi bearing down on them in the other lane. Not until it was too late, him sliding across the ice into the other lane, the semi smashing into them, virtually severing the car in half.

He lived; she died.

Dierdre; oh, Dierdre ...

If Hellboy was sure that Steve would see her again—even in the form of a demon—Steve didn't care ... Just to hold her, tell her how sorry he was for what had happened ...

"You sure you're all right?" asked Colonel Blaine. "We can get somebody else if you'd rather get some rest tonight."

"Oh, I'm fine, sir. Just fine. Really."

And he was. Dierdre awaited him ...

Promptly at seven o'clock, the teams hit the long, neon-red street where the main taverns were located. The teams consisted of the soldier who was there to be bait, to draw out the demon, and another soldier to keep an eye on the bait, to report back immediately if it looked like contact could be made.

Hellboy and Colonel Blaine waited nervously for word that night, but none came. No contact of any kind was made.

The three soldiers nursed beers, walked around, kept themselves as accessible as possible. Each of them were approached by various prostitutes, but these girls were familiar types. The only thing spooky about them was all the makeup and cheap perfume they wore.

Nobody was more disappointed that night than Wentworth. He lay in bed smoking one cigarette after another, listening to his long-play album of the Four Freshmen. Nobody could croon like those lads, using jazzy riffs to extend and clarify the sentimental songs of lost loves and what-might-have-beens.

He was so exhausted by the time he got to sleep, he rolled over and slammed off the alarm when six o'clock came. He didn't come to until nearly nine-thirty. At least he felt rested. He showered, dressed, headed to his office. Fortunately, Colonel Blaine was involved in a meeting at the mayor's office. Once a month, every third Tuesday, the mayor and the Colonel met to work through any problems the Army was causing the town or the town causing the Army. He didn't get to the office until eleven.

Steve Wentworth didn't get much work done. All he could focus on was what the meeting would be like when he finally met Dierdre. He would get the chance to tell her how sorry he was for what he'd done. And then she would be his again.

At Finnegan's Tap Lieutenant Steve Wentworth was well on his way to winning twenty dollars at bumper pool. He wasn't worth a damn at real pool, but he was the Babe Ruth of bumper pool. Even Sergeant Mallory, who stood at the far end of the bar watching over him, was impressed. He'd give a thumbs up every time Wentworth made a good shot.

He was lucky his skill hadn't left him. This was the third bar they'd been in tonight and there was no sign of any woman coming on to him. A few of them gave him the kind of looks that all attractive men or women get, but they didn't show any real interest.

He'd play a few more games here and, if nothing happened, he'd move on to the fourth and final bar.

Dierdre, he thought. Dierdre.

Back to the game.

He lined up his shot. Six ball in the corner pocket. Not much of a challenge.

He shot. Then something strange happened.

He scratched.

Badly.

So badly, in fact, that the tip of his cue tore open the bright green billiard fabric the same as if he'd cut it with a switchblade.

The others around him were too drunk to notice how Wentworth's expression had changed just before he made the shot. He'd just been about to apply cue to ball when his eyes rose and caught sight of her standing at the end of the table.

Distantly, he saw the cue seem to shoot itself.

And miss the ball entirely.

Then rip right through the billiard fabric.

Strange, indeed.

But not nearly as strange as seeing a ghost.

Hellboy was a creature of the night. Not because of his origins, but because he loved late-night television. He'd been watching *Broadway Open House* for about a year now and thought that Morey Amsterdam was one hell of a funny guy.

It was after one a.m. when Colonel Blaine stuck his head into Hellboy's borrowed office. Hellboy was on the telephone and gestured for the Colonel to come in and sit down.

"Right," Hellboy said into the phone. "No problem. Okay, we'll try again tomorrow. Ciao."

"Any luck?" Blaine asked, lowering himself into a chair.

"None," Hellboy said, dropping the phone back onto the cradle. He leaned back in the office chair and propped his hooves up on the edge of the desk. "That was Wilkes checking in. He just left Harrington's Pub babysitting Lieutenant Callahan. No sign of any demons. Although he did say a few of the women looked demonic until you'd had a couple of beers."

"What about Wentworth? You heard anything from Sergeant Mallory yet?"

"No. But I'm sure he'll be calling in. Be time to wrap up the night pretty soon. Maybe she's not going to show tonight, either."

But she wasn't a ghost.

Steve Wentworth let his cue fall to the floor. He started walking to mid-point at the bar. He felt as if he was in one of those corny old romance movies where even in a crowded room the only two people you notice are the two lovers who are coming urgently together.

He bumped people but he didn't notice. He stepped on toes but he didn't notice. He even nudged a guy into spilling some beer on himself, but he didn't notice that, either.

All there was was Dierdre.

And then she was there. Real. Complete. Ethereal in her elegant beauty.

"Hello, Steve. I knew I'd see you again someday."

"I had the same feeling."

"I have a place we could go. But that sergeant keeps moving closer to us. I don't think he wants us to be together."

"Just wait here a minute. Then we'll go."

He felt light-headed, unreal. All that mattered was Dierdre.

He made quick work of Mallory. Walked right up to him and said, "She's an old friend of mine. Not the one we were waiting for. You can go sit down now."

The blunt-faced Mallory checked out the young officer's face. "You don't look right, Lieutenant. Maybe you better let me take over from here."

"I've told you, Sergeant. There's no problem. So just go drink a beer and relax."

He'd spoken so sharply that the soldiers around him were tuning in now. They sensed a fight about to happen. Who could resist watching a bar fight? Not even Uncle Miltie, presently on the TV up in the far corner of the bar, could be as entertaining as a good old-fashioned bar brawl.

But there was no brawl. Steve Wentworth smashed Mallory squarely in the mouth with such force that he knocked the sergeant back into the crowd. Thick blood began splashing from the man's mouth. His eyes rolled back into his head as the soldiers behind him caught him.

Steve wasted no time. The soldiers crowded along the bar gave him plenty of space. He moved quickly back to Dierdre, grabbed her wrist, and dragged her toward the back door.

Sergeant Mallory was unconscious for the next five minutes, and by then Steve and Dierdre were long gone.

For the next thirty-six hours, Hellboy and Colonel Blaine stayed close to the telephones. Not wanting the local police involved—think of how the public would react if the story of a succubus ever got out, a storm of panic, or a storm of hooting, howling laughter—Blaine discreetly ordered his Military Police to prowl the streets looking for Steve Wentworth. All of them knew what Wentworth looked like, so identifying him wouldn't be any trouble.

Sergeant Mallory was interviewed three times. Blaine could see that the enlisted man—a man with a commendable record—was embarrassed to have let down his commander this way. He just kept repeating that he certainly didn't expect Wentworth to have wielded that amount of power with a single punch. He seemed to be in shock.

Steve Wentworth could not believe how much his life had changed. The night he and Dierdre had left Finnegan's Bar together, he had broken down completely. He'd talked and cried for hours, begging for her forgiveness and pledging his undying love. After that, they'd held each other into the morning; the future was theirs once more.

By the next day he had practically moved in with Dierdre.

She had a small apartment a mile from the post, which is where they spent their first night together. When he entered it, Wentworth felt as if he'd dropped into a fantastic dream. Her beauty, her elegance, her gentle love for him—he was in love with her even more than he'd been back in college. When she took him so gently to bed, he felt not only sated but renewed, as if being with her gave him a strength and tranquility and purpose that life had deprived him of before.

Thank God she hadn't died in the car accident, after all. She lay in his arms their first night together and she told him what had happened to her.

"The doctor who treated me had a drinking problem," she explained. "He confused me with a patient who didn't make it."

"But why?" he asked. "Why didn't you tell me?"

"It was a chance to get away, from my smothering parents, from my relationship with you. Remember, we were fighting a lot at the time. And I was so confused! It was really a chance to start my own life, don't you see?"

"But I still can't understand—"

"No," she said, "you can't. You can't know how much I've missed you or how long I've searched. But now we're together again, and I'll always be here. Always!"

His life seemed so simple now, and good. He was with Dierdre again, with her in all respects, and never more so than when they were making love in the shadows of her one-room apartment, away from the rest of humanity.

It was on their third night together that he sensed she was troubled. A terrible fear came over him. Was she going to leave him, after all?

But then he was lost in the warmth and comfort of their love. Only later did the fear of her leaving come back. "Is everything all right, sweetheart?"

"It's nothing, just something I have to work out on my own."

"Your own? I thought we were together again."

She smiled. Touched his cheek. He literally felt her sadness and melancholy. It was on the air itself. "There's a ... a creature, a monster. He's after me."

"A creature?" he said, surprised by her choice of words. "What kind of creature?"

"They call him Hellboy," she said. "I met him briefly in Europe a few years ago. He became obsessed with me. At first I thought it was flattering. But then—" She covered her face with her hands, and his sense of her fear and heartache seemed like a spike in his heart. "But then, he—he kidnapped me."

"*Kidnapped* you? Hellboy?"

"Yes. I managed to escape, but I've been hiding from him ever since. The military is convinced he's so honorable—if they only knew."

Her gentle voice became tearful now. "He always finds me. He's here now. He's convinced everyone that I'm this evil person, this demon. So they help him. Someday he'll kidnap me again and I won't be able to escape. Then he'll have me forever."

Wentworth was horrified.

I should've told her right from the start why I was in that bar, he thought. *Dammit, I was one of the people helping Hellboy find her!*

He gathered her up in his arms and held her close.

I didn't know what he was really up to then, but I know now. I'm going to make sure he never gets his hands on her again, he vowed.

Dierdre looked up at him, and her eyes were full of love and lust and need. He blinked, and for a moment he imagined that he saw fire in them, and that her teeth were as thin and sharp as daggers.

Then she took him down into her sweet, sad, scented beauty, and all his thoughts were lost.

After the first night, when they were unable to find him, Hellboy and Colonel Blaine knew that they had lost Steve Wentworth. Two more days of searching for him had turned up nothing. Apparently, the Lieutenant hadn't returned to camp since the scene with Sergeant Mallory. His clothes were still in his quarters and the bed had clearly not been slept in. By the third day there were at least two dozen pieces of mail lying on his desk, unopened.

"It looks like I'm going barhopping," Blaine said.

"I'd love to join you," said Hellboy. "I could use a beer or three. But I'd probably attract some attention."

Blaine smiled uncertainly. "Yeah, come to think of it, you probably would."

B laine dressed in a gray Irish-tweed jacket, a black crewneck sweater, chinos, and sand-colored desert boots. With the leather patches on his elbows and the pipe in his mouth, he thought he looked like a college professor.

He hadn't been bar-hopping since before his wedding eleven years ago. Some of the soldiers in the bars recognized him, but most didn't. He kept to the shadows unless he was talking to a server or bartender.

Blaine had brought plenty of twenty-dollar bills. He'd never tried to bribe anybody before. It was kind of fun. Like being in a detective movie. Like Mike Hammer, Blaine being a secret reader of the Mickey Spillane novels that presently dominated all the best-seller lists.

He handed out seven twenties that night. First in Charley's, then at The Clover Leaf Club. And always with the same line: You help me find this Lieutenant Wentworth, you'll get four more twenties just like this one. Then he'd hand the person his card with both his office and camp phone numbers on it.

The Colonel hadn't been inside Finnegan's bar for more than five minutes when the bartender directed him to an attractive blond girl who was moving around the tables, serving drinks to the crowd of GIs.

"Sure, I know Steve," she said after they'd slipped into one of the bar's shadowy corners and Blaine introduced himself. Then, more suspiciously: "He's a nice guy. He goes to our basketball games sometimes. I'm a junior at the college here. I just work here part time. Cindy's my name, by the way, Colonel."

Blaine said smoothly, "Cindy, our daughter's in town for twenty-four hours. We'd like to introduce them. You haven't seen him around, have you?"

"Not today. The other night I did. He was playing bumper pool, right there." She pointed to the table. It wasn't being used because of the tear in the fabric surface. A handwritten "Out of Order" sign was propped up between the bumpers.

"Did he do that?" Blaine said, nodding at the tear.

"Yes. And he hit this other soldier hard enough to knock him out with one punch. Then he grabbed this really beautiful girl and ran out the back way. It wasn't like Steve at all. It was as if he was another person."

Damn, Blaine thought. *Wentworth could be anywhere by now. Or dead.* "Did you happen to notice which way they went?"

Cindy looked at him, her expression suggesting she didn't consider him the sharpest stick in the room. "Well, yes, of *course* I know which way he went!"

"You do? That's terrific!" Blaine pulled a small notebook from his back pocket and got his ballpoint pen ready. "So which way did they go?"

Cindy shook her head. "The girl he left with lives in my building." She gave him the address. "Juniors can live off campus. It's a lot better than living in the dorm."

"Thanks, Cindy." He tried not to sound excited. He didn't want her to know how urgent the situation was.

He slid a twenty-dollar bill under his beer when she was momentarily distracted and said, "Somebody left you this."

She smiled. "You don't have to bribe me, Colonel. I've got a brother in Korea. I'm just glad to help any way I can."

She left the twenty on the table.

It was well after three a.m. by the time Hellboy joined Blaine in the dark alleyway across the street from the modest two-story brownstone apartment building.

"She rents the corner one," Blaine said, pointing up at the second floor. "The one in front there."

Hellboy opened the left side of his trench coat, revealing an enormous holster containing the largest handgun Blaine had ever seen.

"You think bullets will actually work on her—uh, it?" he said skeptically.

"Nah," Hellboy said, pulling the gun from the holster and cracking open the chamber. "But I brought along a special surprise." He tapped on one of the bullets, which were made of a clear material filled with glowing, blue liquid.

"It's the blood of an incubus," Hellboy explained. "The male version of our demon. The succubus and incubus love human pain and suffering, but they can't touch each other's blood. It's sorta like giving a human a cyanide cocktail. Except instead of dying, they're forced back into hell. Permanently." Rising to his full, imposing height, Hellboy grinned. "Time to get this show on the road."

"We can provide cover if you need it," Blaine said.

"Cover?" Hellboy actually managed to look hurt. "Me?"

"I stand corrected," Blaine said, amused.

"How soon they forget," muttered Hellboy. Hefting the pistol chest-high, he strode out of the alley and into the night.

In the dream, Steve Wentworth was floating. Dierdre was standing over him, her smile beatific, her gaze loving. Before he could speak or even smile, her face changed. The skin seemed to melt away like candle wax, revealing a hellish creature so terrifyingly hideous that his tongue retreated into his throat, choking him.

Unable to scream, he rolled away and found himself falling into a bottomless pit lined with fire. To his horror, the thing that had once been Dierdre fell with him, sinking its claws into his chest, into his face. Its breath stank of rotting meat.

They say you wake up from a dream of falling before you hit the ground. But that wasn't what roused Wentworth from his terrible nightmare; it was the sound of splintering wood and the loud crash of the shattered front door hitting the wall of the living room. He rolled over, moving instinctively to shield Dierdre from harm.

To his surprise, she wasn't in bed.

He reached under his pillow, fumbling in the darkness for his Browning semi-automatic pistol. He didn't need to see what had kicked in the front door; he already knew.

Hellboy.

The creature had come for Dierdre, just as she'd feared.

"Help! Keep him away from me, Steve! Please!"

Wentworth stepped into the dark living room and saw Dierdre. She was in her nightgown, crouched in front of the window. Backlit by the faint light filtering in from the streetlamps, she seemed more radiant and beautiful than he could ever remember.

"Don't worry," he said, "I'll protect you."

He paused, listening intently. He wanted to go to the nearest light switch, but couldn't risk making any more sound. Staring into the darkness, straining his ears, he waited for some indication of movement.

When Hellboy came through the destroyed front door, he was much faster than Wentworth would have believed possible. But then again, he—*it*—wasn't human. It was a freak of hell, come to steal away his one true love.

"You can't have her!" he screamed and fired the Browning wildly in Hellboy's direction. "She's mine, and I'm never going to let her go!"

As the muzzle flashed, Wentworth saw Hellboy rolling across the living room. Then the hammer clicked on an empty chamber and the room was plunged back into darkness.

Breathing raggedly, he turned and started for the bedroom to get more bullets. It was impossible to tell if any of the ones he'd fired had found their mark.

Then Hellboy was rising up in front of him. Wentworth saw him and his heart froze.

Hellboy was aiming a gun. At Dierdre. At his beloved.

"Noooo!" Wentworth shrieked and threw himself in front of Dierdre just as Hellboy pulled the trigger. The bullet punched through Wentworth's shoulder, tearing a bloody path two inches wide and spinning him around onto the floor. Then the bullet struck Dierdre and exploded in a shower of blue fire.

The effect on her was instantaneous.

Sprawled on the floor in a pool of his own blood, Wentworth watched in horror and despair as Dierdre's entire body flickered, a dying candle. Just like in his dreams.

"Dierdre," he moaned.

Wentworth had lost his beloved once, had nearly killed her because of his drinking and his selfishness. Now he was losing her once again, and it was more than he could bear. Pushing himself up on his good arm, he inched toward the flickering form of his beloved.

He heard Hellboy yell, "Wentworth, don't! She'll take you with her!"

He no longer cared. To live with the memory of Dierdre's face, to have known her beauty once more, only to relive the pain of losing her all over again, that would be a living death.

With a final sob, he reached out and touched the edge of her shimmering nightgown.

Hellboy stood in the darkened apartment, staring down at the empty spot where the succubus had been standing. The blue drops of blood splattered across the walls were already disappearing, fading back into hell. But the blood of Steve Wentworth was still dark and bright on the polished floor.

"Dammit," Hellboy said softly. He slipped his gun back into its holster and knelt down. Reaching out, he rolled Wentworth's lifeless body over and stared into his wide, flame-filled eyes.

Failure was not something Hellboy was accustomed to. Not that this was entirely a failure; he *had* killed the demon, after all. Still, it felt wrong, incomplete.

Someone once said that true love never dies. As Hellboy looked into Wentworth's eyes, he thought maybe he could see love there, even in the flames of hell.

That wasn't much consolation. But for now, it would have to be enough.

SAINT HELLBOY
TOM PICCIRILLI

Father Tommy Guerra hung his head in shame while his grandmother levitated at the top of the stairs. She twirled with her black dress flowing about her, the rosary beads swinging around her waist. She screamed in Italian and continued stirring a pot of pasta and red sauce that spattered onto the carpet.

Hellboy, still wet from the rain outside, stared and asked, "Should we try to get her down?"

"No," Tommy said, "it'll only encourage her."

"Please tell me I'm not going to have to punch out an old lady."

"I'm really hoping we can avoid that."

Hellboy wasn't so sure. The situation appeared just ridiculous enough to have some serious malevolence at work. These kinds of cases started off looking silly and ended with fire and a lot of blood. Usually his.

The elderly woman floated down the steps and, moaning at a fierce inhuman pitch, began kicking Father Tommy in the head. "Grandma Lucia, stop!"

Hellboy reached up to grab at her feet, and she stomped down on him hard with her heels. He flailed backwards and nearly fell into a life-size statue of St. Francis of Assisi. "Those are pediatric pumps. They hurt!"

He felt the sudden rage brewing inside and stepped away. He watched Tom leap and struggle with the crazed woman, whose eyes showed white as she wailed. Hellboy clenched his massive stone right hand and put it behind his back. He really didn't want to get into a fight with a priest's eighty-two-year-old grandmother, even if she was possessed.

He'd known Father Tommy Guerra for almost ten years. They'd been side by side in Jerusalem in '97 when the Whore of Babylon slithered out of the olive trees at the Garden of Gethsemane. They'd worked together well in South America against the death squads of Itzpaplotl, and most recently had teamed in Japan eighteen months ago, where they'd faced Aragami, the fury of wild violence, the God of Battle, slayer of 872 men. He wasn't so tough.

Now, after all that, Tommy had dragged him home to Brooklyn.

Grandma Lucia flipped upside down without spilling any pasta and drifted back up the stairway into the dark recesses of the mansion. Her mewling laments echoed for another half minute and then ended with an unholy cry.

The storm kicked up another notch and the lightning skewered the surrounding woodlands of Prospect Park, thunder bellowing out over the lake. Don Pietro Guerra's men ran around on the estate checking for intruders. There were occasional shouts and the squealing of tires as their Jeeps buzzed around the various driveways and paths.

"They tell me it started slow," Father Tom said. "She became reclusive, acting unlike herself. She's gregarious, really tough where it counts, and she's held the family together through more than one rough patch. When she took to her room they thought it might be her arthritis. Small things happened around the house. Weird voices, milk and meat spoiling in minutes."

"Pretty standard," Hellboy said.

"My grandfather called my cousin and me back home—we're the only close relatives he has left. We both got in this morning. I thought I'd call you, just in case—"

"In case something drastic had to be done and you didn't want to do it?"

The priest met his eyes. "Frankly, yes."

"It's all right, Tommy." He tried to sound sympathetic, but it came off bitter, and he didn't know why.

"I never told you much about my family, did I?"

"Not that they floated, anyway." Hellboy knew Tom had always held back on his past, but everyone who ever operated with the Bureau did. You either kept your secrets or the secrets kept you. Hellboy still wasn't certain which way it was going for him.

"She usually doesn't."

"Yeah."

"Let's go inside and talk with my grandfather. I'll give you a quick rundown."

They walked through corridors past glass cases and shelves containing Renaissance artwork, statuary, and shrines of Catholic significance. Family photos took up most of the remaining space on the shelves. Lots of dour-faced people standing around frowning at the camera.

"They wear a lot of black," Hellboy whispered.

"A lot of them have died violent deaths. Six in the last couple of years. There's been some in-fighting among the New York families. Plus, Catholics like to mourn."

"You've had it rough."

"It's the name. Guerra means war. There's a power in names."

"Sure," said Hellboy, also known as Anung Un Rama, who wears the Crown of the Apocalypse.

He listened as Tom laid it out on the line with a hint of remorse, talking about his Mafia family, touching on some of the dealings his relations had been involved with going back to the last century. Tommy looked at him once, trying to gauge his reaction, but Hellboy wasn't about to act shocked over extortion and cigarette smuggling after fighting resurrected Nazis and a couple of fallen angels. Tom was too close to the matter to realize he had nothing to sound guilty about.

They stepped into a broad living area that was dark with cherry paneling and burgundy carpeting, waves of rain slashing at the bay windows. A deep sense of anguished expectation spun in the air. Three men stood surrounding a fourth in his wheelchair. You could tell he was the one who gave the orders, made the big decisions.

Hellboy looked at the players and decided that all this trouble was probably coming from one of them. He didn't try to figure out which because, no matter who he chose, he'd be wrong and the grief would hit him broadside from another direction. He was best off just waiting for it.

Father Tommy made rapid introductions all around, starting with the low man and working up.

Joey Fresco, Don Pietro Guerra's capo, was the guy in charge of the dirty work. He ran the legbreakers and the hitters, and clearly enjoyed his work. Joey had a smug smile and overconfident eyes that danced with a kind of mischievous light. He was thin, but his jacket bulged with hardware, and his leather holsters creaked and rasped when he moved.

The consigliere was Angelo Del Mare, the Don's right-hand man, an attorney who managed to make everything look legal when the Feds and the IRS came knocking. Runty and soft, with bland eyes and a rugged complexion like he'd taken a lot of knocks when he was a kid. Del Mare said, "Pleased to meet you, Mr. Boy," and moved forward as if to shake hands. Hellboy held out his right fist. Del Mare's face crumpled and he slid back uncomfortably, suddenly fascinated with the knot of his tie. Hellboy put his hand down.

Tom's cousin, Dante, wore the shadows like a shroud. Fresh out of a Sicilian monastery, he assumed the guise of a man who'd drawn away from the world and didn't like being pulled back into it. He had on a monk's robes and cowl so that his face remained half-hidden in darkness. Hellboy smelled blood on him and leaned in closer. It took him a second to realize that Dante's order was made up of ascetics, the extreme penitents and hardcore flagellants, and that Dante had sewn thistles and broken bits of pottery into his frock.

The head honcho, Don Pietro Guerra, still seemed powerful even crippled in his wheelchair, with the years worn into him like desert sandstorms cutting into rock. Weakness threaded his features, and his teeth were gritted against pain. He must've been one rough, intimidating bastard back in his prime.

It was a little jarring, Hellboy thought, to learn that the mob had been in business less than a mile from Trevor Bruttenholm's mansion. He'd been fighting Nazis, dragons, and insane sorcerers for so long that he'd never quite noticed this common sphere of crime.

The Don nodded and said, "My grandson Tommaso speaks highly of you. Thank you for coming. I hope you can help us." His voice had a lot of strength left in it.

"So do I," Hellboy said. "This is a big place. These the only people here? Besides the old lady?"

"I sent everyone else away. There are guards who patrol the estate, but they board in a converted guest house. I ordered them to stay outside no matter what they might hear."

"Smart."

"My wife Lucia has never harmed anyone." Don Pietro trembled with emotion, and the cool appearance of murder spread itself across his face and formed an indignant scowl. "She is a good woman, devout and loving. She does not deserve this ordeal. It began three days ago, this outright madness. I believe one of my enemies, in this world or the next, is tormenting her as a means to destroy me."

"Maybe," Hellboy told him.

He glanced around the place now and wondered when the troubles were going to get kicking into high gear. His presence alone was generally enough to stir things up.

"What do you suggest we do first?" the Don asked.

"I don't know. What exactly does your wife do? You know, besides fly around."

The Don started to answer but couldn't quite get the words out. He gave a small bark of confusion, anger, and something else. It sounded like laughter. Del Mare answered for him. "She cooks."

"Say again?"

"Grandma Lucia cooks all day long, when she's not ... ah ... hovering. She can't seem to stop herself and shrieks for more food and ingredients. It's all that seems to call her down. We've kept the corner grocer quite busy this week."

A cooking demon? Hellboy stepped over to the huge windows at the back of the room, watching as the streaming water lashed the glass, and the lightning gouged and ruptured the sky.

They all waited like that until Joey Fresco decided to tighten the tension a little and flex his attitude. He walked up and said, "You just wasting time here or are you gonna help us take care of this situation?"

"Settle down, Shorty."

"Yeah?"

"Yeah. I'll hammer you into the floor like a carpet tack."

He never had been much good at hurling threats.

Joey gave a grin, and the stink of blood grew stronger in the room. Someone shouted outside, and his words were lost in the thunder. Then the house thrummed, and it sounded like a '57 Chevy was being driven through the east side of the house. A clamor of metal striking metal erupted, and the wild hissing of steam surged. Whatever it was, it was coming out of the pipes and starting to rattle the pots and pans together.

"The kitchen," Father Tom said.

"Everybody stay here, I'll check it out."

Joey Fresco didn't take orders from anyone but Don Pietro Guerra, so he bolted down the hall and made it to the kitchen way ahead of Hellboy. Three shots went off instantly followed by heinous squeals of delight. Hellboy recognized the sounds.

He got to the swinging kitchen door, braced his shoulder against it, and accidentally burst the wood into splinters.

"Goddamn," Joey said. "The hell's the matter with you?"

"Sorry."

He took a quick look around. About twenty knee-high creatures ran around the large kitchen savagely tearing at the drawers and cabinets, clambering over the counter tops and ripping at jars and the sugar and flour bins, wriggling into the refrigerator. They scratched and chewed at each other as well, pulling at one another's tails, fighting for room inside the freezer and meat locker.

They were still pouring out from the broken sink, and hot water continued funneling out in a gushing arc striking against the ceiling.

Hairless, fanged, and hungry, the creatures savagely screeched and ate everything they could. It didn't take long before they were gnawing on the linoleum and swallowing the cheap silverware. The good stuff would've liquified them on the spot.

"What are these things?"

"You've got imps," Hellboy said.

"I tried shooting them. I splattered their brains, but they just put them back in and keep on eating."

"Let me try." He drew his pistol and aimed at the closest imp. The beastie chittered at him and started nibbling on his ankle. He pulled the trigger and nothing happened. When you threw a punch it was natural—everything else was a pain. He always forgot about the safety. He snapped it off but the pistol still wouldn't fire. "Aww, crap!" He hadn't loaded it. He stuffed in four shells but the breach wouldn't close. "I hate guns!"

"I like 'em. Gimme that." Joey took the powerful sidearm and smoothly loaded, aimed, and fired four times in rapid succession. The imps he'd shot vanished in a haze of blue blood and gristle. The rest screeched and escaped back down the drain.

"I need to get one of these!" Joey Fresco showed off his white teeth in a brutal leer of pride, holding the pistol up before his eyes and snickering. "What the hell kind of gun is it?"

"I don't know."

"Those ugly little critters dissolved. What kind of ammo does it take?"

"I'm not sure."

Sealing his lips into a bloodless line, Joey Fresco thrust the pistol back into Hellboy's hands. "You good for anything around here?"

"A bad day just keeps getting worse. This sort of occult flare-up invites other breeds of magic. These imps are only here because this family's problem somehow deals with food."

"So we all like a good plate of pasta! That's not the occult, that's just being Sicilian."

Okay, Hellboy thought, so me and the hitman aren't going to have many intellectual conversations this evening. "Turn the water off under the sink and let's go. I want to talk to the old lady."

"Show some respect to Donna Lucia."

"Come on, already."

They returned to the living room, and the oppressive weight of the storm had driven the men into a silent huddle. Dante stooped at his grandfather's knee as if in prayer, speaking quiet words to the Don. He stood when Hellboy entered, and drifted from the shadows again as the lightning backlit him in a brazen silver. "It appears your presence is making matters worse."

"Usually does."

"Perhaps you should go then."

"No."

A regular guy would've sighed or thrown out his chest, but the monk remained tranquil and moved in an odd fashion beneath his robes. Hellboy frowned. Dante slithered inside his vestments, scraping himself against the barbs, opening new wounds.

"Can you do any good against these forces?" the monk asked.

"Yes, whatever they are."

"Your hubris may be your ultimate downfall."

"Screw that."

Sorrow marked the monk's presence like a brand. "Perhaps there are evils you cannot overcome."

"I can always give it a whirl. Why are you here, Dante?"

"My family asked that I return home, so I came. We do what we can to share one another's burden."

Hellboy thought he should call the Bureau, ask a couple of questions, and get them to do some research for him. "Are the phones out yet?"

Del Mare crossed the room with stooped shoulders, like he was trying to stay out of the way of something coming up behind him. He picked up the receiver. "It's not working." With a worried snort he held his cell phone against his ear and immediately drew it away. "There's a strange kind of static. It sounds like ... I'm not sure."

"Like what?" the Don asked.

"Sniffling ... like several children sniffling ... sobbing."

"Children? Are they being drawn into this now?"

Tommy drew up beside Hellboy. "Figured we wouldn't be able to call out, huh?"

"I wanted to ask somebody at the Bureau a question. Whenever I want to contact them, the phones die." Lightning lacerated the landscape even worse, the thunder battering at the glass. It should've given way by now. "That bulletproof?"

Father Tom nodded. "And Dante's right. Things have turned up a notch since you walked in."

"Since you came in, too."

"Huh." Tom kind of froze at that. The thought hadn't crossed his mind before, and it struck him off-kilter. His eyes widened at the idea that he might be shaking the energies up in the house. "Maybe we should go find her."

Sweat stood out on Don Pietro's ashen face, and he raised a hand to motion them to him. "Do not hurt her. No matter the cost, do not harm my Lucia. She is not at fault."

"No one will harm Grandma," Tom said without a trace of uncertainty. Hellboy kept silent.

A new noise pervaded the home, spiraling closer and closer. It took shape and became an echo of the old woman's cries, but not the sound itself. As if she was howling from long ago, or a time yet to come. Del Mare grabbed a bottle of pills off the antique oak sideboard. "Your medication, Pietro."

"I'm fine, I just need to rest a while," the Don said. A moment later he slumped in his seat and passed out.

Clutching a pair of .45s, Joey stood torn between protecting the boss and going out after the action. The nervous exertion made him do a tap dance against the slate border on the floor, his heels clicking as he fidgeted in place. Hellboy didn't want a shooter like that running around the house in case there were any more outbreaks of black magic. It might be better to have this guy close by where he could keep an eye on him.

"Okay," he said, "let's go find Donna Lucia."

He could feel it now much stronger than before.

The brunt and strain of colliding energies. They parted and swarmed as he moved through the dim mansion that reminded him so much of where Trevor Bruttenholm had died. That gentle, warming draw of his rage tugged at him once more.

The old woman started screaming upstairs, the bellowing growing louder until the ceiling creaked with her anguish, and the framed paintings clattered on the walls.

"She's sure pissed off about something," Joey said.

"It's a sin what's happening to her." Father Tom was at the border of finally giving in to his own frustration and worry. "Someone has to pay. No one should have to stand for it." He had plenty of faith, and it always proved to be his greatest strength, but an attack like this could wear at your nerves, your conviction, and your hope.

Hellboy stopped at the shelves of statuary. "I don't recognize most of these saints."

"Some of them are from La Vecchia Religione, the Old Religion. We're all pagans under the skin. When the Roman Empire collapsed, it took centuries for the Sicilians to absorb Christian tenets. St. Apollinarius presides over the healing ways of Apollo."

"I never heard a priest talk that way before," Joey the killer said with an edge of disapproval.

"You wouldn't in Brooklyn," Tommy said. "But you should hear them down in South America when they've got Aztec death gods going after their kids."

The shooter just shrugged and let it go at that. He stared up the stairwell as Grandma Lucia let out another shriek. "Someone's moving up there."

Down here too. Hellboy watched several of the plastic and stone saints grow animated and fall to their plastic knees. More magic overspill. They turned to glare at him and their tiny mouths moved without sound. Tom spotted the figures as well while Joey proceeded up the first step, guns thrust before him. The priest said, "I can read their lips. They're hungry and begging to be fed."

Hellboy nodded.

"If you can save my grandmother—"

"We will."

"Then she'll build you a shrine."

"I'm telling you now, I'm not going to put on a black suit."

Joey Fresco was nearly at the top of the stairway and called down, "You two coming? Or you gonna leave me to handle this by myself?"

Father Tommy took the steps two at a time and Hellboy followed, staring up at the rafters and waiting for an old lady to come flying down at him. The place rumbled all around them, the storm settling right above, and Donna Lucia's bizarre, timeless cries circled the corridors. When they got to the second floor, the lights flickered as if in fearful expectation.

Joey Fresco had one gun aimed toward the far end of the dark hallway, the other at Hellboy's chest. His chin was tilted into a mocking grin.

Bringing him along had been a bad idea after all. "You don't want to point that at me," Hellboy told him, and drew his Right Hand of Doom into a fist.

"Shut up, you big red mook. You got a statue of St. Anthony crawling up your coat. It looks like it's trying to chew on you. You want me to ping him off or not?"

Hellboy yanked the figure off him and tossed it over his shoulder. This whole situation was starting to get more annoying than anything.

He'd taken his eyes off the ceiling for a minute, and Grandma came swooping down out of nowhere, kicking at him with those shoes again. Her features had folded into a mask of heartache and regret, the white hair coming undone from the tight black net. She kept shouting the same words in Italian over and over. Some sauce dripped down on him and, despite himself, his stomach growled. He hadn't had any good home cooking in months.

"My God." Tom crossed himself and held his hands up in a gesture of pity. "Is she still stirring sauce? She's been doing that for two solid days now."

"The bowl's almost empty."

Even the hitman appeared humbled. "The Don had us go out and get more for her. We left it at the top of the stairs, and she'd take it away. There was plenty more in the kitchen before, but those little squealing creeps ate everything."

Hellboy really didn't want to slug her. There was a power in names, all right, and though he'd never been much good at the subtle approach, he decided to talk to the old lady instead of punch her through a wall.

"Who are you?" he asked.

Donna Lucia cocked her head and swooped in low. Smoke rose from the dish and wafted up into her face, split by her heaving breaths. The rosary swayed in time with her stirring. She whipped the pasta so fast that the food steamed from the heat.

She calmed for an instant, peered into his eyes and said, "*Did you take my bowl?*"

"You have one."

"*Not this. The one that feeds! Did you take my bowl!*"

"No."

"*Bugiardo! Bastardo!*"

"Hey now," Hellboy said, genuinely offended. "Grandma, that's just mean!"

A searing flare of golden-white light spiked down and exploded in an insane roaring blast. Deafening thunder rocked the room, and a ball of fire broke wide, hurling heaps of flame. Everyone was thrown off his feet and cried out, even Hellboy. The bolt had climbed through one of the bedroom windows and hurtled through the hall to crash directly at Grandma's feet. The blast tore the hardwood floor up into charred smashed planks. Coiling billows of smoke heaved around them.

"Tommy, are you all right!"

The priest had splashes of blood on his face but his expression was determined. "Yes—look what's happening to her."

The old woman had begun to transmogrify. They always transmogrified. No matter what you were dealing with, before you were done, it changed into something else, usually much uglier than before. It got predictable, but there it was.

Echoes clustered, converged, and then flowed off. Donna Lucia had altered into an even more ancient woman, a creature millennia old but still with a glint of youth and devotion in her gaze. Tight gray flesh and yards of brittle colorless hair covered it, the fingernails dried and long and cracked. The ladle she'd been stirring with snapped in her wizened claw.

Groggy and coughing, Joey held his guns up directly in front of Donna Lucia's face and then suddenly realized what he was about to do. "Jeez!"

"The children, I will protect the children, even if I must blight you all!"

"Listen up, lady, whoever you are. I lived through three hits from Benny the Penny Castigliano, and I survived Catholic school. You ain't got the brass to take me out!"

The bowl dropped and shattered. She turned on Tom, and the madness clouded her eyes. Hellboy understood he had to make a move, or his friend was going to get wrecked.

"Grandma, stop!" Tommy shouted.

Hellboy let loose with a growl deep in his chest. "I knew this was going to happen!"

He tried tapping her gently on the chin with his left fist, and the ancient woman ignored him. So he held his breath and slapped her with his right stone hand, letting himself go a little, fighting to hold back the anger, and Grandma Lucia shot across the hall.

Saints and religious icons toppled and began to crawl. She returned to normal, looking exhausted but defiant, whispered, "Tommaso," and flopped backward onto the carpet.

Tom and Joey spent a few minutes checking her over while Hellboy used his coat to put out the fires before they could spread. Some of the tiny plastic figures scrambled away from the flames, waving their miniature arms.

"She seems okay," Tommy said.

"Good." Hellboy picked up the lady, carried her to the nearest bedroom, and put her on the bed. He turned to the hitter and told him, "Guard her. Don't leave her alone."

"I won't. What're you two gonna be doing?"

"Finishing this."

"Okay. You want me to load your gun for you?"

"Screw you."

They left, and the saints followed for a time before finally dropping back and running off in different directions. Hellboy had heard the tale before but still couldn't quite get it to click into place. Somebody at the Bureau would've known. "I remember something about a witch with a magic bowl."

Father Tom thought about it for a minute. "That's right, an old Sicilian legend. I should've picked up on it. That was stupid."

"Nobody expects centuries-old legends to come walking into their houses."

"I should've. Her name is Nona Strega, but according to the folklore she's a loving, devoted being. She has a bowl that never runs out of pasta. She feeds the hungry village children across the countryside."

"So somebody stole her bowl. And she's scared the kids will starve."

"Apparently so. But who took it?"

That was easy enough to answer now, but Tom still couldn't see it. "Let's go ask."

The smell of blood met Hellboy before he entered the living room.

Don Pietro remained unconscious, perhaps only sleeping, maybe hexed or dying. The monk stood stoic, apart from the rest of the turnings of humanity. Del Mare the consigliere wore a worried grimace and said, "We heard a horrible commotion upstairs. Was the house actually hit by lightning?"

"Yes," Hellboy told him. "You're going to need a good contractor."

"We've got plenty, but there's never enough insurance."

There was nothing to say to that. He figured he had a line on the problem now and decided to play out his string, wherever it led. He walked over to Dante and watched him squirming under his cloak again, the stink wafting from him. Hellboy grabbed hold of the monk's vestments and yanked them open.

The robes parted to reveal the abominable dissection wounds across Dante's stomach and chest where the flesh had been carefully peeled back.

Now it made some sense.

The monk stood, eviscerated, his chest cavity opened wide with the flaps of muscle and gristle hanging open by a snapped silver thread. Hellboy knew that the needle used to perform this ritual would be engraved with the ten holy names of the Divine Order.

All of Dante's major organs had been carefully removed. They would be kept in ancient pottery, probably back at his monastery in Sicily, each vessel of terra cotta inscribed with Sumerian and Latin phrases. His rib cage would've been sawed in half and set upon the Seal of Solomon drawn out in silver nitrate upon stone that never saw sunlight. All his organs would still be alive and healthy despite being extracted. The heart beating, the lungs working as if they were still inside him.

Del Mare said, "Madonna Mary protect us," and vomited. He tried to make it back to his feet but couldn't, so he just sat there dazed and shaking.

Tom paled and his mouth dropped open, his voice filling with disgust and terror. "Dante? Who ... who did this to you?"

"He did it to himself," Hellboy answered. "He removed his own organs and replaced them with Nona Strega's bowl."

"My God, no ... Dante ..."

"It had to be done," the monk said. "I had to awaken her wrath."

"For Christ's sake, why?!"

"No, not for Christ exactly, but for the sake of the starving children. Disease is rampant in southern Italy. You've been waging war with infernal beasts and ghosts and goblins, Tom. You've forgotten what happens to people when they are hungry."

You've traveled to exotic lands while I've held the sick and the dying and been powerless to do anything to ease their suffering. My holy order works closely with orphanages, hospitals, and even prisons. Heaven may be growing stronger thanks to your work, but the world is only becoming more callous and desperate. Have you forgotten Guerra means war?"

"No," Tommy said, "I haven't forgotten."

"Nona Strega was asleep. I needed her aid so I awoke her, summoned her, showed her what it was to live and nurture and provide again, with grandmother's help."

The priest recovered pretty nicely, the same way he had after stumbling over the Whore of Babylon as she slinked out of the groves of Gethsemane. "Where did you get the bowl?"

"The monastery has had it for centuries, but the abbots considered it only a relic. After recently discovering some texts in our library, I stumbled onto its true power. The witch's bones lie in our cemetery. Once she was a saint."

"Maybe she still is."

"I pray it's so."

Tom swung his head about as if hunting for a gun or any weapon that might put an end to his powerlessness, gaping at Hellboy, turning back to his cousin. "And after all this? After using your loved ones this way? What'll you do now?"

"Go back and return the artifact to her. And restore myself."

Hellboy wasn't sure whether he should slap the crap out of this guy or let it go and leave it to the family. Father Tommy Guerra seemed to be stuck himself, still unsure of his next move. A ripple of contempt passed over his face, and then one of charity, and then something in-between. Sometimes this job could get to you, especially when your own friends or relatives were involved.

"Go now," Tom said. "Don't ever speak to grandmother again, for the rest of your life. I hate that you were willing to use her like this, but I'll try to forgive you. Put your heart back where it belongs, and be human enough again to feel remorse."

"I do."

"I'm not letting this go. I'll visit you in three days, to help with the orphans."

"Thank you," the monk said, and stepped away until he faded into shadow and vanished.

It took about an hour to get the rest of it settled, make sure Don Pietro and Grandma Lucia were okay, get Del Mare cleaned up after his little regurgitation display, and make sure that the imps were completely gone.

Hellboy carried the old lady downstairs and reunited her with the Don. She didn't remember anything about the incident except a vague memory that the ceiling needed to be dusted. She also threw a fit when she saw all the statues scattered all over the floor, the paintings hanging askew, scorch marks and a hole in the floor, and the kitchen ripped to pieces. She got out her feather duster and vacuum and started cleaning, cursing the whole time, and kept smacking Joey in the back of the head.

"But Donna Lucia, I didn't do anything!"

"So you say!"

Dante was right, in his own way. For years Hellboy had been so busy fighting the infernal, the dead, the undead, trolls, ogres, and dragons that he'd forgotten there were kids without bread. He didn't know what he should do about it, but maybe he'd work something out with the Bureau. He had to stay hooked in to the world. It was easy to get too caught up in paranormal events and forget about the orphanages.

Before Hellboy could leave, they opened a bottle of red wine and insisted on him sharing a drink. He hated the taste but he sipped it anyway, trying not to think about where the money had come from for this estate and everything in it, doing his best not to pass judgment on the people he'd just helped. Sometimes the job made his brain hurt.

"So it had nothing to do with her ring?" Don Pietro asked. When he got nothing but surprised looks, he immediately realized his mistake.

"What's this?" Grandma Lucia pulled a face that made her appear much nastier than when she was possessed. Even Joey Fresco took a step back. "What's this!"

The Don's eyes filled with panic. "Nothing!"

"There's something wrong with my wedding ring?"

"No, no, of course not!"

Hellboy looked at the diamond. He took out an iron pentacle etched with the names of seven archangels. The diamond clouded with a swirling foggy pall, and a blue spark angrily shot from it.

"Insurance won't cover this," Del Mare said, and he went a touch green again.

"My wedding ring is cursed?" Grandma started forward, fists on her hips.

Don Pietro rolled himself away, trying hard to hold onto his composure, keep some of his pride. It wasn't working. "Only a little."

Hellboy headed for the door, and Father Tommy Guerra put a hand on his shoulder. "Stick around. I'll have someone run out and do some shopping. We owe you a good meal at least."

"No thanks," Hellboy said. "I'm not hungry."

He walked into the night wanting to feel the wet wind on his face, but it had stopped raining.

SLEEPLESS IN MANHATTAN

NANCY KILPATRICK

Two a.m. Hellboy can't sleep again. The dreams, same as before, of the priest and the nun at the ruins of the church in East Bromwich, the dreams he had when he visited there a few years ago ...

Hellboy decides on an after-dark walk through New York's Central Park. He doesn't feel like company and figures nobody in their right mind will be out and about at this hour, especially on such a cold night. But as he strolls around Turtle Pond, a craggy voice catches him. It originates not from the bench, but behind it, where a ratty sleeping bag has been spread out and a tiny, grizzly old woman reclines, propping up her head with its mop of gray hair with one fist.

"You're Satan, right?" The old lady brushes aside a bit of hair to adjust her glasses. Hellboy has never seen such black skin on a human being, even Africans—it seems to be blacker than the night. "I seen your picture. 'Cept your horns wasn't broke off like that."

"Yeah, right. I'm Satan. Maybe you should go back to sleep, grandma."

"Can't sleep. Fate of the elderly, you see. We're waiting for our creator. Is that you?"

"Uh, sorry, I'm not an artist, but I've been known to collect odd items."

"Me too. Wanna see my Voodoo dollies?"

Hellboy's five senses focus. He glances in all directions. Looking. Listening. Smelling the air. Is this a setup? Maybe he's being paranoid. Just a crazy old coot with no one to talk to; why not hear her out?

"Sure. Okay, grandma, show me what you got."

"Have a seat," the old woman says, gesturing to the bench as if it's a sofa in her living room.

Hellboy lifts his tail and the tails of his oilskin coat and sits, one arm draped over the back of the bench, waiting while the diminutive woman hauls herself to her feet with difficulty. She can't be more than four feet tall, if that, a vertically challenged person. She hefts a beat-up canvas backpack onto the bench with a sigh, then perches at the opposite end from Hellboy, who immediately catches the *eau de gar-bage* wafting through the air. It is bad manners to mention the odor; Bruttenholm taught him to be polite. He lights a cigar, and the smell of burning tobacco helps.

"You oughta quit. Them thing'll kill ya," the old woman says knowingly.

"Yeah."

"Got a spare?"

Hellboy finds another in his pocket. He offers it and she snatches it up, smelling it as if she hasn't savored tobacco in years. Finally she sticks it between her thin lips and begins to chew.

Hellboy pulls out a lighter, but the frail old lady waves it away. "Don't smoke 'em, just like the smell."

"Whatever." He slips the lighter back into his coat pocket and shakes his head.

While the old girl rummages through her backpack, Hellboy takes in the quiet of the park and the stillness of the pond he is facing. He started out up in Spanish Harlem, at 110th Street, climbing the steep hill to enter from the north end of Central Park. Up there, it's all rough terrain, where most New Yorkers never venture, and Hellboy likes it best because he knows he probably won't run into a soul for the first ten blocks—unless you count the souls of animals, which he is inclined to do. The peace and quiet give him a chance to think, which isn't always a good thing.

Tonight's insomnia is triggered by the sense of aloneness that never leaves him, especially since Trevor Bruttenholm's death. The man took him in, raised him, was a father to him in every way, and his loss has left Hellboy even more alone, but for a few friends. It's hard being the only one of your kind, with no ancestry, no sense of where or who you came from but for the snatches in dreams and visions. Bruttenholm was as related as it got. The feeling of floating solo in the universe rears its ugly head big time on occasion and keeps Hellboy pacing the floors, dissatisfied with the latest episodes of *Law and Order*. This evening those floors were at the Manhattan Branch Office of the Bureau for Paranormal Research and Defense, where he'd been sent to chat with a nervous curator of the Museo de las

Momies in Guanajuato, Mexico. Half the time, when there's a paranormal case to investigate, his thoughts don't get out of hand. Tonight, though, with time to kill until the curator arrives, Hellboy feels the desire to be out in the open sans people. Maybe he can walk his troubles away.

He finds it amazing the numbers of humanity that locate shelter and safety in the middle-of-the-night darkness of this huge green space in the heart of one of the world's largest cities. They crawl under fallen logs, hide beneath decaying leaves, behind shrubs they use as walls. Thinking about it, maybe he isn't so bad off after all. At least he has a home, a place to crash when sleep overtakes him, a place to rest and heal when he does battle with creatures hellbent on his destruction, or the destruction of human beings. He had a dad, someone who cared about him. And there are friends: Abe, Dr. Kate Corrigan, and Liz. It's good to have friends.

Hellboy'd just been circling Turtle Pond, about to head back up north and give it up to the TV at the Bureau Branch, when this old woman insists on showing him her dolls, a dozen of which are now lined up on the bench between them.

"That's quite a collection."

"Yep. Been huntin' 'em down whenever I can. Had more, back when I lived down on Delancey. These're all that's left, but they're the best."

A row of a dozen Barbie-sized bundles lie wrapped like mummies, hands crossed over chests, ankles together. The swaddling ranges from gray to black to the red of old blood and the blue/purple of healing bruises, but mostly the fabric is just plain dirty and the colors fading. None have exposed heads, but little pin holes were made in the wrap over the skull and the hair pulled through, likely by a crochet hook or some other fine instrument. It leaves the hair flowing over a wrapped form.

"Like 'em?"

Hellboy doesn't know quite what to say. "They're ... different. How come you collect these? You into Voodoo?"

"Hah! I like 'em 'cause they're pretty like me. Don't ya think they're pretty?"

"The eye of the beholder," Hellboy says.

"Huh?"

"Nothing. Listen, this has been an education, but I've got a date with reruns of *Survivor*."

"Hold on there, young fellow with a tail." The woman touches Hellboy's arm with unanticipated strength, which sends a warning through his body as if he is being microwaved. "Wanna give you one."

"Gee, thanks, but I couldn't—"

"Here!" The gnarled hands close around one of the dolls lying on its front and the old lady shoves it at Hellboy.

"Right." He takes it reluctantly, and when he turns over the plastic effigy wrapped in dark red gauze, he feels even more reluctant. "What the ...?"

The mummy-wrapped doll with fire-red hair flying every which way resembles all the rest but for one thing: two horns emerge from the wrap where the forehead and hairline meet. Hellboy stares at the doll as if mesmerized. "How the hell did you ..."

The bench next to him is empty. The old woman has disappeared. So have the other dolls. He looks over the back of the bench; no sign of the sleeping bag. The few other bench sleepers haven't stirred.

From all around him comes a crooning voice eerily like the old woman's, singing about love and family and connection and home being where they have to take you in.

Hellboy jumps to his feet. He races around the pond, then through the bushes, smashing tree branches aside, his ears pricked for the voice, which seems to come from here, then there, from everywhere. Just when it grows louder, when he almost reaches it, instead of being in front of him, it now comes from behind.

Half a minute of this run-around is enough, and he stops in his tracks. "Okay, be an invisible old lady, see if I care."

The response is a cackle that to other ears might be the wind blowing a candy wrapper across the concrete path. It fades, and with it the sense of a presence, and Hellboy knows he is alone again.

He looks down at the mummy doll he holds in his hand. Boy, does it resemble him! "If this isn't a paranormal experience, I don't know what is."

"**H**elldoll?" Liz turns the little red-headed, red-wrapped mummy with mini horns over and over in her hands.

"That's why you wanted us to come down from Fairfield?" Abe Sapien says, joining them, his moves graceful as a fish gliding through water.

"Let's have a look," Dr. Kate Corrigan says. The esteemed author of books on folklore and occult history takes the little doll from Liz's hands, examines it, then begins to search for the end of the wrapping. "This is not a Voodoo doll."

"Could have fooled me," Hellboy says.

"Ditto," adds Liz, lighting a cigarette.

"A real Voudun doll," Kate continues, "is formed to represent the one upon whom the spell is to be cast."

"It has horns," Liz says.

"Horns that are complete, not clipped like Hellboy's. A doll also has to include something of the person, for instance, hair, blood, or fingernail clippings."

"The fabric might be soaked in Hellboy's blood. It isn't as if he's never been wounded in a fight," Abe suggests.

"I sprayed it with Luminal. It's not blood. This doll is not Hellboy. The horns are a giveaway. It also has no nail clippings that I can find, and it has long, bright red hair." Kate shoots him a look. "I take it this isn't your hair."

"Only my hairdresser knows for sure," Hellboy says. "So if it's not me, who?"

"Maybe it's a coincidence. My guess is that she's just an old lady crazed from living on the streets who likes to collect dolls. This is no more a Voudun doll than a regular Barbie or Ken doll."

"That's not what she said. And what about the laughter I heard?"

"Could it have been something else?" Liz asks. "You said it reminded you of paper."

"I guess ... But she vanished."

"Did she?" Abe wants to know. "It was late—"

"Come on! I didn't imagine this!"

Liz places a soothing hand on his arm. "You said you hadn't slept in almost forty-eight hours. You were exhausted, H.B. The woman probably has an escape route, some wormhole all these park people know about for fast getaways when they feel threatened."

"Maybe ..." Hellboy feels unsure. Is he so caught up in machinations, dwelling on his unknown past, that he is making things up?

"Look!" Kate holds the fully unwrapped doll out for them to have a look. Sure enough, it is just a red-headed doll some nut bar wrapped in dirty gauze. Other than the horns.

"You know," Kate continues, "it could just have been a prank."

"Yeah, well, tonight I'm taking another walk through the park to look for the prankster. Anybody want to join me?"

"The pond looks inviting," Abe says. He steps to the edge. "If there are turtles here, I don't see any."

"Maybe there used to be turtles." Liz lights a cigarette from her fingertip just, it seems, for the hell of it. "There used to be a lot of things in this world."

"Hellboy, I don't see anyone who resembles your geriatric." Kate peers at the few homeless forms draped across benches in the darkness. She checks her watch and wraps her jacket tighter around her against the chilly evening. "It's almost five a.m. Maybe we should call it an evening."

"But she was here last night!"

"That was then, H.B.," Liz says, "she's not here now. I agree with Kate. I think we should go back."

"I don't see any sign of disturbance," Abe says, still scanning the pond's surface for turtles and apparently still finding none.

"Look, you all go. I'm staying here until I find that old woman."

"Suit yourself, H.B.," Liz says, crushing her butt underfoot. "We'll see you back there, okay?"

"Sure."

Once he is alone, Hellboy walks the perimeter of Turtle Pond for the fourth time, but there is nothing new to see in or out of the water. Finally, he sits on the same bench he occupied last night with the old lady, in the same spot. He has already checked the ground for "wormholes" as Liz calls them. Nothing. Maybe he was so tired last night and absorbed by the doll long enough that the woman just up and left and Hellboy didn't notice. That's not like him, but anything is possible.

Maybe I'm losing it, he thinks. First the old man is killed, then all the cases that seem to invite questions about my origins ... Could be it's all catching up to him. Maybe he needs some time off from the Bureau to search—search for what? Search how? And where? He doesn't even know where to begin. He's already been back to East Bromwich in England where he had visions. Of the priest and the nun. And of the human woman who might or might not be his mother and the ... what? Demon from Hell is what he'll stick to, that claimed to be his father. The demon that spoke directly to him. If those visions were true—and who could trust a demon?—that would make him at best half demon, at worst what so many have insinuated is his destiny: the Beast of the Apocalypse.

That's all he knows, or thinks he knows. Hellboy's origins are a mystery, as much as what has been deemed his Right Hand of Doom, the horns he files down so he will not be so outrageous looking to ordinary mortals, as much as his fiery red skin and his tail. Everything about him is a mystery. If only another of his kind existed. Not like Liz with her fire-starting abilities, or Abe, whose history is also shrouded in unknowns of a totally different type. Wouldn't it be great to find a being similar to himself, somebody he could talk to, who might know some truth about where he comes from, who he is? Someone who would let him know that he isn't the only one of his kind, his species, whatever! The only one in the universe.

Suddenly his ears twig to a sound. How long has it been going on? Paper scraping concrete. He spins in all directions, seeing nothing.

Then he catches a flash of red emerging from the pond, rising swiftly. As big as him. No, bigger ... Huge! And ...

"What the...?"

In seconds, he is face to face with ... well ... himself, or something close. But the new arrival is bigger ... much bigger. The horns are curved and sharp. It looks a lot like the demon he saw in East Bromwich, but this guy has long, bright red hair. So he's not exactly like Hellboy ... but then there's that one enormous hand like his.

"Oh, come on! I don't believe this!"

"Believe it," comes a voice that sounds familiar, as familiar as his own voice.

The big guy steps from the pond onto the opposite bank, across the water. Hellboy braces himself. His body automatically takes a stance in preparation for a fight.

"Hey, I'm on your side!" the new arrival says.

"Yeah? How's that?"

"Notice a resemblance?"

"What? You're gonna tell me you're my long-lost brother or something? I don't believe it."

"Not your brother, just *like* you. I'm the same species, or haven't you noticed? We're from the same world."

Hellboy feels stunned, and it keeps him from moving forward, from reacting to the threat his senses perceive.

"Listen, aren't you curious, about where you come from, what it's like there? About your father?"

"I know my father. Trevor Bruttenholm is—"

"—not your real father. I know your real father, and he's nothing like these puny humans. He's full of power and majesty. He rules the universe. It is the destiny of our kind to rule over the lesser beasts, the human beasts. You're the offspring of a deity."

"Why should I believe you?"

"Just look at me. Tell me you don't think I know more about you than they do." He gestures dramatically with the hand that is identical to Hellboy's to take in all of humanity. "What's to distrust?"

Hellboy scowls and holds up his massive right hand. "Well, no denying the resemblance, but I'm pretty sure there's only one of these."

Just then, one of the bodies lying on a bench behind and to the left of the big guy sits up, his upper body weaving. "Shut up, shut up, shut up! People are trying to sleep!" Even from his side of the pond, Hellboy picks up the scent—the guy reeks of the wine he consumed in abundance that is now seeping from the pores of his skin.

"Relax!" Hellboy says. "We're just having a conversation."

"Yeah, well take that and your big, ugly red butt someplace else, buddy!"

Hellboy turns back to the big guy. "Look, let's go up to the north end of the park where it's usually deserted and—"

Before he can finish, the big guy leaps into the air, his heavy hand raised. He brings it down hard onto the drunk, pulverizing him, the bench, and the ground beneath it in a split second. Hellboy is stunned as bits of flesh, wood, metal, and dirt fly up into the air and a hole forms in the ground where the fist landed.

He is about to leap across the pond when from behind him he hears a small cry: "Help! Help me!"

He scans the trees behind, to the left, then to the right where the sound has shifted. Then laughter cuts the night air, causing him to spin in all directions. In the five seconds it takes all of this to happen and for Hellboy to determine that there is no one about to attack him from the rear, and then to turn back to the wino, the big guy vanishes. Then, from the street, he hears a noise that reminds him of an earthquake. The ground is wet, and he follows the moist tracks, racing out of the park to the Upper East Side in time to see an apartment building collapsing on itself, its occupants buried beneath the rubble. There is no sign of the big guy.

Within seconds Hellboy is lifting heavy metal beams and slabs of concrete, rescuing as many people as he can, which is pretty well all of them. Then he waits for the police and the ambulances to arrive.

"Hellboy 2?" Liz says.

"Liz, please."

"Sorry, H.B. This is so weird. Did you search for him?"

"Of course I searched for him! I'm sorry, I didn't mean to yell. I'm upset."

"He's obviously dangerous," Abe says. "He's moody and destructive. Not to mention the megalomania."

"No kidding. And I was too mesmerized to stop him. And he says I'm just like him." Gloomily, Hellboy collapses into a chair.

"You're nothing like him," Liz tells him adamantly. "You're your own man."

"But he said my father is—"

"Yeah, you told us." Kate looks up from the book on the occult she is reading while Hellboy has been relating his experience over the last hour. "I might be wrong, but I think you're up against not one but two creatures."

"Great! And both of them can vanish whenever they want to."

"Maybe. I think what you met tonight was nothing more than a powerful demon."

"Who looks a lot like me, only bigger? No problem, then. I'm relieved."

"I didn't say it isn't dangerous, just that if we know what we're dealing with, that might help you take it down."

"You said two creatures," Abe reminds the doctor.

"Yes. First, the old woman. I think she's an imp."

"You mean like a gargoyle come to life?" Liz asks.

"Not a bad analogy. Imps were sometimes depicted in stone on medieval churches. They're lesser demons. Some have said they're the souls of evil children who have died but returned to earth to create problems for the living. Their skin is supposed to be a very deep black, blacker than any natural black, and they don't cast a shadow, because they are shadows. They're also changelings, which would explain how the old woman disappeared so quickly—she probably took on the appearance of another sleeper in the park."

"Why do you think the old lady is an imp?" Abe asks.

"Because she's not the source of the problem, just a distraction. That's often the role of the imp. They work for a major demon."

"I'd like to see their job description," Hellboy says. "So, what's this major demon about?"

"That's what we have to figure out," Kate continues. "From what has happened so far, it's clear this demon knows something about you."

"Yeah, well, he said he's of the same species and everything." Hellboy sighs. "Sharing my DNA with this guy does not fulfill my fantasies of a pedigree."

"He's not related," Liz chimes in.

"Yeah, but we're genetically the same."

"So the new guy says. Sounds like some kind of scam to me. He knows just enough about you, things anybody might guess."

"I'm curious," Kate says, sipping tea from her China cup. "You've met the imp both times by Turtle Pond. And this demon came out of the pond. It's odd, don't you think, that if he wanted to contact you, he'd wait until you were in a more populated area of the park?"

"And when you said you should go somewhere else and talk, he didn't want to do that, did he?" Abe adds.

"He didn't like the idea at all," Hellboy remembers. "He didn't want to leave that area."

"And yet," Kate sets her cup onto the saucer, "he left the park and demolished the first building across Fifth Avenue, but only that building, and then vanished."

"That might mean his range is limited. To the area surrounding Turtle Pond. He did use a lot of fish imagery."

Kate nods. "His range might be limited to the source of his energy. Abe, you noticed there were no turtles in the pond. Did you notice anything else about that water?"

Abe thinks for a moment. "It was pretty murky. I couldn't see anything below the surface. But nothing was moving, I'm certain of that. No fish or even insects, let alone turtles."

"Here's what I'm thinking," Kate says. "In the Middle Ages it was thought that the earth was divided into four elements: gnomes rule earth, salamanders rule fire, sylphs the air, and undines the water. The undine is related to the mermaid and the Greek nereid, the German nixie. It can't survive long outside of water."

"Which is why he didn't go far from the pond," Liz says. "It's his world."

"Seems that way," Kate adds. "The undine doesn't change form, but more clouds the mind so a person sees what he wants to see. It can tap into dreams and fantasy and become whatever you need it to be. A lover, a friend, a long-dead family member—"

"I was thinking about where I come from, wishing there was someone like me out there ..." Hellboy holds his head in his hands.

"It's natural, H.B." Liz tells him, touching him on the shoulder, her voice soft with understanding. "We all wonder about our powers, and about where they stem from. And with you and Abe, you both also have a lot of questions about where you come from."

"Our strength here," Kate says, "lies in the fact that the undine is severely limited to the element that sustains it, water. I doubt it can travel far from that pond. Likely Fifth Avenue depleted it, and it was forced to return."

"Sounds like we have a fighting chance." Hellboy stands. "But how can we be sure it's an undine we're dealing with?"

"Simple enough." Kate slams the book closed, absently places it on the table, and knocks over the cup, spilling tea onto her trousers. While she wipes it off she says, "Abe goes in for a look. I'd be worse than useless with an undine. I'm human, but I can keep a lookout. And, Liz, if this demon is the water spirit I think it is, it might be powerful enough to douse your fire—"

"Look, I'm still coming—"

"Of course! There's always the imp to take care of." Kate turns to Hellboy. "If it's in there, Abe can drive it to the surface for you."

"I can hardly wait." Hellboy grumbles in a monotone, thinking of the thing twice his size. He yawns. "Somebody bring along the first-aid kit."

They arrive at the park at just after three a.m. Tonight, most of the benches are empty of street people; probably because the temperature plummeted to below freezing, and they headed off to shelters.

"I wish I'd worn another sweater." Kate tucks her hands under her arms and shivers.

"Why?" Abe looks at the three of them, one after the other, his eyes rounder than usual with innocence.

"Us warm-blooded, you cold-blooded," Hellboy says.

"Ah. I keep forgetting." Abe is dressed in only a thin jacket for appearances. "I guess I'm the only one here who knows how this undine exists. Not that I empathize with its actions."

"So," Hellboy says, "you go in, I wait here for what comes out."

"Right," Abe says. He walks to the edge of the pond and instantly dives in. It's the most graceful dive Hellboy has ever seen.

Kate paces in little movements, trying to warm herself. Liz lights a cigarette and looks where Hellboy is looking, at the pond. The murky water's surface holds crusts of thin ice here and there.

Suddenly they all hear it, a sound, like a ton of crumpled paper being scraped over concrete. The three spin in every direction, searching for the source. "I see something!" Liz shouts, dashing into the trees after the flash of black on black.

Hellboy is torn: wait to see what Abe drives to the surface, or rush into the trees to help Liz.

"Hellboy, wait here! You have to wait!" Kate shouts. Her voice is obliterated by the sound of roiling water that results in a geyser in the pond shooting straight up into the air. Riding the top of the geyser is a thing that Hellboy recognizes for its size, which is more than double his. Tonight he sees it in its true form. The undine is no red-skinned horned replica of him. It has a tail, split at the end, like a fish. And a few tentacles that resemble shortened arms—fins really—scaly. The flesh is iridescent and elongated, fish-like, but not. But what strikes Hellboy most is the mouth. No, not the mouth, the *teeth*, three sets of them, row after row after row, shark-like, disappearing inward in the mouth. Teeth that are headed his way.

Hellboy leaps left to avoid that ferocious mouth. The jaw crashes to the cement. A hole is left, like the other one, and Hellboy realizes it was no otherworldly hand he saw that night, just this powerful maw hitting the ground.

He gears up for a punch, and lands one on what might be the undine's solar plexus. It makes a *Grawwwwwhhhh* sound and rears back. But not for long. One of the tentacles flaps by, knocking Hellboy into the air. He plummets six feet back, plowing into a tree, the breath knocked from his lungs. "Lucky punch!" he snarls, leaping to his feet.

Suddenly, a dark shadow races between Hellboy and the undine, with Liz in hot pursuit. Hellboy figures that Liz can take the imp out. He also sees that the undine knows it, too, and is ready to spray Liz with enough liquid to maybe nullify her fiery powers.

"Hey, big fish, small pond! Catch this!" He hurls a large rock into its gaping mouth, breaking a couple of those ultra-sharp teeth. While the undine reels from the pain, Hellboy hurls himself forward, knocking the monster back, onto land. But he falls in the water, struggling for purchase, sinking like a stone. Suddenly, from underneath, Hellboy is lifted out of the turbulent pond, high enough that he can leap to land.

"Thanks, Abe! I owe you."

"What're friends for?" the aquatic one says. "Watch out!"

Hellboy ducks instinctively. One of the undine's fins scrapes up his arm, ripping the coat sleeve to shreds, cutting deep into flesh from elbow to shoulder. Instantly, the wounds gush blood, but Hellboy has no time to feel the pain.

"It's trying to get back into the pond!" Kate calls out. "It's weaker on land, especially when forced out of the water."

And in fact the undine seems to be struggling to retreat into the pond.

Hellboy uses both hands and clamps onto its tail. The tail is powerful, the force of a rushing river, and every muscle in Hellboy's body aches as he yanks the slippery, scaly creature hard, over his shoulder, lifting the undine off the ground. Another loud *Grawwwwwhhhh!* cracks the air. Hellboy twirls the monster around and around in mid-air like a lariat, spinning it fast then faster until the water creature becomes a blur. Liquid flies out of its body in all directions like horizontal rain, a hurricane, soaking the land, the trees, and Kate.

"You're depleting it!" Kate yells. "Don't stop!"

The sound it makes begins to fade as more and more water leaves its body. Hellboy keeps spinning the undine. His arms feel as if they will drop out of the sockets, but he does not stop. And then a curious thing happens: his burden grows lighter. As the seconds tick by, the undine loses weight until it feels feather-light.

"Let her fly!" Liz cries out, a dark lump tucked beneath her arm.

Hellboy uses his heavy hand like a bat to send the water spirit soaring high into the air. Only then can he see what the undine has become, a shriveled, dried, filleted fish, dehydrated.

A burst of fire shoots straight up from the ground into the air, frying the fish as it catapults to earth. The corpse of the undine splatters onto the concrete, breaking apart. One eye lands near Abe, who is still in the pond. He leans over for a closer look.

Hellboy tips his imaginary hat. "Here's lookin' at you, kid!"

The four pause for a moment only. "What have you got, Liz?" Kate asks.

"A hellion," Liz says.

The squirming bundle under her arm mumbles, "Let me outta here, bitch!"

Kate hurries over. She reaches in and pulls out a head, blacker than midnight, the eyes like cats' eyes furtively darting around in the darkness.

"So, you're a real imp. Straight from the nether regions," Hellboy says.

"Go to hell, Redboy!" The voice has altered to that of a furious child. It squirms in Liz's arm, trying to bite anything within mouth range, and now it takes Kate as well to hold onto it.

"So," Kate says to Hellboy, "what do you want to do with this ... imp?"

Hellboy holds onto his upper arm to stem the blood flow. The wound suddenly burns like, well, hell. "Let it go," he says.

"Huh?" Liz asks.

Hellboy strides to Liz. He reaches out and the imp growls at him, snapping like a dog. He yanks a chunk of hair from the coal-black form.

"Uh, H.B., what are you doing?" Liz asks.

"I'm gonna make me a Voodoo doll."

"Red bastard!" The imp screams. Then an ear-splitting shriek causes the three of them to put their hands over their ears, and Abe to immerse himself in the pond.

Liz releases the minor demon. "I'll be back!" the childish imp voice yells. "This isn't over!"

"Get going!" Hellboy says.

"You'll be sorry—"

"Ah, what the hell ..." Hellboy hauls off and knocks out the imp with his Hand of Doom.

Silence rings through the park. It is as if the world has come to a halt. Out of the stillness, a small voice originating from a nearby bench says, "Hey, can't you guys keep it down? Some of us are trying to sleep."

"Sleep," Hellboy says.

Liz takes his good arm and leads him from the park.

THE WISH HOUNDS
SHARYN MCCRUMB

O *ak. Ash. And thorn.* Those were the hard ones. His classmates had all been assigned yard trees, he thought. Pine needles. Maple leaves. Things that even a first-grader could find, but he was the one who made the best grades and hardly had to open a book, so Teacher had given him the toughest task.

His assignment might take a bit more time than pulling leaves off your mother's rose bush, but he would manage. He'd had the school bus ride home to think it over, and by the time the bus reached his house, he had figured out where to find those trees. The big oaks grew on the steep hillside above the barn, and in the fall their changing leaves made a banner of gold beside the green pines and the dull brown of the locust trees on the higher mountain beyond. On his ninth birthday—last October—his grandfather had pointed out the golden oaks on that hill, noting that one of the old ones, lightning-struck, was dying, and would make good firewood for the coming winter. That was how he knew where to find oak.

He had gone there first, scrambling up the hillside and yanking a smooth, undamaged leaf from one of the lower branches. He tucked it between the pages of his science workbook. Later tonight he would glue it in and label the page: *Quercus.* English oak. Had these oaks always grown here, or did the settlers bring acorns with them to the New World? Teacher was one of the new people from the development up the mountain, and she was always going on about how people tamed the wilderness, but, though he didn't dispute her in class, he thought there was another side to that story. Kudzu, for instance. The dumbest kid in the class got sent to find that leaf, because it was everywhere. Brought over from Asia to stop erosion a hundred years back by well-meaning new people. Idiots. The thing stopped erosion all right. Then it engulfed all the local plants, and now it looked like it was going to swallow up everything, even covering the ruins of old buildings out in the fields.

His grandfather said that they ought to have named the fancy development up on the ridge "Kudzu City" instead of "Hunting Hills." *Be more fitting*, he said. Strangers often meant trouble, even if they were just plants.

A sweat bee buzzing around his forehead reminded him that time was passing, and that it would take maybe an hour's ramble through the old fields to finish the rest of the task. He shouldered his backpack and started down the hill toward the creek. The sun was slantwise in the sky now, almost low enough to blind one walking westward. Maybe an hour of daylight left, maybe less. Night came fast in the valley, once the sun slid below the mountain tops, and then, homework or no homework, his mother would expect him on the doorstep, hands washed and ready for supper.

Ash. Ash was next on the list. The valley didn't have any of the tall straight ash trees—the kind they make baseball bats out of. Those grew higher up the slopes—too far to go in late afternoon for one fool leaf. He would make do with the other kind—mountain ash. The crooked little trees that flowered white in May just when school was letting out for the summer, and sprouted red berries right before it was time to start back in the fall. If you followed the creek out of the pasture and through the woods, you came to the ruins of a log cabin in an abandoned field. Whoever had built the place had planted a mountain ash tree on either side of the cabin door. The birds had probably eaten all the berries by now, but he didn't need them anyhow. Just a single small branch with the thin, raggedy leaves, like fraying threads on an old green blanket.

He wondered if Teacher would even know the difference between ash and mountain ash her own self. He supposed she could look it up in a book, but he could always argue that she hadn't specified which sort of ash she meant. It was a silly sort of assignment anyhow. Leaf gathering. Sending the whole science class scurrying all over creation hunting up willow fronds, dogwood leaves, redbud. *Fanciful*, his folks would have said. Just what you'd expect from one of the kudzu people from the big development on the side of Scratch Mountain, where the houses were as big as barns, but the lots were the size of postage stamps. Hunting Hills, indeed. And there was a curved brass hunter's horn mounted on the stone wall by the gate house at the entrance to the development. The houses cost a fortune, but they were all squashed together so close that you could smell what the neighbors were having for dinner. Maybe she was trying to learn all the local trees her own self, he thought. Maybe trying to figure out what would look best in her little bitty yard. The people on Scratch Mountain might live in the country, but it seemed like they did their best not to set foot in it.

Thorn. When she assigned it to him, one of the girls had asked her if she meant a rose bush, but Teacher just smiled and shook her head, and then Tamara Harrison, who lived with her grandmother up in one of the coves, started waving her hand in the air (as usual) and said, "We call it *blackthorn* around here, ma'am."

So then he had known what she wanted without having to put himself out by asking. Blackthorn. Teacher had called it hawthorne, but then when they found it in the tree book and saw the nicknames it went by, she allowed as how it was the American cousin of the plant she had in mind, and if he could find one of those, it would do. She'd looked embarrassed about it, as if they'd caught her out, and he'd begun to think that she wasn't altogether sure what grew in these parts and what didn't. Thorn was in the valley all right, but it would still take more effort than most of the other ones assigned.

The sun was lower in the sky now, bleeding the color out of the spring grass and turning the trees into dancing shadows.

Easiest place to find blackthorn was in the oldest fields, the ones that had been pasture land before barbed wire was invented. He hadn't known that, either. He'd stopped in at Harnett's Store on the way home and asked old man Harnett, who was old enough to remember outhouses and oil lamps.

"Why h'it's organic bob wire," the old man had said. "Them thorns work just the same as the wire, so in the old days folks planted blackthorn trees in a line, and kept 'em trimmed into hedgerows to fence in the pasture. Couldn't no cow walk through a thorn hedge."

Sure enough, in the old field between the tumbled down cabin and the creek, there was a line of shrubs so unkempt and weedy that it looked like underbrush gone wild, but when he got up close, he could see the sharp little thorns along the shoots of greenery. He had his pocket knife to cut it with, but he still managed to prick his thumb trying to hold the stem so he could lop off a twig.

He stuffed the spiky branch into the sack with the rest of the leaves, and turned to look at the red glow of clouds on the horizon. All done now. Oak. Ash. And thorn. An hour or so pasting the leaves down on colored paper and lettering each page, and he'd be done with his tree project. But he'd never make it home before dark, not even if he ran flat out in a beeline for the family land. It was for school, though, he told himself. Even his mother couldn't object to his doing his homework, but she'd still be mad about him being out after dark. Ever since that little girl from over in the Red Bird community had gone missing last spring, the parents had been hellbent on getting the young'uns home before nightfall, even big fifth-graders like himself, who had his own .22 and went squirrel hunting with the menfolk.

He wished he had the .22 with him now. All of a sudden he had noticed how almighty quiet it had become out here in the fields. Not even a mourning dove to break the silence. Only the rustle of the wind in dry grass and the thud of his own heart, and—

Far off. So faint that at first he thought he had only imagined it, a deep, low tone echoing across the ripple of mountains. One long, lowing, musical, but also in the gathering darkness, chilling. The sound was growing louder now. Closer.

It was time to go home.

The boy looked around at the black shapes of trees on the ridge above the creek. Was something moving up there? A lost bull, he thought. Perhaps a buffalo. There used to be buffalo here once—in Daniel Boone's time. Elk, too. Surely that bugling call was some great hoofed beast bawling in its solitude. Closer, now. Now the metallic tone was unmistakable. A horn. Hunters' horn.

Now, dropping his sack of leaves, he ran for the path at the far end of the pasture. There was a cluster of odd-shaped boulders there, big enough to hide under, so that horses couldn't run him down. His grandfather had once told him that if he ever got scared out in the fields—from a thunderstorm, maybe—that he should seek shelter among those stones. So he ran.

He did not look back again. No time. No time. Running flat out now, his breath knifing through his chest. Faster. A few more seconds would see him safe. No looking back, but he could not help hearing the other sounds now, a descant below the blaring of the horn. Hoofbeats. But not cow. Not elk.

Horses.

Maybe a dozen of them. Coming closer.

Coming straight at him.

He almost made it to the circle of stones.

When the Winstead boy went missing last week, that made the fifth child to be taken from here in a space of a year, and not even the state police could find anything that led to an explanation of who took them or where they went. We're talking desperate here. Parents afraid to let their kids out even in broad daylight. The Winsteads and the other grieving families out of their minds with fear and sorrow, and screaming for blood. The community knew it had to do something. Well, the old community, anyhow. Nobody had gone missing from the fancy development, so they weren't overly concerned about some missing locals. But everybody else went to the meeting in the Free Will Baptist Church, and decided that extreme measures were called for.

"Badger," Preacher said to me the next day, "We're calling in some specialists in supernatural goings-on." Told me that they'd sent for a big strange-looking fellow, kin to the devil, and hailing from the place that is eternally hot.

"Well, bring him on," I says to him. "I've met folks from Florida before."

Turns out, though, that this Hellboy fellow was a sight more tolerable than the tourist types we usually get around here. He didn't seem to think that the place was a theme park, for one thing. And he didn't want to buy large chunks of land and then try to duplicate Tampa in a cooler climate. He had even heard of our valley before.

"Abbots Ford," he said, turning the words over in his mouth until he could place them. "Wasn't there a quantum physicist who came from here? MacKenzie something?—No. Joshua MacKenzie."

"Oh, you heard of him?" I said.

"Only that he disappeared about twenty years ago. He was working on some kind of army project dealing with—what was it? String theory or something, and one day he just wasn't there."

"Maybe he got zapped by his own machine," I said. "But, yes, he was born and raised here. Went off to the university, and people say he never looked back. Maybe they'll put up a historical marker to him out at the main road some day. But that's not what you've come about."

He grunted. "No. Missing children take precedence over misplaced scientists. Odd that there weren't any ransom notes. You'd think—" He nodded at the McMansions straddling the crest of Scratch Mountain.

"You've got the wrong end of the cow, son," I told him. "I expect most of the people who live up there could raise a few hundred thousand to get their child back. But the thing is: none of the missing children came from up there. They were the farm kids from down here in the cove. Families that have been here two hundred years."

We started down the road that stretched between the hills, dividing meadows from well-kept yards and white frame houses. He digested this information. "Only the old families. Did this kind of thing happen in the past? Previous generations?"

I stared at him. It's amazing how many people put their mouths in gear with their brains in neutral. "Well, no, it never happened before. Do you think people would still be living here if they knew that the place would take their children?"

He shrugged. "I never take common sense for granted. Do you?"

"Me? Oh, I mostly mind my own business," I said. "I wouldn't even be out and about talking to you except for this trouble the community is in. Since I'm an old-timer without a day job, people trusted me to show you around."

"Where do you live?"

"Oh, just an old cabin up in the woods," I said. "Nobody goes there, but I'm easy to find. Try the general store any time you want me."

We ambled along while he looked at the ground and touched the odd leaf here and there, as if he thought the signs from the Winstead boy's disappearance would still be evident. I thought about telling him how many rainstorms we'd had since then, but then I decided that he was just trying to get in tune with the land, so I held my peace.

"I have a case file on the missing children," he said at last. "But I'd like you to tell me again."

"Not much to tell," I said. "The police can't make head nor tail of it. We've lost half a dozen children in three years. Ages range from three years old to eleven. Boys. Girls. There's no rhyme or reason that we can discern in the disappearances. You'd think if it was a human predator they'd be more—what's the word I want? Specialized, maybe."

He nodded. "If the explanation were that simple, they wouldn't have called us in. We don't do run-of-the-mill human monsters."

"What do you do?"

"Vampires. Goblins. Things that people don't believe in—if they're lucky."

I nodded. I was thinking that taking one look at this guy would make everything in the fairy-tale books seem downright plausible. If he was possible, what wasn't? Hellboy was built like a thumb, lobster red with two polled horns there on the front of his head, a great fist that looked as if it was made of stone, and a long tail, just as if he'd been a Hereford bull in a former life and didn't quite make the transition. He didn't scare me, though. I was just glad that we were on the same side.

"So how long have people lived in this valley?" he asked me, looking at a split-rail fence bordering one of the old fields.

"Two hundred years or so," I said. "The settlers mostly came down from Pennsylvania, following the long valleys that go like corridors between the mountains. Before that, they were in the mountains of Wales or Scotland, so I suppose they felt at home when they got here."

He nodded. "I wonder if they brought anything with them."

"Not much in the way of material possessions. But they carried a lot in their heads. Fiddle tunes. Quilt patterns. The formula for whisky. Old stories."

"Some memories are better left behind," he muttered.

"Well, people were pretty happy here as long as they got left alone. Of course, property taxes may get to be a problem. Ever since they built that excrescence on the ridge up there, the land values around here have gone up like a SCUD missile."

"Well, if children keep disappearing around here, I doubt you'll get too many prospective buyers—Hey, what's this?"

"Rocks," I said.

He gave me a look, so I elaborated on my answer. "Just some boulders, Hellboy. They've been there as long as anybody can remember. People used to have picnics out here and sit on them as if they were benches."

He was counting the stones, then running his huge hands along the smooth gray surface of the nearest one. "Have they ever stood upright?"

I shook my head. "Not that I've ever heard. You mean like Stonehenge? You don't think they're just a natural formation?"

"I don't know. They look too well-matched to me. Smooth and elongated—like fallen statues. This was once Cherokee country, wasn't it?"

"Yes, but they didn't go in for great stone circles. Now out in Ohio, you had the mound builders—giant earthworks in animal shapes. But not here."

"Okay. Forget the stones, then. Any old Indian legends about monsters?"

"Sure. Everybody has monster stories. They had a cattywampus—that was a big cat. I have my own idea about that, though. Around twelve thousand years ago, when the ice age was on the wane, and the first people moved into these mountains, there *were* monsters here. Mastodons. Birds of prey with a twenty-five-foot wingspan. And sabertooth tigers. I think one of those ancient tribesmen saw a sabertooth one day, and talked about it for the rest of his days. That story filtered down to us as a monster tale, but the core of the tale has a grain of truth. Of course, there aren't any more tigers or mastodons around here. Turned out that people were more deadly than the monsters."

Hellboy grunted. "I hear you," he said.

Hellboy wanted to talk to the people up in the McMansions on Scratch Mountain, even though they hadn't lost any children to whatever-it-was. "Will they talk to me?" he wanted to know.

Silly question.

He might be straight from hell and smell of smoke, but he was something of a celebrity, wasn't he? Not a strip miner or a real-estate baron or a mine owner, not anybody really bad enough to be staggeringly rich and politically useful, but they reasoned that if the rumors about Hellboy were correct, then his father was a former angel, which was something like being the kid of an ex-senator—or better yet, the old man was presently the ruler of hell, which made Hellboy just another dictator's kid. Might as well make the acquaintance of the ruling family of a place you may one day have to visit, right?

Damned if they didn't give him a reception.

I went along with him, since I was nominally his guide—not that they expected me to know which fork to use, either. We didn't get too dressed up for the occasion, since it was only an afternoon affair. I went back to my cabin and put on a clean shirt. Hellboy kept on his trenchcoat, and off we went.

The party was held in the Hunting Hills clubhouse, with all residents present to get a look at the visiting celebrity, ask him fool questions, and cast about for a mutual acquaintance. Hellboy stood there glowering over a cup of punch and answered all the twittering with a few curt words.

After a very few minutes of small talk, he worked his way to the portly man in the dark suit who was holding a brandy snifter instead of a cup of fruit punch.

Seeing Hellboy approach, the man broke off his conversation and thrust out his hand, but one look at Hellboy's massive fist made him change the gesture to a pat on the arm. "Glad to see you, Hellboy," he said. "Benjy Geare. I'm president of the residents' association. I'd be glad to show you around."

Hellboy grunted. "We need to talk about the missing children."

Geare's face assumed a suitably solemn expression. "One feels for the parents, of course," he murmured. "But I would have thought the police or perhaps the FBI might be handling it. We thought perhaps a child pornography ring?"

"The children vanished from the valley. No strangers seen. No tire tracks. We've pretty much ruled out the simple answers," said Hellboy. "I just thought it was funny that no children from up here have gone missing."

Geare shrugged. "We have been fortunate. Or perhaps more careful. Are they keeping the children indoors these days?"

"I think the Scouts are still having their campout tonight," I told him. "But they'll all be together."

A smiling blond woman thrust a silver tray of hors d'oeuvres between the two of them. "Canape, Master?" he said.

I reached for one, but Geare waved her way.

Hellboy stared after the retreating woman. "*Master?*" he said.

Geare shifted uncomfortably. "Just a nickname," he said quickly. "Now, I wanted to—"

He was interrupted again, this time by a sleek couple who tapped his arm and said, "Good night, Master."

Hellboy did not react to their farewells addressed to him. He was staring out the clubhouse window at a bright sunny afternoon. For the few more minutes that he stayed at the reception he seemed distracted. Finally he mumbled his thanks for the party and strode out the front door, with me hustling along trying to keep up with those long strides of his.

"I was born in England," he muttered. Then he said, "You go home. I'm going to walk around and think about this."

Some of the oldest land on earth. These hills were the western remnant of a mountain chain that had once soared higher than Everest, broken apart by tectonic forces and now divided by the width of an ocean. The Appalachians, islands in a sea of time, were moored on one side of the Atlantic, while on its eastern shore lay the other half of that ancient chain—the mountains of Britain. In the 18th century when the pioneers arrived in this wilderness, they knew they were far from home, but something about these mountains looked right and felt right, and so they homesteaded there in the fold of the hills—these exiled Scots and Irish, the Welsh and the Cornishmen, all drawn to a strange but familiar place, and never knowing that they were right back in the same mountains they had just left.

But perhaps these people's frontier ancestors weren't the only immigrants who had found sanctuary in these remnants of the ancient mountains. Other beings had left the shores of Britain ... banished to the lands in the west, according to the legends ... to the lands in the west ...

He walked along the dirt road in the gathering twilight, thinking about strangers in a strange land, and wondering what other wanderers had found themselves a home in these ancient mountains. Some things are best left behind.

The wind had picked up now, and he hunched his shoulders and trudged on toward the hillside pasture, listening for the sound of distant horns. The fading light had leached the color out of the landscape, so that leaves and grass were only different shades of gray, and the sky was the color of pewter.

"Master," Hellboy muttered, and his customary scowl deepened. People who said, "Good night, Master," in the broad daylight of a sunny afternoon.

He'd only heard that greeting once, and that was back in his childhood in England, years ago when Trevor Bruttenholm had taken him on a visit to a country house in Sussex. The professor had driven up the long track through ancient oaks and into the circular carriage drive in front of the wide stone steps of the manor house. The lord of the manor, a minor aristocrat named Foley, had been expecting them, but first he'd had to take his leave of his other visitors. Foley, it seemed, was the master of foxhounds with the local hunt, and the side lawn of the manor was now filled with red-jacketed fox hunters astride thoroughbred hunters. Hellboy remembered comparing his own out-sized fist to the rock-like hoof of a bay horse and wondering if they were kindred spirits. It had been a friendly horse, not at all discomfited by the sight of a small red demon capering at its feet. He had stroked its plaited mane and allowed it to sniff at his stubbed horns.

It had been a bright, crisp autumn afternoon, but the departing riders had each saluted their host and said, "Good night, Master."

"But it isn't night," Hellboy had murmured to Bruttenholm.

"It's an old custom," the professor told him. "No matter what time it is, the traditional valediction when one takes leave of the master of the hounds is *Good night, Master.*"

Hellboy had not thought of that oddity from that day to this, but suddenly hearing the phrase again in the club room of Hunting Hills had made him realize who these people were. *What* they were.

There it was ... only a faint moan, muffled by the trees on the nearest ridge, but unmistakably a musical thrum sounding in the distance ... *Hunting horns.*

Hellboy nodded grimly, a suspicion confirmed. Hunting Hills might be a newly built community of outsiders, but this gathering was very old, indeed, only it had always been associated with a different place—with these mountains' kindred hills an ocean away in Britain. *The Wish Hounds ... the Wild Hunt ... the Devil's Huntsmen* ... They went by many names in the folklore of England and Scotland and Wales, where they still told tales of spectral beings who rode across the moors on dark nights, with a pack of phantom hounds baying at their horses' heels, hunting—not foxes—but humans out wandering alone in the night, never to be seen again.

Hellboy scowled in the direction of the dark hillside. "Bring it on," he muttered to himself. He was heading for the cluster of elongated stones that hadn't looked accidental to him. *Maybe once, long ago, somebody here remembered*, he thought.

The bugling of the horns was louder now, and he could hear the clatter of hoofbeats in the distance. Maybe the hunters were headed for that Scout encampment, where many of the local children would be gathered around tents and campfires, but the hunt would have to pass by here first. He didn't have much time to stop them, but he did have a hunch about what might work.

He reached the cluster of toppled boulders, and ran his hand along the nearest one, feeling its cold rough surface, and faintly a tingle of *something*, as if it vibrated in response to the spectral music. He knelt beside one of the fallen stones and, pushing with all his strength against it, he began to shoulder the massive rock upright into a vertical position. And then he propped up another, opposite the first monolith, creating a portal. Stone after stone, pushed upright like petrified giants—as they must have been erected by the first people to settle this ancient valley. The Cherokee? The Scots-Irish pioneers? Long ago someone had known about the hunters of men.

The last and smallest stone he hefted easily—three men could have done it by themselves, he supposed. With a bound he executed a perfect lay-up, setting the elongated boulder neatly atop the two parallel stones—the lintel crowns the posts. The stone archway was once more in place.

He could see the riders now. He wondered if they would also be visible to ordinary people, or if they would only be sensed as a force of terror. But Hellboy could see them: gray riders on dark horses thundering across the colorless field in the twilight. They were heading straight for him.

He stood in front of the stone henge, arms folded, waiting for the huntsmen.

As they clattered closer, he could see that the riders swathed in black cloaks were human-shaped, but not in any sense *human*. Their eyes burned in white death masks and each grinning mouth was a rictus caricature of a smile. The black hounds flowed across the landscape with gaping jaws and glowing eyes.

Several of the riders started to cut away from the pack as if to ride around the stone arch, but he sprinted off in front of the horses and punched one of them squarely between the eyes. The black beast staggered for an instant, and then the rider drew rein and galloped back toward the others.

Hellboy chivied and punched, kicked at phantom hounds and charged at demonic horses until finally the huntsmen galloped through the stone archway—and vanished.

The stones crackled with blue flames as Hellboy edged toward them, and then with one great kick he toppled the standing stones. There was a flash and a rumble, and then darkness and the night silence of a country meadow. Off somewhere an owl called out. The Wild Hunt was gone.

Hellboy nodded with satisfaction. "One other thing Bruttenholm told me about the customs of the hunt," he muttered. "Whoever opens the gate always has to close ity."

A while later he knocked at the door of a small ramshackle cabin on a ridge near the creek. When the old man peered out through the half-open door, Hellboy said, "It's taken care of, Badger."

"It was the new people, wasn't it?"

Hellboy nodded. "But you knew that, didn't you—*Dr. MacKenzie?*"

The old man sighed. "You'd better come in."

The cabin, a rustic ruin on the outside, was all chrome and glass and polished oak within. Rows of bookshelves lined the walls around the fireplace, and a computer held pride of place on the round walnut table. "I wanted to come home," he said simply. "I wanted to spin out my little theories on physics in pure abstraction, but the people I worked for wanted weapons made. So I left."

"And they never found you?"

"Well, they're looking for a Fulbright scholar and a quantum physicist, not a crazy old coot in a shack. And the new people—even the human ones—would never look for a scholar *here*." His accent had flattened out now, and the eyes of a shrewd and learned man looked out of his lined, genial face. "The killers weren't human, were they?"

"No. You knew that, I suppose. You took me to those stones."

"Well, I knew nobody else would believe me if I started babbling about supernatural beings, so I thought: *fight fire with fire.* Hence: you, Hellboy. I did think there might be some sort of interdimensional quality to those monoliths, and I had to hope you'd figure it out and that you'd have the power to send them through it into wherever they came from."

"I did. You're safe now."

The old man gave him a sad smile and pointed to a coffee mug emblazoned with the logo of Hunting Hills. "Oh, don't you believe it, Hellboy," he said. "There are some gates that can never be closed."

Hellboy nodded. "Good luck with the new people," he said.

ACT OF MERCY

THOMAS E. SNIEGOSKI

Fletcher Christian was typing.

Tap, tap, tap-tap, tap, tap, tap-tap, tap, tap, tap, tap-tap.

That's weird, Hellboy thought vaguely, nearly asleep upon the sectional sofa in his private quarters at the Bureau for Paranormal Research and Defense headquarters in Fairfield, Connecticut. He didn't remember any scenes in the 1935 version of *Mutiny on the Bounty* involving typewriters, but he might have been wrong.

Tap, tap, tap-tap, tap, tap, tap-tap, tap, tap, tap-tap.

Pulling himself from that strange, foggy place between wakefulness and slumber, he opened his yellow eyes a crack to gaze at the screen of the nineteen-inch Sylvania console squatting on the floor across the room.

Movie-star handsome Clark Gable as Fletcher Christian was having a heated conversation with a not-so-pretty Charles Laughton as the despicable Captain Bligh, and, as Hellboy suspected, neither of them was typing.

Tap-tap, tap, tap, tap, tap-tap, tap-tap, tap.

Hellboy leaned forward on the couch, searching the darkened room for the source of the strange noise. He grabbed the remote control from the cushion beside him and turned down the volume on the DVD player, listening carefully for the sound to be repeated.

Tap, tap, tap, tap-tap, tap-tap, tap, tap-tap.

"What the hell is that?" he grumbled, flexing his tail and pushing himself up from the sofa. Slowly, he worked his way across the room, illuminated only by the pulsing light of the television screen. He froze as the sound came again.

Tap, tap, tap, tap-tap, tap-tap, tap.

It was definitely coming from the window. His hoof landed on the latest issue of *Cat Fancy*, where he had dropped it earlier, and he almost lost his footing, but caught himself. *I gotta clean this place*, he thought, quickening his pace, careful not to step on any other debris littering his living-room floor. *What a sty*.

Hellboy stood mere inches from the window but could see nothing save darkness beyond it.

"C'mon, c'mon," he grumbled impatiently, itching for a glimpse of whatever had interrupted his precious movie snooze time.

Without warning, something blacker than the night collided with the glass, and Hellboy leapt back, kicking over Chinese takeout boxes of General Gau's chicken and specialty house rice. *I was gonna eat that*, he thought, his attention diverted for a fraction of a second.

The object threw itself at the window even harder. This time the glass shattered inward with the force of the blow.

"Jesus Christ!" Hellboy roared, shielding his eyes from flying glass as a large, black shape swooped into his apartment. It was a bird—a crow, one of the biggest he had ever seen, and it flew crazily about the room, banging into the ceiling, careening through the air. Its incessant cawing was ear splitting.

He was close to calling Abe for help when the bird suddenly dove toward the pulsing light of the television screen. The dry twig sound of its neck snapping as it hit full force made him wince, the savage impact leaving a bloody smear on Captain Bligh's face, as the bird fell limp and unmoving to the floor.

Hellboy glanced out into the night through the broken window, just to be sure that it held no more surprises. Finding none, he turned his curiosity to the body of the crow. Its wingspan was easily five feet, but that wasn't what caught his attention.

"What've we got here?" he said, kneeling down beside the dead bird. The crow held something in its taloned feet, something that looked like a scroll.

"Let go," he cursed, struggling with the bird's death grip. It wouldn't oblige, and he found himself having to peel back the clawed toes, the hollow bones cracking wetly as they were broken.

It was indeed a scroll, and as Hellboy rose to his feet and began to unroll the message, his sense of smell was assaulted by an offensive yet familiar odor. It was the smell of desiccated human flesh. The scroll in his hands was not made of parchment, but of skin, and judging by the length and width of it, it had likely been peeled from somebody's back. "This just keeps getting better and better," he grumbled as he read the message.

His Romanian was a bit rusty, but he got the gist of it.

Scrawled upon the parchment of skin was a challenge.

Written in blood.

Hellboy stood behind Kate Corrigan's chair, watching as her fingers fluttered delicately over the computer keyboard.

"Sorry to get you in here so early," he said. Kate was Assistant Director of Field Operations.

"No problem," Kate said, her eyes on the screen as she typed in her password, preparing to peruse the B.P.R.D.'s mission-archive database. "I was up anyway doing some file review for Manning. Still haven't gotten your official report on the Grottendieck Stone Thrower, by the way," she admonished, double clicking the mouse and entering the archives.

"Hmmm." He wasn't thrilled with the prospect of paperwork. It was the part of the job that he hated the most. "Did Abe do his yet?" he asked, hoping to gain a little time.

"Turned it in two weeks ago."

"Brown nose," he grumbled.

Kate chuckled, turning to the scroll that Hellboy had placed on her desk. "Let's make sure we get the correct spelling of your challenger's name before we begin." Carefully she unrolled the macabre skin scroll.

"Dyavo Mahr."

"The name doesn't ring any bells?" she asked, entering it into the search box on her computer screen.

"Nothing," Hellboy answered. "But judging from the tone of the message, it must be someone I pissed off pretty good."

"You do have that effect on people," Kate said as she watched her information appear. "Bingo."

Hellboy leaned in closer. "Son of a gun," he said in surprise. "Guess I do know this guy."

"Yep. 1978. Romanian mining village called Balanbanya. You were assigned to investigate a number of disappearances that occurred after an old shaft was reopened."

He brought his large, stone hand to his face and rubbed his chin, deep in concentration. "Balanbanya," he said once, and then a second time, hoping to stir some memory. "Was that the place with the really good cabbage rolls?"

"I couldn't tell you," Kate said. "It says here that you fought Dyavo Mahr in the mine shaft and killed it." She turned in her chair to look at him.

"Guess he got over it," Hellboy shrugged. "What kind of beastie are we talking about?"

"You really don't remember this thing?" she asked incredulously.

"Guys like this are a dime a dozen. After a while they all kinda blend together. You punch one demon face, you punched 'em all, know what I'm sayin'?"

"If you say so." Kate returned her attention to the computer screen. "It also says that Dyavo is your typical fiend of the night with a penchant for human flesh. For a time, it was considered quite the boogeyman in that region of Romania."

"I guess poundin' the crap out of him in '78 didn't do much for his image," Hellboy said, reading over his friend's shoulder.

"Nope. Probably why he wants a rematch," Kate added. She turned back to him. "So, what are you going to do?"

Hellboy reached for the scroll. "Can you hook me up with a flight?" he asked, rolling the message up tight.

"You're going?" she asked, surprise in her tone.

"When someone bothers to send an invitation by giant bird on such nice stationery, I'd have to say they're real serious about getting attention." He slipped the scroll into one of the deep pockets of his overcoat. "Don't think I have much of a choice."

In a matter of hours, Kate had provided Hellboy with a private flight to Romania, as well as a ride from the tiny airfield to the village of Posaga, the closest spot to the Apuseni Mountains, where the challenge was to occur.

The flight was relatively uneventful, but now Hellboy held on for dear life as the powder-blue Yugo barreled down a country road that was in a serious state of disrepair. He was sure the car was going to fall apart completely as it rolled over huge potholes and ruts. The driver's name was Anatoly, and he was in the midst of explaining something that only he seemed to find incredibly funny.

"And then he rescued the big monkey from the laboratory and there was much laughing on my part," the chubby man said, wiping tears of laughter from his eyes as he drove. "And then there are his pants. I am laughing now with just the thought of them."

Hellboy tore his eyes away from the road illuminated in the Yugo's headlights to look at the driver. "This Urkel must be one funny guy," he said.

They had been driving for a little over an hour, the surroundings becoming progressively more rustic, and he found himself getting itchy.

"How much farther to Posaga?" Hellboy asked as he tried to reposition his bulk. The passenger seat had been slid back as far as it could go, and he still found that his legs were cramped, the top of his head scraping the ceiling.

Anatoly shifted noisily into second gear and the car bucked and whined as it began to climb a mountain road. "Not long now."

"Maybe I should get out and push," Hellboy suggested, and the driver laughed.

"You are very funny, Mr. Hellboy of the B.P.R.D., almost as funny as the Urkel—but not quite."

That was good to know, he thought as he tried to keep his head from bouncing off the car ceiling. *Almost as funny as some guy named Urkel.*

They drove for a while longer; the sun was just starting to peek out over the horizon, casting their surroundings in the eerie shadows seemingly distinct to this part of the world. *I wouldn't be surprised in the least to see Boris Karloff come stumbling out of the thick woods in full monster of Frankenstein makeup, chased by villagers with pitchforks and torches.*

It was hard to believe, but the road was actually getting worse. Anatoly drove the Yugo like he was driving an all-terrain vehicle, and Hellboy could have sworn he heard pieces of the car clattering off into what passed as a road behind them. He didn't have the courage, or the room, to turn around and check.

"We are now between Turda and Campeni," Anatoly announced. "A curve in road up ahead will take us through a stone archway into Posaga village, I think." Hellboy peered through the early morning murk, but saw nothing.

"Hold onto your hat," Anatoly cried with a throaty chuckle, and cut the wheel suddenly to the right, hurling Hellboy's mass against the passenger door. His head banged off the ceiling again as the car fishtailed, kicking up dust and dirt in its wake. "Easy there, Mario," he barked, and Hellboy began to wonder if he would reach his destination in one piece.

They bounced down the ancient dirt road, surrounded on either side by thick brush and trees, and as they came up over a slight rise, the Yugo's headlights illuminated the forms of several darkly clad villagers carrying a wooden casket.

They were standing in the road.

"Holy crap, look out!" Hellboy yelled, reaching over to grab hold of the steering wheel, pulling it roughly to the right, hoping to avoid the people in the Yugo's path.

The wheel broke loose from the steering column.

"Cheap foreign junk," he mumbled, not sure what to do with the wheel, as Anatoly stomped his foot on the brake.

The Yugo spun around, brakes screeching like a cat stuck in a fan belt, its tail coming to an abrupt stop mere inches from the villagers, who had not moved an inch from their place in the center of the dirt road.

Hellboy and Anatoly sat for a moment in silence until Hellboy handed the driver his steering wheel. "Sorry about that."

Anatoly tentatively took the hard plastic wheel from him and attempted to place it back on the steering column with little success.

Hellboy threw open the door and slowly began to extricate himself from the close quarters of the front seat. Anatoly got out of the car as well, and with steering wheel still in hand, walked toward the crowd of mourners.

"Have you lost your minds?" he yelled in the language of the region. "Do you want to be killed?" He shook his steering wheel in annoyance at them.

"Cut 'em some slack, Anatoly," Hellboy said, joining the driver. He gestured toward the wooden coffin in the road behind the villagers. It was draped in a purple cloth, adorned with religious symbols of the orthodox faith. "Doesn't look like they're havin' the best of days either."

The gaggle of villagers stared silently at him with blank eyes, as if all emotional response had been drained from them.

"What is wrong with you people?" Anatoly berated them. "Haven't you ever seen an agent of the B.P.R.D. before?"

Hellboy watched as the crowd began to part, and an old woman, her back twisted and bent, hobbled forward with the help of a cane as gnarled as her spine. Her head and shoulders were enshrouded in a shawl of black, the clothing she wore the same dour color—the color of mourning.

She stopped mere inches from Hellboy and leaning upon her cane, tilted her leathery face up to gaze into his eyes. Her own were covered with the thick, milky film of cataracts, but there was no mistaking that she could see him just fine.

"It brings us great joy to know that you have come," she said in the dialect of her village.

He was much better at understanding Romanian than he was speaking it, and asked his driver for a hand. "Anatoly, ask her how she knew I was coming."

Anatoly put forth the question and the woman responded.

"The night lurker said that you would come to face him—that you would come to help the children."

"She said that the night lurker ...," Anatoly began.

"I got that part," Hellboy interrupted. "But did she just say something about kids?" he asked with growing dread. "What kids?"

Again the driver posed the question to the old woman, and translated her response.

"He came in the night and stole away the youngest children of our village," she said, pointing with her cane up the road to where the village of Posaga sat. "Father John tried to stop him, but the creature tore the flesh from his body." She shuddered.

The villagers blessed themselves as they stepped aside to give Hellboy a better view of the coffin, and he suspected that he knew where Dyavo Mahr had gotten the materials he needed to write his challenge.

The old woman went on.

"He said that the beast of the end times, who had rejected evil and now fought on the side of the angels, would be called forth to face him, and if he did not come, the children would die for his cowardice."

"Son of a bitch," Hellboy growled. There was nothing worse than someone who hid behind kids to get what he wanted. Dyavo Mahr was quickly moving to the top of his must-punch-hard list.

The elderly woman shuffled closer and placed a gnarled hand on his broad chest, as if to feel his heartbeat. "But you have come," she said, "and will return our babies to us."

"I'll see what I can do." Hellboy patted her aged hand reassuringly. "Might as well get this show on the road."

The villagers picked up the coffin from the ground and continued on their way through the woods to the cemetery.

"How will you know where to go?" Anatoly asked him, once they were alone in the road. "The Apuseni, they are very vast."

Hellboy looked toward the mountains that loomed behind the tiny village and wondered the very same thing. In the distance, a black shape disengaged itself from a patch of shadows, soaring down toward them to perch in a nearby tree.

A crow, even bigger than the one that crashed my apartment.

It fluttered its jet-black wings, cocking its head and fixing Hellboy in a piercing stare. Then the bird lifted its wing and pointed, and he saw that it was directing him toward a winding forest path that disappeared into the thick of the wood.

"Guess that answers your question," Hellboy said to Anatoly. With a final farewell, he proceeded up the path that would hopefully lead him to his challenger.

"Hey, bird!" Hellboy called into the thick forest, hands cupped to his mouth. "Where'd you go?"

He looked around, scanning the trees for signs of his black-feathered chaperone. The crow had been leading him deeper, higher, into the forest of the Apuseni Mountains, but now it was nowhere to be seen.

"Great," he groaned, shielding his eyes as he gazed at the turquoise sky through the canopy of branches. He had been walking for hours, and still had no idea where he was headed. Hellboy sat down on the rotting trunk of a fallen tree, disheartened and thinking of the children in the clutches of the ancient demon.

His stomach grumbled noisily, and he remembered that he hadn't eaten anything since the stale cheese Danish on the flight over. He reached into the satchel at his side and found a chocolate bar that he kept there for just such emergencies. "This oughta hold me until I can get some real grub." He peeled away the candy wrapper and broke off a piece, popping it into his mouth.

"Would you be willing to trade a piece of that candy bar for some help?"

Hellboy leapt up from his seat upon the log to see that a large, spotted lynx was talking to him. The cat sat calmly beside the fallen tree, looking up at him with wide, sea-green eyes.

"How do you know I need help?" he asked, amused that he was not in the least bit surprised that the animal was talking to him. Doing the kind of job that he did, it took a helluva lot to get a rise out of him.

"You're sitting all alone on a log in the middle of nowhere with a candy bar," the lynx observed. "And don't tell me you're just enjoying the scenery."

Hellboy sat back down on the log and considered what was left of his chocolate. "I guess I could give you some." He broke off a piece and tossed it to the ground in front of the cat.

The lynx dexterously grabbed the piece of candy with its paw and brought it to its mouth.

"Didn't know lynxes liked chocolate," Hellboy said.

"I wouldn't know," the animal said offhandedly as it chewed. "I'm a Krukis—a forest spirit. I just look like a lynx."

"Got it," Hellboy said with a nod, and popped the last bite of candy into his own mouth. "So, now that you've had part of my snack, you're gonna help me find what I'm looking for, right?"

"Of course I am," the Krukis replied, licking some stray chocolate from its paw. "That *was* the deal."

The two continued on their way, climbing higher into the western mountains. The sun was starting to set, the shadows of the forest growing more bold.

"He's very upset, you know," the lynx said as they crossed a clearing filled with tall brown grass.

"Who is?" Hellboy asked, running the palm of his left hand along the top of the waist-high grass.

"Dyavo Mahr."

"Holding out on me, eh?" Hellboy said as they entered another, thicker section of woods. "Last piece of candy you'll get from me."

A stray leaf blew by in the cool, gentle wind, and the lynx pounced on it. "I've heard some things," it said, leaning down to smell its prey. "He's angry because he's been forgotten. It's quite sad, really."

"My heart's breakin'," Hellboy said, ducking his head to avoid a low-hanging branch. "So have you talked to him recently?"

Forgetting the leaf, the Krukis padded along beside him. "Last night I encountered him with the children from the village."

It had become like night in this part of the woods, the darkness again victorious over the day.

"He hasn't hurt them, has he?"

"Not yet," said the lynx.

"The clock's ticking then. I gotta hurry."

Slowly but steadily they were climbing higher into the Apuseni. As far as mountains went, they were not all that high, so he figured they had to be getting closer.

"Oh yes," the lynx said in agreement. "The clock is ticking, for everybody. Dyavo wants to be feared again before his end, to remind the world that he once held them in a grip of terror."

"Grip of terror," Hellboy repeated. "Got it."

The forest began to thin and they found themselves standing before what appeared to be a wall of solid limestone. Hellboy reached out with his left hand to touch the cool, white rock. "What's up?" he asked his forest guide. "Do we go around, or what?"

The lynx sat on the ground and began to groom itself. "I'm not going anywhere," it said with finality. "You've reached your destination."

Hellboy was about to ask the forest spirit for an explanation when a thick patch of clouds parted in the night sky, and rays of pale, yellow moonlight shone upon the rock face. "Would you look at that," he said as the sudden light revealed an opening in the limestone. "Why am I always so surprised?"

He unclipped a flashlight from the side of his work belt and shone it inside. "It's a cave all right. Let's get going."

"I go no further," the Krukis said. "How far did you think a little piece of chocolate would get you? I've done more than enough. Good luck," the creature said, casually sauntering back into the forest.

Hellboy watched the spirit go. "Thanks for the help," he called after it, a little disappointed to be losing his companion.

The lynx turned and stared at him, its animal eyes glowing an eerie red in the moonlit wood. "I didn't know creatures from Hell could be so pleasant," it said, sounding genuinely surprised.

Hellboy shrugged. "I'm just a guy doing a job."

"Interesting," said the Krukis. It padded deeper into the forest, and, blending with the shadows, was gone.

According to Kate, the Apuseni Mountains were like a great white chunk of Swiss cheese, thoroughly carved through by underground rivers over thousands of years, and from what Hellboy could see, her intel was right on the money.

He shone the beam of his flashlight around the vast cave, the sound of distant, underground streams making him feel as though his ear was pressed to a seashell. The path he took descended into the base of the mountain, crossing a huge, natural bridge where, at one time, a powerful river had eroded itself passage. He directed his light over the edge of the bridge to see how far it was to the bottom, but all he saw was a sea of black.

"Don't want to be going down there," he muttered, returning the light to his path.

He was looking for some kind of sign, something to prove he was on the right track, when the beam of his flashlight fell upon something startlingly colorful against the yellow-white limestone of the bridge. He snatched up a piece of blue ribbon, the kind worn in a little girl's hair, knowing at that moment that this was where he was supposed to be.

The passage dipped down precariously, the floor slick beneath his hooves, and he was careful to not lose his footing. The darkness seemed to be closing in on him, and he stopped to the check the flashlight.

"Stupid batteries," he complained, slapping the light against his palm, thinking that would somehow fix it. But it only made matters worse, the light dimming to nearly nothing. Knowing that he was fresh out of new batteries, Hellboy tossed the flashlight. "Can't believe this," he griped, reaching into his satchel for the matches he carried. "C'mon, c'mon." His fingers fumbled over stray silver bullets, a pack of Tic Tacs, a button from his coat ...

Hellboy continued to move forward as he searched his bag, and in the darkness, his foot caught on a rock. He tried to catch himself, but to no avail. "You stupid son of ...," he hollered, tumbling down the incline in the pitch black of the cave.

The floor finally leveled slightly, and he was able at last to stop himself. More embarrassed than anything else, he clambered to his feet, dusting himself off as he glanced around. It was lighter here, an eerie glow coming from an area not too far up ahead and around a bend.

Hellboy moved slowly toward the source of light, cautiously turning the corner. The passage before him led down into an open cavern lit with candles—candles inside of human skulls.

"Cute," he said, proceeding down the path, fire flickering inside the eyes of the skulls to light his way.

"These are the heads of my fallen enemies." The voice from inside the chamber was like fingernails on a blackboard, and he felt the hair on the back of his neck bristle. "Enter so that I may add your own to my collection."

"Sorry," Hellboy said as he stepped into the low-ceilinged chamber. "The Smithsonian's already got first dibs on my coconut."

Skull lanterns were placed throughout the chamber, and the floor was littered with a variety of bones, some from local wildlife, and some not. "Nice place you got here. Are heat and utilities included?"

The monster offered no response, but Hellboy could sense his enemy somewhere in the pools of shadow on the ledges overlooking the cavern, watching his every move.

Hellboy was ready, tensed to repel the inevitable attack, when he heard the tiniest of whimpers. Zeroing in on the pathetic sound, he found the children from the village. There were five of them, three girls and two boys, the oldest not more than seven. They were tied up and crammed inside a cage that was, surprise, surprise, also made of bones. He was relieved to see that, though scratched, bruised, and filthy, they appeared to be otherwise unharmed.

As he walked toward the cage, they began to scream and cry.

"Shhhhh, that's enough of that," Hellboy said, holding up his hands in a non-threatening gesture. "I'm here to make sure you get back to your folks."

The children continued to carry on, pressing themselves to the sides of the bone cage, refusing to look at him. He reached out, grabbed hold of the door, and tore it away from the cage. "C'mon out, it's all right," he said, speaking softly. The children stared with teary, fear-filled eyes. They didn't trust him, and really, who could blame them.

"Isn't it strange," came that creepy voice again. It was closer now, but he still couldn't pinpoint its exact location. "You have come to save the babies, but they are just as afraid of you as they are of the one who snatched them from their beds."

Hellboy looked back into the cage. A boy, obviously the oldest of the five, was looking at him inquisitively, a glimmer of something that could have been trust in his eyes. "What's your name, kid?" he asked the child in rusty Romanian.

"Jon," the boy answered in little more than a whisper.

"Is what he said true, Jon? Am I as scary as him?" He pointed out into the darkness of the cave.

Jon thought for a moment and shook his head. The other children cowering behind him slowly did the same.

"Come on out then," he coaxed.

The children tentatively inched toward the opening.

"Promise I won't bite," Hellboy said, carefully helping them out of the cage, one at a time.

Something moved on the darkened ledge above them.

"But I have made no such promise," hissed the voice of the monster, as it leapt down to the floor of the cave.

Hellboy reacted instinctively, pulling the last of the children from the cage, and stood between them and the attacking beast. He brought back his right hand, ready to pound the monster's face, but found himself pulling the punch instead.

"Dyavo Mahr?" he asked the thin, leering beast who landed in a stumbling crouch before him. The B.P.R.D. file had described Dyavo Mahr as a powerful demonic entity, a dangerous predator that was to be approached with extreme caution.

Confused, Hellboy studied the figure before him; its sickly gray skin stretched tightly over sharp, angular bones, sparse, downy tufts of hair atop its sore-covered skull reminding Hellboy of something he had once seen growing on an old piece of fruit in his refrigerator.

The monster smiled, a near toothless grin. "You remember me," he hissed gleefully, nodding as he spoke. "As I remember you."

"What the hell happened?" Hellboy asked incredulously. "You've been sick?"

Dyavo Mahr sneered, a thick, pointed tongue the color of rancid meat passing over scabbed and bleeding lips. "Sick of the world, and how easily its inhabitants dismiss that which once caused them to cower in the darkness of their hovels, hearts filled with terror, praying for the coming of dawn.

"I am sick from being forgotten," he spat. "And will stand for it no more." One of the children began to cry, and Hellboy couldn't blame the kid; he was getting pretty sick of this business himself.

"Why don't you guys go wait for me over there," Hellboy suggested, gesturing back to the chamber entrance. "I'll take you home just as soon as I'm finished here."

"They are going nowhere!" Dyavo Mahr roared, scrambling toward them, spider-like, across the floor of the cave, bits of dry bone scattering with his frenetic approach. "Once you are dead, I will feast upon their soft, delicate flesh in celebration."

Hellboy reached for his gun, with one fluid motion, pulling it from the holster hanging at his side and aiming it at the approaching demon.

"That's close enough," he warned, squinting down the thick barrel of the pistol, his finger twitching on the hairpin trigger. At this range he doubted that even he could miss.

Dyavo recoiled, hissing like a vampire with a face full of crucifix. Then he began to cough uncontrollably.

Keeping one eye on the hacking beast, Hellboy again motioned the children in the direction of the cave entrance. "Go on," he said. "Wait for me over there." He had no idea how this was going to turn out, and he didn't want them to see anything that would give them nightmares, although being taken from their beds by a demon and put inside a cage made of bones had likely placed them well on the road to lifelong therapy.

The older kid, Jon, was taking on the role of team leader, corralling the others and ushering them toward the cave mouth as Hellboy turned back to the pathetic creature that had summoned him here.

Dyavo Mahr was still trying to catch his breath. He had fallen to his knees, rocking from side to side as he attempted to suppress the bone-rattling coughs.

"Need a glass of water?" Hellboy asked, as he lowered his gun. *What do you say to a demon that's on the verge of barking up a lung?*

The monster gulped at the air. "Mock me while you can, hellbeast," he growled between gurgling breaths. "You may have beaten me once, but this day, victory will be mine."

Hellboy looked around and then back to the demon kneeling on the ground before him, wracking his memory for any trace of the familiar, and finding nothing. This place—this monster's lair—could have been one of thousands he had entered throughout his career with the B.P.R.D. But Dyavo Mahr was so pitiful, he almost felt guilty for not remembering.

Hellboy returned the gun to its holster.

"You seem to remember the time we fought pretty good," he said to the demon as it slowly rose to its feet upon trembling, bowed legs. "Why don't you refresh my memory?"

Dyavo smiled horribly, his large head atop a pencil-thin neck nodding in understanding. "Of course, you wish to delay the inevitability of your demise. I suppose I could find it within myself to grant you this last request."

Hellboy rolled his eyes and motioned for the demon to go on.

A milky film seemed to cloud the demon's bulging eyes. "It was a day still talked about by the dark denizens of this region, and even by those beyond it," he said wistfully. "The miners of Balanbanya had stumbled across one of my many lairs littering these mountains, awakening me from my centuries-long slumber."

Dyavo rubbed his bony hands together, thick trails of saliva oozing from the corners of his mouth as he spoke. "I fed upon them for their impertinence, gorging myself with their delicious flesh and bones. It had been long since I last feasted on the meat of humans, and it awakened in me a hunger most voracious." He wiped the spittle from his chin with the back of a spotted hand.

"So you ate some miners, and then they called me," Hellboy interjected, attempting to move the story along.

The monster nodded, a look of annoyance upon his wan features. "Yes, they summoned you, their monstrous champion, and the mountains shook with the intensity of our battle."

Dyavo Mahr smiled again, his dark eyes glistening wetly. The skin on his face was pulled so tight that Hellboy was surprised it didn't rip. "You remember that battle, don't you?" he said, pointing a clawed finger at him. "I can see it in your eyes. Oh, yes."

Hellboy shook his head. "No. Not really, but if you say so. No offense, but I've kicked a lot of grave-monkey ass over the last twenty years or so, and I'm sorry to say I've kinda forgotten most of 'em."

On spindly legs the demon again lunged forward. "You lie!" he screeched, his face twisted in a strange mixture of rage and disbelief. "You have to remember—the mountains, they trembled with the ferocity of our battle."

Hellboy recoiled as the demon grabbed the front of his coat with skeletal hands. "You *must* remember!"

The first rock hit Dyavo Mahr in the face, just below the cheekbone. The demon released Hellboy and stumbled back. A large gash had been opened in the paper-thin flesh at the jutting cheekbone, and black blood as thick as tar began to ooze from the wound. The second rock struck him in the shoulder, followed by another to the head that knocked him to the ground.

Hellboy turned to see the oldest child, Jon, let fly with another stone.

"Leave him alone!" the boy cried, reaching down to the cave floor for more ammunition. "He has come to help us, you wicked ugly thing!"

The other children were now throwing rocks with varying degrees of success, a rain of stones falling upon the pathetic beast.

"Hey, knock it off!" Hellboy bellowed, his booming command reverberating throughout the underground cavern. The children froze, another volley of rocks dropping from their hands.

"He was going to hurt you," Jon said in all seriousness as Hellboy approached.

"Yeah, thanks for your concern," he said, picking up one of the candle skulls and handing it to the boy. "Take this and follow the tunnel," he instructed. "This is no place for you."

"Are you going to kill him?" Jon asked, his eyes glinting maliciously in the candlelight.

Hellboy didn't know how to answer and chose to ignore the question. "I'll catch up with you in a bit," he said instead, giving the boy a slight push.

Jon did as he was told and headed out of the cave, holding the illuminated skull to his chest, a line of younger children following behind him.

"Be careful," Hellboy yelled after them, remembering the tumble he had taken earlier. He wasn't too sure how safe the kids would be alone, but didn't imagine that he would be here much longer. They would be all right till then.

He then returned his attention to Dyavo Mahr. The monster was curled in a ball on the ground, its frail frame again wracked with powerful fits of coughing. He suspected that there wasn't much time left for the monster, that nature would soon be running its course.

"Oh, how they feared me," Dyavo croaked. "When the night fell across the Apuseni, they would gather up their young and barricade themselves in their homes."

Dyavo slowly, painfully climbed to his feet, his body covered with bleeding welts and bruises from the children's anger.

"It was *me* they feared," he said, touching his sunken chest with long, trembling fingers. "*I* was the terror that came for them in the night."

"Yeah," Hellboy said, sharing a strange moment of empathy with the demon. "You musta been something."

It made him feel kinda dirty.

Dyavo Mahr slowly nodded his large head. "Yes," he hissed. "Yes I was." He started to cough again, and Hellboy saw that there was blood now leaking from his mouth. The demon fell against the cave wall, too weak to stand. "But that was long ago."

Hellboy turned to leave.

"Wait!" Dyavo cried, gasping for air. "Where are you going?"

Hellboy didn't even turn around. "I'm done here," he said, staring into the darkness of the passage that would take him from the monster's lair beneath the Apuseni. He thought he could hear the kids in the distance. It sounded like they were singing.

Cute.

"How dare you turn your back on me," the creature warned.

He listened to the sounds as Dyavo came away from the wall.

"I was he whose name they refused to say, in fear that I would overhear, and come for their wives and children."

Hellboy was ready to go; the stink of death was so bad here it was starting to make him feel sick.

"Not even their prayers to the great Christian God could chase me away," Dyavo Mahr growled. "I hid beneath the earth and slept, waiting for them to grow complacent—then I showed them what fear truly was."

He could hear the demon's ragged breathing, his stumbling gait, as he came closer.

"You will show me the respect I deserve."

The demon's clawed hand fell hard upon his shoulder.

"Give me what I most desire," he demanded. The words echoed in the cavern.

At last Hellboy turned, looking deeply into the eyes of the creature, understanding the true reason why the monster had summoned him here.

The gun slid from its holster with ease. "You're too much of a threat to live," Hellboy said to the demon of the mountains as he aimed and pulled the trigger. He was certain he saw the demon smile as it staggered toward him.

Weak, yet putting on its best mask of savagery, Dyavo Mahr lunged.

The single gunshot sounded like a clap of thunder within the confines of the cave, a precursor to the most savage of storms.

The force of the shot threw Dyavo Mahr backward onto a pile of bones, a smoldering black hole in the center of his sunken chest.

"I was the scourge of the night," Dyavo whispered, black blood bubbling over his lips, as he at last died atop a bed of his victims' bones.

"Yep, you were something," Hellboy agreed.

The demon breathed its last. The decay of its flesh was instantaneous, oily wisps of foul-smelling smoke rising up to writhe cobra-like in the air of the cave.

Hellboy felt a strange satisfaction, a sense that he had done something right—something humane. He had no idea why he'd given Dyavo Mahr that small mercy. But he wondered if he'd be that lucky when his time came, if he'd go out with some dignity.

He turned toward the chamber entrance, moving forward into the darkness of the tunnel, drawn to the sounds of children's voices raised in song.

He wondered.

THE THRICE-NAMED HILL

GRAHAM JOYCE

Liz Sherman was waiting for Hellboy as he climbed out of the helicopter. With her, collar of a trench-coat turned up around her ears, was Gina Brown, a medium from the British Paranormal Society. By way of greeting, Liz extended a long, elegant finger in the direction of the sodden, uncanny mound of earth behind her. "There is your thrice-named hill," she said.

The limestone hill was a freak of nature in the otherwise flat Midlands geography. The land had pushed up this weird and solitary outcrop of rock, an eruption in the earth that seemed in the lilac dusk and rain to swell like a singular dark tumor. A small village clustered around the foot and lower slopes of the hill. At the very top, perched almost precariously, was an ancient church. The place was called Breedon-on-the-hill.

A fresh squall had brought with it more rain. "I'm afraid you're not seeing the best of our English weather," Gina Brown said. Gina was a statuesque and beautiful English woman of about the same age as Liz Sherman.

"Never have," Hellboy said gruffly. "But you're forgetting that I was born near this place." Hellboy knew it was an English trait to talk endlessly about the weather. So far as he remembered, there were only three types of weather in England: light rain, heavy rain, and raining six-inch nails.

"It's probably a good thing," Liz said. "It will keep people away."

"The villagers are spooked. They won't go near it," Gina said. "Are you ready to go up?"

"Am I ever," Hellboy said.

The church squatting on the crest of the steep hill was already cast in gloomy silhouette. Moment by moment the rain-streaked sky was turning the color of heated steel. Hewn from gray local stone, its rough outline and squat tower formed a knuckled fist raised at the scudding clouds. The church couldn't be said to grace the hill: it burdened it, and almost threatened to topple.

A direct ascent being too steep, the church was approached by a worn path coiling the hill. "Odd place to settle a church," Hellboy said.

"Everything about this place is odd," Liz said grimly.

"The locals say there's a reason for it being built up there," Gina said. "There's a legend."

Liz Sherman turned up her collar like Gina's. "There always is."

Hellboy was present because the B.P.R.D. had responded to an unusual British request. A small archaeological team from the University of Leicester had gone missing while cutting a trench into the ancient hill. The hill itself was partly natural terrain, but had been built higher and reinforced by the Ancient Britons long before the arrival of the Romans. Whether it was developed as a burial mound or as a defensive fortification was unknown. The presence of the medieval church—itself over seven hundred years old—had restricted excavation immediately below its stone floor.

Archaeologists from the university had been called in when the graveyard on the eastern side of the church had begun to sink. Graves had either dropped a few feet through the topsoil or in some cases seemed to have been swallowed altogether. This led to suspicion that a hollowed chamber in the mound below the church was causing the subsidence.

Hellboy was intrigued. Breedon-on-the-hill was no more than fifty miles from his birthplace of East Bromwich. The return to the familiar landscape of the English Midlands pleased and perturbed him at the same time. Though he'd been raised in the U.S., he'd returned several times over the years, trying to gather rare threads of information about his origins.

Sometimes Hellboy just wanted to sniff the wind.

"Tell us about that legend," Liz asked Gina, breathing hard as they made their ascent. The path coiled round the hill several times.

"The church was built to cap or contain some evil force," Gina said. "The other side of the hill has been quarried from time to time over the centuries, with the occasional disappearance of workmen, just frequent enough to keep the story alive. The villagers are twitchy. They'll talk about it, but you can't get past the superstitions."

Hellboy, meanwhile, was strangely quiet. Liz flicked a nervous glance in his direction. She'd seen this mood in him before.

"We know the settlement here is very old," Gina continued. "There are iron-age ramparts near the top of the hill. The word Bree is the Ancient Briton word for 'hill.' Centuries later the Saxons forgot the meaning of the word and added their own name 'don,' which also means hill. Centuries passed again, and the English speakers added their word. Thus the thrice-named hill."

"Great," Hellboy said. "So I've come all this way just to walk up hill-hill-on-the-hill."

"That's about it," Gina said. Then she turned to Liz. "Is Hellboy always this much fun?"

"Not usually," Liz replied.

On reaching the top, Gina produced an iron key for the huge oak door of the church. As she rattled the iron in the lock, fresh gusts of wind lashed rain in their faces. Though they were in a hurry to get inside, Hellboy seemed to falter.

"What is it?" Liz whispered.

"I don't know. Come on. Let's go in."

Gina banged the church door behind them, shutting out the foul weather. A couple of bulbs burned a dull light at the altar end of the church. As they surveyed the church, Liz's eyes were drawn to the collection of pale stone carvings, some complete, some fragments. The ornate, decorative scrollwork included figures of saints and more enigmatic human forms, plus friezes of hybrid birds, serpents, and animals. Some of the bird or dragon figures had long tails coiling around themselves several times. "These carvings are older than the church," Liz said.

"Much older," Gina agreed. "These are Saxon carvings from a monastery that was here long before the church was built."

"There's something even older here," Hellboy said.

"You feel it, too?" Gina said.

"Feel it? I can breathe it. I know it, but I don't know how."

The ancient stone carvings appeared to add up to some kind of a story. But too many of them were missing. The weird, hybrid birds and the fierce-looking saints glowered back from the shadows folded into the pale stone.

Liz wandered deeper into the church. "Hey!" she shouted. "Come and look at this! Remind you of anyone?"

Hellboy and Gina crossed the church to look at another carving Liz had found. It showed a serpent-like figure in combat with a horned man. Time had chewed away at the carving so that it was impossible to see clearly. The man was either holding a club or his arm was powerfully distended.

"You know something?" Hellboy said, not entirely amused. "I'd like to be left alone here to figure things out."

"Not a good idea," Gina said, squinting about her. "I feel some hideous menace in this place." She sniffed the air. "It's almost like a ... like a—"

"Like a perfume," Hellboy answered with distracted formality. "Please. If you wouldn't mind."

Liz put a hand on Gina's arm. "We'll be nearby. We've arranged to stay at the Three Horseshoes Inn."

They left. The oak door of the church banged shut behind them.

Hellboy listened. He listened to the silence. There was something familiar about this place, something he couldn't identify. It wasn't the building: he'd never been here before. Neither was it the carvings, the stones he'd never before looked upon. It was something else.

The altar of the church was a simple table draped in a fine cloth of royal blue. The cloth bore a heraldic, Celtic-style cross. Beside the altar was a carved chair, like a throne, upholstered in rich scarlet. Hellboy seated himself in the chair, brooding on the secret of the place, the perturbing familiarity.

That scent. That familiar odor. Nothing like the incense normally associated with churches and temples. It was a musky, almost-animal smell he felt he knew deep down, or had known for thousands of years. It was there, lurking amid the ancient church smells of old plaster and damp stone and beeswax polish. He could trace it all around him now. It seemed to be leaking from the darkest corners of the church. How he knew that scent! If only he could remember what it was, he could easily solve the secret of the thrice-named hill.

Hellboy got out of his seat and began to prowl the church once more. Outside, the wind howled around the tower and rain lashed at the stained-glass windows. Under his feet was an inscription in the stone floor. The words were almost effaced by the passage of feet, but Hellboy could make out some of them. "Sanctus Aerdulfus Rex," the inscription read. Hellboy stooped to read more. The inscription was too worn. He traced his finger over words that might have been "wyrm-slayer," and then, perhaps, "conjoiner of peace."

The great slab on which the words were chiseled seemed to Hellboy to stand slightly proud of the others. It rocked slightly as he shifted his weight. "Okay," Hellboy growled. "Let's get you out of there."

The thick slab was perhaps eight foot by four, and two inches thick, but its removal presented no problem for Hellboy. The stone made a grinding noise as he slid it from its bed. Underneath was a lead coffin. Hellboy knew instantly that the coffin was empty. The lid of the coffin had been dislodged only by an inch or so, but enough to reveal an empty case. There was however something mysterious about the base of the coffin. The metal was twisted and perforated with small holes. Hellboy reached down to run his hand along the base of the coffin.

It was a mistake.

As soon as his hand touched the base of the coffin, the metal crumpled like foil and his hand went straight through. Taken by surprise, Hellboy was propelled into the coffin itself, which splintered along with the stone floor all around it. Hellboy plunged his arms straight through the earth underneath, and fell, dragging other slabs along with him in a grinding and clattering of earth and masonry as part of the floor of the church dropped through into a wide chamber beneath.

When Hellboy emerged from the rubble, he took a look round.

"Looks like someone has been busy!"

He was in a dome-like cavern. It was dark, but dimly lit by a strange blue phosphorescent light that seemed to emanate from irregular, odd patches on the floor and on the walls. The blue light had about it a faint pulsing, like a mysterious signaling.

But Hellboy wasn't looking at the light. He was more concerned with making an assessment of the piles of human bones in the place. Full skeletons and detached bones littered the floor. Hundreds of them. This was no ossuary: the bones had not been carefully placed there by some diligent monk tending the remains of his holy predecessors. They had been scattered around with abandon. There were also in the dome two or three massive horseshoe-shaped bands of rusting iron.

All of the skulls, when examined, proved to share a common feature. They had a hole punctured in the rear cortex. Some of the skeletons were still attired in rags. Others again were draped in more modern garments, maybe clothes from the last century or even more recent. There were more to find: Hellboy had discovered the fate of the team of archaeologists.

"You were right, boys and girls. There is a chamber inside the hill. Though you're not going to be able to tell anyone now. Not unless we can find your brains and squirt 'em back into your skulls."

Hellboy examined one of the corpses. The skin on the female archaeologist's face was intact, but it hung over the skull and neck like a flag from a pole on a windless afternoon. A hole had been made near the base of the skull and though the brain remained in place, all moisture had been drained from it. It was dry and hard, like a large walnut. Hellboy shook it. The withered organ of absconded intelligence rattled against the inside of the skull.

Hellboy tossed the thing away. "Looks like something had you guys for the main course," he said. His voice echoed around the chamber. He kicked lightly at one of the giant iron horseshoes. "Wonder what they have in mind for dessert."

"I think we know the answer to that," said a female voice from behind him.

Hellboy turned.

It was a woman, obscured by shadows. She lay in the corner, on her belly, propped up by her elbows. She was smiling at him. The eerie, blue light rippled across her face. She shook her long dark hair, a mass of raven tresses, and smiled again.

Hellboy thought she was perhaps the most beautiful woman he had ever seen. And she seemed oddly familiar.

"It's been a long time," she said.

"We know each other?" Hellboy said.

"Oh yes."

"No. I don't think so." He gestured at the mound of bones and the exsanguinated corpses. "This your handiwork?"

She ignored the question. "Though you looked very different last time we were together. I'm not sure I like the way you are now. Perhaps I'll get used to it."

"Get used to it? Here's a newsflash. You and me are not going to be spending a lot of time together."

Hellboy wanted to sound confident, but she had him wrong-footed. Who was she? Why did she feel he knew her so well? Then it occurred to him, the scent he'd picked up and recognized in the church above—he knew now that it was her scent, her special odor. Somehow it had the capacity to attract him and repel him at the same time.

"You're remembering," she said.

"Why don't you come out of the shadows?" he said. "Let me take a closer look at you."

She licked her lips with her tongue. "I'm comfortable where I am. And I've just dined. I'd rather relax if you don't mind."

Hellboy stepped forward, squinting at her in the blue light, trying to remember where he'd seen those features, haunting and beautiful, before. Then he understood where the phosphorescent light in the dome was coming from. It was emanating from her. A gentle sheen of blue light crossed her face.

He knew that light, in the same way he knew that scent.

She shook her mass of jet-black curls again, and there on her upper brow, hidden until now by her luxuriant head of hair, Hellboy glimpsed a pair of sparkling horns.

"I think your relaxing days are done," Hellboy said.

She inched her body forward, and the walls of the cavern rippled at the same time. Indeed Hellboy got the distinct impression that the walls had moved inward, toward him. She wriggled forward again. The walls moved inward again at the same time.

"Good trick," Hellboy said, suddenly feeling a little less confident than he'd been a moment earlier. "How do you make that happen?"

"I'm full of surprises," she said. This time she reared up in front of Hellboy, until she'd drawn herself up to his height. Then she rose higher, and still higher. Hellboy saw now that the lower half of her body was all serpent's tail, scaled and glittering, and it was the scales that were winking and gleaming with blue light. The walls moved closer as she ascended higher over him, and Hellboy suddenly understood that the walls were not constructed of brick or earth or any other building material; they were organic. The living walls comprised her tail, coiled round and round, all the time moving in toward him.

Hellboy ran at the soft tissue of the tail-wall and punched a hole between the coils with his unstoppable right fist.

Liz and Gina were taking a quiet drink in the nearby Three Horseshoes Inn. They'd managed to fend off the questions of the landlord, and the hostile stares of one or two locals had given way. The inn itself sailed under the sign of the Worshipful Masters of the Association of Farriers: a good-fortune symbol of three iron horseshoes in triangle formation, all points downwards. The iron horseshoe was, in these parts, a traditional amulet against evil.

Liz and Gina, tucked into a snug corner of the old alehouse, were discussing this when they heard the fearful scream. The burly landlord, collecting glasses from the tables, was just passing at that same moment. A beer glass slipped from his fingers, and it splintered on the tile floor.

When the landlord recovered, it was merely to bellow, "See your beers orf, ladies and gentlemen! We're about to close!"

"You're 'alf an hour early," one youth protested, stubbornly replacing his full glass of bitter on the table before him. "You ain't called time yit!"

The landlord stepped across the room and without warning enclosed the lad in a fierce headlock. He then waltzed the youth to the door and bundled him outside. After slamming the door after the lad the landlord shouted. "Time! Anyone else want to argue? No? Well sup up and sod off, 'cos tonight it's early doors!"

The handful of other drinkers finished their drinks and made their way out, and as they did so the landlord spoke to Liz and Gina in a hushed tone. "Excuse me, ladies, but as you're staying the night, I'll be locking you in."

"What's happening?" Liz wanted to know. "What was that scream?"

The landlord gave no answer. He checked outside the door after his last customer, switched off the outside lights, and slammed home the giant bolts on the pub door. Then he helped himself to a bottle of scotch, produced a shotgun from behind the bar, and proceeded to climb the stairs. "Goodnight, ladies. Don't be too long."

"Give him a moment to settle down," Liz whispered. "But we're going to have to go back up to the church."

They found a back way out of the Three Horseshoes, took the key, and locked the door behind them. Within a few minutes they were ascending the hill once more, re-ascending the spiral path.

The dreadful shriek had come from the serpent woman. She shrieked loud and long, but her tail merely responded in a whiplash movement that tightened a noose around Hellboy. In a slithering, swishing instant she had coiled her tail around him, whisking him off his feet and in the air.

Hellboy smashed down at her with his mighty fist, and she released him and shrank back. Reaching for one of the giant horseshoes, Hellboy used it to pin her by the throat, punching the prongs of the horseshoe through the earth ceiling. She was trapped. Her eyes fizzed with fire and she turned her stare on him. Then she opened her jaws and released a cloud of venomous gas directly into his face.

The gas was enough to make him retreat. But when he inhaled it, he identified it as the source of the perfume that had been troubling him so long. It had the power to disorient him, and he lost his hold on the horseshoe at her throat. It came clanging to the floor as she reared up again, lashing her tail around him. This time she made no mistake, coiling her tail around his arms, trapping his strongest weapon against his side.

He was helpless. He couldn't fight back. His mighty arm had been rendered useless and the breath was slowly being squeezed out of him. Her grip was stronger than that of any python, and she was several times larger. With Hellboy limp inside the coils of her tail, she reared up and began to nuzzle gently at the base of his skull.

Hellboy felt himself fainting away, the scent of the serpent woman drenching him as he almost lost consciousness. Almost senseless from the effects of the venomous gas, Hellboy tossed back his head, and, using his neck as a spring, he powered his mouth into her scaly tail, biting down hard, shredding skin, biting deeper.

She howled with pain. Hellboy felt her blood gush into his mouth. The taste of it stunned him again. The moment he tasted her blood, he knew who she was, and also knew that he could no more kill her than she could kill him.

As she writhed and screamed, Hellboy struggled to break free from her grip. Already he felt his strength returning and more, her blood making him stronger.

The rain had eased slightly by the time Liz and Gina reached the church at the top of the hill. They heard the second scream before they had the creaking, heavy door open. Inside they found the hole through which Hellboy had fallen, in the middle of the aisle, near the altar. Earth and slabs had been kicked up after he'd dropped clean through. Some of the neighboring slabs had dislodged but seemed secure. Cautiously, fearing further collapse, they peered over the edge together.

"He's got to be down there somewhere," Liz said.

"Where is that light coming from?" Gina wanted to know. "It's all over the place. And what's that strange smell?"

"I'm going to have to go down there. Stay here. Gina, I might need you to help me out."

"How will you get down?"

Liz glanced around the church. Then she looked toward the tower. "Bell ropes."

They were able to climb the tower and unhook the bell ropes. Gina anchored the thick sturdy rope to the leg of a pew while Liz tied the other end round her waist. They used the column of the heavy stone font to pay out the line.

Liz found herself being lowered into the winking, phosphorescent gloom.

"Can you see him?" she heard Gina calling from above.

"Not yet," she whispered. "I'm going to have a look around."

Liz trod carefully in the dim light. Something crunched underfoot. She soon became aware that she was treading on a carpet of bones. Unless her eyes were deceiving her, the blue walls seemed to be expanding and contracting very slightly, like a set of lungs.

At last she saw Hellboy propped awkwardly in the corner. He seemed to be sleepy. He blinked lazily. Liz was about to open her mouth when she saw something terrible behind him.

It was a huge serpent—or rather it was a giant, gleaming worm with the body of a woman. Hellboy hadn't seemed to realize that the snake-woman was rearing behind him, poised to strike. The woman part of the hybrid creature was strangely beautiful. She was naked and her skin glowed an ethereal blue. She was so focused on Hellboy that she didn't seem aware that Liz had entered the chamber. Liz took a tiny step closer, trying to roll her tread across the bones underfoot, terrified that a bone would crack out a warning.

The serpent-woman moved very slowly. Her eyes had a soft glow to them, like the eyes of someone satiated, almost loving, Liz thought. But there was a flicker in her mouth of a forked tongue. Liz knew as she reared slowly behind Hellboy that she was choosing a spot to strike.

Liz knew she could marshal her pyrotechnic powers to put a fire in the mouth of the serpent. But Hellboy was too close. The snake-thing was but a hair's breadth away from him.

Liz tried to speak in an underbreath, willing Hellboy to hear her. "Hellboy," she said. "Don't move."

Hellboy stirred lazily. He hadn't heard. He was grasping his ribs. She could see he was wounded.

"Hellboy!" Liz said again, in a louder whisper. This time she'd caught his attention. "Don't move an inch!"

"Liz!" said Hellboy.

"Keep perfectly still." She rolled her eyes to signal the enemy behind him.

Hellboy blinked. "Behind me? Oh, you mean her?"

The serpent-woman recoiled slightly and turned her glare on Liz.

"Don't be thinking of burning anybody," Hellboy said, holding up the palm of his hand. "Let me introduce you two."

"Your *sister*?" Liz said.

"That's right," Hellboy said. "I should have known immediately. But it's been so long."

"But Bruttenholm found you in 1944 and you were just a kid then," Liz said. "She's got to have been down here a thousand years at least. How can she be your sister? How could you recognize her?"

"Not her," Hellboy said. "The smell of her. I knew I recognized it. It's ... from before. It's family."

"Our father was worshipped all across this land. He had many children. My little brother may be the youngest, but we have brothers and sisters scattered far and wide," the snake-woman said. "Our father was worshipped at this place, and I, too, once had a shrine here. I am as old as memory, and my name has changed more times than this hill. But in the change of ages I was buried here by incantation, imprisoned by holy ritual. They trapped me beneath the church and coiled my body around the hill. Then they covered it with earth and called in sorcerer-farriers to stake my coiled body to the ground with giant horseshoes of detested iron. The spiral path you see around the hill is only the worm-cast of my form.

"For centuries the local people ceremonially walked the spiral path in an annual ritual designed to hammer the horseshoes in place by the weight of their footfall. But the people forgot. Terror faded. Stories changed to superstitions, and the rituals died out. Meanwhile the iron pins rusted, and the earth beneath the church shifted.

"At last I was able to move again, set free by the same bungled ritual that drew my brother to this plane. The worm-cast spiral path became a tunnel through which I could drag myself. I dug out this chamber beneath the church. My needs were few. With the graveyard overhead I could feed myself on the recently buried. Occasionally I might supplement my diet with the feckless priest or two, or hapless lovers fornicating in the graveyard, or quarriers or other diggers who came too near my lair."

"The archaeologists," said Liz.

"Then came ... my brother," she said. "And my memory was stirred."

And here she turned on Hellboy an expression of such tender love and devotion that Liz was shocked. The snake-woman nestled her head on his shoulder, and she drew her tail closer to him. Liz felt a prickle of rivalry.

"And my memory, too," Hellboy said. "I don't like the reminder of what I am, but I can't deny she is what she says."

"But what will you do?" Liz blurted. "We were sent here to destroy her!"

"I know that," the snake-woman said. "And for that reason I have put myself under his protection."

"She had the power to destroy me," Hellboy said. "Easily. She squeezed the wind out of me, but when I tasted her blood I knew who she was. Knew what that smell meant. And now nothing is simple."

It was true: normally for Hellboy it was easy. Confronted by a monster or a beast or a chimera, he pulverized it and walked away. This was different. And agonizing.

"But we can't just walk away from this," Liz said.

"Where's Gina?" Hellboy wanted to know.

"She's waiting for us in the church."

"She doesn't have to know anything."

"No," said Liz.

"The Bureau's my home, Liz. And it's yours, too. How different is my sister from me? I've got to think things through. I may need help with this. She's agreed to let me put her back to sleep, under the earth, until I can figure out what to do."

Liz looked at the subdued snake-woman.

"I trust my brother," she said, reading Liz's mind.

"You can," Liz said. "You can."

"All right," Hellboy said. "There are some things we have to do here. I'll come and speak to Gina. You'll need her to talk to the locals. I'll fix the hole in the church. You must tell them: no more quarrying or archaeology. Tell them it will cause mudslides and bring the church down on top of them. At least that's true."

Liz nodded slowly. "I'll help any way I can."

Hellboy and Liz returned to the hole in the chamber and called Gina. "We're coming up!"

Liz and Hellboy told Gina that they had found nothing, but that the hillside was in danger of crumbling. She blinked. If she didn't believe them, she knew better than to argue. Liz and Gina returned to the Three Horseshoes and prepared their story for the next day. Hellboy also repaired the hole in the church and replaced the stone slabs there. But not before he had made good his farewells.

After she had coiled herself in her spiraling earth tunnel, wrapped around the hill, she said, "Kiss me, brother. We're made of the same essence, you and I."

Hellboy got ready to replace the incantatory slabs over her head. He was not certain that what she said was precisely true, but it was not entirely false, either.

"I wait for you," she said.

He kissed his sister. She lay down her head in the broken, bone-strewn chamber beneath the church. Hellboy climbed out of the chamber, rebuilt the floor with the solid planks of hefty, wooden pews, covered them over with earth, and re-laid the slabs. The last stone fell into place with a thud that scraped the bottom of his heart.

They left Breedon-on-the-hill the following day. The weather had brightened. Before departing Hellboy looked back over his shoulder at the limestone outcrop commanding the land all around. His mood was sullen. The sun imprinted deep shadows on the spiraling coils of the pathway around the hill. The sign of the Three Horseshoes Inn creaked as it swung gently in the breeze.

"When you come back," Liz said, "I'll be with you."

OF BLOOD, OF CLAY

JAMES A. MOORE

They screamed and they died and he reveled in their agonies. The German soldiers ran from him in most cases, though a few were foolish enough to actually fire their weapons in his direction. They soon found that the creature was not as easily dropped by bullets as the ones who had brought him into the world—into this second World War—had been. Though blood soaked into his skin, it was not his own. The bullets often punctured his body, but few of them went very deep. Most merely flattened and fell to the ground or stuck to him like declarations of his power.

One of the soldiers, young and brave and enraged by the death of his comrades, charged the creature, roaring an incoherent challenge. He smiled and waited for the fool to come closer. When the boy was within reach of the bloodied hands that had already crushed a hundred enemies or more, he grabbed the foolish young man and bent him backward until his scream became pain and fear instead of rage. Then he bent him some more until the screams were crushed along with the spinal column.

The man's death was small payment for what had been done to the creature's people, and he sneered at the thought that there could ever be enough payment to make up for the atrocities committed by the likes of the corpse he dropped at his feet. He took pleasure in the feeling of the soldier's weak flesh splitting under his tread. He was not without some pity. He left the women and the children alive. Those who were innocent had nothing to fear from him.

The armies of the world seemed determined to kill each other, and he had chosen his side. Let those who were foolish enough to cross his path pay with their lives; let those who wore the wrong uniforms pay as well.

Somewhere in this town, Von Holdt was hiding, and he would see the man crushed for his vile orders and his experiments. Ten feet to the creature's left and just slightly ahead of him, the stranger in the brown leather outfit with the odd marking on the chest was fighting the same fight. He, too, sought Von Holdt. He would see the butcher brought to justice, and for the moment that was sufficient.

But the odd man called Lobster Johnson would not stop him from destroying the murderers, would not stop him from holding Von Holdt's head between his hands and squeezing until blood and brains slid like pulp from a crushed orange.

Lobster Johnson gestured for him to follow and he did, moving down a narrow stone hallway that would have withstood a barrage of shells from a Sherman tank. The man was trying to open a steel door that barred his way.

"This way, stranger! This way if we're to stop Von Holdt from escaping the Lobster's Claw!" The man was not sane, of that the creature had little doubt, but he was useful just the same. Lobster Johnson stepped aside and let him reach with his massive hands. He pulled at the steel doors until they screamed their agonized protest. He flexed, and the metal bent back, peeling away from the passage that would lead to final retribution.

Lobster Johnson was past him in an instant, pistol in his hand, prepared to kill anyone that tried fighting back. The doors were tossed aside, useless debris that bounced across the courtyard and crushed two more of the Nazi soldiers before grinding to a halt.

From far, far above them the howls of falling missiles called out a song of destruction. If luck was with him he could still reach Von Holdt before the building around them fell in and destroyed them all.

He was not lucky. The roof above them shook and dropped fragments of stone like granite snow that dusted his head and his powerful shoulders. Lobster Johnson called out a warning, and he tried to step aside in the narrow, stone tunnel. There was nowhere to go when the explosion rocked the foundations of the castle, nowhere to hide when the tons of stone came crashing down. Somewhere ahead of him, he heard Von Holdt's insane laughter and knew he died in vain.

The military jet banked to the left and Roger compensated as he pulled the pictures out of the manila envelope and looked at them again, for what had to be the hundredth time. He understood the nature of violence all too well, but sometimes he was perplexed by what could motivate a being to commit such atrocities.

There were dozens of pictures, each a study in carnage and overkill. Roger searched for a pattern amidst the violence that would tell him anything at all about the perpetrator, other than that he was far stronger than a human being. Most of what had been done required absolutely outrageous strength, but little of it required finesse. The victims looked like they'd been hit with anvils or sledgehammers. Flesh hadn't been cut; it had been pulverized. Bones were not hacked apart as much as they were shattered within the meat casings.

He had no way to be certain, but he doubted even Hellboy could inflict that sort of damage. Then again, his friend would not have lashed out so casually, would have done all he could to prevent the deaths of so many youths.

Henry Middleton leaned over and looked at the photographs. "Jesus, Roger. What could cause that sort of damage?"

Roger looked back at the agent next to him. He knew that Henry was playing watchdog, making sure that he didn't lose control. He understood the precaution. There had been ... issues when he first awoke in the modern world. A few hundred years of starvation and sensory deprivation could lead to terrible accidents.

"I don't know, but I don't want to meet it. You're my field coordinator on this, Henry. Please be careful."

Henry nodded, his broad, craggy face shaking like a basset hound's. "Trust me, Roger. I'll leave the fighting to you."

Roger nodded his head and slid the photographs aside, looking at the next batch, which showed two police officers that had been beaten to death, their uniforms destroyed by savage blow after savage blow. "I think it liked the deaths. It likes killing."

"Yeah. I got that." Middleton shook his head. "What sort of animal gets off on doing that much harm to other living beings?"

"People do, Henry. Watch the news."

"You're kidding, right?"

"This started near Auschwitz. See my point?" At times Roger wished he were more eloquent, but he normally got his message across.

Henry shut up after that and Roger wondered if he had offended the man. Very few creatures he had run across so far were ever happy to hear about their own flaws or those of their species.

Three hours later they were at the scene of the massacre. That was really the only thing it could be called. The amphitheatre was in the woods, and the parking lot remained full of the victims of the violence. Inside, the bodies were still in the same locations. They looked much worse in person than they had managed to appear in the pictures. The bodies of close to a hundred people were decimated, broken, bent, and torn, then scattered across the ground like leftovers from a party.

In this case a recruiting party. Though each and every one of the banners that had been placed around the area had been desecrated—some covered in blood, others torn in half—Roger could still see the swastikas.

He moved around the area slowly, examining everything he could, though not touching very much aside from the ruined signs. He had no desire to examine the dead and no idea what he would be looking for aside from the obvious wounds that could not be missed. Yet even as he had that thought, the hands of one of the dead called his attention and he squatted, lifting the delicate, broken fingers of a young woman. Her fingernails were torn off, broken down at the level of the cuticle in some cases, and her fingers themselves were filthy. But it wasn't just dirt. It was sticky, half-dried clay.

"What are you thinking, Roger?"

Roger looked over at the agent assigned to babysit him and shrugged. "I don't like Nazis. Never will. But this is wrong." He gestured and picked up a torn flag. "They didn't do anything. Their grandfathers did."

"Their grandfathers?"

"Yes. They died because of the flag." He pointed to the ruined signs. "Every single symbol is ruined. Even the tattoos on their bodies."

"So somebody *really* doesn't like Nazis. What makes you think this goes all the way back to the original Nazis?"

"Auschwitz."

"But the place where it came up—that construction site where they found signs of whatever it is coming up out of the ground—that spot's several miles from the concentration camp."

"Yes, I know." Roger looked around again and headed for the door, he had seen enough. The report said the construction team had seen a man come out of the ground and head toward the site of the concentration camp. "It found police along the way and killed them because of their clothes. Their uniforms reminded it of Nazi soldiers. No soldiers at Auschwitz, so it left."

"Why do you think that?" Henry lit a cigar and walked with him, blowing a plume of smoke into the air.

"No soldiers. It left to find more. Nazis, Henry. It hates Nazis. If that had been what I was created for, I would have gone searching for them. That's what this thing has done."

"You would have done the same thing?" Henry's voice had a nervous edge.

"*If* I was made to kill Nazis. I wasn't. This thing was. I think."

"If you were created to kill ...? What? You think this was the work of a homunculus like you?"

"No. Not like me." Roger stepped outside into the fresh air, grateful to be away from the death. He looked toward Henry Middleton and shrugged. "What do you do when you're not working, Henry?"

"When I'm off duty?" Henry looked at Roger and grinned. "I go home to Karen and the kids. You know that."

"I do not have a Karen or any children, Henry. I spend my spare time reading."

"What's your point?"

"Most of what I read is for work. I read up on old religions. It's useful to know."

"Okay."

Henry wasn't getting it, but Roger wasn't surprised, and the one thing Roger was very good at was being patient, so he explained. "I read on old religions and legends, just in case I meet them." He thought about the clay under the dead girl's fingernails again and nodded to himself.

"Yeah. So you think this is what? A demon?"

"No. A golem."

"A golem?"

"Yes, a man created from clay, very strong and unrelenting. Kabalistic mages made them as servants. Defenders."

"Why would they have needed a golem?"

Roger thought about the thin fingers, bloodied and covered in mud and worse. "The Nazis were killing them off, Henry. The Nazis were killing them all off and they had no choice."

"Well, hell, Roger. Someone needs to tell this golem thing that the war is over."

"That's why we're here, isn't it, Henry?"

"Yeah. I guess maybe it is."

"We need a map. To see where other Nazi camps were. I want to see where it will go next." Roger sighed and looked at the ground in the parking lot. There wasn't much clay to prove his theory, but there was a great deal of blood that still hadn't been washed away. "I won't like this, I think."

"Why not?"

"Because it will be mad with me. I don't think it will like what I say."

Roger waited in the darkness, dressed in a long coat and a policeman's cap. The town was quiet and had been for several hours, but Roger thought he knew where the thing would strike. It was easy to figure. While they had been looking at the site of the worst massacre, two more police officers had been killed, this time outside a train station. It hated uniforms. More importantly, the third murder scene let them see that the monster was walking a line toward a police station that had once been a military outpost. Roger was betting that it knew that. That it remembered. The station had to be the target.

He waited because he knew the golem would probably come to this spot. It was one thing to be a different race and quite another to be a separate species entirely. Henry might not have liked what he said about humans and their capacity for wanton destruction, but the history books spoke volumes about their track record. Most of them seemed all right, and he could even have called a few of them his friends, but that was when they were one-on-one and not when they were gathered together into mobs. Once they set their minds on a path, once they were primed and ready to cause harm, little seemed to stop them except the threat of being injured themselves. Roger was trying to understand them, but so far they remained more of a mystery than he liked to think about.

The clothes were the largest sizes available, but he had not been created to wear clothing. Still the tailors had done a fine job of adjusting the coat. It was large enough that it fit and it hid his weapons, such as they were. Hellboy carried charms and grenades along with an enormous handgun. Roger did not. He was carrying a shovel and a pickaxe; the shovel was to cut into clay. The pickaxe was to break open the clay if it had hardened over the years. He didn't know if they would actually do him much good, but he would use them if he had to. The hat hid his features, hid the fact that he was a monster. Or at least the fact that he wasn't a human monster. From a distance it would look enough like a uniform to suit his needs.

It was a gamble, wearing the outfit. But Roger could think of no better way to catch the prey he sought without involving more humans.

He had been walking around outside the police station in Waldsburg for hours. So far he had been accosted by nothing stronger than an irate group of late-night revelers who offered him a drink, and three different dogs that had no idea what to make of his scent. The closest thing to an actual assault had been from the schnauzer that decided to mark his leg. He wondered if the murderer had left the area. There were certain to be more gatherings of uniforms in other towns. If nothing here attracted the golem, and assuming he was right in his guess as to what the thing might be, then the creature would go elsewhere.

Not too far behind him he heard a scuffling noise, and while he was fairly certain it was only another mongrel wandering the streets, Roger made sure he stayed alert. The good news for Roger was that he did, in fact, pay attention to the sound that came from behind him. The bad news was that it most definitely wasn't a stray dog.

The deep rumbling voice that spoke to him was slow and angry, the sounds strained with a wish to cause violence. "How many have you killed, Nazi?" The words were in Polish, a language Roger knew from long ago.

Roger turned and faced the creature he'd been hunting, staring it square in the abdomen, which was not at all what he'd expected. The thing was much, much larger than a man, or even a homunculus. "Two people, but one was an accident, and she got better." As he spoke, Roger started removing the coat and hat he'd had made for the occasion. "I am not a Nazi, my friend, but I had to get your attention."

The golem was bathed in shadows, but he could see that somewhere along the way he had made a mistake about the creature. It was partially clay, but also made up of so much more. There were parts of the body that were comprised almost completely of roughly broken stone and debris, and there were parts that seemed almost wholly formed from the remains of a dozen farm implements that had been broken and tied together. Perhaps it had been a challenge for the Kabalistic sorcerer who created the thing to find enough clay and he had resorted to whatever was at hand, or maybe the creature had been repairing itself while underground for so many years.

"Liar!" The brute stepped forward amid a small spill of granite dust and other detritus. "All of your kind are liars, and murderers besides."

The thing grinned then, baring a maw filled with bone and the blades of a dozen bayonets. It had definitely been making improvements to the original model. In the legends he had studied, the golem had a word written across its forehead. Roger couldn't see any markings on this creature, only a vast expanse of clay and stone. Also according to the legends, the monster was unstoppable until part of the marking had been removed. This was not, by Roger's way of thinking, a good development.

Roger finished disrobing as quickly as he could, stripping down only to his tan vest, with the numerous pockets and the B.P.R.D. logo. "Do I look like a Nazi to you? Have you ever seen a German soldier with skin this color, or eyes like mine?" He stood revealed; the gray tones of his flesh, the hairless body, the circular patch of metal on his chest that housed the generator that kept him mobile. Below his waist where a man would have had reproductive organs, Roger had a block of wood and a large metal ring that had once been used to keep him locked in place and unable to escape from his creator. Like the golem that stood before him, he could never be mistaken for human.

"I am a homunculus, sent here to stop you from killing anyone else. The war you want to fight is over, my friend. The Nazis lost." He shrugged.

"The war is over?" The thing towering over him sounded uncertain. "But what of the people I saw with their markings and their words about purity of race and purpose?"

The creature spoke eloquently, and Roger had to wonder if the spirit of the wizard who had created it was tied to the very act of creation. There had been an accident when Roger was first awakened, a sort of mental calling from the woman Elizabeth Sherman, that he had responded to. She had wanted to rid herself of the power that dwelled within her body and he had obliged her, unwittingly almost causing her death. But he had been changed by that contact. His mind was altered by taking her power from her and holding it inside. He didn't know if he had somehow retained a part of her life force, her soul as some called it, but he knew that the experience had made him better than he was created to be. Did the golem share some of that sorcerer's identity? Or had it merely had a lifetime or so to learn? Roger didn't know and wished he could ask, but the brute was still looking at him as a possible new target for his wrath. Questions of philosophy would have to wait.

"They are foolish, but they are not the Nazis who killed your people." And were they the golem's people? Would it have been accepted as a hero had things turned out differently? For the first time since he had stood against his own brother, there was another like him, another he could almost find a connection to, and he hated to lose the opportunity to learn from the golem.

"Then they are just as foolish! You did not hear their words, you did not see their faces as they spoke of a master race."

"You've already paid them for their folly, my friend. They are dead. They cannot hurt the people you would protect." Roger held out a hand to the golem, an offering of peace. "Come with me, I can take you to people who can show you how the world has changed."

The golem looked at his hand and stood perfectly still. Finally, it stepped back. "I cannot. I was not created to live in this world." Though the creature spoke with passion its words were a monotone. Roger couldn't tell if it felt regret or simply confusion. "I was not made to do anything but take revenge upon the killers of my master's people."

"But there is no revenge, my friend. Don't you see? The war is over, and the Jews have returned to their Promised Land."

"No." The creature shook its head, stepping back a second time. "No, you lie. And there can be no peace until all of your kind have paid for the atrocities."

"You're not listening to me. There are no more Nazis. The men you killed, they were only police trying to protect everyone. I can help you, if you will let me." And he so wanted to help the creature, he was grateful for the chance. When all others would have left him to suffer, it was Hellboy who had decided to intervene and protect Roger. As misguided as the golem was, Roger wanted to return the favor that had been done him. He wanted to help the thing that stood shaking and confused in front of him despite the bloodstains that had soaked into its arms and chest.

Some things are simply not meant to be. The golem shook its head again and then roared, massive hands curling into fists that were large enough to shatter a man with a single blow. The golem lashed out, and Roger was not fast enough to avoid the impact. The force of the strike sent him sailing, lifted him from the ground, and hurled him across the street and into the side of a building.

Roger was not a man. He stood back up, and reached for his pick and his shovel. The golem looked his way, surprised, no doubt, to see anything that could recover from the blow it had dealt.

"I had hoped to avoid this. I truly had. Please forgive me, my friend."

The golem started for him again, and charged. They moved on a collision course. The golem reached out, trying to grab Roger's skull in its hands. Roger dodged to the left and swung hard with the pickaxe, leaving it buried several inches into the creature's chest. The clay monstrosity was much faster than he would have guessed, and it was also much craftier in a fight. The thing elbowed him in the back of the head.

Roger hit the ground hard enough to crack the pavement under him, his face slamming down hard. He started to push off but didn't get very far before the golem pressed a heavy foot into the back of his skull and leaned over him. "You are a liar. And I will make you pay for your treachery."

Roger had no idea if the golem could feel physical pain, but he surely could feel it himself. He grunted hard as his face was pushed against the street. The pressure was overwhelming, and whether or not he was tougher than the agents he worked with quickly became a moot point. If he didn't get the giant off him soon he was going to die.

He set his hands against the ground and tried to push up. The golem pushed down harder. Roger heard gunfire from behind him and blinked. The golem stepped off of him, leaving him free to get back to his feet. Twenty yards away, he saw Henry Middleton standing in a proper firing stance, legs wide and shoulders squared, firing another bullet at the monster. The missile struck the forehead of the creature and knocked free a large piece of stone that landed on Roger's foot.

Once again the golem made a noise as it moved forward. Henry stood his ground, though Roger could see he was terrified. Henry Middleton had a Karen and children at home, waiting for him to be back at their side, but he faced off against a creature they knew was effectively bulletproof and gave Roger a chance to recover.

Roger picked up the stone that had landed on his foot, looking at both of the broader sections, the one that had faced the air and the one that had been concealed against the clay flesh of the golem. He saw the ghost of a marking on the clay-stained side and nodded. There were lines in the clay, spots that were clear of any debris, though they too were lined with dried blood.

The Golem of Prague had paper strips placed under its tongue. It was mute and he had been destroyed by saying the very prayers that brought it to life a second time. Other stories he'd read about golems stated that the word *emeth* had to be written across the forehead, and that by removing the first character and leaving only *meth*, the golem could be stopped. Roger picked his shovel up and started toward the creature, even as Henry started backing away.

Of course the legends also say that only the creator of the golem can destroy it, he thought. *Which could be very bad.*

"Hey!"

The golem turned back toward him, snarling again as it saw he was still alive. "Don't you ever die?"

"I'm stronger than most cops." Roger swung the shovel with everything he had and caught the creature across the forehead, slicing deep into the clay and knocking shards of stone away from the area the golem had sought to cover and protect. The golem wrapped its hands around his shoulders and lifted him from the ground, shaking him overhead like a rag doll. Roger held on to the shovel, though it wasn't easy.

"I want you to die!" The monster roared the words, baring the teeth it had fashioned for itself from the bones of its enemies and the bayonets they had carried. Roger looked past the mouth that roared and into the eyes of the golem. He saw no soul, only hatred raw and angry and pained by the death of the one that had created it.

Roger nodded. "I know, my friend. I'm sorry but I can't help you with that." He drove the shovel down into the bare spot he had made on the creature's forehead and cut through the first letter written across the golem's brow.

The golem stopped moving. Just stopped. It stood perfectly still and Roger looked down into its eyes, wondering if he would see any change in them. The anger and hatred there faded away, replaced by nothing at all.

"Hey, Roger? You okay up there?"

Roger craned his neck around and looked down at Henry below him. "Yes. I'm all right, Henry. But I might need your help."

"What's wrong?"

"I'm stuck. The golem is dead, but it's still holding on to me."

Henry walked closer and looked at him. "Okay. I'll get a ladder. It might take a little while though. All the stores are closed."

"Could you make it fast? This is embarrassing."

"Is it?" Henry grinned and reached into his pocket. He pulled out a digital camera. "I was just thinking you'd look great on the wall in my office that way."

"You wouldn't."

Henry proved him wrong by taking several snapshots. "Hey, we need some sort of proof for the files ..."

"I think you're just being rude now." Roger struggled, trying to get free and finally reached for the handle of the pickaxe still embedded in the golem's arm. He managed to break his way out after only a few hard blows.

"Guess you won't be needing that ladder after all." Henry tucked his camera away.

"I could take the camera from you, you know." Roger climbed down from his perch on the golem's body, and Henry suddenly looked solemn as he moved closer.

"Do you think it hurt much? I mean, it's got all sorts of wounds on it, and there are easily a hundred bullets stuck in the chest and legs alone ..." Henry looked worried.

"I don't think the scrapes and cuts hurt it at all, Henry."

"No?" Henry's fingers brushed the chest of the thing, tracing the bullet holes and knocking loose a fingernail that had once belonged to a young woman in Waldsburg who had let herself believe in terrible things.

"No." Roger picked up the broken nail from the ground and held it in his fingers, studying it. "No, Henry. I think he was already in too much pain to notice."

A FULL AND SATISFYING LIFE

RAY GARTON

1 0:33 p.m.—*Rio Vista Christian Boarding Academy*

Body parts were strewn up and down the main fourth-floor hallway of the four-story boys' dormitory. An arm here, a leg there. Part of a head, a shoe still containing a foot. The smell of blood hung in the air like a heavy mist—cloying and metallic, slightly sweet. Blood darkened the brown-and-tan carpet of the hallway and spattered the beige walls in nightmarish Rorschach sprays.

Forensics investigators were still gathering evidence in the hallway—two men, two women, all wearing dark vests with C.S.U. printed in bold white letters on the back.

Hellboy's upper lip curled slightly in response to the smell. He stood at the top of the open stairwell in the center of the hallway and looked first to the right, then the left.

The hallway looked like a slaughterhouse.

Dick Snodgrass, the boys' dean, stood on Hellboy's left. He was a small, skinny, jittery man in his mid-fifties. He wore a rumpled, brown suit and had not taken his eyes off Hellboy since he'd arrived. They were suspicious eyes, wary, and just a little fearful, especially when they lingered on the fat, round stumps of Hellboy's horns on his forehead, or on his enormous right hand, or on his long tail. Hellboy got that a lot, especially from religious people. It took them a while to warm up to him, if they did at all. Even now, with all the carnage in front of them, Snodgrass watched him carefully. The dean's eyes were also red, puffy, and moist, and he looked tired, his face drawn. He'd seen more death and bloodshed that evening than most people see in a lifetime.

On Hellboy's right stood eighteen-year-old Joey Priven, the youngest agent of the Bureau for Paranormal Research and Defense. He was tall and slender and wore a long, black wool coat. His dark hair was wet and mussed by the rain and wind outside, his face bleached white by the sight of all the body parts, the smell of the blood. He pressed one hand over his mouth. He was a handsome boy, if a bit gawky and uncertain.

"Getting anything, Joey?" Hellboy asked.

Joey slowly lowered his hand from his mouth. "Pain," he said, his voice hoarse. "And fear. A lot of fear. Terror. It ... it happened so fast. So fast, it was over before some of them knew what was going on. So fast that some of them didn't even see it. Some died without getting a look at what was killing them. Just a couple minutes altogether, maybe less." He closed his eyes. His brow wrinkled, then his eyes clenched. "Screaming. A lot of screaming ... pleading ... praying."

Frowning, Snodgrass nodded. He took a deep breath and let it out slowly, tremulously. "I heard the screaming down in my office. At first, I thought the guys were just fooling around, you know? Sometimes they let off steam and get rowdy." His voice broke and he scrubbed a hand up and down his face a couple times. "By the time I got up here, it was all over. It was gone. But we don't know where it went or how it got out. It didn't come down the stairs, and it didn't go out any of the windows."

Hellboy turned to Joey again. "Any idea what did this?"

Joey opened his eyes, slowly shook his head. He squinted a little, as if staring at something a great distance away. "It moved fast. But it was big. Powerful. And silent. And it was ... long."

"Long?" Hellboy said.

"Yeah. Long, with ... teeth. A lot of them. A blur of sharp, bloody teeth."

Hellboy looked down at Snodgrass. "How many on this floor?"

Snodgrass had been staring intensely at Joey, listening, and flinched. "Huh? I'm sorry, what?"

"How many boys live on this floor?"

"Forty-two. But not all of them were here at the time, of course. Some were still in the cafeteria having dinner, others were already in the gymnasium for the evening activity period."

"And how many were killed again?"

"Twenty-three. Twenty-four counting Dean Stevewell, who was up here when it happened." He nodded at the mess in the hallway, but didn't look at it. He massaged the back of his neck with his right hand and took another deep breath. "This is all that was left. They were just ... gone. Some didn't even leave behind this much."

Hellboy's eyes narrowed. Twenty-four lives snuffed out in minutes, bodies consumed by something fast and powerful.

Snodgrass frowned, fidgeted a little. "Look, you mind if I get a better look at your I.D.?"

Hellboy removed his wallet, opened it, and showed Snodgrass his B.P.R.D. badge and I.D. card again.

Snodgrass took a long look, then nodded. "Okay. I don't mean to seem suspicious, it's just, um ... well, you know."

Hellboy nodded as he flipped his wallet closed and put it back in the pocket of his trench coat. Once again, he surveyed the damage.

It had happened more than four hours ago. Something had made its way quickly from one end of the floor to the other, killing and devouring teenage boys and an assistant dean on its way. It had disappeared as suddenly as it had come. The B.P.R.D. in Fairfield, Connecticut had been notified immediately and Hellboy had been given the assignment. He and Joey had been in Denver, where they'd just wrapped up an investigation of a destructive ghost in a department store. They'd been preparing to return to headquarters in Connecticut, but instead a flight had been arranged to take them to the school in northern California to investigate.

Joey was as pale as flour and kept gulping hard. He was a psychic sensitive. Experts at the Bureau were still honing his abilities. He was still learning the finer points of controlling his talent, of using it, but Hellboy was quite impressed with him.

"You gonna be okay?" Hellboy said.

Joey nodded, but did not look confident. "I could use a drink of water."

"You want to go downstairs and wait in the lobby?"

"I ... I think I better. I don't feel so well, you wanna know the truth."

"Okay, go ahead. I'll be down in a while, and we'll go talk to the witnesses."

Joey nodded again. "Thanks." He turned and went down the stairs.

Hellboy turned to Snodgrass again. "Where are the witnesses?"

The little man's shoulders were slumped, as if he carried a great weight on them. "A few of them have already gone home. Their parents came and got them. The rest are staying in the homes of staff up on Faculty Hill until their parents arrive. Some had to be treated for shock, but they're okay now. As okay as can be expected, anyway."

"We'll need to talk to them," Hellboy said as he started down the hall to the right. "Get them together. Maybe in the cafeteria. That okay?"

"Sure, whatever you need. I hope you don't mind if I don't join you, but I'd rather not walk through all that ... well, I'll just stay right here, if that's okay." He took a cell phone from the pocket of his suit coat and made a call, speaking quietly.

The bloody carpet squished beneath Hellboy's hooves as he went to the nearest C.S.U. investigator, a tall bald man with a fringe of salt-and-pepper hair and glasses. He took out his wallet, flashed his badge. "Hellboy, B.P.R.D."

The man looked him up and down. "Howard Rolley, C.S.U."

"Uncovering anything interesting?"

"I think it's a good thing you're here," Rolley said. "This is definitely one for the B.P.R.D. I've never seen anything like this before in my life. This was no ordinary animal."

Hellboy shook his head. "No. It wasn't." He walked toward the north end of the hall, head turning slowly from side to side. The doors of the rooms were all open, the rooms unoccupied. He saw unmade beds, books stacked on desks, messy closets. He came to a half-open door that had a section missing from the edge just beneath the doorknob and approached it for a closer look. A jagged semicircle of wood more than two feet wide had been taken from the edge of the door. Hellboy looked closer at the serrated edge and quickly came to the conclusion that the chunk of wood had been bitten out.

"Holy crap," he muttered.

The jaws of the creature that had bitten the door were enormous and powerful. He remembered what Joey had said about a "blur of sharp, bloody teeth."

Hellboy walked on until he saw something in the wall and stopped, went to it. A long, slender quill, like that of a porcupine, only longer, was stuck in the plaster wall. He closed his thumb and index finger on it and plucked it out. It was about eleven, maybe twelve inches long and black, with a coarse surface and tiny barbs around the red, needle-like tip.

"We found a few of those."

He turned to see a black female C.S.U. investigator standing beside him. She carried a black case with her and appeared to be on her way out.

"Any idea what they are?" he said.

"None, unless they came off the world's biggest porcupine. You're B.P.R.D.?"

He nodded.

"Well, I'm taking some back to the lab, but you might have better luck with it." She walked away, heading for the staircase.

Hellboy studied the quill a moment, then put it in a leather pouch attached to his belt. He looked around a moment longer, then turned and went back to Snodgrass. They went down the stairs together.

"Anyone in particular live up here?" Hellboy said.

"I'm not sure I understand what you mean," Snodgrass said.

"I'm not sure I do, either, to be honest. I'm groping."

"The third floor is occupied exclusively by seniors, if that's what you're getting at."

Hellboy nodded. "Okay. So, you have forty-two senior boys?"

"We're a small school, Mr. Hellboy."

Joey sat slumped on a couch in the lobby. He still looked queasy. He stood when he saw them and came to Hellboy's side.

Hellboy took the quill from the pouch and held it out to Joey. "Can you get anything from this?"

Joey reached out and touched the quill with the tips of the first two fingers of his right hand. He gasped and jerked his hand back.

"What?" Hellboy said.

Cautiously, Joey touched it again and closed his eyes. His mouth pulled back in a grimace. "Hunger. An *awful* hunger that's never satisfied. And ..." He smacked his lips a couple times, licked them. " ... The taste of blood." He cried out suddenly and stumbled backward. "Oh, my God." His eyes widened as they locked onto Hellboy's. "It was called here. *Called* by someone. And it's going to happen again."

"Where?"

"I don't know. Close, I think. Somewhere close by."

"Here in the dorm again?"

"I don't know."

"How much time do we have?"

"It feels like it's going to happen soon, that's all I know." He stuffed his hands into the pockets of his coat. "I don't want to touch that thing again."

Hellboy nodded and said, "Okay. Let's get moving, then." He put the quill back in the pouch.

"The witnesses should be gathering in the cafeteria by now," Snodgrass said. He went into his office and came out with two umbrellas—a small collapsible one for himself, a larger one he handed to Hellboy to share with Joey.

Snodgrass led them out of the gloomy basalt-block building and into the rainy night.

On the plane ride from Colorado, Joey had fidgeted restlessly in the seat beside Hellboy.

"Nervous?" Hellboy had said.

"A little. This is the first assignment I've had where people have ... well, you know ... been killed."

"I'm glad you're here. You might be able to pick something up, help us out, like you did in Denver. Great job, by the way."

Joey nodded. A full minute passed before he spoke again. "You've been doing this a long time, haven't you?"

"I started young. Like you."

"Do you like it?"

Hellboy shrugged. "Haven't known anything else. What about you? You like it so far?"

Joey thought about it a while before responding. "My dad was a colonel in the army. We moved around a lot when I was a kid. My parents and sister were killed in a car accident when I was nine. I had no other family. I ended up with the B.P.R.D. and started working on my talent. Before that, it was kind of ... out of control. Information was constantly bombarding me. It made it hard to concentrate in school. It made everything difficult, really. The hardest part, though, was ... I saw the car wreck that killed my family. I saw it three years before it happened. But I didn't understand what it was until afterward. If I'd known back then what I was seeing, I might've been able to—but I can't think that way. I'll drive myself crazy."

"That's tough," Hellboy said. "Who've you been training under?"

"Enid Charles."

"She's good."

Joey nodded. "She's been great. I don't know what I would've done without her. I just don't know if ..." He stopped, looked down at his lap for a while.

"You don't know if what?"

"If ... I want to end up like you."

"Like me? What do you mean?"

"You said the B.P.R.D. is all you've ever known. Well, it's not *all* I've ever known, but from the age of ten on ... it's close."

Half of Hellboy's mouth curled up in a smile. "Don't worry, Joey. It's not that bad. You travel and meet a lot of fascinating people. You see and do things most people never even dream of. And you can have your own life, too. I mean, you do things on your own, don't you?"

Joey shrugged. "Not much, not really."

"Well, don't worry, you will. You're still learning, still studying. What else would you like to do besides your work in the B.P.R.D.?"

"I've always wanted to be a writer. I write a lot in my spare time, when I *have* spare time. Short stories."

"Hm. Maybe I'll read one sometime."

Joey smiled. "Would you?"

"Sure. This job'll give you plenty to write about. It's a good gig. A full and satisfying life, like Professor Bruttenholm used to say."

Joey returned the smile. "Thanks."

That seemed to put the boy at ease, and he'd sat back in his seat then, and dozed off.

Rio Vista Christian Boarding Academy was spread over the top of a hill overlooking the Russian River outside Santa Rosa. Behind it, along the ridgeline known as Faculty Hill, stood the homes of the teachers and staff. It was a cold and rainy Tuesday night in January and a biting wind made their umbrellas useless as they walked west from the boys' dormitory, past the administration building to the cafeteria. Hellboy's hooves clocked solidly on the concrete.

A phalanx of reporters gathered under umbrellas out in the parking lot, held back by the police. Hellboy had phoned ahead with strict instructions to keep the press well away from the scene of the incident.

As they walked, Hellboy spoke to Joey.

"I want you to talk to these boys," he said. "Try to make them feel comfortable. They're probably not gonna warm up to me right away, and we don't have time for that, anyway."

"Sure," Joey said. "I'll do my best."

The cafeteria was all glass in front, with an A-frame peak that gave it a vague ski-lodge appearance. Dim light oozed out through the front windows and reflected off the slanting rain. They entered through a door on the eastern side of the building.

Only a few of the lights were on in the cafeteria. Five boys sat at a long table as two men stood talking nearby. Sounds came from the kitchen. Snodgrass introduced Hellboy and Joey to the boys—Eddie, Josh, Brandon, Mark, and Kenan—and the two faculty men, principal Mr. Collins and P.E. teacher Mr. Vanderman.

The boys all had a slightly stunned look to them, with a bit too much white showing in their eyes.

First, Hellboy took each boy individually to another table and, with Joey at his side, asked for his version of the incident. As each boy talked, Hellboy made notes in a small notepad he took from his coat pocket. The boys were reluctant to discuss it—they were all terribly shaken and emotional. When Hellboy was done, each boy returned to the table with the others. After the last one, Hellboy and Joey joined them.

"Okay, let's go through it again, together this time," Hellboy said. "Joey and I need you to tell us everything you can about what happened."

Joey said, "Can you tell us again what did this?"

Brandon was a portly blond boy with freckles. He took a breath to speak, but immediately burst into tears. Mr. Vanderman went to him and massaged his shoulders from behind.

"That's okay," Mr. Vanderman said. "It's okay to cry."

"It moved so fast," Kenan said, "it was kinda hard to get a good look at it, y'know?" He was a muscular boy with dark blond hair through which he kept nervously running his fingers. "It was red."

"Red," Hellboy said. "Like me?"

"No, not exactly," Kenan said with a shake of his head. He frowned as he searched for the right words.

Mark sat up in his chair, a short, stocky boy with rusty hair and glasses. "It was more of a ... a purplish-red."

"Purplish-red," Hellboy said.

"That was the color of its skin," Josh said, "but it also had really black hair around its head." He was a skinny boy with curly black hair and braces on his teeth. "The kind of black that's so black it looks blue when the light hits it just right."

"So it had hair *around* its head?" Joey said.

"Yeah," Josh said, "but none on its body, and its head was bald. The hair was like a ... a mane, yeah, that's it, a *mane*."

"What did its body look like?" Hellboy said.

"Like a lion," Kenan said. "A *big* lion. Bigger than any lion I ever saw. It was huge."

"So it had a body like a lion," Joey said.

"But its face," Brandon said, sniffling. "Its head was real big, and its face was like ... it had a face like a man."

A plump woman came out of the kitchen holding a tray with ten steaming white mugs on it. "Hot chocolate for everyone," she said. She put the tray on the table and introduced herself as Mrs. Darlene Claret. "I work in the kitchen," she said, "and Mr. Vanderman called me out tonight to make some cocoa for the boys."

The three men and the boys helped themselves to the hot drinks. Joey took one, too.

"A man's face, y'say?" Hellboy said.

"Yeah, yeah," Josh said, "it was kinda like a man's face, but with that weird red skin, and that mouth that was so—"

Brandon interrupted. "Oh, yeah, that mouth, it was, like, *gigantic*."

Their voices trembled with fear, and their eyes became even wider as they spoke. Hellboy noticed their hands shook as they lifted their mugs to their lips to sip the hot chocolate.

"I don't wanna talk about this anymore," Mark said, his voice breathy. He put his mug down, scooted his chair back, and stood. He folded his arms tightly across his chest and paced as he said, "I wanna go home. Where are my parents?"

"Your sister is coming from Tucson to get you, Mark," Mr. Collins said. "I've talked to your parents, and they're going to fly into Tucson from—"

"I wanna go home *now*, I don't wanna be here anymore."

Joey put his mug on the table, stepped in front of Mark, and put his hands on Mark's shoulders. "Dude, you're gonna be okay. The worst is over. Like he said, your sister'll be here soon, and then you can go. But we need to learn all we can about this thing so we can *do* something about it."

"But Derrin was my best friend," Mark said. Unspilled tears sparkled in his eyes, and his voice quavered. "And that thing ... it *ate* him. In just a few seconds, it gobbled him up like a ... I don't know, like a candy bar. One minute, Derrin was there, screaming and reaching toward me for help, and then that thing was chewing up and gulping him down. And I ran away, into my room, and shut the door. I didn't *do* anything, I just ran away."

"There was nothing you could do," Josh said.

"You couldn't help him, Mark," Kenan said.

"I'm really sorry, man," Joey said. "Nothing we can do or say will bring your friend back. But we've got to do what we can to make sure this doesn't happen to anyone else."

Mark nodded after several seconds and sat down again, sipped his hot chocolate.

Joey picked up his drink and returned to Hellboy's side.

Hellboy turned away from them and stroked his chin. "Body of a lion, face like a man." He turned to the boys again. "What were those teeth like?"

"Oh, God, its teeth," Eddie said, shaking his head. "There were so *many* of 'em. *Rows* of 'em. It ate those guys. Like they were nothing, like they were made of ... of *Jell-O*." It was the first time he'd spoken in the group. He was slender and seemed shy, with a soft, sensitive face, dark hair, large eyes with long lashes, a quiet voice.

Kenan got a faraway look on his face. "I remember the sound of their bones breaking, the ... the crunching and snapping ... the popping." He scooted his chair back and stood suddenly, turned around, and vomited onto the green carpet.

"Oh, dear." Mrs. Claret went to Kenan and put an arm around his shoulders as he apologized. "Don't you worry about that, honey, it's okay." She hurried to the kitchen and came back with a wet washcloth and dabbed Kenan's face. "You sit down now, honey, and just relax, okay? I'll clean this up."

Kenan slowly lowered himself back into his chair, and Mrs. Claret went about cleaning up the mess.

Hellboy said, "What about a tail, did it have a tail?"

"It was like a scorpion's tail," Josh said. "Y'know, segmented. And at the end, there was this, this ... I don't know, this—"

"It was a ball of these ... *spines*," Mark said. "Like some kind of spiny ... what do you call those things in the ocean? Anemones, like a spiny sea anemone."

"Spines?" Hellboy removed the spine from the pouch and held it up for them to see. "Like this?"

They all responded at once in the affirmative.

"It *threw* 'em!" Eddie said.

"Yeah," Brandon said, "it, like, swung its tail back and forth, throwin' those things at the guys, and as soon as the spines hit somebody, they'd, like, drop to the floor. They were out. Then it was on them. Eating them. Eat ... *eating* them."

"But the worst part," Eddie said, staring at his hot chocolate, "was that it didn't make a sound. It didn't roar, it didn't even squeak. Nothing. It was completely silent. The only sounds it made were slurping and chewing."

The others nodded and quietly agreed.

Hellboy caught Joey's eye and jerked his head, beckoning the boy to step aside with him. He lowered his voice nearly to a whisper.

"What they've described is the man-faced Manticore," Hellboy said.

"Manticore?"

"It's a beast of Greek mythology. Red skin, the body of a lion, face of a man, with an enormous mouth and three rows of fangs on top and bottom, with a scorpion's tail that flings *these* things." He held up the quill. "The quills are venomous—a neurotoxin that paralyzes the victims. But the victims do not lose consciousness and are fully aware as the Manticore eats them. Someone has summoned a Manticore to this campus."

"But why?" Joey said.

"To slaughter a lot of students, for one thing." Hellboy put the quill back in the pouch as he turned back to the group. "Mr. Collins, I'll need a list of anyone on your campus of Greek descent."

"I'm Greek," Josh said. "My last name is Demetrious."

Hellboy frowned. "Do you know anything about this you're not telling us, Josh?"

Josh's eyes widened and mouth opened slowly. "Are ... are you outta your mind?"

"That's not necessary, Josh," Mr. Vanderman said.

"No, really, the idea that I'm keeping something from you," Josh said, "that's ... it's crazy."

"He was with me when it happened," Brandon said. "Josh didn't have anything to do with it."

"I'm not the only Greek on campus," Josh said.

Hellboy turned to Mr. Collins. "Is that true?"

"Yes," Collins said. "There are two other Greek boys here at Rio Vista."

"Tell me about them," Hellboy said.

"There's Bill Koulouris," Collins said. "He's a freshman from Wisconsin. And there's Matthew Melonakos, a junior who comes from the Greek town of Molai."

"Matthew Melonidiot," one of the boys muttered, and they all stifled laughs.

"Hey, none of that," Snodgrass said. "That's not his name and you know it." To Hellboy, he said, "Matthew's been here since he was a freshman. His English is still a bit clumsy. His parents sent him here to get a good Christian education. But they don't have much money, so he's only gone home once since he's been here. My wife and I have sort of taken him under our wing. He works in maintenance to pay his tuition."

"Does he like it here?" Hellboy said.

Collins and Snodgrass exchanged a quick look.

"Matthew is a good boy," Snodgrass said. He tossed a look at the boys at the table. "I'm afraid *some* of our students aren't as accepting of him as they should be." Another glance at the boys, this one stern. "I've had words with these boys and others about it, plenty of times."

Hellboy said, "Why would someone come all the way from Greece to go to a school in northern California?"

"We have students here from all over the world," Collins said. "We are a non-denominational Christian school with an excellent reputation for providing top-quality education with Christian values for young people in grades nine through twelve." He sounded like he was giving a speech, and Hellboy was relieved when he did not go on.

Hellboy turned to Snodgrass. "This Matthew Melonakos—is there a chance he's behind this?"

"Matt? Oh, no, Matt is a good kid. He spends a lot of time alone in the boys' dorm chapel, praying. He seems to have taken to our church doctrine quite well. In fact, when this happened tonight, I know for a fact that he was in the chapel alone, praying and reading his Bible."

"What about the other one?" Hellboy said.

"Bill Koulouris?" Snodgrass said. He frowned. "He's a different story. Bill seems to gravitate toward trouble. And if there's no trouble, he tends to make some. He's just a freshman, though, and I'm hoping we can turn him around."

"Mr. Snodgrass," Hellboy said, "could you go get both of those boys and bring them here? I'd like to talk to them."

"Sure, of course." Snodgrass turned and hurried out of the cafeteria with his umbrella.

Joey went to the table and sat down with the boys, put down his hot chocolate. "You guys don't get along with Matt, do you?"

Mark said, "We just don't like him, is all."

Brandon said, "He's, like, not very friendly, for one thing."

"He's *shy*," Collins said. "He'd be a lot friendlier if you guys would give him half a chance." He turned to Hellboy. "Bill Koulouris, on the other hand, has been sent to my office more times than I care to count since the school year started. I get the impression he's been given no discipline at home, because he certainly doesn't react to it well here."

"Look," Joey said to the boys at the table, "I need you guys to be honest with me, okay?"

They silently looked at him.

"*Okay?*" Joey said.

They nodded.

"Matt gets picked on a lot, doesn't he?"

They hesitated—there was no response at first.

"You getting something, Joey?" Hellboy said.

Joey nodded. To the boys, he said, "He gets picked on a lot by you guys and others, doesn't he?"

Slowly, they nodded; first Mark, then Kenan, then the others—except for Eddie.

"Look," Joey said, "I'm psychic. What I'm picking up right now is that you guys really can't stand Matt. You pick on him every chance you get, you make his life miserable. You don't like him because he's different, right? He doesn't speak English well, he's shy, he doesn't fit in. Right?"

"I don't like it," Eddie said as he swiped a hand down over his face wearily. "I guess I should do something about it, speak up when it happens, but I never do. But I don't *like* it. I've talked to him a few times—"

"Talked to who?" Hellboy said.

"Matt Melonakos," Eddie said. "When nobody else was around. It's not *cool* to talk to him, y'know? But I've talked to him a few times. He's not a bad guy, but he doesn't really like it here. He misses home."

"You mean, Greece?" Hellboy said.

"Yeah," Eddie said. "I know what Mr. Snodgrass said about him—that he's really taken to the faith, and all that. But from the things he's said to me ... well, he seemed pretty angry. He puts up a good front, but it's been a big change for him—his parents' conversion from Greek Orthodox—"

"The Greek Orthodox church is Christian," Hellboy said.

"A different kind of Christianity," Eddie said. "Matt didn't like being sent here to go to school. He doesn't like any of it. And the way he's treated by the other students here just makes it worse."

Joey leaned forward and folded his arms on the tabletop. "Who else picks on Matt? Please, this may be important."

Brandon shrugged and said, "Like, who *doesn't*?"

"Girls, too?"

Brandon chuckled and said, "The girls are, like, worse than us. He can never get a date for a banquet."

"Banquet?" Hellboy said.

Collins said, "Some Christian denominations do not approve of dancing, so instead of dances, we hold banquets for the students."

"Matt can't get a date for these banquets?" Joey said.

Mark said, "Heather Spencer weighs about two hundred pounds and never gets a date to anything, and even *she* wouldn't go with him."

Frowning, Josh shook his head and said, "I don't see how he could have anything to do with that thing we saw in the dorm tonight."

"The Manticore appeared from nowhere and then disappeared because it was *summoned* by someone," Hellboy said. "Conjured up. I'm guessing the reason it appeared for only a very short time is that the person who summoned it wasn't able to hold it here for long. My guess is that one or both of those boys, at the very least, know something about it."

"I find that hard to believe," Collins said.

Hellboy turned to him. "Well, somebody called that Manticore here, Mr. Collins."

Collins said nothing.

"We need to talk to them," Hellboy said. "Whoever did it was able to hold the Manticore here for only a couple minutes this time. The next time, he might be able to—"

Joey suddenly clutched his head in both hands and cried out. He stood so abruptly, he knocked his chair over. He nearly fell as he spun around to face Hellboy, mouth gaping, eyes bulging. Although he looked at Hellboy, he seemed to see through him, to look at something else far beyond him.

"It's happening again!" he shouted. "It's happening again right now!"

Hellboy said, "Where? *Where* is it happening?"

Joey clearly did not hear him. "It's happening again!" he shouted as he ran through the cafeteria and went out the door on the western side of the building, shouting, "No! Make it stop! Make it stop!"

"Oh, crap," Hellboy said as he broke into a run after him.

Outside, Joey ran across a patch of grass up ahead to the main sidewalk. He turned left and went west along the sidewalk, swerving this way and that as he ran. As he went after Joey, Hellboy knew what was happening, he'd seen it before with other psychic sensitives—Joey was having a real-time vision, and because it was close by, he was drawn to the location of the event he was seeing. He headed for the other basalt-block building on the campus—what Hellboy assumed was the girls' dormitory.

"Joey, stop! Wait!"

Joey ran even faster. He turned left and stumbled up the concrete steps in front of the dormitory, went through the door, and into the lobby.

As he approached the building, Hellboy heard the screams. They were coming from the fourth floor. He ran up the steps.

He pushed through the glass door to find a heavyset woman in her forties—the dean, he assumed—flailing her arms and shouting, "Call the police! Somebody call the police!" When she saw Hellboy rush by, she let out a startled yelp. He ignored her and went to the stairs. The building was identical to the boys' dorm, with the open stairwell in the center.

On his way up, he heard Joey's footsteps ahead of him, heard him shouting, "No! No! No!" Hellboy passed the second floor, with Joey approaching the third. He knew Joey was not entirely aware of what he was doing. He did not realize he was walking into a dangerous situation.

On his way up, Hellboy passed screaming girls running down the stairs in nightgowns and underwear.

Hellboy shouted, "Joey! Joey, stop! Wait!"

Time slowed down to a crawl when he reached the fourth floor.

The creature apparently had started at the far eastern end of the hallway and was making its way toward Hellboy. In its trail were strewn body parts—arms and legs and heads—and a few girls were leaning out of their dorm rooms, screaming at the creature that had just passed them, while a clot of girls ran straight toward Hellboy, away from the Manticore.

The boys were right—it was huge, monstrous. Well over ten feet long, its hairless, purplish-red body rippled with muscles as it moved down the hallway. Its large eyes were the eyes of a man, large, piercing blue, its nose flat with large nostrils. Its mouth was the stuff of nightmares, a giant Cheshire cat's grin of fangs, three rows on top, three on the bottom, red with blood. Chunks of flesh were lodged between the fangs as it tossed its head back and forth and gulped down a masticated arm. Its ears were human ears, and its mouth stretched from one to the other. Its tail swept back and forth, shooting quills forward through the air. The small missiles found their targets and fleeing girls dropped to the floor, paralyzed, only to be eaten up by the beast. Others tripped over the fallen girls—and over Joey, who had gone down on the floor. The creature's mane of thick, shiny, black hair was rapidly becoming matted with blood and gore as it ate its way through the terrified girls. It was so big, it swallowed up the hallway as it moved rapidly forward and ate voraciously. Blood sprayed through the air as bones cracked. One girl after another went down. It took great bites out of their bodies, swallowed legs, heads, arms, torsos, whole bodies.

It came down on Joey fast.

One second after reaching the fourth floor, Hellboy moved forward against the tide of fleeing girls. He felt as if he were moving through quicksand as he headed for Joey, who got knocked back down every time he tried to get up.

The Manticore headed straight for Joey, and it moved fast.

Too fast.

Joey's scream rose with all the others, shrill and filled with terror, as the creature closed its enormous jaws on Joey's head and shoulders, lifted his body up off the floor, and began to chew.

"*No!*" Hellboy shouted as he shoved girls out of the way and moved forward.

As the beast chewed its way to Joey's waist, tossed its head back, and gobbled up his legs, Hellboy bounded forward through the air toward the Manticore. Joey's left shoe fell off as his feet disappeared into the Manticore's mouth. Hellboy landed on the creature's back and raised his enormous right fist. But when he brought his fist down, it hit the floor on which he was kneeling.

The Manticore was gone.

The cold rain stung Hellboy's face as he walked fast from the girls' dormitory. His rage numbed him to it.

The scene he had left on the dormitory's fourth floor was identical to the one in the boys' dormitory—blood everywhere, limbs scattered here and there.

The surviving girls screamed and cried hysterically. Hellboy's trench coat had been sprayed and splattered with blood, but he had not noticed.

He went into the cafeteria through the western entrance. Snodgrass stood by the table with another boy—tall, with short black hair, sleepy eyes.

"Who's this?" Hellboy asked Snodgrass.

"This is Bill Koulouris," Snodgrass said. "He was asleep in his room. I woke him to bring him here."

"Where's the other one?"

"He wasn't in his room. I was going to go back for him while you talked to Bill."

"Where *is* he?" Hellboy said through clenched teeth.

"I don't know," Snodgrass said, "but I suspect he's in the chapel. Like I said, he spends a lot of time there by himself."

Hellboy took Snodgrass's elbow and led him out the eastern door into the rain. "Take me to him. Now."

Halfway to the boys' dorm, Snodgrass said, "Could you please let go of me? You're hurting me."

"Sorry." Hellboy let go of his arm.

Snodgrass broke into a jog to keep up with him.

They went up the steps in front of the dormitory, through the door, and into the lobby.

"Where's the chapel?" Hellboy said.

"Second floor."

They hurried up the stairs to the second floor.

The chapel took up the entire northern side of the western wing of the second floor. Snodgrass pushed through one of the double doors, and Hellboy hurried past him.

"Wait outside," Hellboy said.

Snodgrass said, "But I want to—"

Hellboy turned to him, gave him a no-nonsense look. "Wait outside. Don't come in here until I come out and say it's okay."

Hesitantly, Snodgrass backed out of the chapel and let the door swing closed.

The chapel was small, but with a high vaulted ceiling that rose up into the dormitory's third floor level. Only the lights over the stage were on. A lone figure sat in front of the western column of pews to Hellboy's right. The figure stood and turned around.

Matthew Melonakos was of medium height and wore a white T-shirt, blue sweatpants, and slippers. He held an open Bible in his left hand. Around his neck, on a leather thong, he wore an amulet of some kind.

Hellboy hurried down the center aisle between the two columns of pews, jaw set.

"Matthew Melonakos?" Hellboy said. "We need to talk. Now."

Matt reached up and clutched the amulet in his right hand, looked down at the open book, and began to read something from it in his native language. He read quickly, in a sing-song cadence.

The air between Hellboy and Matt shimmered and blurred, as if heat vapors were rising from the floor. A great, hulking shape materialized.

Without making a sound, the Manticore lunged for Hellboy. He swung his club-like right fist and hammered the creature in the face. Several of its fangs scattered from its mouth and it made an "Oof!" sound as it fell back. Without hesitating, he hit it again, backhanded this time. The Manticore fell into the western column of pews, knocking them askew with a loud clatter.

Matt continued to chant, still clutching the amulet in his right hand.

Hellboy thought of Joey, heard his final screams. Before the creature could get back on its feet, Hellboy jumped on its back and took from his belt a knife with a long eight-inch curved blade. Riding its back as if it were a horse, he swung his left arm down hard and buried the knife to the hilt in its neck.

The Manticore released a growl so deep, Hellboy felt it rumble in his chest. It bucked and turned in a circle, trying to knock him off. It only knocked over pews. Hellboy felt the sting of several quills as they pierced his trench coat and entered his back. Pain like fire spread over his back and his vision blurred. The quills' venom instantly paralyzed the creature's human prey—but Hellboy was not human. He swayed dizzily from side to side on the Manticore's back as the poison quickly coursed through his system, but he did not fall off. Hot tears stung his blurry eyes as he drove the knife into its neck again, the sound of Joey's scream still ringing in his ears.

The creature fell over on its left side and Hellboy fell off. He struggled to his feet, stumbled and fell, but got up again.

The Manticore got to its feet again, too, but now it faced Matt, who still chanted as he clutched the amulet in his right hand. Hellboy stood behind the creature and to its left.

Knowing only hunger, the Manticore bounded forward, tilted its head to the right, and closed its jaws on both of Matt's legs.

Matt's ululating scream filled the small chapel as he fell to the floor. He stopped chanting and the Bible flew through the air away from him.

The Manticore disappeared immediately, taking Matt's legs with it.

The boy convulsed on the floor as blood cascaded from what remained of his body. His scream did not last long. Neither did he.

The chapel door burst open and Snodgrass hurried in. "Oh, my God!" he cried as he ran to Matt's side. "Oh, dear Jesus!"

Hellboy slowly staggered to the boy who lay legless on the chapel floor, a pool of blood growing below his torn waist. The Bible had landed a few feet away from him. Another book had landed a few inches from it, a book that had been open inside the Bible. It was smaller, little more than a booklet. Hellboy fell, slowly struggled to his hands and knees. He picked up the smaller book.

It was old and the cover appeared to be made of leather, the pages of something similar to parchment. Hellboy could not read the language, but he knew it had been from this book, not the Bible, that Matt had been reading.

The chapel spun dizzily as Hellboy crawled to Matt's side. The boy was already dead. Hellboy dropped the book and clumsily removed the amulet from around Matt's neck. It was made of tarnished silver and was a likeness of the Manticore. The creature's body curved in a circle and its head met its tail, mouth open.

Hellboy's fingers became useless and he dropped the amulet just before he fell flat on the floor, numb.

On the plane back to Connecticut the following day, Hellboy sat alone. He had not felt so alone in a long time. He felt heavy with the responsibility of Joey's death. If only he'd stopped him before he'd gotten to the dormitory. If only he'd reached him in time.

Plenty of if-onlys to go around, he thought. *If only Matthew Melonakos's parents had not sent him to this country, if only he had not gone to that school, which he hated so much. If only ...*

An ambulance had taken Hellboy to the hospital the night before, where doctors were not quite sure what to do with him. It turned out little was required once the quills had been removed from his back. The poison had worked its way out of his system rather quickly. He'd spent the night and the following morning there, and had boarded a plane that afternoon.

Matt's small book and amulet were packed away with Hellboy's things and were going back to B.P.R.D. headquarters with him.

When he got back, he would be given another assignment, and he would go about his work as usual. But although he had not known Joey Priven well, he felt a great loss. The B.P.R.D. had lost a good agent. The world may have lost a good writer, perhaps even a great one. Hellboy had lost someone who might have been a friend.

It was a full life, as he had told Joey. But had been wrong about one thing—it was not always satisfying.

THE GLASS ROAD
TIM LEBBON

"Hey, H.B., how's it hanging?"

"Liz, nice to hear from you. Long time no see."

"Well I miss you, too. But considering what usually happens when we get together, I don't miss you *that* much."

"Sweet talker," Hellboy said.

"So what are you up to?" Liz asked.

"I'm between missions."

"Oh, to have that luxury! So you're relaxing, kicking back, catching up on your correspondence?"

"Spending most of my time having nightmares."

"Oh." There was a long pause, as uncomfortable as a telephone silence can be. Liz broke it. "So, did you have any pets in Hell?"

"Huh?"

She laughed, then apologized. "Sorry, it's just that of all cases, this one's caught me off balance. Don't suppose you could ...?"

Hellboy sighed. Liz could imagine him leaning back in his chair, eyes closed, unable as ever to resist a mystery. How could he when his existence was the biggest mystery of them all?

"Of course. Where are you?"

"Sahara. Tell me when you can fly into Al Jawf, and I'll meet you. And bring your shorts. It's damned hot."

"I've known hotter. I'll be in touch."

Hellboy hung up first. Liz held onto the phone and listened to the broken connection, trying as always to hear the truth behind static's secret whisper. Sometimes she was sure that *everyone* was plotting against them. She supposed paranoia was a natural product of spending so long in this business.

She lit a cigarette, sat back, and wiped her brow. *Damn*, it was hot. The tent gave scant protection from the desert sun, and offered no insulation from the screams. She knew what fire could do; these cries brought back memories she had struggled to subdue for half her life.

If only there was something she could do to help.

Hellboy called the following evening to say that he'd be landing in Al Jawf in the early hours. Liz had no real desire to be driving through the Libyan desert at midnight, but then she'd been the one to ask for Hellboy's help. She owed him the courtesy of a personal reception.

Besides, the only thing she really feared in the desert had yet to manifest itself since that first time a week before. And if it did return now—if it chose this night to gasp its fury onto more unsuspecting victims—at least in the dark she would have ample warning. Of all people, she knew that fire shone bright.

Hellboy stepped off the charter plane, and if he hadn't been so red—Liz would have sworn he looked gray around the gills.

"Bad trip?"

"Nothing a few hours at flight school for the pilot wouldn't solve. I got the distinct impression the whole journey veered on the edge of catastrophe."

"Thanks for coming, H.B." She smiled, and he gave her the disarming grin that changed him completely. Sometimes when he smiled like that, she really thought he might be at peace.

"I didn't have anything better to do. HQ still thinks I'm resting up, but I'm sure they'll find me if they need me." He looked around, shivered. "I thought you said it was hot out here!"

"Well, you would arrive in the middle of the night! Come on, I've got a Jeep. We'll head straight there."

"'There' being?"

Liz looked up at the big demon, her affection for him subtly tempered, as ever, by fear. Not of him, but of what he meant. *If I really think about where he's been ...* But she did not allow herself to pursue the thought. She had been through enough with Hellboy to know never to judge by appearances.

"An old ruin out in the desert. It was uncovered a few weeks ago during a major sandstorm. A team of archaeologists have been there ever since, until last week when ..."

He smiled grimly. "That pause means something bad. So let me try to finish. '... Until last week, when they were all horribly killed.'"

Liz nodded. "Well, most of them. It's the ones still alive I feel sorry for. Come on, it's best you see for yourself. One of the survivors can still talk, though there's not much sense. Hear it from him, and you'll get none of my preconceptions. They've done me no good."

Hellboy stepped into the Jeep, its suspension groaning. He wrapped his coat around his shoulders and settled back for the drive. Liz glanced over at his silhouette. "It's good to see you again."

"You too, Liz," he said. As ever, a man of few words.

"It's a two-hour drive. Do me a favor and watch out for anything that glows in the dark."

Hellboy groaned, and muttered, "This is going to be a bad one, isn't it?"

They crossed the desert. The starlight was brilliant here—Liz was still not used to it—and halfway through their journey she stopped the Jeep, simply to turn off the lights and look. She had never seen so many stars. With zero light pollution, the celestial display was awe-inspiring, and she could make out the great swathe of the Milky Way sweeping from horizon to horizon. Three nights ago, at the camp, she had seen a shooting star, and had wished only for the screams from the survivors' tent to stop.

Even Hellboy seemed awed. He stood next to her and stared skyward. They shared the moment in comfortable silence, neither of them feeling the need to spoil the effect with words. Time seemed to stand still, even though what they saw was from any time but now.

Later, just before they reached the camp, Hellboy said, "It's very beautiful here."

Liz slowed the Jeep, nodded, shrugged. She had very mixed feelings about the place herself. "It'll be dawn soon. Starts warming up pretty quickly, so we'll do what we can before then. Do you need a rest, or—?"

"Hey, I'm on a break. Why would I need to rest?"

"Sarcasm doesn't suit you."

"I'm sorry, it's something I've been practicing."

"Come on, I'll show you the survivors. I'm sorry, Hellboy, but this'll knock the humor out of you." She parked the Jeep and jumped out. The sun was barely smudging the horizon pink, and already the temperature had risen five degrees.

And then Liz noticed that the screaming had stopped.

One of the doctors on her team was sitting outside the survivors' tent, smoking a cigarette and looking in their direction. He seemed exhausted.

"Mark? No screaming?"

"Hi, Liz. Hellboy, Dr. Mark Williams, I came here with Liz a week ago to ..." He took a final, long drag on his cigarette and then stubbed it out on the ground. "Well, to help. It's a pity there was nothing I could do."

"They're not all dead?" Liz said.

"All but Mumbler. And he's still doing his thing."

Liz looked at the ground, thinking of those poor, tortured bodies in the tent, and she was *glad* that they were dead. To live—to survive—damaged as they were, would have been too cruel.

"Well, let's talk to him," she said. She entered the tent, and the big demon followed her in.

The man should not have been alive.

"Holy crap," Hellboy whispered.

"Absolutely."

They called him Mumbler because he had not ceased mumbling since the attack. Incoherent ravings mostly, but sometimes there were words to be made out, though they were never words anyone wanted to hear.

Liz gagged, finding it difficult to breathe, and she tried hard to crush down the memories threatening to stir. They were like wild animals pacing beyond the security fence of her consciousness; if she let her concentration slip for an instant, they would be in. And they were voracious.

Mumbler had suffered extreme burns to most of his body. He lay naked on the bed, but there was little recognizable about him. His fingers and toes had melted away, hands and feet turned into knotty globules of hardened flesh and protruding bone. His genitals had been scorched to nothing, his stomach and chest eaten into by fire, and his head bore only the crude approximations of nose, ears, and mouth. The only patch still recognizable as skin was a swathe across his right temple, a half-moon shape that included the eye. The other eye had been burnt to a crisp, its remains hidden by a smear of pinkish cream. His body shivered constantly, as if cold and craving the return of whatever had done this to him.

The doctor scooped white cream from a tub by the bed and smeared it thickly across Mumbler's body, cringing at the pig-like screech that issued from the charcoal mouth. The cream turned pink almost immediately from the continuous bleeding, and his body seemed to suck it in as though it were his final hope.

But there was no hope. They all saw that, and Liz felt a terrible tension building between her and Hellboy. They had been keeping Mumbler alive because of what the man had seen, no more than that. It was cruel, it was awful, but it was essential. That did not mean any of them had to like it.

The doctor gave the burnt man an injection and then walked away, head bowed.

"What did this to him?" Hellboy asked.

"Fire Dogs," Liz said. "That's what he called them, a few days ago when he made more sense. It's almost like the fire's still eating him, burrowing in and stealing everything he was. Now he mostly just growls and screeches."

"What in Hell are Fire Dogs?"

"Maybe you just answered your own question."

Liz glanced at Hellboy, but Mumbler held his attention. For a demon, he had such humanity in his eyes. Liz tried to stifle a sob, but it broke free anyway, and she stepped out of the tent and breathed deeply of the desert air. It stank in there; scorched flesh and death.

She glanced at the sun cresting the horizon, watched a bird fly gracefully against its crimson stain, and the memories came crashing in. The heat, the fires, the screams as her family died, and the terrible, unforgivable monster that was her ego reveling in every lick of flame.

She cursed the sky, kicked at the ground, and then Hellboy was standing there, touching her with his normal hand. The other hung heavy by his side, clenched as if ready for action.

"Why did they send you to this one?" he said quietly.

"I guess they thought fire and me go together."

"How sensitive of them." He held her for a while longer, letting go just when it would have become uncomfortable. "I'm glad you called me."

"So am I, H.B."

"That dying man in there won't tell us anything. So, tell me what you know."

"Do you mind if we go to my tent? I have some whisky there, and I need a drink."

"The ruin I told you about is a mile south of here. Nobody seems to know where it comes from, how old it is, or what it was. I've seen it, and it's ... strange. There are dozens of separate cells, and rooms that must have been for torture."

"How do you know?"

"There are engravings. You ever been to Pompeii?"

"Nothing's ever taken me there."

"You should go one day just for your own edification. Spend one of your breaks traveling instead of waiting for me to call you, eh? In Pompeii there are brothels with menus carved into the walls, because a lot of the patrons were foreign sailors. They'd peruse the menu and point out their particular preference."

"Was there a specials board?"

"Very droll. This place out in the desert, H.B. ... it has a menu. A menu of torture. And all the torture is by fire."

Hellboy was silent for some time. Liz drank, sighed, fanned her shirt. It was scorching already, but Hellboy seemed untroubled. As he said, he'd known hotter.

"I need to go there," he said.

"Of course."

"So, Mumbler and his dead friends?"

"As I said, archaeologists. Some local traders had started visiting them, and a week ago they found them all lying in the desert, burnt. They did what they could for them, set up a tent, went to get help."

"The traders know anything about—?"

"They've gone. Vanished into the desert. After what they saw, you can hardly blame them."

"And Mumbler said that Fire Dogs did this?"

"Fire Dogs up out of the ground, he said. Or that's the gist of it. There was more, but most of it was indecipherable."

"So where did these Fire Dogs go? Did anyone else see them? You checked the area for any geological oddities, gas pockets, anything like that?"

Liz smiled grimly at Hellboy for a few seconds, finished her drink, and stood. The heat was already molding her clothes to her body, and there he was in his big coat.

"Aren't you hot in that thing?"

"I don't want to get sunburnt. It's bad for the skin."

Liz laughed, a real belly laugh that held more than a taint of mania. Nevertheless, it felt good, and she was thankful to him for that. She'd had precious little to laugh about lately.

"I have to show you the site, H.B. There's so much more, but it's best you see it for yourself."

"So let's go." He stood, horn stumps brushing the tent's ceiling. He grinned at Liz, and she liked that because he meant it.

By the time they approached the ruin it was mid-morning, and the sun had made a furnace of the desert. Even Hellboy had shrugged his coat from his shoulders.

He showed no sign of breaking a sweat—Liz had never seen him sweating—and he stared around at the desert as if he had been here before. Its great expanse of packed ground, loose sand, miles and miles of dunes with little to break the monotony except for occasional patches of undergrowth ... none of this amazed him. She hoped it was because his mind was already moving ahead, examining the problem at hand. She knew that Hellboy had a heart, but his imagination had always been an enigma to her. His sense of wonder was not human, and he never made it out to be so.

His manner changed when the ruin came into view. He sat up straighter, stopped his casual observation of the desert, became focused. Liz saw that he was clenching his big fist, keeping it resting at the ready in his lap.

"There it is," she said. "It's not all that big, just a single building really, split into smaller rooms. No roof, just a few tumbled-down walls. The storm was a real zinger to clear that much sand away. Must have been buried for a long time, and the sand's preserved a lot of the features."

"Looks pretty featureless from here," Hellboy said.

Liz brought the Jeep to a halt. Turning the engine off plunged them into a shocking silence, punctuated only by ticking as the motor began to cool. They sat for a few seconds as if awaiting the usual background noise to kick in, but Liz had been here before, and she knew that there *was* no usual noise. The roaring of Fire Dogs a week ago, yes, and the screams of their victims. Now, nothing.

"Let's go nearer," Liz said. "I'll show you the engravings."

"Any language you know?"

"That would make it all too easy."

Hellboy nodded thoughtfully, heading off across the sand.

Liz had seen the ruin before, but still it made her shiver, as if her sweat had suddenly been cooled by an invisible breeze. It was so alien, unknowable, the engravings so mysterious that their inscrutability made them all the more terrifying. Nothing was as frightening as not knowing.

Hellboy stood by one wall and held out his hand, not quite touching the surface. "It's warm," he said.

"Sucks in the heat of the desert. There's lots of weird stuff out here. It'll be warm tonight as well, when we're as cold as a polar bear's ass."

"It feels *too* warm."

Liz looked around at the desert, watching for heat haze that might not be natural. Mumbler had said nothing that would help her spot the Fire Dogs' return. She thought that her own talents might aid her, and the B.P.R.D. must have considered that as well. But the longer she spent here, wallowing in heat, the more she considered the possibility that the opposite could be true: when they came, she might have no idea at all.

"The inscriptions are here," she said. "Inside the walls." She climbed over a tumbled portion of wall and entered what was left of the building. There was no shelter from the sun, no real sense of being cut off at all from the desert, but she felt suddenly disoriented, vulnerable, and exposed. It was as if with one step she had traveled ten thousand miles.

"Hmm," Hellboy said as he followed her in. "Weird."

"What?"

"That sensation of moving away from things."

"It's just strange finding something so old in the desert, is all."

"Maybe," he said. "I feel like it could be any time now, any era. Odd. I wonder if a plane flew over now, would we see it?"

"You're freaking me, Hellboy. Come here and see the inscriptions, then maybe we can get out of here." She led him into a small enclosed room, pointing out the hideous torture scenes that decorated the walls; flaming heads, burning eyes, piles of blackened corpses. They emerged quickly into a central area where the walls were lined with weird hieroglyphs.

Hellboy glanced down at his feet, as if expecting the ground to open up, and then stood next to Liz and looked at the markings.

"Do you recognize any of them?"

"You think I will if you don't?"

"Well ..."

He looked for a couple of minutes, running his fingers over the carvings, clearing out hardened sand to reveal their full shape.

"It's strange," he said, trailing off, tracing the carvings again. A couple more minutes went by. Liz stepped back from Hellboy and let him look, searching the ruin herself for anything she might have missed her first time here. Even standing by the section of tumbled wall, able to see out across the desert, she still felt trapped and removed from time and place. The Jeep looked a very long way away.

"I don't know this language," Hellboy said, "but it's speaking to me."

He had turned away from the wall and was standing at the ancient building's center, head cocked as if listening.

"What exactly does that mean?"

"Not sure."

"There's something else," Liz said, keener than ever to get them both out of the ruin. "The glass road."

Hellboy raised his brow, but Liz only smiled and shook her head. "This you have to see; I can't describe it. I drove in from this direction on purpose. Come on, it's on the other side of the ruin."

They clambered out, climbing a slope of broken stone and hardened sand, and the sun hitting the desert tried to blind them to its wrongness.

"What in the name of ...?"

"Impressive, huh?" Liz said.

The glass road started almost at their feet, a wide, uneven expanse of melted sand, mostly blackened but with clearer patches here and there. Its dark areas ate the sunlight, the lighter splashes blazing it back out as if magnified by entrapment. It stretched off across the dunes, a wound across pale skin.

"This is where we found most of the bodies," she said quietly. "The ones that survived were beyond the edges of the road."

"You say *road* as if there's design in this."

Liz could have disagreed, but she was not altogether certain herself.

"The Fire Dogs did this," Hellboy said. "Hot. How hot would they have to be?"

"Hotter than fire," Liz said. "This is concentrated. Boosted. You've seen me at my worst. Something like that."

"So where does it go?"

"I guess it leads to the Fire Dogs." Liz knew what Hellboy was going to say next—that was partly why she had brought him out here to see the ruin—but the very idea still gave her a chill of fear.

"Feel like a drive?" he asked.

"Not really. But I've got nothing else planned, other than sweating."

They made their way back to the Jeep, took a drink, and then set off along the glass road. The going was smooth to begin with, and the fact that the hardened sand did not try to suck the wheels down made it fast. Hellboy stared at the horizon, and Liz knew that he was concentrating on those carvings he had run his hands over, again and again.

I don't know this language, but it's speaking to me.

Now that Hellboy was here with her, Liz hoped she would hear nothing of its voice herself.

If the road had a destination, it was confused. It veered east and south, east again, then performed a gradual curve that brought it northward. It passed between huge sand dunes or over them, never seeming to choose the easiest route. Its surface cracked and split beneath the Jeep's wheels, and more than once Liz thought that a tire had been shredded. The Jeep carried two spares and temporary repair kits, but if they lost all four tires they would be stranded. At one point she turned off the road and started along beside it, but Hellboy grunted and shook his head, so she took the road again. The Jeep moved faster over its mostly solid surface.

The rough glass refracted sunlight into a million rainbows, and on occasion Liz was all but blinded by color. Such a beautiful effect from something so dreadful. The horizon was always close, and gorgeous mirages hung above it to show where the road would take them next.

"So what do we do if we find them?" she asked Hellboy at last. The heat of the desert prickled the back of her neck, like hellish eyes boring into her.

"Hmm," Hellboy said. He glanced at Liz, tapped his heavy fingers on the dashboard, scratched absently at a horn stump with his other hand.

"And what does that mean?"

"It means I'm still thinking."

"About the inscriptions?"

He continued tapping, scratching, then he looked abruptly at his left hand, as if the meaning of the carvings would be implanted in his fingers. "These have touched ancient dust," he said. "Words and images put there eons ago. I know a lot of languages, Liz, some of them secret, one or two unknown to anyone else alive, now that Professor Bruttenholm's dead. I know how they work, how they feel, and this one is different from them all. I don't quite have it yet, but ... well, I think I know how this one works already. I touched it with my fingers, traced the carvings, and in doing so I translated them. I just haven't listened to the message properly yet."

"So how do you listen?"

"I stay quiet, and concentrate."

And I drive and keep quiet, Liz thought, but she did not feel hurt. Hellboy could have just told her to shut the hell up.

She was the first to see the smoke in the distance. She kept driving for a while, glancing across at Hellboy to see if he'd noticed. It seemed he had not. His eyes were closed, though she knew he was still awake. His fist clenched and unclenched with the sound of fractured tombstones.

The smoke was several miles distant, a dark haze against the vicious blue sky. There was no breeze at all, so it simply hung above whatever caused it, marking its place for all to see. As they drew closer along the glass road, Liz knew that they would pass right under the smoke, and as soon as they crested the next rise, they would see its source.

"Hellboy."

"I know. Cooked flesh," he said, almost casually. "And still cooking."

Liz was shocked, and not only by the smell. Her own reaction surprised her; fear that the Fire Dogs may still be nearby, as opposed to pity for who- or whatever they had killed. That was not like her.

Her fingertips tingled, sizzled, and she cursed and gripped the wheel tighter. This must be getting to her more than she realized.

Hellboy sat back and closed his eyes once more.

Some of the bodies were still burning.

The glass road scorched its way through the encampment like the tire track of a giant truck. It had blackened humps here and there, vague hints that something may have been there before, but little more. Beside the road were burnt bodies—human and camel—and tents. These fires were out; their intensity must have been so great that any combustible material was quickly used up. Further out from the road, scattered across the sand as if trying to flee, were the burning bodies. None of them moved, but for the flicker of flame and the rising of noxious, greasy smoke, and there were none untouched by the Fire Dogs. Liz counted twenty bodies for sure, and some of the congealed masses on and around the road might also once have been people.

A camel belched blue flame as its stomach ruptured.

"I think we've found the traders," Hellboy said.

Liz did not reply. She was glad that she'd brought the Jeep to a halt before reaching the scene. Even she could smell some of the burning now, and taste it, and in her mind's eye she saw so much more from her past, scenes she had tried keeping deep down, but which always reared their heads when provoked. Guilt could do that to a girl, she guessed. Guilt and a healthy dose of self-loathing.

Every burning body had a family. She knew that only too well.

"Let's take a look," Hellboy said.

"Do we have to?"

"Of course." He seemed surprised that she had even hinted at moving on. "What if there are survivors?"

"Like Mumbler? I'd sooner leave them to die."

"They might be able to tell us what these things look like, how fast they move, how they act. Did you get any of that from Mumbler?"

"No," Liz agreed.

"Then let's go. Liz, I know this is hard, but we need to know what we're up against."

"Those inscriptions haven't told you anything yet?"

Hellboy seemed suddenly evasive, shaking his head and jumping from the Jeep. The road crackled under his weight, snapping like a gunshot.

I guess he'll tell me when he's ready, Liz thought. *But I don't like secrets*. She exited the Jeep and walked beside Hellboy.

One of the camels was still alive, barely, and Hellboy pulled out his revolver and put a bullet in the thing's skull. It sighed as it died.

"So now what?" Liz asked. The sights were getting to her, and the sounds of burning. Rage, guilt, and fear were twisting in her head like a nest of snakes, and there was a hot, insistent knot in her chest, sending tendrils of itself along bones and through veins. Her fingers were hot. She was very scared. *Not here*, she thought. *Not now.*

Hellboy looked at her and saw that something was wrong. Perhaps he guessed, perhaps not, but as her friend he tried not to make it obvious. "Now we get the hell away from here," he said. "Follow the road, see where it's taking us. And I need to concentrate a bit more."

"So, what?" Liz asked. "What do they say?"

"Give me time," he said quietly. "We all have our secrets, Liz."

The sun was setting in the west when they saw the glow to the east.

"Is that usual in the desert?" Hellboy asked.

Liz shrugged. "I haven't seen it before."

"Weird atmospherics, maybe? Mirage?"

Liz did not reply, because Hellboy's tone of voice said what they both knew. The Fire Dogs were ahead of them, just over the horizon. Ten miles distant, maybe even less. And it was getting dark.

"Maybe night will be the best time to deal with them," Hellboy said.

"Deal? How? They'll burn the Jeep, I'll be reduced to a smoldering pile of ash and you ... I don't know what'll happen to you. Roast demon."

"Liz ..." She heard an unfamiliar fear in his voice. Or maybe the fear was her own, and she was hearing it in him to make herself feel better.

"Hellboy, tell me. I'll be straight with you first: I hate it here. Memories I thought I had control of are haunting me. My family ... my brother ... I *hate* it here. Now please tell me what you know, and then we can decide—"

"We can't stop them."

"Oh." She slowed the Jeep to a crawl, stopped, heard it settling into the surface of the glass road. *When we get really close*, she thought, *the road will still be hot.*

"I don't know how I know the language of those inscriptions—and I don't want to think about how—but I traced them with my finger, and they've spoken to me. And they're calling me home."

The word hit Liz like a stone fist. "Home."

Hellboy nodded.

"You mean ...?"

"The ruin is a portal to Hell. From what I can gather the Fire Dogs guard it, and every now and then, when it's exposed, they come out to hunt."

"Home?" Liz said again. *Is he going to—?*

"I'm not going," Hellboy said, scaring her even more.

"So if we can't stop them, why are we following them."

Hellboy tapped his fingers on the dashboard again. Liz felt the vibration through her feet, her legs, her butt on the seat.

"We have to lure them back," he said. "I have no idea how long they'll roam across the desert, nor how far they'll go, before they return to the Underworld. I don't think they've been out for a very long time. Maybe pre-history they came out, destroyed whole populations, civilizations. We can't afford to let them go anywhere."

"And how exactly do we do that?" But Liz knew. She had worked with Hellboy enough to know his methods, and really, when she thought about it, this would be the only way.

"We're bait," he said. "But once we get there, I'll have to act fast, so I need you to drive the Jeep."

A cool finger ran down Liz's spine and nestled in her lower back. Inside her chest it was still hot. She wished that heat could be extinguished forever, but as she was stuck with it, at least she could use it for good. She would never make amends, but assuaging the guilt even a little helped her sleep at night.

"H.B., even if you didn't need me, I'd still be coming along."

"Thanks," he said, smiling. As he turned away, Liz saw something in his expression, something that scared her still. Doubt.

They're calling me home.

L iz drove slowly. Every muscle in her body was telling her to lift her foot and stop the Jeep, but Hellboy sat next to her, tensed and primed for action. And ahead of them, scorching the sky and turning dusk to day, the Fire Dogs frolicked just over the hill.

The Jeep crawled easily up the sand dune, carrying them relentlessly toward the blazing monsters, and Liz wondered whether this would be the last red sunset she ever saw. She had faced death so often before that it had begun to excite some part of her, but this was different: death by fire. Much as she often thought it was all she deserved, it was the last thing in the world she wanted.

They crested the slope, the Jeep leveled out, and Hellboy grunted. Liz could not even do that. She had never seen anything like it.

Before them lay a wide, shallow dip in the land, perhaps a mile across, and it was alight. The Fire Dogs rolled from one side to the other, colliding, rebounding, leaping into the air, burrowing into the fluid ground, scorching it black and spitting showers of molten sand behind them. Sparks floated in the air like flaming dust, and true flames spun higher, a hundred mini-tornadoes of fire that flickered and flitted out as they rose into the evening sky. There were fifteen separate Fire Dogs, maybe twenty, each of them easily as big as the Jeep.

The Jeep's windscreen cracked from the sudden blast of heat, its metal chassis creaked, and Liz felt the film on her eyes drying, skin stretching, hair sizzling. Inside her chest was a ball of fire that could never match what she saw here.

"Hellboy ..."

"They're playing," he said. And he was right. The Dogs were running at each other, spitting fire, snapping with insubstantial jaws and clasping on, rolling through the melted sand and separating again, running in circles around the perimeter of the basin, and above the roaring sounds of conflagration came something more astonishing ... the barking of hounds.

"Turn the Jeep around," Hellboy said.

"We'll never outrun them."

"I don't think we have any choice. Our hand has been forced. Look." Hellboy pointed with one stone finger, and Liz saw the awful truth. Several of the Fire Dogs had come to a stop, and blazing eyes stared their way. The barking died down, leaving only the crackle of flames. Liz felt those eyes boring into her, and she wondered whether they saw what she was.

Her fingers were hot on the wheel, and not only from the heat of the Dogs. Her throat was parched, from the inside as well as without.

"Hellboy," she rasped, "something's—"

"Go!" he shouted.

The first Fire Dog had started crawling up the slope toward them, long fiery legs hauling it up, rump raised, the classic stalking pose.

"Liz, go!"

She rammed the Jeep into reverse and floored the gas. The vehicle bucked and groaned, and then rocketed backwards down the slope, wheels following the glass road by some miracle. Liz turned in her seat and swung her arm across Hellboy's shoulders.

"Don't tell me how close they are," she said, but she could already feel the glow of heat on her neck.

Keep down, she thought, *down, keep down, not now, not yet!* Her fingers cooled and saliva moistened her mouth, and in one movement she left the glass road. The Jeep's rear wheels hit sand, momentum spun them around, and Liz changed gear, flooring the gas again and heading off down the bottom part of the slope.

"Nice move," Hellboy said.

She glanced in the rear-view mirror, and the ridge above and behind them exploded. "I'm sure it impressed them."

"How far to the ruin?" he asked.

"A good forty miles."

"Hmm." Hellboy had turned in his seat, and fire reflected in his eyes. "Floor it!"

Liz took the Jeep out across the desert.

Either they were well matched for speed, or the Fire Dogs were toying with them. *I thought only cats did that,* Liz thought, but she shook her head. No point losing it now.

The Jeep bounced along the glass road, but Liz drove hard. If they had punctures, broke their suspension, or cracked an axle, the Dogs would have them. But if she let up the Dogs would *definitely* catch them, and she had no intention of making it easy.

Behind them, the whole desert was aflame. The Fire Dogs had spread out, running side by side and scorching separate routes into the sand. Liz's snazzy driving had given her and Hellboy a head start, and the Dogs were maybe half a mile behind them, matching their speed and direction perfectly. They had come ten miles already—maybe thirty left to go—and Liz was thinking about what would happen when they reached the ruin.

"Do you think the Jeep will take it?" he asked.

Liz shrugged. "I can't let up. And I can't go any faster." They hit a ridge in the road and bounced from side to side, tires throwing them back and forth for a few seconds before they leveled out again. "I could always lose some ballast." She glanced across at Hellboy and smiled.

"I've been meaning to go on a diet."

The road began to curve ahead of them, and they faced a quick decision. "Stay to the road," Hellboy said.

"You sure?"

"The sand will slow us down too much. And they're so close that they won't cut across the curve. They're right on our tail—they go where we go."

Liz looked in the mirror and saw that he was right. The night brought no darkness to the desert tonight; the Fire Dogs had made it their own. They barked and roared, as if passing amusing comments along the line, and then fell silent again.

"Gas is low," Liz murmured.

"Don't tell me that."

"Okay, forget it."

Thirty miles. Ten to go, maybe less. Liz's muscles were aching from the constant pounding, her arms stiff and burning, her ankle asleep from where it pushed the gas pedal to the floor. Something had started rattling beneath the Jeep, an insistent banging as metal struck metal. The temperature gauge was heading above the safe limit, and the gas warning light had come on three miles earlier. They should reach the ruin—*should*—but driving like this she was burning gas fast.

She could not slow down. If anything, the Fire Dogs were gaining on them.

She could feel the heat of their pursuit, and her own heat rose in her, and she knew that Hellboy was aware of that.

"Can you make it?" he asked.

"I'll have to," she said, afraid that her teeth were on fire.

"Come on, Liz. Fight it. Maybe it'll be useful in a few minutes, but *not right now!*"

Not right now, he had said, and Liz repeated this to herself, telling it to her own inner demon again and again, *not right now*.

The ruin came into view, lit by the Jeep's headlights and the flames of the things pursuing them. The engine stuttered to a halt, dry at last. And Liz felt herself about to explode.

"H.B., I'm going," she said, slipping sideways in her seat and leaning on the door latch. The roar of the Fire Dogs filled her ears and fire blossomed around her, her own flames or those of the Dogs she did not know, and as she tumbled from the Jeep she felt a cold hand curl around her leg.

Fire came down upon them, filling her vision, the vehicle exploding somewhere behind and above her, and Hellboy's voice was raised above the cacophony, shouting out in a language she had never heard. Even though she did not know the words, she knew the rage with which they were spoken.

Taking them home, she thought, *that's how he'll do it. He's taking them home.*

Something smashed against her ear, and she realized it was a bark, so loud that it had felt like a fist. Hellboy's hand had gone from her leg now—she was alone—and from the fires surrounding her a Fire Dog emerged. Its eyes were white pits in the wall of flames, its claws sizzling, skin crawling with Hellish designs. It barked again, and she barked back, sending a gush of fire at its face. It shook its muzzle and stepped away, confused, and Liz was sure she heard an uncertain whine from its white-hot throat.

It disappeared back into the flames, as if something had grabbed it by the tail and hauled it away from her. She was about to bark again—that had felt good, that had felt *right*—when she felt herself being pushed down into the sand. It closed around her, hot, biting into her skin, and she went deeper and deeper.

Hold your breath, something whispered, and though Liz felt the guilt of awful memories coming out to haunt her beyond the flames, she did not want to die. She took a gulp, closed her eyes, and obeyed those final words.

Hellboy brought her up. He smashed the hardened sand around her, tugging it away from her gashed and scraped flesh, lifting her high with his cold stone hand and carrying her into the desert. It was dawn. To the east, natural light kissed the horizon. To the west, the beginnings of a colossal sand storm danced in the sky.

"Are they gone?" she asked.

He nodded. "Gone home."

"How?"

"I told them."

"And they listened?"

Hellboy shrugged, nodded. "They took a little persuading, I guess. They were bad dogs."

"So, did you have any pets in Hell?"

He was quiet for a long time, tending her wounds, using the remnants of the medical box salvaged from the Jeep. She was cut and scraped from when he had forced her underground and from the dogs' attack. She drifted in and out of consciousness, but all the while she marveled at Hellboy's gentle touch. He rested her limbs on his massive stone-like hand and used his other to apply salve, bandages, gauze.

When she decided he had ignored or forgotten her question he looked up at the sun, closed his eyes, and said, "I can't remember."

TASTY TEETH
GUILLERMO DEL TORO & MATTHEW ROBBINS

Dark in here. As usual.

Hellboy wondered if he'd ever get over it, that familiar mix of fear and joy. Something about good old gloom and his own stygian origins ... He shuffled his way down a wet floor, his hooves scraping smooth stone.

What was he supposed to find in this godforsaken place? He was tired *and* hungry, just enough to provoke his famous irritability. Crap, this was looking like another false alarm. Missing children, from Bucharest. *A police matter, something for the Transylvanian milk cartons*—

He felt a cool wind on his face, rising up from somewhere below. Time to light another glow stick.

With a hiss, the chemical light bloomed and he squinted his golden, demon eyes. Before him lay a narrow stairwell, spiraling down into the living rock. This was an ancient, clammy burial vault, some thirty meters below the ruins of a fortress. He wished Abe were here, but the lucky fish man was lolling in warm Mediterranean water, retrieving a ghost-infested Spanish altarpiece from the bowels of a galley ship. Abe hated Romania anyway. Especially Romanian crypts with their corny reputation.

He paused to sniff the musty air. No bat guano, no smell of blood. Just dank mildew, not the sort of atmosphere vampires might favor. He sighed, knowing he had to at least go through the motions. So, onward, through another rank tunnel. Story of his life. He glanced at his bulky shadow and smiled at its looming menace. Like a movie, he thought. Too bad there was no one here to enjoy the show.

Or was there? His red skin tingled, the strange, inexplicable warning he'd come to know in places like this. Wary now, he brought out the big-ass gun. His very own steel security blanket, all ten pounds of it. Hellboy loved its heft, as a firearm and blunt instrument.

The B.P.R.D.'s Kate Corrigan and Captain Mihaileanu, their local contact, were waiting somewhere above, parked in the Land Rover, gazing at gravestones and sipping slivovitz.

"Hellboy? You want to check in, big fella? A little show-and-tell?"

On the radio Kate sounded extra girlish, ultra-American. Hellboy kept his voice low, his lips near the microphone. "Not yet. I'm freezing down here—"

Wait. Did he hear something?

"Come in, H.B., you were just complaining—?"

"Shh ..."

Voices. Definitely. High pitched, whimpering, somewhere up ahead. And a rattle of chains. Creepy. Hellboy threw open the gun and checked his bullets. Hmmm. Maybe not such a good idea, all this garlic juice and boxwood, with no sign of suckheads or bats.

More cries and whispers. Human, he guessed. Again, he spoke into his microphone. "Someone's down here."

He plucked some bullets from his cartridge belt and changed a few rounds. He'd spent the night before on the B.P.R.D. plane, making his own assortment of poisons, not knowing what to expect. Now he decided to change to Ptolemaic silver dust suspended in holy water, an all-purpose, monster-numbing agent.

"H.B., this is Mihaileanu." Yeah, Radu the magician; the guy sounded like a Bela Lugosi impersonator, but he had a heart of gold. He was the one who'd rung the alarm, drawing the B.P.R.D. into this. "If it's kids, they're going to scream when they see you. How much Romanian do you know?"

"I dunno, urm—*La plume de ma tante, dos equis por favor, sieg heil...*"

"Enough. If they're conscious, just ... smile, okay? They'll be famished. Give them a couple of candy bars."

"No way. I'm down to my last two. That's where I draw the line, d—"

Something at his feet. A child's skull, festooned with live spiders. The greenish yellow light picked out an assortment of niches cut into the rock walls. He reached into the nearest one and pulled out a fistful of little bones.

"Guess what, guys. I got baby bones all around me."

On his earpiece—static growing louder—he heard a muttered curse. Then the sound of tearing paper as Kate ripped open their attack plan. Radu spoke hastily: "H.B., look carefully. Are there toothmarks? Fresh ones?"

Hellboy squinted at a child's clavicle. Scored, scratched, and chewed. Old bones, new marks.

"The marrow—has something eaten it?" He could hear quick page-turning. Kate was reading the field manual.

Static growled in his earpiece. And just then—perfect timing—his light stick went out. Grumbling, he lit another flare and looked around. Miniature rib cages and dusty, wooden toys were strewn all over the floor. He chuckled as he felt his heart thumping faster. Yeah, that old feeling again: both jazzed and scared. He instinctively flexed his knuckles.

"Radu? Yes. The bones—nibble nibble, crunch crunch." More nasty muttering. "What's the matter, Kate? This making you hungry?"

"Shut up and watch out. It's *tooth fairies.*"

Hellboy smiled. That's what he loved about the B.P.R.D.'s field-ops director: she took it all so seriously, even when the B.P.R.D. analysts went off the deep end, like now.

The ceiling had been barely high enough to accommodate his size, and now, in another rough-hewn sub-cellar, the walls closed in. He'd heard all the tooth-fairy stories, each one a grotesque joke and, in the end, an expensive waste of time. Some perverse fascination to the notion, he had to admit, dragging a beloved childhood fantasy into the Bureau's mire of demonic lore. What would they turn up next? A sabre-toothed Easter Bunny?

Kate was reading: "Okay, we've got the Concord of 1226, an agreement between Pope Honorius and Pauxtis Salgudis, king of the fairies ..." Hellboy laughed again. King of the fairies: sorry, he just couldn't help it.

Then he noticed iron rings hammered into the ceiling, glistening in the weird, sour light.

The history lesson continued: "The endless predations of the fairies, their quest for the sweet, tasty calcium found *only* in the bones of young children. They made life impossible in late medieval Constantinople. Children were stolen from their beds, murdered, their bones consumed ... Honorius wrote a pact in which a silver coin, left under each child's pillow, would serve as payment from the hungry tooth fairies in exchange for a fresh milk tooth. Hellboy, did you copy that?"

He'd heard enough. Clicking off the earpiece, he set down his equipment pack, conscious now of shallow breathing from somewhere nearby. Working slowly and deliberately, he cracked two more light sticks and tossed them out into the gloomy chamber. That's when he spotted the cells.

Iron bars were set at regular intervals along the walls, like a subterranean kennel. Behind them, in each little cage, lay a pathetic heap of bones, some of them still draped in rotted pajamas. He moved closer, knowing now what he'd find.

Just above his head, in one of the cells, there was movement. Eyes stared out—two pale children, each about six years of age. A boy and a girl lay in chains, whimpering and looking at him in horror. He stepped closer and the children shrank back, weakly pressing themselves against the rear wall, ready to die.

"Easy now, Uncle Red's not gonna hurt you. Look, I brought candy." He pulled his candy bars from his overcoat and held them near the cage, waiting. But the children just gawked, glassy-eyed.

"What's the matter? Afraid they'll rot your teeth?"

He smiled broadly, pointing to his mouth. "Teeth, you know? Er, um—brusha brusha?" The kids were trembling; the boy pointed to something behind him.

Hellboy turned in time to see a shape dart along the floor, like a high-speed rat. Moments later, another dark figure scurried past. Hearing a faint chorus of laughter, he stepped over to a drain and looked down.

Something was moving down there, and he was aware of the sound of whispering, like the rustle of tissue paper. He held out a light stick and dropped it in. No more than five seconds later the light winked out, but in that brief glimpse, he knew he was in trouble.

A glittering array of wings and pale, bobbing heads were swarming up from below, intent on some nameless mission.

He backed away, grabbed one of the bars of the cage and pulled. But nothing happened. It was old iron, sturdy and fat. Using two hands, he tried again, as piping voices echoed in the pit behind him. They were getting closer. Straining and groaning, he realized he wasn't cold any more. In fact, he had started to sweat.

In a sudden explosion of rock dust, he managed to dislodge the iron bar, enough to bend it away and reach into the cage. After a brief scuffle, he scooped out the little boy, snapping his tether. But he felt a touch on his leg as something ran delicately up to his waist. Without dropping the child, he brushed whatever it was to the floor and leveled his gun.

Staring up at him was a cheerful, wicked little face under a mop of scraggly, white hair. It had tiny fingers and a blur of light at its back, where gossamer wings were beating at hummingbird speed. In a moment, the fairy was joined by half a dozen more, who came skittering out of the drain, taking to the air like newly hatched mayflies.

Under their pallid, membranous skin, fine bluish veins were pulsating with excitement. Their little jaws parted, revealing row after row of thin, tightly clustered teeth stained orange with centuries-old blood.

Revolted, Hellboy squeezed the trigger, and the gun boomed off the rock walls. In the muzzle flash, he was able to see the floor alive with more running, buzzing creatures, far too many for one magic bullet, no matter what its contents. As the smoke cleared, he saw he had vaporized a few, but others were already landing on his back, running on his shoulders and scurrying up the sleeves of his heavy leather duster.

He reached into the cell and grabbed the little girl by the collar, hauling her out. By now he was ankle-deep in the critters. He felt them greedily gnawing at the skin on his neck, legs, arms. His blood and sweat mingled, soaking him. "Damn, you hurt!" he roared. In a rage, he fired a few rounds.

The gun clicked on an empty chamber—already?! No time to reload. Hellboy charged for the stairs, both children under one massive arm and his equipment bag in the other. Behind him, a cloud of little creatures took wing, like grasshoppers rising from a wheat field.

He'd always been fast, but there was no outrunning the swooping, darting creatures that came buzzing behind him. He swatted at them and knew, from their soprano squeals and the suddenly slippery floor, that he was crushing some underfoot. But there were too many.

One of the creatures sank a grimy incisor deep into Hellboy's forearm. An instant later, the right hand of doom ground the hapless fairy to paste. Hellboy examined the fresh, jagged wound: the thing had chewed through flesh, muscle, and tendon. "Ugh. That ain't gonna scar so nice," thought Hellboy. "Trophy wound."

He felt himself slowing down as they pulled at his coat, trying to drag him back. Growling and shrugging, feeling like Gulliver among the Lilliputians, Hellboy fought on, passing marble friezes with Roman funerary inscriptions. Someday, he thought, it would be interesting to come back here and learn about ancient Dacia ...

Crap. He wasn't getting anywhere. The fairies were everywhere, dancing on his head, swinging from his forearms, crawling down his collar. Glancing down, he could see them alighting on the tear-streaked faces of the children. The little boy's mouth was open in nightmarish, howling anguish. Hellboy spotted a few shiny, white teeth hanging precariously from his gums.

Seeing his chance, he pushed his big, clumsy fingers into the child's mouth, probing until he grasped a loose molar. He plucked it out, fast enough so that the gagging boy hardly knew what had happened. For a split second, Hellboy held it aloft, hoping it would shine like a nugget of gold.

Sudden silence. The myriad of fairies seemed to freeze, as if hypnotized by the sight of something so exquisite, so tasty. Hellboy managed a smile.

"So you want something to chew on?"

He tossed it away into the darkness.

The tiny tooth clattered like a white pebble on the stone floor, only to disappear under a roiling heap of frenzied, buzzing bodies. The excited fairy chatter was indecipherable, but it somehow told a tale of ancient lust and, for the lucky ones, delicious satisfaction. Hellboy wedged himself into the nearest corner and stuffed both children under his coat. Reaching into the equipment bag, he brought forth a double Vulcan 64 grenade, yanked the pin, and rolled it across the floor.

Both kids were screaming now, more frightened than ever. They'd probably caught a glimpse of his tail. Damn. Too bad Abe wasn't here—he had that gentle, soothing voice—

With a deafening roar the grenade went off. The searing heat rolled over Hellboy's body as the burial vault bloomed in orange flame. Ah, combustion, his old friend, so handy in times like these. He stayed low, holding the children down and letting his fireproof body shield them from harm. He glanced up as the flames began to subside.

The air was filled with dying fairies.

They were thudding to the ground all around him, their wings spraying sparks and wisps of smoke. The floor was littered with their charred bodies, some twitching like jumbo roaches.

Something was glinting among their dead. He kicked aside a small leather pouch and heard the familiar clink of coins. He reached down and gathered up a few shiny pieces of silver, marveling at their mint condition. Even though he was no expert he could recognize the famous profile of the Emperor Constantine. Souvenirs—he loved 'em.

Someone was tugging on the hem of his overcoat. Of course, the kids. He glanced down and saw them looking up at him, groping for his big hand. He knelt down and looked them over. Not too bad, despite their pallor and recent trauma.

"Easy, easy ... Uncle Hellboy hasn't forgotten. Show me your smile and let's see what the tooth fairy has left you, okay?" He handed over his last two candy bars. A never-before-seen gesture that would be debated and whispered about in the B.P.R.D. corridors for years to come.

Outside, the sun was coming up. A few coils of mist rose among the gravestones as the birds began to chirp. Kate, riding shotgun in the Range Rover, stared out across the graveyard at a plume of black smoke pouring out from a half-ruined mausoleum. And suddenly, there was Hellboy, striding toward her, a child on each shoulder. And both kids were grinning and gap-toothed, chewing away at the soft nougat and chocolate. Hellboy felt full of reassurance and smiled: Professor Bruttenholm used to tell him about dawns like this, when a new day can bring magic into the world.

He was ready to have a great morning.

CONTRIBUTORS

SCOTT ALLIE writes and edits comics and stories for Dark Horse Comics and other publishers, including *The Devil's Footprints* with Brian Horton, Paul Lee, and Dave Stewart. He lives in Portland, Oregon with his wife Melinda and their phantom cat, Shadow. Visit him at scottallie.com.

✠

JAMES L. CAMBIAS is a writer and role-playing-game designer. He grew up in New Orleans, but doesn't recall meeting any vampires there. Mr. Cambias currently lives in western Massachusetts, where the shambling black shapes in the yard at night are probably just bears.

✠

Author, editor, critic/essayist, poet, and now—with the award-winning PS imprint—publisher, PETER CROWTHER has edited more than twenty anthologies and produced almost one hundred short stories and novellas (two of which have been adapted for British TV), plus the novels *Escardy Gap* (in collaboration with James Lovegrove) and *Darkness, Darkness*. Two story collections (one SF and the other horror/dark fantasy) appeared in 2004, and he's now putting together another, while working on the second installment of his *Forever Twilight* SF/horror series, a mainstream novel, a couple of new anthologies, and another TV project. Pete jumped at the opportunity to write about Hellboy—after all, he's a long-time fan of comic books and graphic novels (he used to own full runs of DC's *Strange Adventures* and *Mystery in Space*, but he sold them, many years ago, when he needed an injection of cash—he's almost recovered from the aftereffects of that transaction, though he still sobs uncontrollably when anyone mentions *Captain Comet* or *Space Cabby*, and he regularly dreams about trying to catch the Zeta beam to return to his beloved Rann ...). He lives in England with his wife Nicky and many thousands of books, comics, DVDs, record albums, and CDs.

✠

Three-time Oscar nominee FRANK DARABONT was born in a refugee camp in France in 1959, the son of Hungarian parents who had fled Budapest during the failed 1956 Hungarian uprising. Brought to America as an infant, he settled with his family in Los Angeles and attended Hollywood High School. His first job in movies was as a production assistant on the 1981 film, *Hell Night*, starring Linda Blair. He spent the next six years working in low-budget films in the "art department" (building and dressing sets) while struggling to establish himself as a writer. His first produced writing credit (shared) was on 1987's *Nightmare on Elm Street 3: Dream Warriors*, directed by co-writer and friend Chuck Russell.

Darabont is one of only six filmmakers in history with the unique distinction of having his first two feature films receive nominations for the Best Picture Academy Award: 1994's *The Shawshank Redemption* (with a total of seven nominations) and 1999's *The Green Mile* (four nominations). His most recent feature as director, *The Majestic*, starring Jim Carrey, was released in December 2001. The next film he hopes to direct is his adaptation of Ray Bradbury's classic science-fiction novel *Fahrenheit 451*. Also intended for future production are film adaptations of Robert McCammon's intense female-driven thriller *Mine*, and Stephen King's *The Mist*.

Frank still lives in Los Angeles and is a big damn Hellboy fan. A collector and lover of original art, his house is filled with pieces by such awesome artists as Bernie Wrightson, Drew Struzan, Sanjulian ... and, of course, Mike Mignola.

CHARLES DE LINT is a full-time writer and musician who presently makes his home in Ottawa, Canada with his wife MaryAnn Harris, an artist and musician. His most recent books are *The Blue Girl*, *Medicine Road*, and *Spirits in the Wires*. Other recent publications include the collections *Waifs & Strays* and *Tapping the Dream Tree*, and *A Circle of Cats*, a picture book illustrated by Charles Vess. For more information about his work, visit his website at www.charlesdelint.com.

✠

Born in Guadalajara, Mexico, 1964, **GUILLERMO DEL TORO** is a devoted fan of Mario Bava, Luis Buñuel, James Whale, Alfred Hitchcock, and Terence Fisher. His fascination with classic horror cinema was already evident in his first film, *Cronos* (1992), which won the Grand Prize at the critics' week at the Cannes Film Festival along with nine Mexican Academy Awards. The film was replete with insect biology, outlandish monstrosities, and Catholic imagery, which have continued to appear in his films: *Mimic* (1997), *The Devil's Backbone* (2001), *Blade 2* (2002), and *Hellboy* (2004). A self-confessed horror addict, del Toro has written articles or film commentary for magazines as diverse as *Fangoria* and *Sight and Sound*. He is currently adapting (along with Matthew Robbins) H. P. Lovecraft's novel *At the Mountains of Madness* while preparing the screenplay for *Hellboy II*.

✠

RAY GARTON is the author of over forty books, including the Bram Stoker Award-nominated *Live Girls*, *Shackled*, *Sex and Violence in Hollywood*, and most recently, *Scissors*. Among his books are the short-story collections *Methods of Madness*, *Pieces of Hate*, and the upcoming *Slivers of Bone* and *The Girl in the Basement and Other Stories*. Under the name Joseph Locke, he has written a number of young-adult novels, including *Kill the Teacher's Pet*, *Game Over*, and *1-900-Killer*. His movie novelizations and TV tie-ins include *Warlock* and *Buffy the Vampire Slayer: Resurrecting Ravana*. He lives in northern California with his wife Dawn and their nine cats.

✠

ED GORMAN has been writing full-time for twenty years, during which he has produced thirty novels in the suspense and western fields and six collections of his own stories. His work has won a variety of awards, including the Shamus, Spur, Anthony, and the International Writers Award in horror. He's been nominated twice for the Edgar and once for the Golden Dagger (UK). *Kirkus Reviews* has called him "One of the most original crime writers around," and *The Bloomsbury Review* has called him "The poet of dark suspense." His lives with his wife Carol, a much-celebrated young-adult writer, in Cedar Rapids, Iowa. He is presently working on a long, dark suspense novel.

✠

GRAHAM JOYCE was born in Keresley, England, a mining village near Coventry, and grew up there. He received an MA in Modern English and American Literature from Leicester University and a PhD in English from Nottingham Trent University. For seven years he devoted himself to youth work until he burned out and decided to throw it all over to concentrate on writing. In 1988 he married Suzanne Johnsen and left England to spend a year on the Greek island of Lesbos, living in a shack on the beach they shared with scorpions while he worked on his novel. They were still in Greece when he got word the following year the novel had sold, and they used the advance money to travel to the Middle East before returning to England. He has won the British Fantasy Society's August Derleth Award four times, for *Dark Sister*, *Requiem*, *The Tooth Fairy*, and *Indigo*. He won the French award Grand Prix De L'Imaginaire for his novella *Leningrad Nights*. He won the World Fantasy Award for his recent novel *The Facts of Life*. He currently lives in Leicester with his wife, daughter Ella, and son Joseph.

NANCY KILPATRICK is the award-winning author of fourteen novels, five collections, about one hundred and fifty short stories, and she has just edited her eighth anthology, this one along with fellow writer Nancy Holder. She has also written much non-fiction, a stage play, a couple of radio programs, and three issues of the *VampErotica* comics series, the stories based on her collection *Sex & The Single Vampire*. Her most recent title is the non-fiction opus *The Goth Bible: A Compendium for the Darkly Inclined* (St. Martin's Press, October 2004). Many of her titles are being reprinted, including her vampire series *Power of the Blood* and her erotic horror series *The Darker Passions*, written under the nom de plume Amarantha Knight. She lives in lovely Montreal, Canada with her cranky black cat Bella, where surely Hellboy will one day show up, because the Euro-like city throbs with preternatural, bilingual energy.

✠

TIM LEBBON's books include the novels *Face*, *The Nature of Balance*, *Mesmer*, and *Until She Sleeps*; the collections *Faith in the Flesh*, *As the Sun Goes Down*, *White and Other Tales of Ruin*, and *Fears Unnamed*; and the novellas *Naming of Parts*, *White*, *Exorcising Angels* (with Simon Clark), *Changing of Faces*, and *Dead Man's Hand*. He has three new novels forthcoming from Leisure Books: the first, *Desolation*, is due out early 2005, and will also appear in a limited edition from Borderlands Press. *Berserk* will appear in 2006, and *Echo City Falls* in 2007. Other forthcoming publications include *Into the Wild Green Yonder* (with Peter Crowther), new novellas from PS Publishing and Necessary Evil Press, and novellas in the collections *Night Visions 11* and *Fourbodings*. Lebbon has won two British Fantasy Awards, a Bram Stoker Award, and a Tombstone Award, and his work has been optioned for the screen on both sides of the Atlantic. He is currently serving as vice president of the Horror Writers Association. For more details and news visit his website at www.timlebbon.net.

✠

SHARYN McCRUMB's award-winning novels celebrating the history and folklore of Appalachia have received scholarly acclaim and ranked on the *New York Times* bestseller lists. The author of *Ghost Riders*, *The Songcatcher*, *The Ballad of Frankie Silver*, *The Rosewood Casket*, *She Walks These Hills*, *The Hangman's Beautiful Daughter*, and *If Ever I Return, Pretty Peggy-O*, as well as many other acclaimed works, McCrumb's novels have been named Notable Books for the Year by the *New York Times* and the *Los Angeles Times*. In her newest novel, *St. Dale* (Kensington, Feb. 2005*)*, Sharyn McCrumb has crafted a moving tale of transformation and everyday miracles that finds the seam of humanity behind our need for perfect heroes. Suffused with incisive southern wit and eccentric characters, *St. Dale* looks into the very heart of America—its secular saints and cereal-box heroes, wild dreams and unrealized ambitions, heartbreaking losses, and second chances—and celebrates its unbreakable spirit.

Her novels, studied in universities throughout the world, are translated into German, Dutch, Japanese, and Italian. Her work has twice received the AWA's Best Appalachian Novel Award. In November 2003, she was presented with the Wilma Dykeman Award for Regional Historical Literature by the East Tennessee Historical Society.

✠

Although he began working as a professional comic-book artist in the early 1980s, drawing "a little bit of everything for just about everybody," **MIKE MIGNOLA** is best known as the award-winning creator/writer/artist of *Hellboy*. He was also a production designer on the Disney film *Atlantis: The Lost Empire* and visual consultant to Guillermo del Toro on both *Blade 2* and the film version of *Hellboy*.

Mignola lives in New York City with his wife and daughter.

JAMES A. MOORE has been writing professionally for the last fifteen years. His novels include the Bram Stoker Award-nominated *Serenity Falls*, as well as *Fireworks*, *Possessions*, and *Under the Overtree*, and several media tie-in novels. He's worked heavily in the gaming field, mainly for White Wolf Games, and his work in comics includes *Clive Barker's Nightbreed* and *Clive Barker's Hellraiser*. Jim is currently working on several different novels, including a handful of collaborations. He lives in the suburbs of Atlanta, Georgia with his wife, Bonnie.

✠

TOM PICCIRILLI is the author of a dozen novels including *A Choir of Ill Children*, *November Mourns*, *The Night Class*, and *Coffin Blues*. He's been a World Fantasy Award finalist and is a three-time winner of the Bram Stoker Award for Novel, Short Fiction, and Poetry. Learn more about him and his work at his official website: www.tompiccirilli.com.

✠

MATTHEW ROBBINS was born in New York City and went to the Johns Hopkins University, where he received a BA degree in Romance Languages. Shortly after getting his MFA at the USC School of Cinema, he began writing screenplays. *The Sugarland Express* was the first to be produced; starring Goldie Hawn, it was Steven Spielberg's first feature film and won Best Screenplay at the Cannes Film Festival. There followed more scripts for Universal Studios, MGM, and Paramount. Mr. Robbins' films as writer/director include *Dragonslayer* and *Batteries Not Included*. Collaborating with writer/director Guillermo del Toro, he wrote *Mimic* for Dimension Pictures. They are currently writing *At the Mountains of Madness* for DreamWorks, from the novel by H. P. Lovecraft. Matthew Robbins lives in San Francisco with his wife, Janet. They have two children.

✠

DAVID J. SCHOW's short stories have been regularly selected for over twenty-five volumes of "year's best" anthologies across two decades, and have won the World Fantasy Award, the Dimension Award from *Twilight Zone* magazine, plus a 2002 International Horror Guild Award for his collection of *Fangoria* columns, *Wild Hairs*. His novels include *The Kill Riff*, *The Shaft*, *Rock Breaks Scissors Cut*, and *Bullets of Rain*. His short stories are collected in *Seeing Red*, *Lost Angels*, *Black Leather Required*, *Crypt Orchids*, *Eye*, *Zombie Jam* (2004), and *Havoc Swims Jaded* (2005). He is the author of the exhaustively detailed *Outer Limits Companion* and has written extensively for film (*Leatherface: Texas Chainsaw Massacre III*, *The Crow*) and television (*Perversions of Science*, *The Hunger*). You can see him talking and moving around on documentaries and DVDs for everything from *Creature from the Black Lagoon* and *Incubus* to *The Shawshank Redemption* and *Scream and Scream Again*, a BBC4 special about the horror film boom of the eighties. He is also the editor of the *Lost Bloch* series for Subterranean Press and *Elvisland* by John Farris (Babbage, 2004). He has co-produced supplements for such DVDs as *Reservoir Dogs*, *From Hell*, *I, Robot*, and the forthcoming *Chronicles of Narnia*. His bibliography and many other fascinating details are available online at his official site, *Black Leather Required*: www.davidjschow.com.

✠

THOMAS E. SNIEGOSKI is the author of more than a dozen novels, including the teen-fantasy quartet *The Fallen*. With his frequent collaborator Christopher Golden, he is the author of the new dark-fantasy series *The Menagerie*, as well as the young-readers fantasy series *OutCast*, both of which have had their first installments published in 2004. Sniegoski and Golden also co-wrote the *Hellboy* spinoff graphic novel *B.P.R.D.: Hollow Earth*. Sniegoski has written or co-written a great many books and comic books related to the TV series *Buffy the Vampire Slayer* and *Angel*, as well as the scripts for two *Buffy* video games. As a comic-book writer, his work includes *Stupid, Stupid Rat Tails*, a prequel miniseries to the international hit, *Bone*, the only writer to work on the series other than *Bone* creator Jeff Smith. He has also written tales featuring such characters as Batman, Daredevil, Wolverine, and The Punisher. Tom was born and raised in Massachusetts, where he still lives, with his wife LeeAnne and their Labrador retriever, Mulder. He is currently at work on *Sleeper*, a new thriller for Penguin Books. Please visit him at www.sniegoski.com.

✠

RICHARD DEAN STARR is a former member of the Science Fiction and Fantasy Writers of America and the Georgia Press Association. His work has appeared in magazines including *Starlog*, *Science Fiction Chronicle*, and *Twilight Zone*. In addition to his magazine work, he is the former entertainment editor and film critic for *The Southeast Georgian* and *Camden County Tribune* newspapers. Richard is currently President of WebPanther.com Internet Services, which includes WeHostWriters.com, a web-hosting company for authors. His next story, "Fear Itself," will be published by *Cemetery Dance* magazine in 2005.

MORE TALES OF THE STRANGE AND TERRIFYING FEATURING HELLBOY AND THE B.P.R.D.!

HELLBOY BY MIKE MIGNOLA

Seed of Destruction
ISBN: 1-59307-094-2 $17.95

Wake the Devil
ISBN: 1-59307-095-0 $17.95

The Chained Coffin and Others
ISBN: 1-59307-091-8 $17.95

The Right Hand of Doom
ISBN: 1-59307-093-4 $17.95

Conqueror Worm
ISBN: 1-59307-092-6 $17.95

The Art of Hellboy
ISBN: 1-59307-089-6 $29.95

**Hellboy Weird Tales
Volume 1**
by John Cassaday, Jason Pearson,
Eric Powell, and others
ISBN: 1-56971-622-6 $17.95

**Hellboy Weird Tales
Volume 2**
by John Cassaday, Jim Starlin,
Evan Dorkin, and others
ISBN: 1-56971-953-5 $17.95

Hellboy: Odd Jobs
short stories by Mike Mignola,
Poppy Z. Brite, Chris Golden,
and others
ISBN: 1-56971-440-1 $14.95

Hellboy: Odder Jobs
short stories by Mike Mignola,
Frank Darabont, Guillermo del Toro,
and others
ISBN: 1-59307-226-0 $14.95

Hellboy: The Art of the Movie
featuring the screenplay by
Guillermo del Toro
ISBN: 1-59307-188-4 $24.95

**B.P.R.D.: Hollow Earth and Other
Stories**
by Mike Mignola, Chris Golden,
Ryan Sook, and others
ISBN: 1-56971-862-8 $17.95

**B.P.R.D.: The Soul of Venice and
Other Stories**
by Mike Oeming, Guy Davis,
Scott Kolins, and others
ISBN: 1-59307-132-9 $17.95

B.P.R.D.: Plague of Frogs
by Mike Mignola and Guy Davis
ISBN: 1-59307-288-0 $17.95

ALSO FROM DARK HORSE

The Devil's Footprints
by Scott Allie, Paul Lee,
and Brian Horton
ISBN: 1-56971-933-0 $14.95

Angel: Hunting Ground
by Christopher Golden,
Tom Sniegoski, and others
ISBN: 1-56971-547-5 $9.95

**Buffy the Vampire Slayer: Blood of
Carthage**
by Christopher Golden, Paul Lee,
Brian Horton, and others
ISBN: 1-56971-534-3 $12.95

AVAILABLE AT YOUR LOCAL COMICS SHOP OR BOOKSTORE!

To find a comics shop in your area, call 1-888-266-4226
For more information or to order direct:
• On the web: darkhorse.com • Email: mailorder@darkhorse.com
• Phone: 1-800-962-0052 Mon.-Sat. 9 A.M. to 5 P.M. Pacific Time
*Prices and availability subject to change without notice